Total-E-Bound Publishing books by Aurelia T. Evans:

Calling the Dragons Home

I0607627

Sanctuary

WINTER HOWL

AURELIA T. EVANS

Winter Howl
ISBN # 978-1-78184-578-3
©Copyright Aurelia T. Evans 2012
Cover Art by Posh Gosh ©Copyright November 2012
Interior text design by Claire Siemaszkiewicz
Total-E-Bound Publishing

This is a work of fiction. All characters, places and events are from the author's imagination and should not be confused with fact. Any resemblance to persons, living or dead, events or places is purely coincidental.

All rights reserved. No part of this publication may be reproduced in any material form, whether by printing, photocopying, scanning or otherwise without the written permission of the publisher, Total-E-Bound Publishing.

Applications should be addressed in the first instance, in writing, to Total-E-Bound Publishing. Unauthorised or restricted acts in relation to this publication may result in civil proceedings and/or criminal prosecution.

The author and illustrator have asserted their respective rights under the Copyright Designs and Patents Acts 1988 (as amended) to be identified as the author of this book and illustrator of the artwork.

Published in 2013 by Total-E-Bound Publishing, Think Tank, Ruston Way, Lincoln, LN6 7FL, United Kingdom.

No part of this book may be reproduced, scanned, or distributed in any printed or electronic form without permission. Please do not participate in or encourage piracy of copyrighted materials in violation of the authors' rights. Purchase only authorised copies.

Total-E-Bound Publishing is an imprint of Total-E-Ntwined Limited.

If you purchased this book without a cover you should be aware that this book is stolen property. It was reported as "unsold and destroyed" to the publisher and neither the author nor the publisher has received any payment for this "stripped book".

WINTER HOWL

Dedication

For Shannon, for getting me started.

Chapter One

Renee took the last sip from her Samuel Adams and set the finished bottle down next to the first one. She smiled and nodded at Marie, who had come over to take the empty bottles and leave the receipt. There were no words between them. Usually Marie would chat to her customers, but she'd learned when she'd moved to Antoine five years ago that Renee Chambers would not look at her, half of the time wouldn't talk and the other half of the time would stumble through some painful attempt at conversation. Renee had got better as she'd come to know Marie, but it was still more comfortable for both of them when Renee didn't try to talk and Marie didn't try to make her.

Renee left the cash tip on the table, clenched the leash and slid out of the booth. Her legs stiffened when she saw Josh Beall and Marcus Levinson a few booths down. She had not seen them come in, and although she had heard their laughter, she hadn't recognised it as theirs. She would have to walk by them to leave. The warm body against her leg reassured her, nudged her in the right direction. She took one step, then two. Her knees loosened and let her walk. She instinctively — and fruitlessly — tried to hide in her long, light blue coat.

"...saw her at the supply store getting her checklist squared away," she heard Josh say.

"What's it been, two months since she last came down here?" Marcus asked.

"Three months. Won't come back down till spring. You can practically set your seasons by her." He belched, then coughed, pounding his chest a bit.

"What does she do up there all alone, anyway?" Marcus asked.

"Roswell says she gets a lot of mail," Josh said. "He says she has help, but I don't believe it. She wouldn't let anyone up there. I bet she does it all herself. Completely crazy."

Renee closed her eyes and breathed in. She was not so egotistical as to believe that everyone in Antoine talked about her, but it was just her luck that she had to walk by these two rubes when they were. Neither was too far into his mug for slurred speech, but they were far enough that they couldn't gauge their volume.

"Maybe she does porn," Marcus suggested. "You know, video stuff."

Josh snorted. "Frigid bitch like her? Don't think so." He leant forward conspiratorially. "Hey, what if we went up—?"

"Hey, Renee," Marcus said, even more loudly then they had already been speaking. Josh turned around, his scruffy but reasonably attractive face lighting up with a sly grin when he saw her huddled against the booth table behind them.

"Speak of the scared little devil," he said, raising his glass. "Want a drink? You look a little tense."

Renee's eyes darted from Josh to Marcus to Marie to the door. At another nudge to her leg, and she stepped towards the door.

"Yeah, come on, sweetie," Marcus said, misinterpreting her direction. "We'll make it worth your while."

How? Renee thought. *By drooling on me and trying to feel me up with all those smooth moves you've cultivated over the last ten years?* She didn't say anything, of course, just kept inching along until she finally started past the table.

She lurched forward when Marcus delivered a hearty smack to her ass. It didn't hurt, but Renee could feel her face start to burn and her chest tighten. At least she could move her legs faster now that she was past them.

"Hey, now, none of that in here," Marie called from behind the bar. "Have a good day, Renee. Don't be such a stranger."

"You always run away," Josh shouted after her.

"I wonder why," Renee muttered, her tongue looser now that she was out of the bar and no one was looking at her. "Come on, Britt, one more stop before we go home."

"Hey, Mommy, can I pet the dog?"

Renee winced at the high frequency of the voice and hoped that the mother would know the appropriate way to answer her child. No such luck.

"Hello, miss. Can my daughter pet your dog?"

Antoine was not exactly a highly populated town, but it had a fair tourist trade, particularly downtown Main Street, which was described in most tourist guidebooks as colourful, cheerful, folksy, and unique. Renee did not know about unique or folksy, but many tourists liked to come by for the ambience. And like most townies, the Antoine population had both respect for tourist dollars and frustration with the tourists themselves.

Especially when tourists did not know a service dog when they saw one.

"I'm sorry, ma'am," Renee said, emphatically not looking at the woman. That sometimes helped, and the warm feeling of Britt against her leg reassured her. "She's working."

"Oh, I'm sorry... Hey, wait, you're not blind." The overly polite apology turned into a similarly grating voice of parental annoyance. "If you didn't want Lisa to pet her, you could've just said. There's no need to lie."

"I'm not lying," Renee said. In fact, she was a terrible liar, but that was not the issue at hand. "They do more than help blind people. Please... I need to..."

"Well, that's just rude, having a dog around when you're not really blind and then not letting a little girl pet it," the mother said indignantly.

"I'm sorry. She's working." The words came out short and clipped and curt, but Renee was not really that angry. Her throat was just tightening, and she could feel her shoulders curling in.

"Bitch," the woman muttered under her breath as she grabbed her daughter's free hand — the girl's other hand had been playing with Britt's tail. The little girl was lucky that Britt was an extremely well-behaved dog. The woman led her daughter across the street.

"Good girl," Renee whispered, rubbing Britt's ear gently. "Ready to go?"

She barely had to tug the leash in the direction of the grocery store. Britt had a deep bond with Renee, had been with her most of her life and been her service dog for about five years. She could feel where Renee wanted to go.

Renee admired Britt's beauty beneath the deep green service vest. So many people confused her for a Siberian husky, and Renee understood the mistake. They were both northern sled dogs, but malamutes were bigger, with thicker fur. Britt was a little larger than average, and the darkest parts of her fur—set off by the usual white accents—were almost black. Malamutes were not traditionally service dogs. But Renee had loved Britt since the first time she'd met her, and the feeling had been mutual. There was friendship and respect between them, a connection that she had never managed to make with any of the people at school. It was really no wonder she spent all her time around dogs—she understood them and got along with them so much better than she did with most people.

With Britt in front of her, Renee felt secure in her steps. The sides of her coat hood blocked out her periphery, like blinders on a horse, and she felt a little more confident where she put her feet. Besides, with a large dog like Britt with her—a dog that was occasionally confused for a wolf—she felt more protected. Like a celebrity with a bodyguard, thankfully without the paparazzi.

They made it to the grocery store in about a ten-minute walk. That was what she liked about Main Street. Almost everything was within walking distance, so all she had to do was drive into Antoine, walk around a bit, then drive back home when she was finished, rather than drive from one place to another, and another, and another. Renee was able to stretch her legs after the long drive into town, and certainly Britt needed the exercise as well.

Renee did not need to go to the grocery store often, and she did not necessarily need to go now, which just went to show how much better she had become in public places. But she wanted to get a few treats to tide herself over before all her orders were shipped in. That was actually how she did most of her shopping — online through bulk providers. She had the space, the money and the resources, and most of the things shipped in *needed* to be shipped in bulk. Besides, it was such a long drive between Antoine and where she lived.

There had been a time right after her father had died when she could not even walk into a grocery store without panicking, a time when she could not walk off her property without feeling everything coming in to crush her, as if the entire world had a force field of inhospitality. That was what each successive building had felt like once she stepped out into the world — like a heavy, unpleasant curtain surrounded each of them, and it would take all her effort to pass through. And sometimes she couldn't.

With Britt, though, she was able to walk into places much more easily about ninety per cent of the time.

A grocery store should have been easier, in theory. All those people should have made her feel less conspicuous — she should be able to do better in crowds where she was anonymous and no one really cared. She should do worse with one-to-one interactions. But quite irrationally, it was the other way around. While she was quite bad at one-to-one interactions outside her sanctuary, she was even worse in places that tended to attract more people. Marie's bar, The Benefit, was small and close, and although it tended to get more crowded by around four in the afternoon, Renee avoided it at that time.

The grocery store, however, was another matter altogether. It was more than just a public place — it was a *frequented* public place, and that meant that the unwelcome energy surrounding it seemed to pulse against her.

Swallowing, Renee squinted at the people she could see inside. None of them were looking, none of them were judging. They were all going about their business. She was not the centre of the universe, she reminded herself sternly. The muscle of her heart felt as though it was forcing itself against the thin walls of her lungs, rattling her ribs.

Britt whined slightly as Renee retrieved a shopping cart. She could do this with Britt at her side. Then she could leave. If she could just get through this, she could go back home. That was good motivation to do what she needed to do. Her heart was still racing and her breathing was still a little shallow, but Britt stayed next to her, with her fur brushing Renee's jeans.

When she had finally finished, she pushed her cart to the self-checkout. Once she wheeled the cart out into the parking lot — relieved to be outside and breathing open air again — she saw a few dry flakes of snow fall on her coat sleeves. She guessed there was not going to be anything more than a flurry, but it would only be a sample of what was to come in future months.

Renee took the bags out of the cart and opened her duffel to pack them in. The bag was heavy on her shoulder when she started walking again, but aside from altering her gait, it did not bother her much.

The cold air felt great on her face, since she was beginning to sweat a little. She went around Main Street this time, behind the shops, among the employee parking and the dumpsters.

She rushed through the alleyway and finally reached the intersection between downtown Main Street and the beginning of Antoine proper. Her blue 2000 F150 was waiting at the end of the downtown parking lot. She was going to break into a jog to reach her truck that much faster, but two things held her back. One, Britt did not let her hurry. And two, Josh stepped out from behind the hood, where he had been leaning against the driver's side door.

"Hello, peaches," Josh said. "Plan to leave town for the rest of the winter and use the snow as an excuse?"

Renee hesitated at the edge of the last building, as if she had run into a glass window—but then she pushed through and circled around the truck, away from Josh. There was a chest in the covered bed of her truck that she usually put her groceries in. Her keys clinked as she pulled them out of her coat pocket and unlocked the back of the truck.

"Sit," she murmured to Britt. She needed both her hands to climb into the bed.

"Just going to ignore me?" Josh asked. "That'd be nothing new."

Renee opened the bed and lifted her duffel up into it, then crawled up to open the chest at the other end of the bed.

A low growl that made even the truck vibrate alerted Renee to the fact that something was wrong. She glanced back as Josh pushed himself up into the bed and started to crawl in after her. Renee had to hand it to him. He was crawling after a woman with a wolf-like dog growling at him, and although his face showed a trace of concern, he did not seem scared enough. He was either very persistent or just very stupid. Britt's brows twitched as she looked from Josh to Renee, waiting for Renee to decide what to do with the situation and whether she could handle it herself. But what Josh had not anticipated was that the truck was part of Renee's space, just like her land. And Josh had just entered her space.

"Don't you ever get lonely up there those dark winter nights?" Josh asked. "Don't you ever wish — ?"

"I didn't go out with you in high school. What makes you think I'm considering it now?" Renee said.

Josh blinked.

"Time," he said, overcoming his surprise. "You're all alone, and it's been what? Seven years? Things change. *I've* changed."

"I'm not alone," Renee said.

"Oh, that's right," Josh said. "Your dogs. As though that's a substitute for good human companionship, especially in front of the fire with no lights on and sweet music playing... Unless they are a substitute, and I severely misjudged you."

Renee's face twisted in automatic disgust.

"Well, that's a relief."

"You haven't changed," Renee spat, unloading her groceries into the chest, then shoving his arm. "You haven't changed at all."

"And neither have you," Josh said. He grabbed her arm, and although it didn't hurt Renee, Britt's growl kicked up a notch. "Up there, nothing ever changes, and nothing ever happens. It's all safe and easy and alone, and don't you wish something would happen? Something new, exciting, different?"

Renee slid out of the bed and tugged Josh out. She felt a little shaky, but she knew Josh was mostly talk, no action, so she did not feel as threatened as she might have with Marcus or someone like that.

"Every day," Renee said. "You have no idea. But it's also not you I'm looking for. God, it's so not you."

Josh's jaw twitched as he clenched his teeth. She tried to pass by him, but he grabbed her arm again. His face was too close, and his gaze drifted down to her lips.

"You sure about that? You really sure about that? 'Cause it is awfully out of the way where you live, and if..."

It was Renee's turn to blink. Maybe she had underestimated him, with that glint in his brown eyes, the set of his jaw.

But she narrowed her eyes and murmured, her voice almost inaudible outside the truck, "You try and come on my land, and I promise it will go badly. And it won't be any fault of mine. I'm sorry."

She tugged herself away, and he let her go without much of a fuss. Renee looked around to see whether anyone had been watching their little altercation, because if they had, she would have been mortified. But where she was parked, the last building on Main blocked most of the view.

"So I guess this is the royal brush-off again," Josh said, leaning back against the truck as she fumbled with her keys. "Frigid bitch."

She unlocked the door and whistled to Britt, who came over and jumped into the driver's seat, then into the shotgun seat, settling down and keeping a sharp eye on Josh. Renee pulled herself up—it was a big truck for a small girl. Before she shut the door, she said, "Don't I know it."

Renee thought she heard Josh snort before she revved the engine and left him and Main Street behind. She breathed a sigh of relief and felt a muscle in her body unwind for every second she headed out of Antoine.

* * * *

In spite of the fact that Renee had always thought Josh looked down on her, she had been surprised when he'd asked her to the winter dance, a gathering between the two Antoine high schools — East and West — Barrington High School and Lex High School. At first, she'd been convinced that it was a *Carrie*-like joke, but by the third time he'd asked, she had discovered that in spite of the shiftiness of his glance when he'd asked her, he'd been serious. And she'd had no idea why. Why he would want a girl who seemed afraid of her own shadow — *seemed*, not *was*. Why he would want a girl who rarely talked and generally avoided his crowd — or any crowd, for that matter. Why he would want a girl who never stopped to give him a second glance, other than to get out of his way.

The third time she'd tried to walk past him in an effort to ignore what she thought was mockery, Josh had touched her cheek to stop her. And it had worked, because she hadn't been used to other people touching her at all. The next thing she'd known, he'd been kissing her. His lips had been soft and a little sloppy, but it hadn't been as bad as she had thought kissing might be. In spite of her nerves singing to get away from him, there'd been a strange warmth running from her lips down her spine to pool low in her belly. It hadn't quite been arousal, as she had discovered later, but it had been interest, new and a little exciting. Her panic had only magnified the feeling, as it magnified everything.

In spite of herself, in spite of the nervousness that Renee had taken for granted most of her life as just a part of her, she'd felt herself lean closer. The kiss had been nothing special. But they'd only been sixteen, and it was her first. Her fingertips had brushed against his neck. She'd felt the warm velvet of his tongue on her lips, and that was when she'd jerked back. It hadn't been that she didn't like it, but she had reached her quota for closeness. Her nerves had reached a screaming pitch.

Renee had not given him an answer, and while her father had bought her a dress for the dance, she hadn't gone. She'd sat at home in her dark blue, silky dress with the thin straps, corset-tie back and sparkles, and watched *Prom Night* and *Ever After*, in that order. She'd regretted not going to the dance, but she had known she would not be able to handle it, no matter what her father had said about it. The next school day, Renee had learned that Josh had gone with Kristin Fontaine. And she'd been just fine with that, although the touch of his lips had haunted her for months as she'd hidden under her covers and tried to sleep. After a while, the memory had faded. She hadn't even missed it.

She still did not miss it. Josh might have been more interested in her than any of her other classmates had been, but that did not mean she was interested back. It did not mean that Josh was anything good for her—he was quite innocently misogynistic, intentionally anti-intellectual, although Renee remembered he had been good at math. A lowest common denominator. Her father had told her to never settle, and she intended to keep to that advice. Not to mention that she was not nearly as lonely as Josh thought she was.

* * * *

After an hour of driving through the Northern Highland region, alternating between radio stations and a Celtic album and memories, she felt at peace with herself. Most of the forest was state and national parks, but her land was nestled just on the edge of the Chequamegon-Nicolet National Forest.

Britt became restless the closer they got to her land, and at the first sight of the massive wrought-iron gate protected by electronic security, she gave a high whine.

"Almost there," Renee said. "Bought sirloin steak for tonight. Looking forward to that."

She pushed the door opener on her visor, and the gates swung outward. In spite of the appearance of the gate, her land did not have heavy security. Just a standard, primitive barbed wire fence spanning its circumference. It didn't need to be too protected.

They passed through the gates, and as the iron squeaked to a close, the paved street gave way to a greyish dirt road.

Over hundreds of acres, with a mix of sugar maples, aspens, basswood, pines, birch, and scattered with hemlock, there was nothing but state-protected land and private ownership. Aside from the odd call by geographically distant relatives, there wasn't much to remind her that there were other places in the world. A few planes passed by overhead, trucks came by to bring her supplies, the mail came every day, and a few people visited the sanctuary, but mostly her world was just hers. It was like Josh had said, as infuriating as it was for him to be right—it was easy for her to pretend that her land was all there was in the universe.

On the side of the dirt road—Renee guessed she could call it a very long driveway—there was a wake of turkey vultures, and Renee slowed down to get a look at what they were picking at. Britt shifted to watch the movement of the birds as well as they shuffled away from the truck, although they did not shuffle far, persistent creatures that they were. Renee breathed a sigh of relief when she saw that it was just a hare. Just as this was a little too far north for turkey vultures in this season, it was a little south for hares, and she did not see them very often. The dead animal was big enough to confuse her only for a moment. There was something about the animal's face, though. It was gruesome to see that the mouth looked oddly human, more gruesome than the belly, which had been gutted and strewn a bit on the dirt in a harsh orange-red, and not entirely by the turkey vultures. Renee was not too concerned, though. Dead animals were all too common in her area, and they were usually taken care of by the garbage disposals of the animal kingdom, such as the buzzards.

Renee sped up again and continued on her way home. It took about seven minutes to drive from the gate to the compound.

Her house and the series of large buildings behind it loomed on one of the forest's highest hills — which was not saying much, but it made the sight more impressive. The house itself was pretty big, although not so big that it wasn't dwarfed by the three buildings behind it.

As she neared the house, she had to slow the car down to a crawl, but a grin spread over her face. It was like frozen glass shattering. She was happy to be home.

At least twenty dogs of varying sizes ran up to her truck and started barking, with the excitement and energy only dogs and young children seemed to manage. They jumped up with their front paws, and Renee had to be careful not to crush the smaller ones, but for the most part, they kept out of the way of the front of the truck and stayed to the sides. She finally stopped about twenty yards from her house. She would drive it into the garage shed later.

She opened her coat and slid herself from the sleeves, then unwound her scarf before opening the door, so that all that got the brunt of her canine friends' excitement was her T-shirt and jeans. She did not let them jump on her — she had a strict rule and trained as many of them as she could to stay down, at least the ones who jumped at all — but excitement and greeting was not a crime on the sanctuary land, and she wanted her dogs to be happy.

Most of the dogs who came to greet her, all of whom she knew by name, bounded off to whatever else they desperately had to do at the moment. A few calmer dogs stuck by her side, along with Rufus, a long-haired chihuahua who was never calm. There was Ki, a mutt on the smaller end of the medium scale with Jack Russell markings, who was followed by Max, a black Yorkie terrier. On the other side of her — beside Britt, who had climbed out of the truck — was Leslie, a chocolate brown male boxer with a perpetually comical look on his face. Renee was sure that Malcolm, a grey whippet-Australian shepherd mix, was not far behind.

Rufus saw one of his favourite large dogs, a St Bernard and German shepherd mix named Pom, and bounded off like a fuzzy, excitable rat to be with him, leaving Renee to most of her primary pack, the one that had been with her for more or less her whole life that she could remember clearly. There was only one missing, and he was walking out of the door of the cabin, wearing only his jeans and carrying a hot chocolate in his hands, just the way she liked when she came home from her winter trip. He also had a midnight-blue dressing gown draped over his arms, which he tossed past Renee to the quite naked woman who had appeared behind her.

"Don't suppose you have some chocolate for me, too?" the woman said, wrapping the dressing gown around herself. While Renee did not have a strict policy of wearing clothing on her property — although she herself preferred to stay clothed — the cooler weather made it more necessary than during the summer months.

"Waiting inside," Jake said. "The rest of us have had our share." He leant down and gave Renee a light kiss on her cheek as he handed her the hot chocolate. "I see you made it through another day."

"Somehow I survived," Renee said. "Thanks. Hope you don't mind that I brought steak for the pack tonight. Means you have to cook them."

"Such a trial," Jake replied. "I'll find a way to bolster my strength and manage." He walked over and kissed Britt, the girl who had sprouted from her fur coat into a woman. This kiss was a bit more than a simple peck on the cheek. Renee gave Ki a scratch behind the ears, then headed into her house with her hot chocolate.

The other dogs followed her in, transforming on the way and grabbing their respective dressing gowns from the coat rack. Britt pushed past them for the hot chocolate waiting for her on a coffee table coaster. She settled into the living room armchair, breathing a sigh of relief in her other skin. The living room was decorated like a rustic lodge, with an asymmetrical coffee table and carved wooden furniture softened with red cotton and denim cushions. One of the house cats, a fourteen-year-old arthritic Maine Coon named Claire, was sleeping on the sofa.

Renee joined the cat on the sofa adjacent to the armchair, sipping from her own hot chocolate. While she had lived with Britt since they were both seven years old, there was something about the woman's self-confidence and presentation that could sometimes be a little off-putting. Renee was a small person, around five feet three inches tall, and petite. Britt was tall for a woman at five feet ten inches, and built with the classic hourglass figure. She could have gone out and become a model or an actress, but instead, she stayed in the wilderness with Renee to help her take care of the sanctuary, heedless of the physical blessings with which she was endowed. It was just another skin to her.

Ki, Max, Leslie, Malcolm, and Jake joined them in the living room. They were all usually hard at work around this time, but Renee's quarterly forays into town translated into fairly relaxed evenings for them. They would pick up work again tomorrow.

* * * *

When Renee was seven, Seward and Frances Chambers had already started their collective dream to create a dog sanctuary—a no-kill shelter for all kinds of dogs from mutts to purebreds, as long as they were of a reasonable disposition. The only exceptions were the rogues, the ones who had been raised wrong and showed signs of violence. Cesar Millan might have been able to handle them, but Seward and Frances were just dog lovers, not whisperers. A little exuberance, a little bad training, that was okay. They took the supposedly violent dogs that were just defending themselves, the large dogs no one else wanted, and sometimes people from other shelters came by to ask the Chamberses if they could take some overflow. On the seven hundred acres of pure forestland, with the exception of the more cultivated house hill, there was plenty of space for them to just be dogs, to enjoy fresh air, to live out their days in peace without threat of being put down. The Chambers Dog Sanctuary did have an adoption programme, and it was supported by both regular and irregular donations from all over the country and for all kinds of reasons. They had a special relationship with the three local vets, in Antoine and the other nearby towns, who regularly came up to check on the dogs for a reduced fee and sterilise the newcomers — at least, the ones who were just dogs. The sanctuary sometimes even took cats, although dogs were its focus.

One day after school, when it was beginning to get dark, Renee had been walking one of myriad trails, humming to herself and listening to her portable cassette player, when she'd seen a half-grown puppy panting in bushes. There might have been a lot of dogs at the sanctuary, but Renee knew every one of them, the same way she could differentiate between all the people in her school. This little pup had been new. It looked almost like a wolf puppy, but from the way the dog moved, wagging its tail in its happy way and licking its muzzle, Renee had known it was not a wolf. The puppy had crept towards her, cautious but generally friendly, and Renee had not been afraid. It had done as dogs do and sniffed her hand, then her leg, then her ass, which made her laugh and wriggle away, only to gasp as the dog had become a girl right before her eyes. If she had blinked, she would have missed the transition, it had been so seamless.

The girl had been skinny and dirty and scraggly and naked and cold, and Renee had led her back to the house without a thought. She did not even consider whether the little girl was dangerous or not. Seward and Frances had been more than a little alarmed, but Frances had taken in the little girl, given her a bath and dressed her in some of Renee's clothes—that had been around the time they'd been the same size.

The little girl had told the Chambers family her story—that she'd come to them from a home that did not want her or understand why or how she changed. She had run away before they'd been able to throw her out, thinking she was some kind of witch. She had heard through fellow canine shapeshifters living on the streets as strays that there was a dog sanctuary in Wisconsin, and some dog shapeshifters went there when they did not want to live on the street anymore. They'd said it was safe. So she had followed the rumours until she'd reached the sanctuary. Her name was Brittany Lewis, and she'd been hungry and thirsty and had wanted to know whether she could stay.

Seward and Frances Chambers had initially thought the mention of shapeshifters was just a little girl's fancy, a way to escape from terrible reality, maybe from a home that had abused her in more than a spiritual or emotional sense. But when Seward had asked her gently if she could shapeshift for them, Britt had done so without a thought.

The Chamberses were stunned. Then they'd slowly asked Britt whether other shapeshifters were there, at their sanctuary. Britt had shrugged, but if Britt had made it to the sanctuary, other shapeshifters might have as well. They'd left Renee to stay with Britt and get her acquainted with Baal and Beelzebub, the two original lazy house cats that preferred being inside to mousing.

As it turned out, among the twenty-five dogs that had been living in the barn—which was a loose term for the huge building they used to house the dogs during the winter or bad weather—three had been canine shapeshifters like Britt.

Seward and Frances had initially not known what to do with this new information—they had arranged for a dog sanctuary, not a people sanctuary. Or a nudist sanctuary, as they discovered that shapeshifters could not shift their clothes and appeared before Seward and Frances completely naked, if a little chagrined at the situation. One had been named Henry, and he was relatively old at sixty-three. He was much happier in his canine form than in his human one, which was ill, while his canine form was not. The other two were teenagers, Ki and Max, who had met at a shapeshifter community meeting.

"They have shapeshifter community meetings?" Frances had asked incredulously.

"They're like conventions, with more fur," Max had answered.

They had come there because their parents, who were also shapeshifters, had wanted them to be humans more than dogs and become valuable members of human society like they had done. Max and Ki thought that their dog sides were just as valuable as their human sides, and as much a part of them. They had not run away, per se, but they had left. Their respective parents, somewhat bewildered at the choices of their children, had wished them well and had been donating regularly to the Chambers Dog

Sanctuary ever since their children had sneaked to the phone in the cabin and called their parents to tell them where they were and that they were all right. Once the Chamberses got an Internet connection, it was even easier to keep in contact with their families.

After learning about the new developments in their sanctuary, Seward and Frances had been forced to decide whether they were going to work with it or deny the canine shapeshifters access. If the sanctuary had already developed a reputation on the street, surely that reputation could be changed by word of mouth. But if these people needed a place to go, if they had been a part of the sanctuary without the Chamberses' knowledge, it was questionable whether they could really stop it, even if they tried. And then there was the question of whether they wanted to. The three shapeshifters had actually been very good dogs, and once they'd shifted into human form, they had answered questions about the other dogs in the sanctuary and assisted Seward and Frances with their unique perspectives.

In the end, the purpose of the sanctuary had changed. Not only did it offer shelter for unwanted dogs, it offered shelter for canine shapeshifters. They were, however, expected to help around the sanctuary in exchange for their presence there. They watched other packs, made sure everyone was healthy, and helped weed out the dogs that were not a fit for the sanctuary. In addition, they helped in the garden and greenhouse and did other odd jobs within their means. The more work they did, the more privileges they had — the system worked well because those who wanted to do less work were those who usually preferred their canine side and were fairly typical dogs. Those who embraced both sides of themselves and also wanted to be human on occasion could have human privileges in exchange for their work. Over time, the other two barns had been built—one for farm animals like cows and chickens, which the shapeshifters took care of and protected, and another for the shapeshifters who wanted a place for their human skins.

Britt had been accepted as almost a member of the family, and while they were not sisters, she and Renee had been the closest of friends even through their teenage years. Perhaps it had been easier for them to get along because they were not blood-related. Ki and Max had been too old for them at first, but the older Britt and Renee became, the more Ki and Max had hung out with them in human form. When the three shapeshifters were in canine form, however, they'd hung out just fine, with Ki and Max keeping Britt company and acting the leaders.

When Jake had arrived, around the time that Renee and Britt were eighteen, he and Britt had almost instantly connected. He was able to turn into a golden retriever, which could have been funny, except the human mind in conjunction with the dog's made him more of an animal to be reckoned with. He was an undeniable alpha as a dog. He was something of an alpha with his pack as a human, too, although Britt would not let him be too much of one. But he was always somewhat reserved with Renee, solicitous and deferential, in spite of the fact that he towered over her at more than six feet.

Britt had suggested to Renee one evening that Jake might have a thing for her, in such a way that she was the alpha in their relationship without even trying to be. Renee did not know what to think about that. Renee sometimes had the sense that Britt had a thing for her, too, like how Ki mostly stayed with Max but sometimes was with Malcolm.

After Seward, Renee's dad, had died of a heart attack when she was twenty, roughly eleven years after the death of her mother, Renee had inherited the entire operation. The shapeshifters had been indispensable in taking care of the sanctuary and keeping all things canine running more smoothly than Renee could have done on her own, especially since that had been the point when Renee's agoraphobia had become so much worse.

The sanctuary had grown from the initial seven dogs to an average of seventy-five dogs. Right now, there were seventy, of whom eighteen were shapeshifters. There were approximately five packs, varying from the six dogs in Renee's primary pack to sixteen dogs in the largest pack. The fences were good enough to keep most dogs from leaving, but a shapeshifter was another matter. The ease of coming and going was more useful for the shapeshifters.

With a more official presence among the shapeshifter community, Renee received more donations more regularly than she would have with an ordinary dog sanctuary. Especially from Jake's parents, who were more than a little rich and wanted only the best for their baby, even if their baby was almost thirty.

Renee's primary duties were in the legal and advertising aspects of her sanctuary. She wrote press releases, handled the bills, taxes, and paperwork, and dealt with everything computer-related, including the sanctuary's website and online bulk purchases. She was also the public face of the sanctuary, as reluctant as she was to be a part of the public. She helped facilitate adoptions, both on the computer and in person. As long as she could stay on her land, she was all right, if a little awkward.

She was not the only one who helped the sanctuary on the computer. In order to contribute to the expenses, Leslie and Ki did online freelance work. Ki helped her with the finances near tax time and the end of the fiscal year, and with writing grant letters. Leslie had actually published a book, which had been a moderate success, and was working on his next. He generously donated half the proceeds to the sanctuary. In addition, he wrote articles for green and country living magazines. Like Malcolm, he was something of a loner and more eccentric than was typical for someone who spent as much time as a human as he did a dog, but he was passionate about the sanctuary.

Malcolm had more of a managerial role—he kept track of the names, health and disposition statuses of the dogs, and he was the main person to whom Renee went when she was updating the database for adoption purposes. Max and Jake tended to manage physical labour among the other shapeshifters, and Jake was the main cook for the house, while Ki was the main cook for the shapeshifter barn, although she had two other shapeshifters working with her at all times. Britt was attached to Renee's hip most of the time when she was not running the perimeter of the sanctuary to exercise the dogs.

Their pack was the most concrete pack in the compound, and while some of the other shapeshifters were transients or did not want a bigger role, they all provided a solid foundation for Renee to run something that could have easily overwhelmed her on her own, but something worth doing. Besides, dogs were much easier for her to understand and be around than people, including some of the shapeshifters in the compound. Not many people truly enjoyed following in their parents' footsteps, but Renee felt that it was work worth doing.

* * * *

"As difficult as it is to be," Malcolm said, "you're a little quieter than usual. What happened in town? Did everything go smoothly?"

"I'm fine. Josh made an appearance," Renee said.

"Backwoods bastard," Britt snapped. "All you have to do is give the signal and I'll bite him right where it hurts. I can do more than just sit back and look loyal."

"It would only get you put down," Leslie said. "You know you can't do that." He sometimes had trouble discerning what was sarcasm and what wasn't.

"Then I wouldn't bite. I'd just hold and pull."

That earned a smile from Renee before she drank the last bit of her hot chocolate. She set the empty mug on one of the coffee table coasters.

"So did anything momentous happen in the six hours I was gone?" Renee asked.

"Ah, business," Jake said. "Always something to do. Well, I'll tell you one thing, we've either got a wolf or coyote in the north sector, or we've got a large dog who isn't in one of the packs. There've been some ravaged animals that haven't been eaten. We should keep an eye out for a sick dog or wolf, and if you go out that far as a human, remember to take your gun in case it's rabid. Britt, if you want to do guard duty, keep that in mind." He looked at Renee. "You still have the rabies shots, just in case?"

She nodded. One of the vets had provided her with rabies shots to keep on hand and had taught her how to use them.

"Wait, what? They're just killing animals but not eating them?" Ki asked.

"We saw a dead hare on the way back," Britt added.

"All I know is that the animals—I saw a few rabbits, a fox and a hare, plenty of squirrels—are gutted and their faces are bitten, but they don't seem to have been eaten very much, if at all. It's not normal. Hence, the carefulness," Jake said. "Now, did I hear you say something about sirloin?"

"In the truck bed," Renee said. "I should go check out the barns, see if everyone has everything they need. There were some flurries, so we should try to get everything shipped in that we can before the weather really starts getting bad. Max, have you looked at building three's solar panel yet? We used more electricity over there than usual, and I want to make sure that it's working one hundred per cent if this winter is as harsh as I'm expecting it'll be."

"On it," Max said with a sigh.

"Break over," Ki added, following him out of the door. Malcolm followed also, sensing that the top dogs and their human needed to talk.

Leslie wandered off into the computer room and office, where Renee had set up three different computers—one for Leslie, who had bought his own, one for her, and one for general use during the day among her staff and the other shapeshifters.

Renee, Britt, and Jake were left lounging in the room. The sun would go down soon and make the air more than just brisk. Jake would set up a fire once the sun set.

"So what's really up?" Jake asked. "Usually we all sit and chill, I make dinner, Ki makes popcorn and ice cream shakes, and it's all a good time." Sometimes they would play games—Clue, Monopoly, Risk. It was not the games so much as the interaction that they enjoyed, since they kept pretty busy the rest of the time.

"We can still do that," Renee said. "I just want to get some work done, that's all."

"Yeah, but honey, aren't you exhausted?" Britt asked. "All that tension you get when you go out, and *I'm* tired, too, you know. You could let me try to give you that massage again..."

"No," Renee interrupted a little too quickly. The last time Britt had done that, it had hurt like hell, and Britt had asked whether she ever relaxed because she was hard as a rock. Renee had raised her eyebrow, and Britt had let it go. "I'm fine. Josh just shook me a little, and I wanted to do a few things before this evening. You can let them back in around dinner time, okay? I'm fine."

"Come on, Renee, we know you," Jake said, leaning forward in his seat and staring at her intently. "You can't hide when something's bothering you."

"Brought up some issues," Renee said. "Things I didn't want to think about."

"What, calling you a frigid bitch and then trying to kiss you?" Britt asked.

Renee glared at Britt. "Thanks."

"So...you're afraid he might be right?" Jake asked.

"No," Renee said.

"And I would agree," he said quietly. "You're not."

"Not that there's anything wrong with being a bitch," Britt added, stretching and grinning. The statement made Renee smile again. "You're an honorary bitch, honey. Ki and I just come by it naturally."

"Yes, you're our bitch, although someone here is more bitch than others," Jake said with a pointed glance at his girl. Britt just flipped him the finger. "But you're not the ice queen of the Northern Highlands, if that's what you're thinking."

"The way I am when I'm out. The way I treat people, here and there," Renee said. "I haven't done anything that would indicate that I'm *not* some…"

"You're not," Jake insisted.

Renee curled up in the armchair. "Why?" she asked.

"Just because you have different needs than other people, just because you were born a little different, doesn't mean you aren't a passionate person."

"If I can't let people near me, if I can only stand being around people who aren't people half the time, then what difference does it make whether I'm passionate or not?" Renee asked.

"Renee," Britt interrupted, "I know why you're concerned, but you aren't anything near an ice queen. It was your idea to have the detachable showerhead in the bathroom."

Jake tried not to snort and failed.

"People are different than showerheads because they're something you can't control," Britt continued through Jake's snickering. "You know how you are about control. But just because you have standards and certain issues doesn't mean you're frigid or anything like that. Trust us. When we're dogs, we can smell when you are anything but frigid."

Renee blushed. "Really?"

"Yes," Britt replied, kissing her on the forehead lightly. "Don't worry, we don't mind and neither should you. You're only twenty-six. New shapeshifters come in every year. And then there's us, the ones who stay." She stroked Renee's hair, fingernails scratching pleasantly on her scalp through the red strands. "You have time to decide what you want and when you want to take it. And when you decide to take control of whoever the lucky bastard is, I promise that you'll find out you're nothing like frigid."

Britt did not usually touch Renee at all when she was out of her dog skin, respecting Renee's strict boundaries, and this just added fuel to Renee's curiosity about whether Britt was interested in more than just their close friendship.

She was not against the notion of women with women — she just did not know where *she* fit into the notion of women with women. Sexuality in general was relaxed among her shapeshifters, in part because the issues people had with sex were often not an issue among their canine companions. Hence the red faces and apologies in polite society when Duke tried to mount Spot or when Cinnamon tried to mount Lily. Renee, having been raised around dogs who naturally engaged in sexual activity amongst themselves and shapeshifters who did the same, was not fazed by the theory or practice of sex. She had just never engaged in much more than masturbatory exploration, which had been okay with her, for the most part. The idea of being attracted to someone was an abstraction with very few exceptions in her life, the kiss with Josh being one of them and the attraction that Jake and Britt had for her and each other being another.

The hair stroking did feel good, though. But another part of her was beginning to make her skin hum a little less pleasantly. She felt frozen in place, caught between liking the strokes and disliking the sensation of not having a handle on the moment.

Britt removed the hand, and her placatory grin was a little wry. "Sorry, was I pushing things?"

The 'no' caught in Renee's throat, but she was able to say, "Wasn't sure what to make of it. I need to go check supplies in the shifters' barn."

"Sorry," Britt said.

"No. Don't be." And that she said it meant that it was true.

* * * *

Renee left the house and retrieved her scarf and coat from the truck. The sun was going down fast, and she was going to get chilly very soon.

Her feet crunched on stray brown leaves as she walked down to the second barn, where the set-up favoured the shapeshifters who occasionally preferred to be human. Renee provided each shapeshifter with a bathrobe, but as long as it was okay for them, and they felt no shame in their human skins, they were free to eschew clothing altogether. Renee had no trouble looking at naked people with their beauty and their flaws, ever since Henry, one of their first shapeshifters. It had taken Seward and Frances a little time to accept this, especially with their young Renee seeing everything. But after a while, they relaxed the necessity for some kind of clothing cover. If they were okay with Renee seeing nature take its course with the dogs, they figured that knowing the human body would not be too traumatic for a seven-year-old.

Renee entered the barn to hear Ki clanking pots and pans as she fixed a stir-fry for the dozen or so shapeshifters who did not eat with the core pack. There were forty cots on one side of the room and five beds. Renee was working on getting five more. Some of the shapeshifters slept with the dogs, on the property or in the dog barn, but most slept in their human skins in the shifters' barn because the sleep was more satisfying. The beds were usually reserved according to seniority or physical need. Most of the transients slept on the cots softened by additional mattress pallets, which were more comfortable than they sounded. Every once in a while, Renee bought more clothing from secondhand stores during her summer visits to town, and she kept these in boxes on the shelves along the barn wall. People could take what they needed and put it in the small chests at the end of their beds.

If any of the shapeshifters had been confrontational, the set-up might not have worked so well, but in general, shapeshifters who came to the sanctuary wanted to avoid conflict. There were fights now and then, typical as much in human nature as in canine, but they were usually easily resolved. At least, Renee had never heard any complaints. There had only been one shapeshifter that they had ever had to throw out—she had been placid when sober but raging when drunk. The sanctuary had had to reject more dogs than people.

The laundry machines—three washers, three dryers, all donated—were adjacent to the kitchen area, and a door next to the two stoves led to a huge walk-in freezer for the bulk supplies, which would last a season and sometimes more. It was connected to a separate emergency generator in case the electricity went out during storms.

"Everything kosher, commander?" asked one of the older shapeshifters—Dusty, who could turn into a dachshund and hound mix—as he rested on a bed. He had hurt his foot by stepping on it wrong when climbing out of one of the trees during a routine trim. It did not seem to be broken, but it was swollen, so it might have been strained or sprained. He was supposed to stay off his feet until he was better—at least, until he could put his weight on it again. They could not bring a doctor up. The shapeshifters did not want to be noticed. They only involved hospitals when there was an absolute emergency.

Renee nodded. "New blankets needed?"

"Sir, no, sir," Dusty replied.

"Stand down, soldier," Renee said, with a completely straight face. Dusty looked as if he wasn't sure whether she was being serious or not.

Renee left the shifters' barn and walked a little way to the dog barn. Most of the dogs were out and about, although that would end soon when Max and Malcolm began feeding them. That could be something of an arduous process, especially when it came to giving everyone their fair share.

The dog barn, unlike the human barn—which could resemble a decent halfway house at the best of times—was something of a dog heaven, although most of their play time was outside. There were old couches, chairs, and dog beds, all donated or bought from Freecycle and Craigslist—it did not matter how beaten up the couch was as long as it was clean. There were also plenty of dog toys, donated new from people around the country as well as purchased with monetary donations, strewn all over a sawdust- and hay-covered dirt floor. At the back, there were two rooms for new puppies. There were another two rooms above the puppy rooms that acted as sickrooms for quarantine.

There were only a few dogs in the dog barn at the moment, and one cat. Butch Cassidy was a tough tom who looked as if he had had a hard life, which was part of the reason why he had never been adopted through the website. The funny thing about Butch Cassidy was that he was a tremendously affectionate cat—although he did not get along well with other cats, he very much liked spending time with the dogs and humans. He hit dogs across the face whenever they got uppity, but he was a purring fuzzball the rest of the time. He only looked ragged and diseased, even though most of his bald spots were from old fights and he was given a clean bill of health every time the vet came by.

One of the chocolate labs, Betsy, was nursing a paw, licking it and biting at it, and Renee caught sight of a little blood, so she went over and stroked Betsy's head gently to distract her. Upon closer inspection, it just looked as if there had been a splinter or a misstep, so Renee kissed Betsy behind the ear and let her take care of it as nature intended. She would have to notify Malcolm of the problem, if he did not already know.

Renee shook her head as she returned to the house— two thousand five hundred square feet of log cabin, with three bedrooms, three bathrooms, a great living room and dining room open area, a patio, and a greenhouse connecting to the kitchen. In addition to her computer duties, she was the one who mostly took care of the greenhouse and garden, although Max and Jake helped with some of the heavy grunt work during harvest. Since the bulk of the harvest had finished around a month ago, most of the outside garden work had ended for the season, at least until it was time to plant seeds again. But the greenhouse duties never ended, and Renee liked that kind of hands-on work.

She walked into the house and heard that some members of her staff were enjoying a different kind of hands-on work. The realisation that sex of the noncanine variety happened in her sanctuary—in her home—had made her blush in her late years of high school after she had walked in on Ki and Max, then later on, Jake and Britt. It had since become something she was used to, and she mostly stayed out of the way when she heard certain sounds coming from the bedrooms in the back of the house or from Renee and Britt's room, which was actually a loft above the great room. It was blocked off by a waist-high wall and a curtain to hide the rest. But a curtain did not always do enough to hide the gasps and pants, and even restrained groans, when Jake and Britt decided to get involved up there rather than in Jake's room, which he shared with Leslie. Which, Renee thought, would be more considerate. At least that room had four walls, a door, and a doorknob to put a sock on.

To their credit, they were trying to be quiet since they were in a less private place. But trying to be quiet and being quiet were two different things. Renee sighed and sat on the sofa to wait them out. The most frustrating part about it was not the way that things creaked or the way their breathing incited a certain number of enticing visuals. The most frustrating part was that she could not go into her room to deal with the tingling between her legs from hearing them.

She had never been very good at getting herself off. Ever since she was thirteen and Britt had asked her, bold as brass, whether she'd ever masturbated, she had tried now and then. But it had only resulted in reaching a certain point and simply plateauing or even falling off, leaving her frustrated, with her pubic bone feeling a little abused and her hands dirty. But she knew that Britt could masturbate just fine, and Renee had never really figured out what the secret was. It was like trying to tickle herself—it was never as good as someone else tickling you. At least, that was Renee's working theory. It wasn't as if she knew.

When Renee had turned eighteen, Britt had gifted her with a standard vibrator in secret—that kind of gift, you did *not* unwrap in front of your father—and that had been a revelation. It had been exactly what she'd needed, and in retrospect, it could have been the first clue that Britt might fancy her just a little bit. Within just two minutes of switching it on and bringing it against her clit, the orgasm had come over her in an overwhelming wave, as though it had just been waiting to flood the dam.

In that way, Renee could understand how Britt could tell her that she wasn't frigid. But being able to bring oneself off was no indication that she could allow someone else to do the same. Or whether she really wanted to. Although if she were to let anyone try, she supposed she could trust Jake or Britt. If she were to let them, they would respect her boundaries and the kinds of things that she needed.

And the very thought of that made Renee look around to make sure she was alone in the great room before sliding a hand under her jeans. This was just a quick, light taste of what she would give to herself when she could get into the bathroom or the closet— the two places where she could truly have privacy. Or when she could get to one of those detachable showerheads that she had put into all the bathrooms, including the stall showers in the shapeshifters' barn. On the sofa, she lightly rubbed the fabric of her underwear up and down and in small circles just above her clitoris, against that sensitive spot where her pubic bone was hard against her fingertips.

The litany of gasps and stifled groans from the loft began to increase in pace, and Renee imagined the way that Britt would be riding Jake. Britt had once told Renee she liked being on top, and in spite of his alpha status as a dog, Renee didn't think Jake would mind relinquishing power in the bedroom. Britt could be wild sometimes, and the creaks of the bed indicated just how wildly Britt was thrusting. Down around Jake's erection, squeezing him with her thighs and with other things, truly riding him. Soon, she would whimper in *that* way, the way she whimpered when she was about to reach her climax, that deliciously clenching feeling right before the orgasm collapsed into a momentary peace. Renee had heard it some nights when the rustling of the bed clothes could not be explained by tossing and turning or scratching an itch—or at least not the itch Britt had meant when she'd initially tried to explain it away. Eventually, both of them had grown used to just letting themselves be girls. If they needed privacy more than convenience, they would kneel in the bathroom or the walk-in closet. But if it was night time, anything was allowed. Heavy breathing from either of their beds was generally ignored, as was a light hum if Renee was using her vibrator.

There it was, that whimper that Renee had been listening for, and the quiet curse from Jake as the noise of the bedsprings quickened forcefully. Britt came before he did, and there was a spike of pleasure as Renee pressed against that spot just above her clit a little harder. Then there were the last few grunts from Jake, which told Renee that he had not been far behind. Britt was always quick, at least for a woman— as far as Renee knew. Renee had always climaxed pretty quickly with a vibrator, although it could take her much longer when she was waiting for a dead vibrator to be replaced.

There were about five minutes of soft whispers, post-coital bliss, and Renee slowed down her strokes. She would have her time as soon as those bastards got out of the room. She smiled tightly as she thought of them walking out right then, finding her with her hand in her pants right after they'd had sex in her room. She was a little self-conscious as she heard the first creaks from the floorboards in the loft, and she withdrew her hand quickly, although she did not try to hide it. Britt would catch on to that immediately if she were to walk out of the room right then.

Then Britt laughed and Renee knew it was probably safe to go up to her room, but she would still wait for them to start coming down the stairs, just to be more polite than they were — going at it in her room when there were steaks to be cooked. Not that it took long when most of them liked rare meat, with the odd exception of Leslie and Ki. And, goddamn it, she needed to come now that she'd got herself started. It was almost unpleasant, the warmth and slight throbbing between her legs. It had been even more unpleasant when she had not known what it meant in her younger years.

"Quite finished?" she asked as Jake pushed back the curtain and started down the stairs with Britt at his heels. The two of them shared a self-satisfied look. There was no guilt — guilt was not an issue in their household. Just inconvenience.

"Quite," Jake replied. "What do you want to go with your steak? We have some eggplant..."

"Go wash your hands before you cook, the both of you," Renee said. "Eggplant is fine." She stood from her place on the sofa and headed up the stairs herself.

"You'll be down soon?" Britt asked.

"Yes. A few minutes."

"And the rest of the evening will go as usual?" Jake asked.

"Yes. Okay."

"You know, I think she heard us," Jake murmured to Britt as they headed into the kitchen together.

"Heard us? I think she was listening," Britt said, not quite as quietly as Jake, which meant that she'd intended for Renee to hear her. Renee grinned, then briskly went up the last few steps.

She retrieved her trusty silver-coloured vibrator from her bedside drawer and escaped into the bathroom, closing the door behind her without turning on the lights. She unzipped her jeans and pushed them down a little bit. She did not bother pushing down her underwear.

Renee turned the vibrator on its highest setting and pressed it against herself, feeling the vibrations up her arm and all around the flesh between her legs. She didn't need anything fancy right now. All she wanted was to come, and come soon. It wouldn't take long.

She thought of what Britt and Jake would have been like if they had not been in the loft. She had heard their noises muted through the logs when they were in Jake's room, and she knew they liked to be vocal. They never screamed, but there were so many other noises to make. She thought of Jake whipping Britt around and plunging deep into her, taking control, whispering dirty things in her ear and losing himself in her warmth as she held him close. If Renee felt anything approaching shame for imagining her friends having sex in order for her to get off, it was lost in the quick tightening, then release, with her cunt clutching at emptiness. It was always over too soon, no matter how much she tried to savour the moment.

Sighing, she stood up, then went to the bathroom while she was there, in part to wipe off the strong-smelling juices that seeped out of her. Now that she knew her friends could smell her after she'd orgasmed, it made her slightly self-conscious.

If she thought of Britt and Jake while touching herself, the world of possibilities for the others suddenly opened up—maybe they thought of her when they were doing the same. It was an odd, slightly sideways thought. She would not let it bother her. They were her friends, and they were loyal friends at that. And she thought she might love them like that. A little thing like sexual fantasy should be nothing. She washed her hands, replaced her vibrator, and went downstairs to check the sanctuary blog and feed the cats.

* * * *

She'd had a wonderful night with the pack. A game of Monopoly could be boring, but it had been worthwhile for the company and being able to bankrupt people and have strange rules like eating a piece of chocolate on every third double or drinking whenever someone got into jail. Not for some of them, on that last part, although it had never been a problem for Jake or Renee. Britt was a surprising lightweight. But of course, any of the imbibing had been optional.

Leslie had won, laughing in his quiet way as the group had showered him with fake money and promised to do some of his chores over the weekend, like vacuuming the rugs in the house and cleaning the bathrooms.

No, no one had forced him into doing those chores—he had chosen them himself, wanting to help out but not really wanting to leave the house. He was very much a homebody when he was in human skin. As a boxer, however, he would run and run and run through the woods until he was frothing and mud was embedded in his paws. So having his chores done for the weekend meant that he could work on his book and a few articles before taking his run.

Leslie was the kind of man—forty-two years old and looking like a fifty-year-old professor—with whom Renee felt completely comfortable just sitting silently in the same room, without feeling the pressure to talk or listen. They sometimes spent hours together doing their respective tasks on the computer. When she needed to use the phone, Leslie was usually so lost in whatever he was writing that he barely noticed. He could not be considered a surrogate father—it was more accurate to say he was a surrogate eccentric uncle.

Leslie, though, was an early bird whereas she was a night owl, so now she was alone in the computer room with the quiet hum of technology around her. The only illumination came from the computer in front of her and various LED lights from the other machines. She was updating information about the various dogs in the sanctuary, and she wanted to add a post on Butch Cassidy. Butch Cassidy, while an unfortunately unadoptable cat to so many ignorant people, seemed to be vastly entertaining nonetheless. People who stopped by her blog loved him and the pictures she'd taken of him. People subscribed. Advertisers asked whether they could advertise on her blog and her website. And it made her money. Not much, but for a non-profit organisation, a little was a lot.

Building her website and keeping her blog updated helped with that. She received donations through the blog and the website. Whenever the Chambers Dog Sanctuary had a little press release in one town or another, either through the newspaper or through a reporter on a news station, donations saw a spike. That was always nice.

Renee's eyelids were finally beginning to droop when she heard the commotion outside. Grabbing her own plush, purple dressing gown, she threw it on over her pyjama tank and navy-striped lounge pants. Running and tying a knot at the same time, her hair loose around her face, she ran to the front door. Just as she reached for the doorknob, she heard something she had only heard maybe twice in her life, and never so close to the sanctuary. Part of the racket was the barking of the dogs—the sound both territorial and fearful. But over the barking, a single, extended piercing howl rent the air and literally made her hairs stand on end. She had heard of that phrase, but had never known the experience until that moment. It was too close, right-outside-her-house close. Too close for Renee to open the door.

"What the hell?" Britt said blearily, running down the stairs.

Renee was paralysed with her hand on the doorknob, but she whispered, "Wolf."

"Are you kidding?" Britt said.

Jake did not even bother with the stairs. He swung down from the top stair and landed hard on the wooden floor. "She's not kidding," Jake said grimly.

The howl keened again, and the noise from the dogs quieted for a moment before coming back in full force.

Jake's hand covered hers on the doorknob. "It's okay. We'll protect you." She felt the muzzle of a rifle against her arm, cold even through the bathrobe sleeve. "It's probably the animal that's been doing all those killings. But if it comes after you, it won't have a second thought. All right?"

She nodded, but it took Jake's help to break through her panicked paralysis. The warmth of Jake and Britt helped, and Ki, Max, and Malcolm were padding over to join them. Leslie was probably sleeping—he could sleep through almost anything.

Heart jerking in arrhythmic beats, she pulled open the door and peeked out. She could not see anything in the yard but shadows, although the waxing silver coin of a moon at least made some shapes visible in the darkness. Jake pulled the door open some more and cocked the gun, ready. Renee cautiously stepped onto the wraparound porch, peering into the yard.

There it was—a large, slouching shape, a hulking silver creature with eyes that mirrored the moon greenly in the glare. Britt fumbled with the light switch near the door, and she turned on the great room light before the porch light. For one terrifying moment, Renee could not see past the steps of her house, but then the porch lights came on, illuminating the part of the yard in front of it. Then she could see the creature even better, and that did not help at all.

At first, Renee thought it was too large to be a wolf, but the mannerisms, the shape, the mouth...they seemed to fit. It looked a bit like a dark version of Britt in her malamute skin, though several times as large. Even as her mind interpreted what she saw as a wolf, she *knew* it was far too big. But she had no other explanation.

From what she could see, there was no foam around its mouth, but foam was only one indicator of one disease, and its gaping maw seemed to be grinning hungrily at her, although she was silly to impart it with some kind of homicidal intent. If it was a wolf, it did not have homicidal intent—it had instincts and wants and needs, and that was all. It did not feel malice.

Jake brought the rifle to his shoulder and pointed it at the wolf. The wolf just sat there, panting slightly. There was no apparent agitation, no anger or pain. Even knowing it was impossible, Renee thought that it *did* appear malicious.

The animal began to walk towards the porch, still grinning. Its mouth was clean of blood, and that was encouraging, but wolves were not supposed to just walk up to humans. It should not have even been so close to the compound in the first place. Something was clearly wrong, and Jake muttered, "If he gets within ten yards of the porch, I may have to shoot."

"Go ahead," Renee said quietly. They were all staring, unable to do much more, since as dogs they could only attack it in numbers because it was too big for them to attack singly. Not that they would want to attack, not with the indifference that the wolf seemed to have for the rising barks of the dogs in the dog barn, some of which had come out but not come any closer. They were not reckless. It was the wolf that was reckless, and when the dogs could not smell fear, they knew something was terribly wrong.

"What is it?" Ki asked, even though she could see it fine. "How can it...?"

"I have no idea," Jake said. "And it's still coming closer. What the hell?"

It stopped at just past ten yards from the porch and grinned at them. Then, not in a blink of an eye, but in a twist of flesh, bone, and sinew and with a creaking that seemed to come from the ground itself, the wolf began to change into a man. A man more completely unashamed of his body than any of the shapeshifters, some of whom had to adjust to living in a place where they were allowed to indulge in their pure human skin. He stood naked in the yellow light from the porch, touched in his shadows by silver from the moon. He was short for a man, maybe five feet and eight inches, but he was built in such a way that his presence was greater than his height. His dark hair was thick, with enough length to show a slight wave. His facial hair was neatly trimmed around his mouth and up the lines of his jaw, which was neither prominent nor weak but structured, like the rest of him. He was strong, compactly proportioned. In spite of the chill of the evening, he did not seem to be cold, with the exception of the tightness of his nipples along the ridges of his chest.

He gave his onlookers a smirk and said, "So, does a place like this have an opening for a guy like me?"

Chapter Two

They were all in the shapeshifters' barn. Malcolm had woken Leslie up so he could join them. But Britt wouldn't let Renee get near the man. He was sitting on the edge of a cot in a pair of jeans and a dark red, worn dress shirt that was about one size too big. They were his own clothes—he had brought a bag with him. From the wear marks on the sides, he'd held it in his teeth. Before the shapeshifters had ushered him into the shifters' barn, he had retrieved it from the edge of the road where he had left it to meet them and put on the clothes while they watched. Renee didn't think he'd put on clothes for the modesty, but perhaps to make himself appear less threatening. If that was the case, he'd failed miserably. He never seemed to stop grinning—even if it was just a slight curve of his mouth or a crease of skin near his eyes.

Jake sat opposite him on another cot, and the other shapeshifters stood awkwardly along the edge of the room. Jake's gun was still trained on the man.

"Judge, jury, and all we're missing is the executioner," the man said. "Unless you'd be that black-hooded man, my friend."

"More like prosecuting attorney, really," Jake replied. He tried to relax his frame, but he could not seem to shake the tension out of his shoulders. The other man, however, lounged in his seat.

"Then where's my defence lawyer?" the man asked. "This isn't a fair trial."

The man laughed a little. "Look, if you all don't want me here, you can just tell me," he said.

"Tell you the truth, I *don't* want you here. But it's not up to me to decide," Jake said.

"No," the man murmured. "It's hers, isn't it?" He looked over at Renee, before Britt pushed Renee behind her.

"Hey!" Renee tried to move to the side again, but Britt stood in her way. "Brittany, what's going on?"

"She's just trying to protect you, love," the man said, "from big, bad me."

"Protect me from what?" Renee asked.

"Look, Renee, trust me," Britt said. "I'm just trying to—"

"Protect me from *what*?" Renee grabbed Britt's arm and whirled her around. "What are you trying to protect me from? So he shapeshifts into a wolf. What about it?"

"Oh no, honey, that's not how it works," Britt said. She led Renee to a cot and sat her down. Renee felt more than a little patronised, and she did not like it.

"Look," Britt said, sitting down next to her and looking her straight in the eye, too intently for Renee's comfort. "Canine shapeshifters aren't the only breed out there. I'm sure you've figured that out by now. Other shapeshifters turn into bears, ferrets, raccoons, house flies, sparrows, warthogs, just about everything out there. Even wolves. But *that*—" She pointed at the man. "That is not just a wolf shapeshifter. If he was, he would look like every other wolf around, and maybe a few that have recently gone extinct. But he doesn't, and he's not. That's not a wolf shapeshifter. That's a werewolf."

"What difference does it make?" Renee asked.

"Long story short—werewolves are bad news. Shapeshifters are born, werewolves are made. And how are they made? By other werewolves attacking and biting people. They're the shapeshifting equivalent of a plague. They're evil, and you don't want one here."

"Now wait just a damn second, bitch," the man said. "No need to hang me for crimes I haven't even committed yet."

"He was probably the one doing all those animal killings," Jake said. "Either that, or we've got *another* rabid wolf on our hands."

"Hey, if you prick me, do I not bleed?" the man said, holding a hand to his heart as if wounded.

"I don't know yet, but if you'd like, I'll go fetch an axe and see," Jake said.

"Okay, okay, I get it. I'm unwelcome by the overprotective sheriffs in town. But you said it yourself. You two aren't the ones I have to impress. None of you are. The only person who can give me the okay to live here is the woman whose picture is on the website, and that would be you, love." He stood up and looked down at Renee, even from a few yards away from her.

Jake grasped his arm hard. "Don't call her your love," he said, through gritted teeth. "You don't even know her. And I swear, if you—"

Jake was taller than he was, but the man was not threatened by Jake's ability to lean over him. "Think she can't decide for herself? Do you trust her judgement so little?"

"Don't do that," Jake said, his voice soft at first. Then he shouted, "Don't you *dare* do that! Don't turn this back on me! She doesn't know what you are!"

"Because you won't let him talk," Renee said quietly, standing up from her place on the cot. She crossed her arms.

"Renee, don't..." Britt whispered, but Renee shook her off.

"I appreciate all your input on this," Renee said. "But I would at least like to know what he has to say before I throw him out. Does that sound like too radical a suggestion? We don't even know this man, and you're condemning him just for what he is. Don't you know that's what people might have done to you a hundred years ago? Hell, fifty years ago? Thirty years ago? Ten years ago? Isn't that why you came here in the first place, Britt? There are still people who would look at you if you changed in front of them, and they'd think 'witch' or something like that. Now, everybody sit down. Because I want to hear this."

It might have been the longest speech Renee had ever made.

"Thank you," the man said.

"Start talking," Renee snapped.

"Your friends are right," the man said. "I'm a werewolf, not some little shapeshifter. I pack more power in my punch. But that doesn't mean I'm a bad guy. Name's Grant Heath. I'm from here and there. I was last a bank accountant in Missouri, and that was after I got bit. I can be respectable, mild-mannered, whatever you like, love. But to be honest, I left the job because it just wasn't me anymore. I wanted to let the wolf out to play. And isn't that what you all wanted from this place? Somewhere you could cut loose, be yourself more than in any of those tidy, domestic places? So why am I so different?"

"Because you're dangerous. Not as a man, maybe, but as a werewolf," Britt said. "Why should we trust you?"

Grant took a second look at Britt, taking his time a little more and clearly enjoying the view before returning his attention to Renee. "I didn't attack you, did I? I guess all you have is my word."

"You haven't earned the trust of your word yet," Britt snarled.

"And you're going to need time for that trust to grow," Grant said. "Which I can't have if you just throw me out without letting me prove myself."

"And if you decide to eat our intestines or make some of us werewolves while you're at it, that will mean you don't get our trust?" Britt said.

"Well, at least you'll know," Grant said mildly. He looked back to Renee. "And I promise not to turn anyone who doesn't want to be turned."

Renee found herself shivering at the intensity in his gaze. It sounded stupid and a little cliché, but it was true. Everything about him was like a bundle of copper wires vibrating with electricity. He was a little dangerous. Maybe a lot dangerous. Renee could sense it. But she did not think that she could just throw him out when she didn't even like some of the shapeshifters who came in, even though they were harmless. She couldn't throw people out on instinct or because of hunches or prejudice. She had to throw them out based on evidence. Evidence that she did not have against him. And underneath all her logic...she was just not sure whether he would leave, even if she told him to.

"Well? Do I pass inspection?" Grant asked.

"This is a dog and dog shapeshifter sanctuary," Renee finally said. She'd thought her voice was going to shake, but it didn't. "But I'll consider letting you stay. You get a week's trial run. Carefully watched. I reserve the right to throw you out at any time."

Grant flashed a toothy smile. "You can watch me all you like, love. I promise you won't be disappointed."

"Hey," Jake said, resigned to Renee's decision but not at all happy with the way that Grant was looking at her. "You treat her with respect. She's the one letting you stay."

As Grant whipped around to face him, Renee knew that the animosity between them had not lessened a bit just because of her permission.

"I'll keep that in mind, Junior," Grant murmured, his jaw tight. Then he relaxed back and put his thumbs in the belt loops of his jeans. "So where do I sleep?"

"In here," Renee said. "With the rest of the shapeshifters. Choose a cot."

"Not in that nice, comfy house up there? Or one of the beds?" Grant asked, leaning back until he was lying on the cot.

"That's a privilege that comes from time and hard work," Renee said. "Or if you'd be more comfortable slipping into your werewolf skin, you've got the whole woods. I don't recommend the dog barn."

"In fact, if you go in there, I hope I can consider that a threat to this facility," Jake said. He checked with Renee, who nodded.

"No problem on that front," Grant said. "I know wolves and dogs don't really mix. No need to cause unnecessary animosity. Don't you agree, Junior?"

"Stop calling me that. Are you even older than me?" Jake said.

"Much older, Junior," Grant answered. "Age works differently when you're turned."

Renee's brow furrowed in curiosity. "How old?"

"Closing in on fifty," Grant said. "I've kind of lost track."

"Fifty?" Ki said, her appraising double-take incredulous. "You're shitting me."

Grant shrugged. "It's part of whatever voodoo that changed me more than just the moon can account for."

"Speaking of moon, do you change—?" Renee began.

Grant responded before she could finish her question. "I have to change when the moon is full and above the horizon, but as long as I'm not under direct midday sunlight, I can transform into the werewolf at just about any time. They're night creatures. *We're* night creatures. But sunlight won't kill us or turn us into dust or anything."

"All the old werewolf stuff applies, though," Britt said. "A silver bullet can kill them, decapitation, explosives, wolfsbane, that kind of thing."

"Hey now, bitch, no need to give away all the family secrets," Grant said brightly.

"Call me a bitch again—"

"It's what you are," Grant interrupted. "No need to get defensive about it. No insult was intended, I assure you."

"Well," Britt said, less defensive this time, although Renee thought she still had the right to be, because Grant obviously *had* meant to get her riled up. "You know how to kill us, so a little reciprocation probably doesn't hurt."

"I suppose not," Grant said.

"How to kill you?" Renee said. "There's a special way?"

"No," Britt explained. "That's the point."

"Oh."

"Shapeshifters have always been this way. They don't trust weres," Grant said, directing his accusation conspiratorially to Renee.

"As though there's nothing inherently wrong with something that was born and bred to prefer the blood and flesh of humans and to propagate itself through vicious attacks," Jake muttered.

"You have heard of mosquitoes, right, Junior?" Grant said.

"Look," Renee said, interrupting the back and forth—or rather, the around and around. "It's about two in the morning, and I think we should all get back in our beds." She nodded at the early birds in her group. "Just shut down for the night. I promised a week-long trial, and that's what I am going to give him. Starting now. Anyone who isn't okay with it is free to sleep in the walk-in freezer. Understood?"

Grant's eyebrow arched in approval, but he did not push his unwelcome luck.

"Fine," Jake said, lowering his gun at last. "When are you coming to bed?"

That perked Grant's interest again. Renee felt a compulsion to qualify Jake's question, but she fought it. There was no reason for her to explain the sleeping arrangements to a perfect stranger like him.

"I'll come to the room when I'm finished," Renee said. "I've got a few more things to put on the website."

Jake headed towards the door, but he bent down to whisper in her ear. "I don't feel you're safe when you're all alone in the office."

"You never seemed to worry about a psychopath coming in to slaughter me before," Renee said. "Even though we've got the perfect horror movie set-up where no one can hear us scream."

"Yeah, well, we never had an actual psychopath we knew was here," Jake said.

"That's just the thing, Jake," Renee snapped. "We don't know. *You* don't know. And I'm not going to make these kinds of judgements on someone *I* don't even know. Sure, he's something of a bastard, but that's not the kind of criteria that immediately rules him out. You know that."

"Listen to the girl, Junior," Grant said. "She's making good points." He pointed to his ears with a grin. "Wolf hearing. Even if you whisper, I'll probably hear you. Made for good blackmail in a corporate setting."

"Shut up," both Renee and Jake said at the same time.

Grant held up his hands in mock surrender, then lay back down on the cot again, propped up by his elbows.

"Extra blankets in the second chest over there," Renee explained. "If you need any food during the night, check the cabinets or the fridge."

"I'll be just fine. I'm hot-blooded," Grant said.

Once again, there was something about the way he was staring at her. As though he wanted to put his mouth on her and bite down hard for his own pleasure. It could have made her shiver again, but instead she just felt heat under her skin. She knew she was blushing in spite of herself and the cold when Grant flashed one of those quick smiles with his brilliant teeth, before turning his face away.

"Look, I'll be fine," Renee whispered at Jake, even though she knew that Grant could probably still hear her. She began to lead them all out of the door. "Isn't there the whole 'they can't come in unless they're invited' thing?"

"That's vampires," Jake said. "Completely different animal."

Renee blinked. "Do vampires exist, too?"

Jake shrugged. "I never met any, and they never really talked about them when I was around our shapeshifter community. So they either don't exist or they aren't of any consequence to shapeshifters. I couldn't tell you."

"They exist," Grant called after them.

Jake and Renee stared at each other for a moment before walking the rest of the way to the house, the others following them up.

"We should plant some wolfsbane in the greenhouse," Britt said. At Renee's expression, she explained, "No, I'm going to try and reserve my judgement. But just in case. It's not like we have a silver bullet on hand or anything."

"Hypothetically, a silver bullet could be made, although it melts at a higher temperature than lead, so it's harder to keep it liquid long enough for a smooth casting," Leslie said. "But they're not very accurate. I wouldn't depend too much on something like a silver bullet. I know some companies add trace amounts of silver to their lead bullets to harden them, but then there's no guarantee that silver particulates would make it into a werewolf's bloodstream to poison them. So they're popular in fiction, but considerably impractical in reality."

"How about a silver knife?" Renee asked.

"That is a better suggestion," Leslie replied, nodding as he contemplated the possibility. "In fact, I think it is a brilliant idea. Well done, Renee. I'll have to write that down somewhere."

"What did you do, old man?" Max asked. "Write a werewolf story?"

"Not yet," Leslie answered, in all seriousness. "But one never knows when the answers that stem from simple curiosity will have a purpose later in one's career."

"No, one never knows." Max hid a grin. The mockery was all in fun and affection. Leslie was just odd enough that the average person might dismiss him, but the core pack knew better than to do so.

"Night, everyone. Again." After everyone had made it in and headed to their respective rooms, Renee closed and locked the door to the cabin behind her. She was unused to having to lock her door, as out of the way as they all were. It was usually too much work for someone to try and invade their area without a damn good reason.

Renee wondered what Grant's reason was. She did not think he really needed the sanctuary that they offered in the woods, and he was so antagonistic to the shapeshifters that it had to be something else. She supposed time would tell.

In spite of what she'd said to Jake, she did not feel at ease. And she did not think that locked doors were going to do anything to help. Sleeping in the same room with Britt and Jake tonight would help, she thought. She didn't think that Jake was going to let his gun leave his side for a while. At least not until Grant either proved himself to be harmless...or until Grant had to be led out of the sanctuary at gunpoint. Or shot into the ground. Renee was not unaware that it was a possibility.

The sanctuary had never felt like anything less. It was going to be a harsh winter, Renee thought. She pulled her bathrobe tighter around her and went into the computer room, intending to hurry through her last activities so that she could sleep with the others around her.

Chapter Three

The next afternoon yielded a few more snow flurries. They didn't stick to the ground, but still spoke of a possibly harsh winter. It had taken Renee some time last night before she'd wanted to go to sleep, then it had taken even longer for her to *get* to sleep, so it was actually noon before she even considered opening her eyes and throwing back the covers.

She had some article-writing to do that day and two new dogs to put up on the website because they had finally completed their three-month socialisation period. She also had to write up some papers on a potential adoption. A woman was coming by in a few days to meet Gumption, a raggedy mutt with a missing leg who had come to the sanctuary two years ago and was still affectionate and playful in spite of his handicap. Renee wanted to have his papers ready even if the adoption did not go through. But usually, when someone came this far out of their way to adopt a dog from the sanctuary, they went through with it. Then she had some plant-tending in the greenhouse to do.

But first she got dressed and threw on her coat before sneaking towards the shifters' barn. 'Sneaking' was not really the right term. There weren't many places to hide in the open spaces between the buildings, but she tried not to disturb the leaves beneath her feet, and she looked around her in case Grant was watching her at that moment. She wanted to see whether he was still there or whether he had gone. She did not think that she had dreamed him or anything silly like that. She just didn't know whether he had really wanted to stay or whether he had slaughtered something while they'd all been asleep.

Then again, if he had slaughtered something, Britt or Jake or Malcolm would have woken her up to tell her. They wouldn't have said, "I told you so," but learning one of her friends or dog charges had been killed would have been a cold awakening enough.

She thought she'd made it all the way to the shifters' barn without being detected, so she opened the door and peered in. Grant was not there, but the bed where he had slept was mussed, and there was a personal chest at the end of the bed with the leg of a pair of jeans caught in the lid, so she assumed that he was at least still in the sanctuary.

"Looking for me?" he asked behind her.

Renee mentally kicked herself for jumping, but was thankful that she had not done anything as pathetic as squeal.

"Just checking whether everything was the way it should be," Renee said.

"Mm-hmm. I'm convinced," Grant said.

It wouldn't matter what reasonable explanation she gave. He wouldn't believe she was out there for anything but him. Narcissistic bastard.

Incredibly close bastard.

Too close.

Renee ducked under his arm. There were benefits to being short.

"Running away from me?" Grant called after her. The question could have sounded mocking, the way it had been when Josh had said it—especially with Grant's amused way of speaking—but it didn't sound mocking to her ears. "Don't tell me all that shit the shapeshifters were saying actually got through."

"It's not you," Renee said quietly on her way up the hill to the house. She knew he heard her, because he came up behind her again.

"Didn't Malcolm have any work for you to do?" Renee asked.

"I thought it wasn't a requirement to work," Grant said.

"It's not. It's just recommended. And it gives you something to do besides follow me."

"You started it, love, not me."

"I wasn't following you. I was checking to see whether you'd run off in the night after causing your little bit of chaos," Renee said.

"*My* little bit of chaos?" Grant said. "If you didn't notice, I wasn't the only one causing problems."

"I did notice," Renee said. "However, they've been reliable judges of character over the last twelve years or so."

"So you trust them unquestioningly, but you don't trust me as far as you can throw me," Grant said.

"That's the short of it. Go talk to Max or Malcolm about helping. You look strong enough, and you might get on their good side in the bargain."

"And what are you going to do with your time?" Grant asked. "Be a good little girl and stay in the kitchen?"

"I don't cook. Jake cooks."

"You must do something," Grant murmured. He pulled the shoulder of her coat down a little to show the slight definition of muscle on her upper arm through her tight-fitting sleeve. "I didn't think I imagined this."

"I garden. And run with the dogs on occasion. By the way, don't run with the dogs."

"I don't run with dogs," Grant said.

"Then why are you here?" Renee asked.

"I told you, I need sanctuary."

"From what, I wonder?" Renee said. She pulled her arm away and went up the porch steps before slamming the door behind her.

She didn't think he'd respect the finality of a closed door, but she hoped he would. He didn't. He threw open the door and followed her in.

"What are you—?" Renee began, but Grant cut her off.

"I hunt," he said. "If you need fresh meat, I can hunt. I like to hunt. In a pinch, I can do your taxes for you."

"I do the taxes for the sanctuary," Renee said, cold at the intrusion of her space that she had not given freely. "But some of us do other things to earn money. When tax time comes, if you're still here, you are welcome to help."

"And hunting?" Grant asked. If his expression could be said to show imploration, this was the time. He did not, however, look innocent. In the room, he was far too large, and she could not help but feel flustered. In her mind's eye, she imagined shoving him out of the door so that he tripped on the step into the house and down the porch steps. She imagined a split in his head from its hitting a stone. There wasn't supposed to be *anyone* who could invade her space without her permission on her own property.

"If you want to hunt, then hunt," Renee said quietly. She would not look at him directly, so she looked at his feet. He had found himself a pair of dark brown hiking boots. "We don't get much fresh meat around here because it's too expensive and I would have to go to town more often. Does your saliva...? I mean..." She did not know quite how to articulate her question, especially when she could tell he was staring at her even though she was not looking directly at him.

"It's not my saliva that changes people," Grant answered. "It's not so simple or scientific as a sharing of fluids. It's the act of the bite. It's a confluence of specific events, not a disease. For instance..." He stepped closer, and Renee could feel his breath cool on her neck. If he got any closer, it would be warm. "If I were to bite you now and break the skin, you wouldn't change. If I were to transform and lick an open wound, you wouldn't change. If your blood were to mix with my blood, you wouldn't change. I would have to bite you and break the skin while in werewolf form."

"So if you get us dinner, it's not going to change us," Renee said. She leaned away from him, but she did not back away yet.

"How often *do* you go into town?" Grant asked, bypassing the issue at hand.

"Not often," Renee answered.

"Why not? There are bars in town. Movies. Streets to walk on. People. So many people it makes your mouth water. Why avoid them?" Grant asked. Now his breath was warm against her cheek and neck, and she backed away. He followed her mercilessly until the back of her legs hit the sofa and she could not move farther away from him.

"I like it here."

Grant inhaled, and Renee could almost hear him purr. "Maybe you like it here," he said. "But I think what really keeps you here is that you don't like it out there. And you don't like it when people get close, like I am now. You have an over-defined sense of personal space. I can tell just by looking at you. What I *don't* know is why you aren't doing anything about it."

The answers were at the back of her mouth, caught on her tongue. But Renee also had the feeling that he already knew.

"Is it because you can't bring yourself to touch me in order to push me away?" he whispered in her ear. She almost felt the brush of his lips there.

Then they both heard movement in the kitchen as someone came in from the back, and Renee jerked back violently. Grant pulled away in a calmer, measured movement. He refused to show any sort of shame for almost being caught doing...*almost* doing something. Menacing the woman who'd let him be there in the first place. If 'menacing' was the right word. He was right in that she was not doing anything to stop him. And she thought that if Josh were here doing the same thing, she really *would* have pushed him out through the door. She did not just *let* people do things to her that she didn't want them to do, no matter her issues with touching people, with being near them.

"So..." Grant said. "How do you and yours feel about hares for dinner?"

"I'll tell Jake and Kit. How many?"

"How many do you need?"

"As many as you can bring as early as possible — we have eighteen other shapeshifters, then me."

He stared at her. "You aren't a...? You're completely human." Grant digested the unexpected information, then shrugged it off. "I was completely human once myself. I'll see what I can do about the meat."

"Do you know how to clean them?" Renee asked.

"I do." Grant backed out of the open front door and shut it in front of him, watching her to the last second.

Renee had to shake the prickle from her skin and press her palm against her mound to push down the gentle throb there. This was no time for an inconvenient and unsuitable reaction.

Breathing shallowly, she passed Leslie in the hall, coming back from his foray into the kitchen for a writing snack. He offered her half of his sandwich, but she shook her head. She would make her own. She was not hungry, but she thought a peanut butter and grape jelly sandwich might help settle her fluttering stomach. The encounter had only solidified her worry that letting Grant stay at the sanctuary was a bad idea. A very bad idea.

Before going to the computer room to join Leslie after making her sandwich, Renee went out through the back door and searched the compound from her vantage point for Jake. When she saw him up on the roof of the farm animal barn, she ran over and waved him down from the roof.

"Grant is getting us meat for dinner," she said. She slid an arm around his waist for a sideways hug to reassure him, knowing that he would not be happy. "Don't complain."

"I'm not exactly leaping for joy," Jake said.

"I know. But he showed a willingness to contribute. Let's just see, okay. For me, wait and see." She gazed up at his slightly flushed face, warm from work in spite of the cold, and smiled a little when she saw the resignation in his face.

"Whatever you want," he muttered. "When is he bringing them in?"

"I told him to bring them in well before dinner. We'll just see."

"Yes," Jake said. "We'll just see. I need to get back to work."

Renee left him to ruminate and returned to the house, this time taking her sandwich with her into the computer room and sitting down properly to work and print things out.

At around four-thirty, Renee went out into the greenhouse to trim, weed, and generally get herself dirty. She did not like using gloves. She could touch so few people that she felt better when she could touch her plants, even if they hurt her hands. Most of her flowers were outside in the flower garden next to the vegetable garden, but Renee liked to keep her roses — full-sized and miniature — in the greenhouse so that she could see them all year round. The greenhouse was warmer than outside, and during the much colder months, the heater kept the room at moderate to warm temperature for the plants. All of the irrigation was from harvested rainwater or melted snow. The greenhouse was her baby, although Britt usually helped her with it.

She wondered where the hell Britt was. When she was nowhere to be found, it usually meant she was taking one of the dog packs for a run. Or taking herself for a run in her human skin. But she usually stopped by in the afternoon for lunch or to say hi to Renee before going back out, and Renee had seen neither hide nor hair of her since she'd woken up.

Later that afternoon, when Renee was hip-deep in dirt and smelling of chlorophyll and compost—the greenhouse was actually quite large, large enough to keep her occupied when she needed the occupation— she heard the stomp of boots on the wooden floors in the kitchen and assumed it was either Max, Jake, or Grant. Rubbing her nose and probably getting some more dirt on her face, she set down her gardening tools and swung her head through the door from the greenhouse to the kitchen. Grant set a brace of hares and three rabbits onto the butcher block. Each of them had their necks snapped with minimal amounts of blood. Not at all the brutal ripping out of intestines like the mutilated animals. It did not mean, however, that Grant was not the one doing the killing. Renee was not that naïve.

Renee noticed that although he had put on a white undershirt, jeans, and the boots before coming in, he had blood smeared on his cheek near his mouth. Grant sniffed the air and turned to see her watching him. He chuckled in amusement.

"What did you do? Bury yourself alive and then dig yourself back up again?" Grant asked.

"What about you? Did you go hunting in your human skin?"

"What?"

"You have blood on your face," Renee said.

"Who are you to talk?" He wasn't argumentative, just sparring for the hell of it.

"I know what I'm covered in," Renee replied. "You just didn't seem to know what was on you."

Grant muttered under his breath something with the word 'you' in it, and Renee did not even want to ask him to speak up. If it was innuendo, she did not want to hear it, and she didn't believe in making people repeat themselves more loudly if they'd intended to keep quiet in the first place. Some things just needed saying aloud, even if they were not meant to be heard.

"Well, aren't you going to thank me for getting dinner for you and your friends?" Grant asked after he'd finished muttering.

"Thank you," Renee said politely. "Start cleaning them before Jake gets in, and you'll get a bigger thank you later."

"Oh, really? Dare I ask what that thank you will be?" Grant said, raising his eyebrows in interest.

"It's not what you're thinking," Renee said, backing out of the door.

"Then I'm not the only one thinking it, love," he called after her.

Renee shook her head as she returned to her work. With Grant's contribution, she supposed that all the shapeshifters would be getting a treat tonight, so she'd better find more makings for a salad.

When Renee finally came out of the greenhouse again, she could not see Grant anywhere, and Jake was finishing up cleaning the meat. Jake was pretty thorough when he dressed meat, and tried to use all the parts that he could, burying the rest near the compost heap. Using hunted or slaughtered meat was nothing new for Jake. The dogs had managed to bring a few hunted animals in over the years, and the shapeshifters sometimes had a yen for new meat rather than thawing frozen meat. Also, they had their small set of farm animals to eat, mainly chickens and turkeys—the latter mostly for holidays—since they used the cows for milk.

"Tell the wolf that he did well," Jake muttered as she passed by him.

"Tell him yourself," Renee said. "I'm not your mediator."

"Will he be eating with all of us?"

"I imagine so."

"So we'll use the big dining table tonight so the others can be invited in?" Jake asked. There was a breakfast table in the kitchen area where the core pack generally ate. But they also had a dining table in the great room that seated twelve, or more if they all squeezed in. Renee did not think that all the shapeshifters would be eating with them with Grant there. The dining room table would work fine.

She nodded and continued through the kitchen. She probably had a few hours before dinner.

As she left the kitchen, she heard Jake muttering, and she knew he was offering something of a prayer — a word or two of gratitude towards the animals for surrendering their lives. It was a ritual that the three shapeshifters who cooked — Jake, Ki, and occasionally Britt — followed regularly. Renee had once asked whether they really believed that the animals could hear them. Britt had answered that everything was energy, and even if the animals could not hear them, it was respectful to show thanks nonetheless for the energy that would go to nourish their bodies. It was not a matter of talking to the spirits of the animals, although some shapeshifters believed that. For Jake in particular, and to some degree Britt, it was just good manners.

Before going completely down the hall, Renee looked into the two bedrooms for the other shapeshifters. There were actually three rooms, but the two that were currently occupied were the largest ones. The one that was unoccupied had been empty for several years, since Renee had moved out of the small room. It had been Britt's idea, back when Renee was around sixteen and only did the occasional 'sleepover' up in Britt's loft. Britt had not liked the idea of Renee sleeping in a place that shut her off from the rest of the world, even from her own sanctuary. She'd thought that Renee would benefit from sleeping in a room with someone else, a room that didn't have proper walls. For the first few months in that room rather than her own, she had slept badly. But over time, she had grown accustomed to it and now enjoyed Britt's company. Even as a human instead of a service dog, Britt grounded her in a way that no one else at the compound had ever been able to, not even her father. Her mother had never seen her at her worst, for which Renee was sometimes relieved.

It had been the perfect little room, though. It held her high, full-sized bed, her dresser, and a small desk in a tight squeeze, but it also had its own small full bath. Just enough to live in for most of the day—which was why Britt had wanted her out and about. Her father had encouraged the move. The room had stayed the way she'd left it, sans the clothing and toiletries and her stuffed teddy bear. Her stuffed polar bear guarded the room now.

Renee climbed the stairs to her loft, grabbed a clear pair of jeans, a royal blue sweater, and a clean pair of panties before heading into the bathroom. She undressed after closing the door behind her and threw the utterly filthy clothes into her hampers.

Looking into the mirror, she could not help but snort at the places where the dirt abruptly ended at her collarbone, her arms—above her elbow because she had removed her jacket—and the area above her ankles where her socks stopped. In contrast with her pale skin, which was slightly sticky with sweat, her dirty skin looked as if it had been smeared with charcoal.

She turned the shower on as hot as she could stand. She cracked the bathroom door open a bit in order to let the moisture from the bathroom out of the room. As she pulled the blue-and-brown patterned shower curtain behind her, she felt the hot spray run over her chilled body. She ran her hands through her loose hair and shuddered at the knots she found.

Around the time she reached down to wash and shave her legs, she thought she heard the door creak. With the shower water pattering against the porcelain bottom of the tub, she could not be sure, but she paused to listen closer. She could not hear anything else, so she just continued with her routine, closing her eyes as she sensed the contours of her legs with her razor. Breathing out into the steamy air within the shower, she ran the razor past her thighs and carefully over the swell of her mound, over the labia. She could not remember exactly when she'd started shaving between her legs. She remembered first trimming it from the ginger bush that it had been until the hair was close against her skin. She'd wanted it to look clean and controlled, but she'd worried that she was going to get a shaving cut in a very inopportune and inappropriate place. She had been surprised when she hadn't cut anything at all the first time she'd tried.

She remembered what it was like the first time she'd used the showerhead on it, then her vibrator. It was as if the feeling had intensified just a little bit more. And she had done it ever since then, and liked the look and the feel for herself. She liked the routine, feeling the guarded blades sliding over the flesh and revealing it to her gaze when she looked down, seeing the tease of lip and clitoris whenever she looked in the mirror. It felt sexy to her somehow, especially since it had not been done for anyone but herself. Britt, who never shaved between her legs herself, had said—on one of the few occasions she had seen Renee naked—that she liked the way it looked on Renee. That it was beautiful, even. Another one of those moments when Renee hadn't been sure about what Britt wanted from her.

Renee circled her clit lightly at the thought and wondered whether she could ever get up the courage to ask Britt. Or take her up on any potential offer. She did not really want to get off now, just a little touch, a little push. Enough to get her going without going off. She considered pulling out the shower head, but she was not in that sort of mood.

Once she'd shut the shower off, she pushed the shower curtain back and peered out to make sure that she had just been hearing things. Everything was as she had left it, the door at about the same distance from the door frame as before. She still felt nervous, because she could not be sure whether the order of her clean clothes on the vanity counter was the way it had been when she'd thrown them there, nor was she sure that the distance between the door frame and the door was that exact distance. But everything was there, and she just figured that she was being paranoid. If someone had been there that she had to worry about, there was no reason that they would just come in to hear her in the shower instead of pulling open the shower curtain to see her.

And of course, when she was thinking 'they', she meant Grant. Then again, Britt could have come in looking for a hairbrush.

She pulled on her clean clothes and slipped into her house shoes before heading downstairs. She paused a bit when she saw how many people were in the cabin. She knew all of her shapeshifters pretty well, but it was different when they were outside to when they were in the home itself, filling space that she was not used to being filled. Or rather, she was not used to so *much* space being filled.

"Hey!" Britt came over and gave her cheek a kiss. "Long time no see, Red." True to form, she was wearing jeans and a loose blouse, but had neglected to button it.

"Where have you been all day?" Renee asked.

"Out and about—needed a good run today, ease out some tension of the stranger variety," Britt answered. "Took a pack out with me in the afternoon. We didn't see whatever animal has been ripping up other animals, and we didn't see any fallout from it either." She sat on the arm of the sofa and trained her dark brown eyes on Renee, running her fingers through her already wild, curly hair.

"So," she said.

Renee waited for her to continue.

"How has the stranger been so far? I heard he got us our dinner," Britt said.

"He's been an arrogant asshole, but he asked what he could do and said he liked to hunt," Renee said, shrugging off the underlying concern in Britt's question.

But Britt knew what Renee needed to hear—a direct question, something she could not shrug off. Britt knew all of Renee's weaknesses, and honesty was one of them. "Did he behave himself? Keep his hands to himself, and that sort of thing? Refrain from killing things that won't be on our table tonight?"

"Well, he wasn't a perfect gentleman," Renee answered quietly, so that the others around them could not overhear. "But it's not like any of us are expecting him to be. And he *was* willing to go out and hunt for the people who don't like him. Please, Britt, work with me here. Give him the benefit of the doubt and let him prove himself guilty."

Britt clenched her teeth, showing off the line of her cheekbones. She was not angry at Renee. That kind of clenching meant that she was trying to withhold an opinion. "Look, honey," Britt murmured. "The way he was looking at you... I'm just worried."

"*You* weren't exactly ignored, if you're talking about wandering eyes," Renee said. "Wandering eyes aren't anything to worry about, and as long as he makes an effort—"

"Wandering eyes, no," Britt said. "But wandering eyes can lead to wandering hands, and you don't exactly have the best natural defences, Renee. At least I can change into dog skin and teeth." It was rare to see Britt so serious. "You might look into investing in some protection. I'm just saying."

Renee did not know how to respond to that. Britt was right when she said Renee was incredibly vulnerable to that kind of danger in a way that the other shapeshifters were not.

When conversation waned in the great room, Renee knew that Grant had come in. He was still wearing the clothes that he had been wearing when he had come into the kitchen earlier. There was a spot of blood on the collar, but he had cleaned his face. He took the collective slight in stride and just went about his business with that small grin on his face. He raised an invisible glass at Renee and Britt from the other side of the room, sat down in an armchair, and waited for conversation to return to normal.

"Look, honey," Britt said, lowering her voice even more so that Renee had to lean in to hear her. "Maybe being a werewolf doesn't automatically make him dangerous. Like you said, maybe that's just another shapeshifter prejudice. But I could *swear* that *he* is dangerous. And I want you safe. I don't want you alone with him at any time."

"He hasn't killed me yet, Britt, and we have been alone together," Renee protested quietly. She held up her hands. "I'll be careful, okay. But I just... I don't want to condemn him before he's even had a chance. I refuse to be afraid just because he's here. I have too many things to do to be afraid here, on my own land where I'm not supposed to be afraid. Someone can't always be with me. I know what you're trying to do, and I know that you care, but..."

Britt touched a hand to her cheek and lifted her face a little so that she could press her lips against Renee's mouth. It was a chaste kiss, certainly more chaste than anything that Renee had witnessed her doing with Jake. Britt was cautious in her impulsive decision, but when Renee relaxed rather than tensed up after the initial surprise, Britt tilted her head more for a closer kiss.

It was a strange sensation, not least because it was only partially unexpected. Renee decided that she did not mind this display of affection from Britt. She almost wanted to slip her arm around Britt's waist so that she could be closer somehow, so that the slow and enticing tingling sensation in her breasts and between her legs could somehow be touched by someone she trusted, and maybe even loved, and maybe even wanted. The feeling was curiosity, but not curiosity about whether she could be sexually attracted to a woman. Just whether what was currently brewing between them could grow into something else, something bigger, or whether it was not to be. There did seem to be more than just a spark between Renee and her best, greatest, closest friend, a connection they'd had since they were young and had first met each other that went beyond just friendship.

That general openness in the sanctuary was part of the reason why, when Renee broke the kiss, there was not too much embarrassment when some of the shapeshifters around them cheered, happy that something they'd believed possible had indeed happened. There had been talk, of course. Close quarters always bred a certain amount of gossip and drama.

Renee tried to school her expression into something controlled, but she could not help the smile that filled her face. And Britt's initial expression of uncertainty relaxed.

"Thank God," Jake said, ruffling Britt's hair with a broad grin on his face. "I thought you'd never do it. Good on you. And you, my little gumdrop." He gave Renee a great big hug, then held her away from him and searched her face as he asked, "Are you okay? With this? With…?"

Renee nodded, a little flustered but okay. "I'm just… I shouldn't have been as surprised, but I was anyway."

"You've been expecting something like that?" Britt asked, honestly startled. "Damn, and I thought I had come up with something original."

Renee shrugged and looked down at her hands. "A little bit. Just little hints."

"And you'd be okay?" Britt asked. "With trying? Maybe?"

Renee chewed on her lower lip, then leant forward and kissed Britt herself. It was brief and a little off the mark, but Britt knew the effort it took for Renee to initiate something like that.

"Just remember that this is new to me," Renee murmured as she pulled back.

"If it makes you feel any better, I'm as nervous as you are," Britt said, laughing slightly. "Believe it or not, it's new to me, too."

"I mean, the whole idea of a relationship with another person…"

"I know what you mean," Britt said. She pushed a lock of hair out of Renee's face, then let her have her space. Britt knew she had to have her space, especially when she was nervous enough that her hands started shaking, which they were doing. She didn't take it personally.

As Britt pulled back, Renee caught the way that Grant was staring at the two of them. The realisation that they were not just being watched by old friends was like a proverbial kick in the gut, and she almost felt as if she was going to be sick at the way he was looking at her — *them* — his eyes dark with arousal. He seemed completely unashamed of the way he felt about what he had seen, although his pants were fashioned in such a way that if he was indeed aroused, she could not really see much. Just a suggestion. A certain knowledge that *that* was exactly how Grant saw what she and Britt had done. It made Renee feel almost slimy. The worst part was that the feeling was not necessarily bad. And Grant knew that Renee knew he had been watching. He stared directly at her without shame.

"By the way, my two favourite girls," Jake said, snapping her eyes away from Grant, "dinner is served."

* * * *

The dinner went surprisingly well, even though Renee was expecting some kind of catastrophe. Britt and Jake flanked her, partly to protect her from Grant and partly in celebration of what had just occurred. Grant sat just across from her. The dining room table was wide as well as long, so he would not be able to reach her even if he stretched out his legs. But he could stare. On the other hand, he could stare from any vantage point at the table if he wanted to. It was not overwhelming, and he did not look at her all the time. But when he was looking at her, at them, she could always tell.

To Britt's credit, she did not do anything like touch Renee's thigh under the table or give her a moony smile during the dinner. Everything was normal, which was part of the reason why Renee loved her. Whether she was *in* love with her was up to time, but love on its own had never been a question.

Hare was not a common meal at the dinner table, but most of them had had it before, either in its original state or cooked in a stew, the way Jake and Ki had cooked it for this evening. Renee's salad fixings helped set off the meal — it might not have been good enough for the royal table, but it was just fine for theirs.

Renee noticed that Grant never touched the vegetables or fruit. He ate around the carrots and celery in his stew when he could and just ate the meat.

Renee wondered whether it was a werewolf trait or just Grant, but she didn't say anything.

The shapeshifters on either side of him were sitting as far away from him as possible, which wasn't very far. Renee felt sorry that Leslie had not been paying attention when he'd sat down to Grant's left. He didn't know what to do with himself. Grant sometimes raised his eyebrow when Leslie did something clumsy while trying to avoid him, and there was that little smirk. But he did not do anything directly to Leslie, which Renee thought she might have to thank him for later. For the meal and for the general politeness. It was a small thing, but Renee felt that he was at least making an effort.

After dinner, Britt kissed Jake and left the rest of them to clean up, leading Renee up by the hand to their shared room. Renee was too focused on the feeling of another person's hand in hers—Britt was pushing the personal boundary deliberately, Renee knew, without pushing too far—to notice any of the people downstairs watching them go up. She did not even have the mental energy to think of what Grant was seeing. Let him look—as she had said to Britt, wandering eyes were nothing to worry about.

Britt led Renee to her own bed, then let go of her hand before moving to sit on the end of hers. A space of about five feet separated the two of them. Britt's blouse was still gaping open, and Renee found herself peering into the shadow to look at the swell of her breasts, the dusky brown of nipples the size of half dollars, tight in the cool air. She had seen Britt naked many times before, but it was as though she were seeing Britt through new eyes—Renee was good at compartmentalising things, so when Britt was just a friend, she was *just* a friend. The possibility of *girlfriend* was new territory now that the subject had been broached, and it changed the way she saw everything.

"Am I going to start as usual, or are you?" Britt asked.

Since Renee did not even know where to begin or what the question really was, she waited for Britt to start.

Britt inhaled to brace herself, then went into it. "Okay, I know I kind of stepped into it by kissing you in the middle of a crowded room when it was the last thing you expected or maybe even wanted. But I can't apologise. It was going to happen sometime. I knew that, and I guess you suspected it might. That makes me question my covertness, but that's not the point. The point is that we have a decision to make. Do you want to pursue this, this new angle of what I think we've always had? I don't know whether you think the same way. You've always kept what you think or feel pretty close to the vest, even though I know that you tell me more than you tell everyone else. But I sometimes have to feel my way through the craziness that is your mind. And I don't usually babble like this, but you know that I'm…"

"Nervous," Renee finished for her.

"Yes." Britt relaxed her shoulders a bit.

Renee bit her lip as she considered what to do. Her lip felt dry, and she licked it a little, sensing how dry her whole mouth was now.

The hum of continued conversation from the other side of the curtains reminded her that they were not really alone, but the fact that no one could see them gave her a little bit of courage, and she stood from her perch on the end of her bed and walked over to where Britt sat, then stepped between Britt's knees. Even sitting, Britt did not have to bend her neck too much to see Renee. And Renee did not have to lean down very far before she was eye-to-eye with Britt. She was surprised at her own daring, her own willingness to push herself through some of the barriers that kept her from really connecting. She threaded her fingers through Britt's hair, burying her hands in the mass of dark brown curls.

Britt had always been a grounding influence, and this was another time that she did not disappoint.

Renee felt the flutter of Britt's breath on her lips as she leaned closer, using her grip on Britt's hair to angle her head just right. Britt slid her fingers over the curve of Renee's hips, pulling her even closer, and they were kissing again. It was completely different when they were alone, much easier for each to experience the sheer sensation of the other, every touch, every sigh that no one else could hear.

Britt had to be the one to bring the kiss to the next level. Renee did not exactly understand the logistics of a kiss in practice, but Britt took her teaching role in stride. The warmth of the woman's tongue against Renee's lower lip was amazing, not at all what she had expected—she had known that tongues were a part of some kisses, but she hadn't thought she would enjoy that. She was pleasantly surprised as Britt slid her tongue against Renee's own.

It took a hand on Renee's to tell her that she was holding too tightly to Britt's hair, and they broke apart, laughing a little.

"Sorry," Renee muttered.

"No," Britt said. "It's okay. It's good that you're excited. I want you excited." She slipped a hand beneath Renee's shirt to press the palm of her hand on the flat of Renee's stomach. "And I want you to do what you want, what feels good for you, Renee. I promise you won't break me, and feeling your way is half the fun. It's okay to make mistakes. You know that you can trust me, and I know that I can trust you. It's the safest place in the world, right here. All right?"

Renee grinned, then pushed the blouse from Britt's shoulders. Britt pulled her arms back so that the shirt could come off completely.

"There's my girl," Britt said, her gorgeous smile shining through. Renee was overcome by the idea that millions of men *and* women would kill for the position she was in right now. It made her feel unusually powerful. Although she was gentle as she guided Britt down, so that she lay on the bed with Renee bent over her, her touch was firm.

"I don't want everything tonight," Renee said as a sort of disclaimer.

"I understand," Britt said. "I'm not sure I do either. But I can say that you're taking things a little further than I had anticipated. I saw this happening a few months from now. You should be proud of yourself." Britt strained upward to swipe her tongue against Renee's cheek affectionately. "And I'm reaping the benefits."

"Mm-hmm," Renee hummed as she kissed Britt again. Already she was starting to get the rhythm of it, just feeling it, rocking in and rocking out. It was more awkward when she was above Britt like this, with her knees on either side of Britt's hips. But it also gave her a bit more control, and she stroked Britt's hair, which was splayed around her head like a corona. It was hard not to touch Britt's bare skin as she tried to press closer, her body wanting the closeness that her lips had with the girl beneath her — that was something very new for Renee, like so much that night.

Britt was brushing her fingertips underneath Renee's shirt, understanding Renee's need for her to pace herself. Renee knew that Britt could be much rougher. She almost wished that Britt could do that now. Although with the way that Renee's heart was beating fast enough to make her head tingle, she thought it might be a bad idea.

She did not even realise how her hips were rocking down with the rest of her body until she undulated against Britt's denim-clad hips, which rose to meet her. She gave a little squeak that sounded patently unsexy to her own ears, and she actually lost balance so that she was flush against Britt's body. It was surprisingly warm, like her mouth, and the buds of her nipples pressed up against Renee's chest. She felt her own small nipples tighten against the fabric of her bra in response.

"Oh. My. God," she whispered, her mouth pressed against Britt's neck. She was already oversensitive to the way everything felt, and to have it thrust upon her — or rather, to thrust it against Britt, since she was the one who'd fallen on top of the woman — almost overloaded her. Not that it was doing nothing to her sexually. She felt if she did not get some friction against her clit, she was going to go crazier.

Britt laughed, rubbing Renee's back and kissing her head lightly. "Do you need to stop?"

Renee answered by canting her hips, pressing her mound against Britt's. From the way Britt exhaled sharply, Renee thought she had done something right. She had certainly found her own spot. It was nothing like using a vibrator to stimulate the spot. Nothing at all like that. But she felt herself come close to the edge anyway, shaking with stress and desire at the same time as she kissed Britt again, drawing both of them to a sitting position, Renee straddling Britt's thighs and Britt bracing herself with a hand behind her. They rocked together, and Renee shyly brought a hand between them to touch the swell of Britt's right breast. It was surprisingly heavy in her hand, the nipple hard and pliant as Renee circled it in the centre of her palm. Renee would have thought that, having breasts of her own, it would not feel so strange, so exciting in its novelty. But it was completely different when she was touching something that belonged to someone else.

"Take it, roll it between your fingers," Britt whispered in her ear before kissing Renee's neck, laving the line of the cord in a way that made Renee want to moan. She didn't, though, not feeling comfortable with making any noise at all, especially with the possibility that someone would hear them. Hear *her*.

Renee did as she was told, feeling the nipple harden even more as Britt jerked her hips under Renee's, putting pressure in just the right places.

"Look, I don't expect us to complete each other, but seriously, Renee, I think I'm going to explode here," Britt murmured. "Who would have thought?"

Who would have thought? Renee repeated in her head. Everything was too much, and it was not too long before she was clutching at Britt's arms as she *pressed* and felt everything on the inside clench and flutter into a release to the thrust of Britt's tongue in her mouth. Renee was perfectly silent, almost afraid to breathe through it as the orgasm curled her toes and made her dig in her nails into Britt's arms a little.

Renee felt Britt bring her free hand between them to circle violently at her own clit through her jeans. As Renee's muscles began to loosen to the flood of endorphins through her system, Britt gasped through her own climax, whispering Renee's name in a rhythm that became almost a chant. Finally finished, Britt fell back onto the bed so that they were again a tangle of limbs. Renee could not help but laugh into Britt's shoulder, punctuating the conclusion with a few soft kisses before resting her head between Britt's breasts and just feeling the warmth and smoothness of her skin itself, without any of the pressure of desire.

After a few minutes of hearing Britt's heart beat under her head, Renee propped herself up and rolled to the side, adjusting her clothes as she flipped her legs over the side of the bed. She did not know what to say. She knew what she wanted, but she had no words for it.

"So..." Britt murmured, her pink lips darker and fuller, as they usually were after Jake had just finished kissing her. And it was from her, Renee, of all people. Her grin was tentative. "I think it's safe to say that we're compatible on this level. God, Renee, I didn't think that you'd...you know. I didn't think you had it in you yet." Britt pushed herself up and rested her chin on Renee's shoulder. "It was amazing," she said quietly, soberly.

"You, too," Renee replied. It was not nearly adequate enough to express the most primitive sense, deep in her stomach, that she wanted to hold Britt against her and keep her there like a stuffed animal all night, but she just couldn't. She physically could not do it, and she physically could not say it. She could just reach up to touch Britt's cheek softly to try and reassure her that everything was fine, that they could keep doing what they had been doing, that they could really try at whatever this could be. She kissed Britt on the corner of her mouth and stood.

She was the luckiest woman alive because Britt understood.

"You probably want a quick shower, just to rinse off after that," Britt said, fingers trailing down the length of Renee's spine and touching an unexpectedly sensitive spot just below the curve of one cheek under her jeans. "Remember, I'm next. Would you rather I not come in while you're still in there, or…?"

"I'd prefer some time alone," Renee said. Everything she said came out wrong, came out cold. She hated it. Even as she was walking towards the bathroom, she stopped herself and turned around, forcing herself to face Britt, who was looking remarkably happy and young in a way that Renee had not noticed in a long time.

"Brittany?" Renee said.

"Yes, Red?" Britt asked. The decade-old pet name made Renee feel a rush of warmth over her face in a flush. Not a bad one.

"I think… I think we can do this," Renee said. The words were hard to get out, but once she did, the next words were even harder—although not painful—no matter how true they were. "And I don't expect anything in our lives separate from each other to change. Jake… I want you two to still…you know, be together. I wouldn't want it to change."

Britt's face became even more beautiful—Renee didn't think 'love' was a facial expression, but if it was, that might have been it. "I'm glad you are the woman that you are, Renee Chambers," Britt said. "Now go clean up. *I* am going to go downstairs and make brownies. We can have some tonight, just the core pack. I think this whole thing calls for chocolate."

Renee smiled. "I agree."

She went into the bathroom, retrieving a clean pair of panties from her dresser first. It occurred to her that she had just had what basically amounted to sex with her best and closest friend, with all her clothes on. And Britt had only lost her shirt. Renee thought that was amazing.

As rare as it was, even as she got into the shower and stood under the spray, Renee found that in the privacy of the moment, she could not stop smiling.

Chapter Four

The world hadn't changed. Renee still had work, and she still did it without mooning. Too much. But it was part of the experience, part of the novelty. She could actually let someone touch her without going a little crazy—at least, not in a bad way. Britt continued to not push her, but they did sometimes take time out of the day to kiss. To keep in practice, Britt said with a grin on her face. Sometimes those kisses led to more, but it was still Britt who shed some of her clothes, more comfortable in skin, while Renee only let Britt touch her underneath her clothing, even though Britt had seen her naked without much fanfare before. For Renee, it was not a matter of modesty or fear. She just felt more comfortable with some kind of layer, although that layer seemed to be becoming more cumbersome by the day, even as she needed it. After all, the weather was getting colder.

Grant regularly brought in meat, but there were some days that he disappeared completely. He had made it through his week trial period, and although he was not exactly well-liked, he mostly kept out of the way. So everyone let him be, warily adjusting to his presence in the sanctuary. Renee was a bit concerned when the full moon came. She and the core pack stayed up just in case Grant tried to kill something under the moon's influence, but as far as she knew, he never stepped foot on the compound.

He still watched her from a distance with an intensity that might as well have been right in front of her. He was somehow there whenever she and Britt were together outside of their room. Renee wasn't innocent. She knew that some men liked watching two women, and she assumed that was the reason that Grant was around so much—that he was gathering fodder for whatever stroke fantasies were simmering in his brain. But as long as he did not invade their privacy and try to make them do something for him, as long as he did not touch her, he could be as uncouth as he wanted. There were assholes in every society. Grant just happened to be one of them. In the end, she and Britt decided to ignore him as best they could.

As more and more flurries swept over the sanctuary, more frequent donations began to come in from her regulars. Most of them knew that the winter was sometimes the hardest time for the sanctuary, because more energy was required to keep things running. Winter was also the time for more adoptions and sometimes more inhabitants due to poor Christmas gift-giving. Renee was happy, though, that three of her dogs had been adopted over the course of three weeks.

Things were normal, and maybe better.

Then someone buzzed her doorbell at the gate. This caused an alarm to go off over the facility. Just a short buzz—nothing loud or obnoxious. Enough to let everyone know that someone was there and to tell them to change if they needed to. Most of the shapeshifters reverted to their dog skins when company came. Renee thought it had something to do with keeping their whereabouts a secret and hiding their identities. Most people probably assumed she had someone working with her—there was no possible way that she could run an operation like this all on her own. But the shapeshifters did not want anyone to know that *they* were ones doing it.

The buzzing sound also told Renee to drive down to meet whoever came. The sanctuary could use a security camera at the gate, but they hadn't come up with the extra money for it, mostly because it was not as needed as all that. Who would take the time to come all the way up to her sanctuary to make trouble? Besides, the dogs themselves were her built-in security. Even those who were not dominant knew an intruder when they saw one—and the shapeshifters had an even better sense of those who were not supposed to be there. A security camera was never high on the priority list of purchases.

Renee looked up when the buzz filled the compound, although the people at the gate probably could not hear it, so far was the facility from the gate. No one was supposed to come today, but maybe someone had not read the website rules about calling to make an appointment. Maybe they thought they could come on their own time. Either way, she would need to tell them to make an appointment, although she might let them in if they seemed okay. After all, it was a long drive back to civilisation.

Britt came into the computer room just as Leslie turned to Renee in confusion.

"What's going on?" Britt said. "I didn't know there was someone coming today."

"Neither did I," Renee replied.

"Do you want me to go down with you?" Britt asked. "I'm beginning to dream about shipping orders and gardenias."

"Sure, if you want to. Human or dog skin?"

"Dog skin," Britt answered. "In case it's someone from town, they should see me in the state they're used to. It could just be a squirrel having fun with the doorbell, though."

"Best to check." Renee minimised the window she was working on and ran to get her proper shoes on. She grabbed her scarf and coat as Britt shed her clothing layers and changed into the malamute. She then trotted behind Renee as she headed to the car.

"What the hell was that?" Grant came out from behind the log home and rubbed the side of his head as though the buzzing had pained him. Renee did not understand why it would — it was not at a frequency that harmed the dogs.

"Doorbell," Renee said. "I have to go down and see what they want. Choose which skin you want to be seen in if someone comes up. Or just...go away."

"I'm going to ride in the back of the truck," Grant said. And before Renee could say anything, he opened the door and jumped into the covered bed, then pulled the door closed behind him.

Renee looked down at Britt, who looked back at her with an inscrutable expression on her face. Finally, Renee shrugged, thinking that saying anything would be more trouble than it was worth to make a fuss. As long as he didn't make her crash. Britt did a little huffy thing with her nose as Renee sighed and opened the driver's door. Britt got in first, and Renee climbed in after her.

Renee could see through the back window that Grant was lying down with his hands cradling his head. He was insane, and she shook her head before buckling herself in and turning the truck on.

The drive there was fairly uneventful. Grant didn't do anything, just lay there in the bed, sitting up near the end in order to brace himself against the unbalanced shaking and sudden stops that came from driving on a dirt road.

When she reached the end of her driveway, Renee groaned. Josh and Marcus and one of their friends, Will, were there, and they leaned against Josh's truck with their arms crossed and faces smug, obviously glad they could waste her time and harass her with their fucking passive-aggressive bullshit. She barely realised that she'd said that out loud before Grant opened the back window and said, "Kiss your mother with that mouth?"

"Shut up," she muttered as she turned off her truck and got out.

"Hey, bitch, got a dog for sale?" Marcus asked. The man didn't need to be drunk to be crass.

"Fuck off," Renee said from the other side of the gate.

Josh raised his eyebrows. The other two did their 'oooooohs', which had been old way back in high school.

"Come on, this is a charity, right?" Will said. "We're here to be charitable."

She did not even try to be polite. "This is a sanctuary. We screen each potential adoption, and you can't get in without an appointment. So. Fuck. Off. I don't have time for you."

"But what if we want a dog? We have money. We can pay," Will said.

"I would never give one of my dogs to you. This isn't a business, it's a non-profit organisation. I decide whether to let the dogs go or not. I'm not doing it for the people that come in, I'm doing it for the dogs that go out. And I would never ruin one of my dogs' lives by letting you bring him home," Renee said.

"God, you're chatty when you're safe behind an iron fence," Josh said. He curled his hands around the wrought iron and pressed his face between the bars. "I'd half a mind to think you were slow."

"You *do* have half a mind," Renee muttered.

"I heard that," Josh said. "You know, I may not be able to get this truck through the gate, but I can find a way over the fence. Primitive system you've got here."

"You do that, Josh," Renee said, stepping closer to the fence and stopping short of his arm's reach. Her voice could shatter ice as she continued, "You could fall and get barbed wire in your balls. Or, if you make it over, one of the dogs could take a bite out of your face. Or ass. Or worse. See, my sanctuary doesn't need anything more than it has. You come in here and find that out."

"If I get a bite out of my ass, I'll sue the sanctuary for reckless endangerment," Josh said. "I could shut you down and have all your doggies put to sleep."

"You would have been trespassing. Anything the dogs did to you would be in protection of my property, and you would be liable for any damages. If you tried to go to court, you would lose," Renee said. She did not think that it was in Josh to do anything like that, anything complex like legal issues. He had probably just watched too much *Judge Judy* and *Law & Order* and thought it was all easy and dramatic. But she knew several lawyers through the shapeshifter community and had their numbers in her personal phone book—they were prepared to represent her for any reason because of what she did for their own.

However, there was a kind of manic energy in Josh's face, underlain with calculation, and Renee started to get nervous.

"Go back to Antoine and play mailbox baseball or throw eggs at houses or something like that," Renee said. "There's nothing for you here."

She turned around to return to her car when she heard a loud clang behind her. She jumped, then spun around to see Marcus with a shovel in his hand. The sound was from hitting the gate with it.

"Don't you walk away from us!" Marcus shouted. "What is it? So afraid of men you won't just let us into your little sanctuary thing?"

"And you think assaulting my gate with a shovel presents a convincing argument? If I called the police, sure, you could get away in time. But I know all your names, and now there's a mark where that shovel hit the gate. You want destruction of property on your rap sheet, Marcus?" Renee didn't actually know whether the mark on the gate would be enough to convict them of anything other than being dicks, especially since the police would get there so late after the fact. But if they were avid *Judge Judy* and *Law & Order* audiences, they probably thought things really worked that way.

"Frigid bitch," Josh said through the bars, a huge, shit-eating grin on his face.

"After all, why wouldn't I want to spend time with a bunch of grown-up boys who sling back shots to get falling-down drunk and try to intimidate a woman who is much smaller than you and doesn't give a shit? Believe me, Josh, it's not me. It's you."

Renee opened her truck door, and when Marcus brought the shovel back to hit the gate again, Britt rushed out through the open door and started snarling and barking. She looked enough like an angry wolf, even for those few moments, that Marcus fell back in a comic pratfall, the shovel slipping from his fingers and hitting the back of Josh's truck. The dent was not bad, especially since Josh's truck was beat up without the help of the shovel. But Josh turned his attention to the damage that Marcus had done, and Renee called to Britt to get back into the car. She left them at the gate yelling at each other about stupidity and shovels and plans.

"So, my love, my darling," Grant said, as she motored up the driveway. She jumped and almost ran the truck into a tree. She hadn't even realised that he had crawled through the window into the small seating area behind the front seats. He must have been lying down until he'd popped up like that. "Care to explain that little interlude?"

"Goddamn it, don't do that! You don't scare people when they're driving!" Renee yelled. "It's dangerous."

"Sorry," Grant said, although he did not sound too sorry. More amused than anything. "So, the brainless no-necks. What do they have against you?"

"Petty high-school vendettas, I guess. And they're clearly bored out of their minds," Renee answered. She was surprised to find that she was actually angry. 'Angry' was not usually a word in Renee's emotional vocabulary. It made her feel a little wired, and not in a good way — as if she had drunk three cups of coffee too many. "What on earth made them think this was a good idea? They had to drive hours to get here just to get in my face..."

"Look in a mirror lately, love?" Grant asked mildly.

Renee opened her mouth, but nothing came out. She closed it, only to open it again. "You can't be serious."

In a blink, Britt transformed into her human skin, expression indignant. "What are you saying?"

"I'm saying, Lady Godiva, that when a man likes a woman, he'll do anything to get her. And I can guarantee that if you could get them all the way up here all by yourself, Red, seeing the two of you together would have them breaking down the fences. What a man will do for a piece of tail, right?"

Renee forced herself to loosen her fingers from the steering wheel. "Are you implying that they came here because they thought they would somehow have sex with me?"

"I'm saying that the one who was staring through the bars at you wants to have sex with you," Grant said. "You'll find that the more men throw the word 'frigid' around, the more they just want to take a ride. Of course, if they're so pitiful as to insult you to try and get you in bed, they aren't worthy."

"Oh, really? Thank you for clearing that up for me," Renee said. "I was actually considering turning this truck around and having it down with all three together. Glad I had you to talk me out of it."

"God, Renee, you should get upset more often," Britt said, crossing her legs. "You've got a brittle tongue."

"Seems good enough for you most of the time," Grant muttered, sitting back in his seat.

"Oh, for fuck's sake, grow up," Britt said.

"I'm only being honest when I say that the idea of the two of you together makes everyone in the sanctuary hot, not just me."

"Most of them don't say so to our faces," Britt said.

"So you don't mind that every single one of us jacks off to the image of you in our minds, just as long as no one says anything," Grant said. "Or is it just me that you mind?"

"Mostly, it's just you," Britt retorted.

"I notice that Renee isn't saying anything about it. So far, the only lady that doth protest is you. The protector. Who can't always protect her, can you?" Grant leant forward again. "You can't protect her from people like me. You probably can't even protect her from those men back there if they decided to sneak in. It would take more than just you to take them down. And you know it."

Britt turned around in her seat and glared at Grant. "Last time I checked," she said slowly, "you weren't doing anything to her but acting a little creepy. You care to up the ante and start doing a little more? You'd find yourself half-eaten in your sleep if you tried anything to hurt her..."

"Who said I wanted to hurt her?" Grant said, bringing his hands behind his head.

"I'm sitting right here," Renee said. "Just stop it, the both of you. I don't need this on top of those boys."

"I'm trying to help," Britt replied, sounding a little hurt.

"I know. I'm not mad or annoyed at you," Renee said.

She was not accustomed to having to reassure Britt. She guessed that her inability to infuse the right kind of emotion into her voice could backfire when Britt felt more vulnerable, when she had something to lose.

"Just don't bother engaging when he tries to get a rise out of you," Renee said. "And that's what he's doing. He gets off on it. Don't you?"

Grant grinned, and Renee saw a surprising array of sharp, white teeth that could not be human in the rearview mirror. But then they changed back to their human size. Renee did not think she had imagined it, but she could not figure out what it meant.

"Well, look at you, Red," Grant said. "You barely speak two words to me, but you know me so well. I like that."

Renee did not say anything to that.

"You know, I'm not harmless if you just ignore me."

"I'm not angry anymore," Renee said by way of explanation.

"Do you want me to make you angry again?" Grant asked.

She did not answer him, refusing to play into his game. The compound was just ahead.

"Look, the drive was a good distraction," Britt said. "Well, it was until a few minutes ago. Could you let me off here? I'll take a pack on a run and do some greenhouse work. See you this evening? Will you be okay?"

Renee slowed the truck. "I think I'll make it the next twenty feet without getting mauled. Go on."

Britt kissed her on the corner of her mouth before opening her door and jumping out. Before she even hit the ground, she was back in her dog skin and running ahead towards the compound.

"I can see why you didn't say no to that," Grant murmured.

"No," Renee said, "you don't." She put the truck in drive and continued her way up.

He was almost right next to her ear now. "I've seen her kissing that pup, the one who thinks he's alpha. The clean Marine kind of guy." It was the closest he had been since that first day he'd been in the sanctuary. It made her skin prickle for him to be that close. Her hair fluttered a little with each word.

"I imagine you have," Renee said.

"Hmm. I wouldn't have thought you'd be the non-monogamous type," Grant said.

"All these years when we were friends, she loved Jake," Renee said. "I never felt like she was spending too much time with him or that he stole time away from me. And Jake actually wanted Britt to start something with me. Why be jealous of him if he's not jealous of me? It's not like she has a limited amount of love to give."

"That just makes me curious, then." His lips were brushing against her ear now, and it was making her hands shake. "Do *you* have a limited amount of love to give?"

"If I had love to give, I wouldn't give it to you," Renee said shortly.

"Somehow, I just don't believe you," Grant whispered.

Renee stopped the car abruptly, earlier than she usually would. She turned off the car, pulled the parking brake on, and got out of the truck without looking back.

It took Grant some real effort to get out of the car through the doors rather than out through the back window. When he did, he ran up behind her and grabbed her shoulder.

"What are you afraid of?" Grant asked.

"It doesn't have to be about fear," Renee said, whirling around and looking up at him straight in the face, which was not her forte. She would be proud about it later, when she lay in bed and shivered at the thought that she did it at all. "Sometimes, a girl just doesn't like you."

Grant lifted his head, and Renee could see his nostrils flare and eyes close as he breathed her in. "Somehow," he repeated, "I just don't believe you."

Renee jerked herself away from him, flushed. "Leave it," she said, softly and firmly, as if she were telling a dog not to chew on a shoe.

She was almost to the house when she heard, "I'm afraid I can't do that."

She slammed the door behind her.

* * * *

Renee lay under her covers, listening to the creaking of Britt's bed across the room. It was not that she was lonely. It was actually kind of nice listening to them be together without trying too hard to be quiet—usually when they tried too hard, they ended up being louder anyway. She just pulled her three quilts around her, disregarding Claire, the arthritic Maine Coon, who wouldn't have budged from her spot at Renee's feet even if Renee was the one who had been doing the midnight dance.

Her evening had mostly gone well. Jake had walked in on Britt and Renee having a little time together, but after a brief check with Renee, Britt had told him to stay, not back out. He had grinned and sat down on Britt's bed. It had been strangely thrilling and invasive at the same time. She did not feel threatened by Jake— she had been honest about that. But she was not sure whether she was ready for him in this new capacity.

Britt had consciously become more demonstrative. Not more forceful, but as though her moves were choreographed. Renee felt that their sort of organic dance became something she was only marginally a part of. Britt had sensed the way she'd withdrawn and asked whether she was okay.

"Not to push you too far, but this kind of thing can be fun with other people. If you would like to try it. And *only* if you would like to try," Britt had said, peppering kisses along her cheek to her ear, where Renee had discovered she was quite sensitive—*and not just with Britt,* that voice in the back of her head had told her. "I know how you…"

"Brittany," Renee had said, pulling Britt up and looking at her straight in the eye. "I may be a little broken in the head, and I appreciate the time you're taking with me. Appreciate it more than you'll ever hear from me most of the time. But I just want you to know that if I want something to stop, I'll say something. If you want to try something new, you don't have to preface it with all that reassurance. Okay?"

Britt had laughed and squeezed Renee's bare arm. They had not quite got to the point that Renee liked having all her clothes off, but nonetheless she'd grown to like the feeling of skin on skin. She had taken to wearing a cami under her shirts, just so that Britt could take off the shirt and there would be something there underneath, but not enough that she could not feel that closeness. It was practical, too, with the cold weather.

When Renee had swivelled to face Jake, he'd been looking at her with something like misgiving, but not quite. More like he wasn't sure where he stood with her. She was the human alpha without even trying, without even being dominant. And there she'd been right before him, waiting.

"Didn't you hear the girl?" Britt had said, looking amused. "She's not going to break."

"What do I...?" He'd laughed at himself. "Where do I start?"

So Renee had started for him, reaching up to pull him down to her height, which was an even greater distance than she had to pull Britt. She'd discovered how much control she would have to give up in order to kiss him properly. She'd had to crane her neck and curve her back so that he'd had to hold her to keep her balanced, and she'd clung to his shoulders. He'd just been so big... And his long blond hair in a tail had been begging for her to hold it, to feel its texture, which had been a little rougher than the texture of hair she was used to.

He'd been so gentle as he'd kissed her, as if he was kissing a china doll, and Renee had found herself impatient. She'd bitten his lip. Not hard, but enough for him to know that he did not have to wear kid gloves with her. With all the 'practice' she'd had with Britt, she was a little more confident in her kissing technique by now, even if she did not know much else in terms of style. She only knew what she wanted to feel, and he'd still been too careful, even as his tongue had met hers when she'd drawn him into her mouth. But to kiss her, he'd had to hold her, and as the kiss had warmed between them, he'd held her closer. All she'd been able to do was hold on and feel the growing hardness of him against her stomach.

Then Britt had been behind her, laving her ear and running her hands up and down Renee's arms until she'd brought goosebumps to the flesh. Britt's breasts had pressed against her back, and she'd been surrounded by two people who Renee thought could love her, who knew what she needed and what she didn't need. It had been warm, together, close, and she'd felt herself rubbing back against Jake where he stood, then pulling away to feel Britt closer. There had been so much more sensation with another in the mix. She hadn't known whether she could deal with this much—the feelings, the neediness, then the subtle, growing sense of claustrophobia. Gentle fingers over her back and over her arms, soft tongues, soft kisses, little moans. She'd felt as if she was a part of something larger, but she had been about to fall at any moment. She'd needed her feet flat on the ground.

She'd pulled away, stumbled for a minute as she had found her footing.

One side of Britt's mouth had lifted as she'd watched Renee adjust her cami and the bra straps underneath, pulling the bottom down over the lifted hem.

"A little too much for now?" Britt asked.

Renee nodded.

"But not bad?"

Renee shook her head. "Just...I need to go. You two should stay. I'll be back out in a few minutes."

The lights had been off when she'd come out from the bathroom—just a quick soak to think about things. But she could hear them anyway. She felt so unsatisfied, yet knew she simply couldn't go the rest of the way. Like her social skills in and out of the sanctuary, she felt she could only go so far without feeling completely out of control. She wondered if there was any loss of control that was actually pleasant. Even when she brought herself to a climax, or when she and Britt reached that place together at their right pace... That did not feel out of control. Her teeth would clench, her fingers tighten, her breath stop. She rarely cried out, never sighed or moaned. Nothing that Britt did. And she wondered whether it was her. Whether she could ever let herself really lose control.

She rolled over so that she was on her stomach, sighing into the pillow and feeling her heart beat against the mattress.

They had finally climaxed—Jake first this time, then Britt. And Jake at least seemed to be the kind of man who fell asleep pretty fast after sex. Orgasm didn't make Britt or Renee tired, but it was also midnight now, so Britt was probably going to sleep, too. Technically, Renee should not even have been in bed. It was not late enough for her. So she just lay there, trying to feel relaxed and listening to all the night sounds of breathing, the house creaking, Claire humming her little snores.

Then she heard it—a wolf's howl. It was like that night again, except the dogs didn't go crazy when they heard it. Since the werewolf had come to the sanctuary, the dogs became agitated when he was around, but they did not respond to its howl anymore, other than to cower in their beds. Malcolm had slept in the dog barn for a few nights after Grant had arrived, to teach them that they did not have to be afraid. Even if some of the staff, including Renee, were concerned that they *should* be afraid.

Renee got out of bed, listening as the howl rose again, higher and almost ringing in her ears. She slipped her house shoes on and went downstairs. Grabbing her dressing gown from the hall coat rack, she opened the front door and stepped out. She didn't turn on the porch light. Even without it on, she could see Grant running around the corner of the dog barn. The moment he saw her, he howled again, sounding as if he had found prey, as though he were calling to a pack.

With a hitch of effort, he walked straight into his human skin, bones and sinew creaking before leaving him a light piece of flesh in the moonlight.

"You know it's not safe to be out here," he said.

She didn't feel any of the chill when she shed her dressing gown on the porch steps, single-minded as she grabbed the sides of his face and pulled him down to her. He was not quite as tall for her as Jake — it felt as though he fit better, a little shorter than Britt. And God, he was all around her, not even stopping to ask as he plundered her mouth, drinking her in and holding her tightly against his rapidly reacting body, as hard as a rock to the touch, hard and warm and smooth. She touched him everywhere, feeling every inch of him as he ripped the camisole off and pushed her bra down to release her breasts to his mouth — hot, passionate, not caring how she was shaking or panting or digging her fingernails into his shoulders. Half pushing him away and half bringing him closer.

He wrenched himself away from her flesh that glistened from his saliva, grinning silver, sharp teeth as he shoved her down on the porch so that he could pull off her pants. He did not even bother taking off her panties, just pushed them aside.

Then he was filling her, filling a place that had been so empty and grasping until he stretched her around him. She whimpered. It should have hurt, but it didn't. She just wanted him to fuck her, fuck her hard, make her feel something.

He bent over her as he did what she wanted without her saying a word. His vulpine teeth sank into her shoulder, and her hips rose to meet his as the coil of ecstasy released. She thrashed against it, with it.

And then there was nothing, and the rise of physical sensation was lost when she opened her eyes to the wooden beams of the roof. She was in her own room. Britt was above her, shaking her. Her orgasm was awful, an unbearable clenching into nothingness without even the benefit of arousal. A bodily response to blood flow, with no feeling of warmth at all.

Renee gripped tightly to Britt's wrist as she rode it out without any pleasure.

"Hey, are you okay?" Britt asked, sounding really concerned. Renee wondered whether she had been making any noise. She remembered bits of the dream—it was already fading away. All she knew was that Grant had been inside her, doing whatever he liked, that she had somehow been turned on, but that the climax had been empty. Stolen.

"Sorry," Renee said as her heart rate began to return to a normal pace. "Nightmare."

"I'll say," Britt murmured. "You were thrashing in your sleep."

"Not to interrupt or imply anything, but it honestly doesn't smell like a nightmare," Jake said. He did look concerned, though.

"Blood flow to the genitalia is biologically normal during sleep. Even for women," Renee said. "It was a bad dream."

"Do you need your medication?" Britt asked.

"I'm calm now," Renee said. "But..." She curled her knees under her to kneel and press her lips against Britt's neck. She stroked a wet line up the curve of Britt's throat with her tongue. Britt gasped at the unexpected sensation.

"Please," Renee whispered. "I don't want to... I've already, you know... But I want to feel you."

Britt wrapped her arms around Renee's waist. "Who am I to resist such a wish?" she asked with a grin.

"Can we…in your bed? Can we fit?" Renee asked. "I don't think I'm ready for Jake to be with me like that…but I don't mind him there. I want him there."

"I wouldn't complain," Jake said. "Come here." He held out his arms. "I'm sorry you had a bad dream." He took her into an embrace, just to comfort her, not with any other thought behind it. Jake was one of the few people she could allow to get so close, especially when she was feeling so vulnerable. Britt was another, of course. Renee brushed her lips against his chest lightly, then pulled away.

He scooted over in the queen-size bed to lie against the other pillow, content with watching for the time being.

Renee lay down on the bed, removing her pyjama pants much more patiently than Grant had in her dreams, then buried her hands in Britt's beautiful hair as Britt climbed over her. She loved Britt's hair, the way it curled around her fingers, how soft it was, how it closed in around them so it was just the two of them in the world. Renee breathed her in as she kissed the woman, smelling skin, smelling Britt's shampoo, smelling a little of Jake. If asked, she would not be able to articulate what those smells were, only that they *were*. She kissed Britt as if drinking her in, and Britt, seeming a little surprised, matched her fervour, responding with the intensity that Renee demanded.

She wrapped her legs around Britt's waist, curling them around the length of Britt's thighs and stroking skin on skin. It was a new sensation, and she had never known just how sensitive her legs could be, particularly her thighs. They clenched against Britt's hip bones as Renee tried to bring her closer, almost like pulling her in. It was as though Renee were trying to merge the two of them, but it was just impossible. Renee broke the kiss in frustration.

"What is this?" Britt whispered. "What's wrong?"

"I'm just... I feel lost. Disconnected. I want to... It's like you can't get close enough." She explored lower with her mouth, running over the line of Britt's collarbone.

"That must have been some dream," Britt breathed.

Renee slid down farther under Britt until her mouth pressed against the flesh of her breasts, tasting the skin there, licking under them where the breast was heavy against her tongue before taking the nipple into her mouth. She was gentle, but Britt almost whined as she flicked her tongue back and forth, enjoying the sensation of the rough, hard nub in her mouth. She ran her nails up Britt's thighs before sliding them over the firm, round flesh of her ass.

"Whoa, girl," Britt said, lifting herself up so that she was on her hands and knees. "Don't start something you can't finish. What's up?"

"I'm sorry," Renee murmured. "I didn't mean to get that carried away."

"No," Britt said, lying down next to her after Renee shifted so that she was between Jake and Britt. "Don't be sorry. It was good. I promise."

"I'll say," Jake muttered. Renee elbowed him in the stomach, but there was not any force to it.

"It's just it wasn't like you. That's all. Was it the dream?"

Renee closed her eyes, her head against the pillow, and both Britt and Jake brought the blankets over them.

"I wanted to get close. And I couldn't do that just staying where I've always been. Why did you let me stop?" Renee asked. She curled her fingers around Britt's until she was holding Britt's hand tightly.

"It was hard to say no, if I'm being honest," Britt said. "But partly because I didn't think you were really ready. Or completely awake. When you and I go further, I would rather do it in the light. Does that make sense?"

"It's harder to teach me when I can't see the chalkboard?" Renee answered.

Jake snorted into laughter behind her, and Britt joined him on the other side of her. "Basically," she said. "I want to know we're both ready and that we're completely conscious. It's important to me. It's important that things go well for you, and I'm not sure whether this was the best time for that."

"But soon?" Renee asked.

"If you're that eager," Britt said, kissing her softly and lingering a little, "I can guarantee it."

"I hope you don't mind if I put some of the quilt between us," Jake said. "Gender hazard."

The sides of Renee's mouth curled up. "It's fine."

Then Claire jumped up on their bed, because it was sure to be warmer where three humans slept than where her last human had vacated, and they had to be still. Renee relaxed into the warmth of the two friends with her. It was only a matter of time before she fell asleep again. Just in that place between sleeping and waking, she thought she heard the howl again. But she fell beyond it before she could tell.

Chapter Five

Renee turned on the intercom. "Attention. In thirty minutes, the last shipment of the season will be coming in. I will need some human skins around, so decide whether you want to be seen or not. Thank you."

Unloading was always a complicated time because the shapeshifters so rarely liked to show their faces to outsiders, but she needed as many of them as possible to help her put everything away as it came out.

The circumstances of their being at the sanctuary determined how comfortable they were being seen by visitors. Usually Jake was okay with showing his face, although Britt was not. Britt did not want her parents to find her under any circumstances, but Jake's family knew where he was. Malcolm usually helped out, as did two other shapeshifters named Nancy and Lotus. They were both regular workers. Ki would usually be in her human skin, but she would not make herself known unless she had to. Max would make himself scarce at these times and would only help move when the shipping guys had gone. Both of their families knew where they were, but they did not want strangers seeing their human faces. They wanted as little record of their human identities as possible.

Once the bell at the gate rang at the arranged time, Renee remotely opened the gate, a mechanism she only used on the days the shipping trucks came, and waited five minutes before closing it. The shipping truck would be up in about ten more minutes. It sometimes took them more effort because of their vehicle's size on such an unsure and sometimes slippery gravel road.

She shed her house shoes for more substantial boots and pulled her denim jacket on over her thin sweater. It would be cold when they started unloading, but after a while, the work would keep her warm enough.

"Are you going to help this time, Les?" Renee asked, closing all the windows on her computer after saving some of the copy for new blog posts and dog profile changes.

"I'm afraid I'm in too far in this scene to leave it like this," Leslie said, not taking his eyes from the computer screen as his fingers typed almost too quickly to see. "Maybe next time."

Renee grinned. He always said that, but she knew Leslie liked to be asked.

"Don't work too hard," she said. "Be sure to eat something."

"Mm-hmm," Leslie replied, already deep inside the fictional world on the page in front of him.

She went out to see all her usual shapeshifters on duty, ready for the afternoon-long effort and knowing that there would be frozen pizza ready for them after all their work. It was both a treat and a thank you from Renee for helping the sanctuary run smoothly. As far as she knew, pizza was a universal language for appreciation, and it was so easy for Ki to cook it for everyone.

The dogs all rushed around them, mouths wide and tails wagging furiously. They would get in the way, of course, but Renee and the group were used to that, as were the shipping guys. They usually loved to come to the sanctuary because they were surrounded by dogs who were all excited to see them. In general, she had a good relationship with this particular shipping company — they had been working with her for all six years that she had run the sanctuary on her own.

Britt was there, too, looking regal and calm near the dog barn wall, watching everything and making sure that the dogs kept in line. Max was nearby as well, also for dog control purposes. They did want to help as much as they could, even if they could not do it in their human skins.

Renee's eyebrows rose when she saw Grant walk around from the back of the log home to join them. He was not wearing anything warm, in spite of the increasingly cold weather. Just one of those white undershirts with his jeans and boots.

"Well, don't look so surprised," Grant said. "I haven't seen human meat in a while. With exception of you and your friends from town, of course."

Renee did not comment on his designation of humans as meat. It was just too much like him. As long as he behaved himself and helped, she was just going to ignore it.

"There they are," said Malcolm.

"Thank you, Malcolm," Lotus, the youngest shapeshifter in the sanctuary at just under eighteen years old, said. "It's not like any of us have eyes or anything."

"I'm just saying," Malcolm retorted.

"I know. But you don't have to."

Nancy, a woman around Leslie's age, punched Lotus in the arm, and she must have punched him more than just playfully, because he winced and didn't continue to goad Malcolm, who sometimes took his managerial role a little too seriously.

Renee raised her hand in greeting as she went up to meet the shipping guys.

"Hey, Miss Chambers," said the taller one, Vic Taylor, who had a face something like a thin basset hound's. "It's good to see you again. Got any early Christmas presents for me this year?"

"Sorry, I just have the usual tip," Renee replied.

"Shame, that," said the other one, Daniel Franklin, whose proud moustache made him look a bit like a fox terrier. "I had my heart set on an Xbox."

"A what?" Renee asked.

"Popular game console," Daniel Franklin said. "I guess you guys are kind of cut off up here. There are advertisements for it all the time on TV."

"We don't watch much television," Renee said.

"Do you even have a television up here?" Vic Taylor asked.

"We have one," Renee said. "It doesn't get used much. We sometimes watch movies."

"Sounds nice," Vic Taylor said. He took a deep breath and clapped his hands together. "So, you ready for this?"

"Whenever you are, boys," Renee said.

It was a long, hard slog, but after two hours they managed to get every box off the truck, in addition to the items that Renee took out of some of the boxes and stored in trash bags in her old room. She didn't want the shapeshifters to see their Christmas gifts when they started unpacking. They knew what Renee was hiding and where, of course, but as far as Renee knew, they'd never peeked. Either that or they could all play a mean poker game, because they always looked surprised and pleased on Christmas morning.

Grant was a bigger help than Renee had thought he was going to be. And he was certainly stronger than he looked. It could have been because the werewolf in him gave him supernatural strength. Or Grant could just be particularly strong. Renee wasn't sure.

Renee thanked the shipping guys after they'd finished unloading everything. Even though not everything—not even *nearly* everything—had been put away, she would not let them stay to finish packing everything away, knowing that she would get a little extra help after they left. She tipped them her usual one hundred dollars in cash for each of them, gracious that they came up every season for her needs and never once complained or seemed resentful of tripping over dogs and stepping around shit that hadn't been picked up yet. Renee guessed the job was routine for them, but it was more than that for her and the sanctuary.

Once the truck had left, Britt and Max went into the house and re-emerged with Ki, clothed and ready to resume the unloading. Things moved more quickly now.

She didn't notice that Grant was behind her as she carried one of the boxes back to the house from the pile of items in the centre of the front yard. He pulled her into the thin space between the shifters' barn and the dog barn.

"What?" Renee asked.

He did not even hesitate. "You know I say what I want, and you probably guessed I don't like to be told no. And you haven't told me no yet. You gave me the benefit of the doubt when you shouldn't have. And I just wanted to say… Thank you. I wanted to say thank you."

Renee blinked. "Sure," she said. Somehow, she could not find the words to say he was welcome when she wasn't sure how sincere he was.

"I know that you and the bitch are getting along," Grant said. "And I can smell him on you, too. Not as much as the bitch, but it's enough." He took the box she was holding from her arms and let it drop to the ground, so that she did not have anything to use as a barrier between them. "So you really are okay with the two of them together as long as you're in the mix."

"It's none of your business," Renee said.

"It's all my business. I can't help what I smell, and as long as I can smell their scents all over you, it becomes my business."

"You don't have to say anything."

"Oh, I think I've been quiet long enough," Grant said.

"So, what? You don't approve?" Renee said. "It's not right? They're not a match for me? I'm going to get hurt? When did you become so altruistic?"

"My goals are completely self-serving," Grant said. "But that doesn't change the fact that they're not good enough for you."

"And you are." Renee did not state it as a question, but it was implied. She turned to pick up the box and leave.

He grabbed her by the arms and spun her around so hard that she almost lost her balance. He gripped the flesh to the bone, his fingers tight and painful. "They can't give you what you need," Grant said. "Because you can't give them what they need, you'll never get what you need."

Renee did not even dignify his unfounded accusation with an answer. There was no way he could know what all three of them needed. He was trying to intimidate her, and he was doing a good job just with his hands. What he was saying seemed secondary. She felt her heart beat against her lungs the way it always did before a panic attack. Her shoulders began to turn inward.

"They may think they're doing right with you," he continued. "But they aren't. They know you too well to give you what you need."

God, this was just perfect timing for a panic attack. A cold sweat surfaced on her face and palms, and she could feel her tongue become heavy. Everything around her seemed to slow down.

"No," Grant said, getting in close so that his face filled her vision. "You aren't going to leave. You are *not* going to lose yourself. Not this way. Do you understand me?"

"I need..." She needed her Xanax, that was what she needed, but there was only him. With the scents of dirt and sweat and hair and fur, and with his unusually dark blue eyes staring straight into her.

"Stop thinking." He tightened his hands even more, sending a stab of pain up and down her arms, which interrupted the progression of the panic attack a little, but she was still on the cusp of falling into something she could not get out of. Why couldn't anyone hear what was going on? Because everything seemed so loud. And there he was, right in front of her. Right there.

"Stop thinking. You think too much," Grant said. "It's not a bad thing in moderation, but that's what people like you do. Think entirely too much. Whatever you're thinking... Just do it. Don't think.

Act. You live your life in your head, why don't you just *live*...?"

She lunged forward, her arms still held tightly at her sides, and kissed him, not even bothering with preliminaries. Just taking him, tasting him, feeling the roughness of the skin around his mouth and the fullness of his lips beneath hers. Then the hot velvet of his tongue on hers as he proceeded to give as good as he got. He was good at what he did, and Renee thought that her legs were going to give way completely as all her blood rushed to the area below her belly in a dizzying wave.

He loosened his hands on her arms, pulled her against him as he reached one of his hands down to feel her ass through her jeans. He was not slow, not careful, not gentle. His teeth were almost sharp when he bit her lower lip hard, not enough to draw blood but enough to make her cry out into his mouth. Not enough to make her pull away. If kissing Britt or Jake felt like becoming part of a whole, then kissing Grant was like falling, drowning, not being able to breathe with everything rushing above her, and she kept opening her mouth to gasp for air, but she only drowned more.

He did not have to hold her anymore. She clutched at him herself, pulled on his shirt until she found skin beneath his collar. She slid her hand beneath the clothing and down the stretch of spine as far as she could reach. She combed her other hand through his hair to find purchase, to keep him against her mouth so that she could breathe him in as though he were air. Whimpers tried to escape her throat, but Renee held them back, a small but persistent part of her still self-conscious. Grant had no such reservations. He groaned into her mouth, tasting her and inviting her to taste him in a torrent of tactile sensation hooked into a deeper response than emotion.

When he finally tore himself away from her mouth, Renee was prepared to pull him back in, but he attacked her neck instead, down to the juncture of collarbone and shoulder, with open-mouthed kisses that were almost bites. He pushed her shirt to the side to bare the rest of a creamy shoulder and the swell of one breast above her bra cup. He laved down until the bra got in the way, then yanked it down so that his mouth closed on the hardening peak of her nipple. She had done this to Britt but had not imagined just how good it could be, each rough suck on her nipple over-stimulating her almost to the point of pain. Her clit seemed engorged and sensitised to every touch of fabric against it. She could feel her cunt softening and opening, minor tremors fluttering through with each press of his teeth against her nipple. Just enough to hurt, just enough to make her skin sing.

As he moved away, the cool air puckered the skin of the areola even more, but now Grant knelt down and pushed up her shirt to kiss and bite down her stomach, laving each red mark that he left behind so clearly on her milky, pale skin. She felt the muscles right above her legs twitch of their own accord. She did not know exactly how she was still standing, even if Grant had backed her against the wall of the barn so that she had something to lean on.

Without thinking, Renee brought a hand up to fondle the breast that Grant had just given up, pinching the nipple to try and simulate the feeling of his teeth. Grant watched her for a beat from where he was occupied, nipping and licking around the rim of her navel.

"That's right," he muttered, voice guttural enough that she could feel it all the way to her spine. "Do what feels good. Don't think. Do it. Do anything."

He fumbled with the button of her jeans almost frantically, and as soon as he managed to unbutton it, he yanked the zipper down, then pushed her jeans down so that he could press his nose against the fabric of her panties, inhaling deeply. It all happened before she could even think to stop it, and by the time it was happening, she didn't *want* to stop it.

He pressed his tongue, which seemed impossibly big and impossibly long when she could not see it, against her clit through her panties, and she could feel the wetness seep through. And that was not the only place she was wet. She squirmed against him, although whether she was unconsciously trying to get closer or get away was still in question. With one hand still occupied with her exposed breast, she pressed the other against her mouth, trying to suppress the whimpers that threatened to come out. She barely realised just how hard she was biting down to keep from making a sound, because Grant was pulling her panties down over her ass, brushing his fingers close to the crease between her cheeks, which was surprisingly sensitive.

Grant pulled back again and stared at her shaved mound, which had only a slight growth near to the lips.

"Well, that's...interesting," Grant said. The statement was almost a hum. "And unexpected."

Renee lowered her hand from her mouth, and she was alarmed at the teeth marks she saw there.

"Bad?" she asked.

"No. I just didn't think you would be someone to do it," Grant said. "I like a woman's pussy either way. *Any* way."

It was around that time that Renee finally realised that anyone could come across them at any minute. And someone might have already done so without her even noticing, so lost in the sheer carnal experience she was. She hurriedly straightened her bra and shirt, then reached for her underwear and jeans.

"There you go, thinking again," Grant said, and before she could clothe herself, he buried his face between her legs, inhaling her scent and swirling air against the engorged flesh. "Mmm... There you are, love." And he slid his hands behind her thighs and dove in, licking and suckling and nibbling as though she were some kind of delicious fruit.

She grasped at the wall but could not find purchase, so she clenched her hands in his hair as best she could as wave after wave of pleasure moved through her from the things his mouth was doing to her. She could feel herself dripping down her inner thighs as he brought her to the brink of orgasm before pulling back just enough to keep her from attaining it. He licked the moisture from her quivering skin before returning to his feast. She did not know how he was even able to breathe when his nose pressed just on that place where she usually used her vibrator because it was so sensitive, or when he thrust his tongue *into* her. All the while, he made a noise that was better than any vibration from a toy — something between a groan, growl, and purr that could not be human, that seemed to come from deep within him and rattled her foundation from her head to the curling of her toes.

"Please," she gasped, finally just needing to come, needing him to bring her off with his mouth before she went completely out of her head. "Please. I need...just..."

"What?" he murmured into her clit. "What do you *need*, love?"

"Let me... I need to come. Please, Grant, just let me..."

"Do you really think you're ready? You seem awfully coherent."

"I can't keep going like this," Renee breathed. "It can't just keep going."

Grant grinned. "I think you'd be surprised how long it can keep going. But since you asked so nicely."

He renewed his onslaught with even more fervour, which Renee could not have begun to imagine just minutes before. There it was—a mewl of pleasure, and her teeth broke the skin on her hand. Under his steady pressure, she was coming, forcing his mouth closer until she finally crested through the pleasure and relaxed against the wall.

As Grant finally stood, his chin smeared with her juices, Renee wordlessly pulled up her jeans and panties, and fastened the jeans before pulling her jacket closer around her. There was nowhere for her to back away as he bent to kiss her again, and she was somewhat mortified to taste herself on his mouth. It did not, however, taste bad to her, although she could not say that it tasted good. A little bitter and a little salty, but mostly tasteless. She surprised herself by licking him as clean of her taste as she could, the feel of his trimmed facial hair on her tongue strange but not off-putting.

"See," he whispered, a hair's breadth from her lips. "That wasn't so difficult." His nostrils flared, and he followed the scent to her hand, which showed dots of welling blood where Renee had bitten through her hand from the force of her climax. His hand and mouth trembled as he brought her hand to his lips. He flicked out his tongue to taste the deep red liquid. It was only a little blood, but he groaned and wrenched himself away from the taste.

"Not hard at all," he continued, a little breathlessly. "Although one of us is. And unless you want that to be fixed right here and now, I suggest you leave."

Renee ducked under his arm but was somehow compelled to pull herself back to kiss him, pressing her hips against the hardness of his erection. He smiled into the kiss, and that was when she pulled away. She almost didn't, but with the release of all the pre-orgasmic tension, she was back inside her own mind and cognisant of the fact that she could see people walking by the shapeshifter and dog barns. No one seemed to have noticed the two of them because they were in shadows—although certainly not in darkness—and because the passersby were otherwise occupied, but there was no guarantee that they had not been noticed or that they were not going to be noticed soon.

"This doesn't have to be the last time this happens," Grant said, backing away. "Think about that. Or better yet, don't think about it. When you feel the itch for what you really need, I'm the one. Not the puppies."

"Fuck off," Renee said, without the venom there would have been before he'd performed a staggering act of cunnilingus without real protest from her. Even though she probably should have protested.

"Gladly." He tipped an imaginary hat and headed around the shifters' barn, leaving her to back out from the other direction.

"Renee!" Britt called, pulling on a coat as she came out of the log home. "Hey, girl, is it getting cold or what?"

"I think I'm going to duck out for the rest of the unloading. I've hidden what needs to be hidden," she said. What she did *not* say was that she really needed to take a shower before one of the shapeshifters smelt Grant on her. Before Britt smelt him on her.

"Sure," Britt replied. "I'll let Jake and Malcolm know. But you're still doing pizza with us tonight, right?"

"Of course," she said, looking at her feet as she hurried into the house. She felt reasonably hopeful that Britt would believe she was being her eccentric self—at least, if she hadn't already smelt something.

She ran up to the bathroom and shed her clothes, prepared to wash all of them after she'd showered. It felt as if she was showering so often lately. She poured an extra amount of soap onto her loofah and scrubbed herself pink, trying to rub every part of him from her skin. Renee made sure to clean between her legs several times over.

Part of her was not ashamed of what she had done—was, in fact, pleased that there was an actual impulsive bone in her body that had somehow passed every brick-wall inhibition. The other part wanted to hide the fact that she had done anything with a man she knew was dangerous and not to be trifled with. 'Trifled with' including—but not limited to—'fucked with'.

She could not let Britt or Jake or any of the other core pack know. Especially not Britt and Jake. At least, not yet. On an intellectual level, she knew it was all such a mistake. But already, when she was making her skin sting with the effort of scrubbing Grant from her, she wanted that drowning feeling again. Because it made her feel free. And at the first taste of freedom, however dangerous or unknown, it would be hard to go back to being her self-confined, impossible self.

However understanding Britt could be, she would take it personally that Renee had been with Grant. If she had been with Malcolm or Leslie, Britt wouldn't have cared at all. But Grant... That was a different story altogether.

Renee thought that she might not just love Britt—she could be in love with her, too, which was just as important to her at this point. She didn't want to compromise that with a questionable decision, an uncharacteristically impulsive decision...to do something that she never, ever did, or at least had never done before.

Renee wished she could understand why she had done what she had, *how* she had done what she had, and whether she could trust herself around Grant. The same part of her that had chosen to let him do those things to her made her think she could not trust herself at all. Not with him. *Especially* not with him.

Maybe her time with her pack, that night and every evening after, would bring her feet back to the ground. Maybe kissing Britt again would remind her of how good it was, how complete she felt when she was with Britt, how safe she felt when Britt and Jake were around. Maybe she would forget what Grant had done to her, the memories fading with the passage of time as if she had woken from a dream—or woken from *that* dream. She shivered at the few memories she had from her dream of Grant fucking her hard, which could never really fade, not when they were imprinted on her memory as though they'd been branded.

She could only hope that she could forget. But she didn't want to forget feeling free. And that just led her straight back to where she'd started. Confused, hot, raw, ashamed...and exhilarated even at the memory.

* * * *

While the core pack and other unloading participants ate their pizza—which had been graciously warmed up by Jake and Ki—Grant finally came in to join them. Renee watched everyone tense up and knew that she was doing the same. And that her cunt seemed to remember exactly what Grant had done to it. Quite against her will, she felt the whole area between her legs get a little aroused just by the way he looked as he sat down between Leslie and Lotus. It took a few minutes to jumpstart the conversation again.

"Looks like the shipments came at just the right time," Grant said after a while, chewing on a piece of pepperoni and sausage pizza. "It's really starting to snow."

Several of them, including Renee, stood up and went to the window. Grant was right. The snow was coming down in dense, swirling flurries, and it wasn't melting. The first real snow of the season, foretelling the snowstorms to come.

"I never get tired of this kind of thing," Britt murmured. When Renee looked at her, it was as if she'd shivered her malamute fur over her human body, a partial shift that sank back into her skin. "Perfect for the dog. I think I'll go out after this. You want to come?" she asked Jake.

"No, thanks," Jake said with a grin. "I think I'll stay in tonight."

"Wait for me upstairs?" she asked. She elbowed him in the ribs.

"Do you even have to ask?" Jake pushed himself from the window sill and headed back to the couch area to return to his meal. Renee followed him, sitting across from Grant, who was leaning back on his own sofa cushion and watching her with a ghost of a grin on his face. The combination of her traitorous sexual side and the nausea churning in her stomach made her finish her pizza quickly, then leave to hide in the computer room. She was joined later by a very uncomfortable-looking Leslie.

"You okay?" she asked.

He shrugged. "I don't like him at all. And somehow, he always ends up sitting next to me."

"It's nothing personal," Renee said.

"Still...very off-putting to have him next to me."

"I can understand that. Have much work to do tonight?"

"Always," Leslie said. "It's very exciting."

Renee smiled. "Good."

"What about you? You escaped in here fast enough," Leslie said.

"Just felt like the room was closing in. Needed to lose myself in cyberspace," she answered.

Leslie nodded. "I can understand that," he said, echoing her. "Well, good luck."

"You, too," she said, and turned back to her own computer to start an online chat with a man who was interested in adopting of one of their older dogs.

Britt came in to say when she was going out, then Jake came in to kiss her on the head and ask if it was all right if he stayed up in the loft that night. Renee nodded, knowing how much Britt liked the first snow and how eager she would be to celebrate its arrival.

She hoped she could convince herself to go upstairs and join them in one capacity or another. Or maybe she would just stay in the computer room until four in the morning, in case she had not scrubbed herself hard enough before. Surely another day or so would make whatever scent that lingered dissipate. She figured that if there was any smell of Grant left, it was faint, because the entire pack had been in the living room, and they had not smelt a thing. But she could not help but be a little paranoid.

Six hours later, having updated several profiles and her blog, then having done some early Christmas gift-wrapping, she was finally beginning to wear down. She thought that Britt had come in. A check from the living room confirmed that she had come back and was working off some excess energy with Jake. Because it was so late, they did not have to put so much effort into keeping quiet. The insulation between logs was pretty good, and sound did not carry so well to the other rooms. With the computer room door almost closed, she could not hear a thing.

But she did hear the howl at two o'clock in the morning, like the howl from her dream. Quite against her better judgement, she shifted in her seat, considering going out to see whether it was Grant out in the snow, which had already covered the lawn in drifts.

It was not until she heard the howl nearer to the house that she closed down her computer and stood up. Leslie was already in bed, so she was the only one in the cabin who was awake.

She pulled on her coat and scarf, which were damp from the other times that evening she had gone out to look at the new-fallen snow. It was always a wonder the first time she saw it each year, no matter how tired of snow she got after a few weeks. It just completely epitomised winter, enclosing the property and making her feel as if she lived in a snow globe. That kind of thought irrationally made her feel safer. But just because she felt safe did not mean she *was* safe.

As she went out onto the porch, she heard the wolf rushing through the snow. It seemed far away, but in the cushion of the snow, it was difficult to trust her senses. Things far away could sound nearby, and vice versa. Renee wrapped her coat more tightly around her, her right hand pressed against her stomach. She went down the porch steps, letting the cold wake her up a little, feeling it clear her sinuses and throat, clear her mind. With the snow reflecting the moonlight that poured, diffused, through the clouds, Renee was surprised at how well she could see.

She was halfway around the log home before she heard him again. Not running. Walking. It was as if she could hear the crunch of every flake of snow from his huge paws, clear in the silence of the night. She froze where she stood. She did not know whether she stopped because of fear or something else. Her practical side was telling her that it was something else, and she needed to get out of there now. Except she did not exactly trust her practical side anymore, not when it was also the voice of her anxiety, the voice of her fear, the voice of everything that made her life outside the sanctuary, and sometimes inside the sanctuary, difficult at best. She stayed.

There he was. He was bigger than she thought he had been the first time she'd seen him in his werewolf skin. His eyes glowed a momentary green with reflection of the moonlight. When she looked closer, she saw that they were actually just as blue as his human eyes. But as he came towards her, she could only see his smiling maw—he was panting slightly, and his teeth glistened. They were too big for his mouth and reminded her of the teeth of a lion, like simulations she had seen on TV of wolves' ancestors during the ice age. That was what it was about Grant—he looked primeval, ancient, preserved over the years to return with icy violence and vitality. And he was just a few feet from her, muscles coiled as if he was ready to crouch and pounce.

She did not back away. Her heart was beating faster against her lungs, but she did not feel the onset of a panic attack. She thought she was afraid, but not afraid enough of him. She knew she should be ready to run. When a predator looked at you like that, you were supposed to run. But she didn't. She couldn't. She just waited.

He came closer, pressing his nose against her coat as he sniffed over her. Her stomach, her breasts, her neck, the warmth coming from the opening in her coat where she had slid her hand, the frozen breath coming from her mouth and nose. He puffed and sneezed a little in her hair, and Renee resisted the impulse to laugh. It sounded funny to her so near her ear, and it tickled. But then she felt the slide of teeth over her neck, and that was when she knew her first real stab of fear.

That was when she pulled her hand from her coat and pressed the knife against the werewolf's neck.

Chapter Six

She took care not to press too hard — she wanted it to be a warning, not something more. Not unless she needed it to be something more.

His fur shifted under her hand, and he stood human before her.

"What is that?" he asked, his eyes still strangely feral in spite of the change.

She did not answer him. He knew perfectly well what the sharp point on his neck belonged to.

"You'll never use it."

"I will." Her voice seemed loud between the two of them, as enclosed by snow and wood as they were. "Aren't you cold?"

Grant was completely naked, as he and the other shapeshifters always were when they shifted back to human skin, and it was about fifteen degrees Fahrenheit outside. And only getting colder. His breath fogged the air between them and mingled with hers. He leaned over and parted the fog.

"I'm never cold," he whispered. He touched her face, claiming her chin, and she felt the warmth of his skin. It seemed impossible. As he gripped tighter, she pressed the edge of the blade closer to his neck. He let go of her.

"If you do decide to use it, love, you better use it hard and fast. But even then, werewolves heal quickly. You might not even come close to killing me."

"It's silver," she said.

Grant paused. "No, it isn't."

"It's sterling silver," Renee explained. "I bought it a week after you came."

In that moment, Renee thought she saw a touch of fear. Then that look turned into something calculating and contemplative before melting into an expression that Renee could not put a finger on. Except that it made her cunt clench.

"So you really do know that I'm a dangerous man." He licked his lips. "Maybe a cruel man."

"I'm not stupid. And I don't have to stab you hard. Just enough to reach the bloodstream. Isn't that right?"

He tried to step forward, the heat from his body reaching her even through her clothes. And she was not looking directly, but she could just see that his cock was certainly not feeling the cold. She pressed a little harder, knowing that if he came closer, she really would nick him, and that would be bad. Partially for him, but also for her. She did not want to hurt him — she didn't like to hurt anybody. But she was shaking, and not because it was cold. She vibrated with tension.

"You know you could kill me with that," Grant murmured.

Renee nodded. She swallowed against a tightened throat.

His eyes seemed to glow red, and there was no question that he was aroused now. "God, I want you," he groaned, voice deep and low and so primal — the baritone shivered down her spine and pooled in her belly. "I can't even tell you how much I want you."

She could not explain where it came from — the same hidden place that had inspired her before — but, still pressing the knife against his neck, she pulled him to her and kissed him as hard as she could. There was no finesse, no skill, no artistry, nothing she could have learnt. There was only the passion that made her squirm where she was, pulling him nearer until he was flush against her, even with the knife clenched in her hand and cold between them. With every groan, that deep half-growl, she tasted him and pressed him closer. He was hot to the touch, and as he grabbed her thighs and pulled her up so that she was straddling him, then pressed her against a wall, his body heated hers until she was sweating under all her layers. All she wanted to do was shed them until it was skin on skin, until the frozen snow around them melted with the fire of whatever abandon he was creating inside her. He splayed his hands across her back, under her coat, under her shirt, pushing the latter up over her breasts. He consumed her with as much artlessness and need as she did him. She had never felt like this, and she was not sure that she liked it very much. But she was sure that she wanted it to continue.

She pulled away. The cold slipped in where he was not touching her, and she almost leant back to kiss him, just to keep that warmth.

He gazed at her lips, seeming unable to look away, his mouth open as though he was going to recapture her at any time.

Renee brought the edge of the knife up over the jugular vein, then touched it to his jaw, then the corner of his mouth. She slid down his body, catching his hard cock between them before her feet reached the ground. He hissed at the chafing from the denim of her jeans.

"You know what this means, love?" Grant said.

Renee covered his mouth with the knife, silencing him. But she reached down with her other hand and touched the head of his cock. The skin was surprisingly smooth and soft to her, and she slid her hand down until she held the firm base of his erection in her palm.

"Don't say anything," she ordered. And she began to lead him back around the house by the cock.

He followed without question or comment, eyes glowing more brightly. As they went up the steps to the porch, then as Renee opened the front door, his almost-growl grew louder.

Renee strained to hear whether Britt and Jake were asleep.

"Don't make a sound," Renee whispered just above a breath. The growl lowered in volume until it was only a vibration through his body to her hand.

· Britt and Jake were talking quietly, and there was a slight movement to the mattress springs that told Renee that they were still making their brand of love. She looked behind her to make sure that no one was coming, that no one knew they were there. She let go of Grant's cock to take his arm and lead him to the room that she had kept closed—her old bedroom. Once she'd shut the door behind her, he slammed his hands against the door on either side of her head.

"So I'm going to be your little secret, am I?" Grant murmured. He pressed his mouth to her ear, licking the edge of it before delving into the hollow right underneath. She exhaled in a slight sigh.

"Is that a problem?" Renee asked.

He relieved her of the coat, then pulled her shirt over her head. She was an active participant in it, and she hardly knew her own body as he pressed his mouth to the swell of one breast, above her bra. The bristle of his chin chafed her, but it only made her more sensitive, and she felt her stomach flutter with each flash of hot tongue on the reddening skin.

"Not particularly," he said.

Renee reached to the side for the light switch and turned on the ceiling fan lights in the room. Everything was much as she had left it, although she washed her comforter a couple of times a year so that it did not get too dusty. The trash bags of Christmas presents were in the corner of the small room, near the dresser. The rest of the décor was somewhat juvenile, but she could not care less as she looked Grant over in proper light.

Everything about him was hard. The line of every muscle was defined, and although they were not overly large, it was undeniable that he was strong. Much stronger than anyone else on the sanctuary, even the ones who did regular physical labour. Renee had never thought she would ever be interested in a man like that.

His erection jutted unashamedly from his body, neither big nor small, but flushed a deep and angry red. Grant seemed unshaken by the physical manifestation of his need—his cock was ready, but his expression was shuttered as he let her look him over. He took the opportunity to do the same to her as she removed her jeans, then her bra and panties—everything practical, unassuming, until it was taken off. Britt had seen her naked before, but never when they'd been sexual together, and Renee had never known how truly vulnerable and even scared she could be without any clothes on. After all, she had no other skin to change into. All she had was this soft, easily torn human skin and no natural defences. Just a silver knife held tightly in her fist.

"While this can be a spectator sport, love, I want to fuck you, and I think you would very much like to fuck me," Grant said.

When he reached for her, Renee thrust the knife between them reflexively, and he yanked back his hand.

"Do you want to kill me, Renee?" he asked quietly. It was as if his entire body was a burning coal, smouldering. She could feel him even a few feet away, pulling her to his heat, and she stepped forward, the knife in hand and pointing at his flat stomach. He took a step back and found the foot of the bed behind his knees.

"Keep moving," she said.

He grinned and leant back, pulling himself further up the bed with an intriguing flex of his arms before lying back against the pillows. He began pumping his cock lazily for her benefit. Renee squeezed her thighs together as she watched him move the uncut foreskin over the head, revealing it and hiding it in turns. She licked her lips unconsciously.

Climbing onto the bed, she adjusted her grip on the knife so that she could slide her other hand over the light fur on his leg, softer that she would have thought, although the hardness of his muscle was as she'd expected and felt good under the velvet of his skin. When she reached his thighs, the muscle there twitched, and she got an eyeful of his erection, moist with the spread of pre-cum as Grant continued his slow up-and-down motion, waiting for her. With his other hand, he grasped her shoulder and tried to pull her to him, but she braced herself on his thigh and brought the tip of the knife to his balls. It would not have been an exaggeration to say that Grant froze.

"Fucking bitch," he breathed, but there was no venom. It was more like a moan, and his cock twitched in his hand.

Renee's red hair fell over her shoulders and draped over his thighs, brushing his sac as she leant down. The scent was strange to her, but not unpleasant. Her entire body was quivering as she brought her mouth to the base of his cock. He released his hold on it and moved his hand away slowly, so that she would not react and castrate him as well as poison him. He left himself open to her exploration.

She slid her tongue over the flesh, testing. She was ambivalent to the way he tasted, but the more she breathed him in, the more she wanted. She took more of him in, laving the root of his cock and mouthing her way up his length, following the pulse in the prominent vein. The contented growl returned, and she did not tell him to quiet down. As she pressed the flat of the blade closer to his balls, she thought he got even harder. Finally, she flicked her tongue over the foreskin, delving a little deeper.

She jerked back at the sudden bitterness, and Grant chuckled low in his throat. His head was thrown back, his throat working as she tried again, now prepared for the taste of his glistening cockhead. She took him in, dipping her head down until she felt him throbbing full in her mouth. He jerked his hips, but another press from her knife, closer to the flesh, persuaded him to hold back his reactions. His entire body shook from the effort, and it gave her a heady sensation of power as she took more of him in, sucking lightly. At the first snag of her teeth, she thought he was going to jump, but instead he just slid his fingers into her hair and pulled her up. Her mouth and chin were wet, her face flushed, and her hair tousled — she could only imagine what she looked like to him, but whatever it was, he seemed to like it.

"How about you put down that knife?" he said quietly. "We have all night to play like that. But I don't want to play right now." He tightened his fingers in her hair until he was almost pulling at the roots — it was just on the good side of pain, and he pulled her up his body until she was poised with her lips above his, the knife still against his drawn testicles. Slowly, she ran the tip up the sensitive vein of his cock, and she almost whimpered from a wave of arousal when he closed his eyes tightly, his jaw clenched through his own wave. She drifted the knife's tip from his cock and drew an invisible line up his stomach, his chest, along his throat. Grant strained to capture her lips, and she tossed the knife to the side to let him.

The second she heard it hit the comforter, he engulfed her in his arms and pulled her flush against him. He was even hotter with skin against skin, and all Renee wanted to do was eat him up as she kissed him, bit his neck, let every impulse have its way. She had never felt like this, unfettered and wild and as dangerous as the man beneath her. He groaned every time she lifted herself to her knees and rubbed his erection with her wet cunt, wanting him inside her more than anything, but not knowing how to begin. As for him, he was no less insistent than she was, except he seemed to know more about what he wanted from her. He held her as though he wanted her to melt into him. She pushed her breasts against his chest until he bit an exhilaratingly painful line down to one nipple and sucked softly, then too hard, pulling it with teeth that felt as if they could be sharp at any moment.

And it did hurt, it all hurt, but she didn't push him away, didn't tell him to stop, felt her juices stick to the inside of her thigh as her cunt tightened around nothing. She dug her nails into his arms, the flesh of his back, tearing the surface with every minor tremor that shook her body. And throughout everything, that deep vibration from within him continued.

It was all messy, hard, unpractised, unchoreographed, hot, panting, secretive, and all she could think was that it was not enough.

"Inside," she whispered into his mouth before he slid his tongue in, before he drank the word from her lips. She reached for the knife again, and at the first touch of the flat edge on his side, Grant's eyes flew open, and he flipped them over so that she was underneath him, surrounded by his weight, his heat, the shadow of his body.

"Forcing me to take you at knifepoint," Grant murmured. He clicked his tongue mockingly. "Now, now, you don't need to convince me."

"Don't care how hard," Renee said. "Please. Just…"

"I hope you're not a virgin, love…" He parted her thighs until her knees were almost on either side of her chest, spreading her for him, exposing her far more than she felt comfortable with. But comfort was far from the front of her mind as he took his cock in his hand and covered her again to slide into her. It had been a while since she had penetrated herself with anything and the aching stretch was almost pleasant, like the first time running after a week of recovering from illness. He did not even let her adjust—she had not expected him to and welcomed the burn of it. He pulled back and slammed into her again, rolling his hips so that he rubbed her clit and something else on the inside, which made her bite his shoulder to hold back from crying out.

She had not known that sex could be like this. She'd had a taste of it with Britt, but Britt had stopped her. She had thought that the earlier encounter with Grant and her previous experience with toys would have prepared her. But it was so different than using one of her vibrators, even one of the more realistic ones. It was the difference between rubbing an ache in her neck and having someone do it for her, like getting someone to scratch the itch she just could not reach herself. She had never experienced it on such a scale, crashed with surge after surge of pleasure that tore her apart on the inside and banished her thinking mind entirely.

And as for Grant, Renee was not convinced that he'd ever used his thinking mind very much. He was rough and thorough, shaking the bed with every thrust. Although he was clearly ripping his own pleasure from her, he kept up an angle that must have been difficult for him, the one that rubbed against that place inside that made her tighten around him in a swirl of wetness. He clenched one hand around her waist and pressed the other into the bed as his mouth roamed greedily over her until she drank in every groan, every growl. He was being quiet for her. She wondered how demonstrative he would be when he did not have to be quiet. She dropped the knife again so that she could cling to him, bracing against every time he thrust in, imagining him taking her in the middle of the living room without any restraint at all.

Her orgasm began climbing before she even recognised its presence. But she latched her teeth on to his shoulder again, rocking her hips to help him help her reach its peak.

There, she thought. *There, right there. God... Grant, there...*

She whimpered through the climax, and he drew it out as long as he could, his cock still rock hard within her. She could not believe that he'd lasted longer than she had when he had been aroused longer. But his eyes were wild and glowing as she came down from the orgasm, and he began to fuck her even harder through her oversensitivity. She grasped for the knife and brought it between them, effectively stilling him in his actions, but she could tell she was not going to hold him back for long. Every one of his muscles shook from the effort of not taking her, using her.

With her eyes fixed on his, she pushed him to the side until she was the one who was over him. He was still buried within her, and she adjusted herself so that she was comfortable again. His hips bucked, but she put the flat of the knife back against his stomach.

"If you're going to kill me after fucking me, bitch, you'd better do it now," he snarled, fingers digging into the flesh of her hips.

"*I'm* ready to play," Renee said. "Sit up." She lifted herself off him a little so that he could pull himself sitting. His expression was twisted with need and anger and frustration, but he did as he was told, a glitter of renewed interest in his eyes.

"There," she murmured, and she began to rock, her arms around his neck and the knife glinting behind him. Slowly at first, drawing herself past the oversensitivity stage and into her own renewed interest. She rubbed her clit tantalisingly against his pubic hair and bone, squeezing herself around him in a deliberate attempt to make him look *that way*—his eyes rolling back, jaw tight, everything about him needing to take her but unable to do so. If he had really wanted to, he could have broken her wrist, held her down, and taken what he wanted. But he was not doing any of those things. He permitted her the power that she had over him when she could easily take his life with the smallest of incisions.

"Tease me any more," he growled, "and I will not be responsible for anything I do, any noise I make to alert the others that you are riding me under threat of death, taunting me when I've brought you off twice today for nothing in return. And…I'm going to…have you in front of that…bitch…so that she… *Fuck*."

All her inner muscles were tight as she began to lift herself up and bring herself down hard, truly riding him now with her breasts bouncing in front of him until he took one nipple into his mouth and sucked, raking short nails with the beginnings of claws down her stomach. She held his head closer as she took him faster and faster, not as violently as he had, but he was thrusting up into her and tasting her and groaning as his balls drew up. His orgasm almost unseated her, and they rolled over as he slammed once, twice, three, four times quickly into her cunt, coming in spurts of heat inside her.

He held himself above her after he'd finished, not slumping over her or crushing her, just staring down at her, all the hunger driven from his expression but the fire still there.

"If I had wanted to kill you, I would have done it before now," he murmured. "And if I had hurt you more than you wanted, you would have killed me. I don't think you need that knife anymore." He took her wrist lightly. He wanted to squeeze the bones of her wrist, she knew, but all he did was bring her arm down to the bed. "Give me the knife, Renee."

"No," she answered. She pushed herself to a sitting position, and he pulled out of her when she moved away. She crawled over and put the knife in the drawer of the night table. "If you take it from me, I'll have Jake blow your brains out with his rifle. And he's an excellent shot."

"You don't need to protect yourself from me," he said, pulling her back beneath him. He rubbed his shoulder lightly, and his hand came away bloody from where her teeth had broken skin. He sucked his fingers into his mouth and cleaned them in the dirtiest way. Grant might have come, but Renee was worked up again. She wanted to taste his fingers as they came back out of his mouth without a trace of his blood. She could not believe that she had bitten him so hard.

"But you're a dangerous man," Renee said. "You told me yourself."

"I am." He lowered himself so that he covered her like a blanket, returning his attention to her neck, slowly working his way down. "But you don't need to protect yourself from me." His mouth made its way down her stomach, circling her navel before hovering above her clit. She bit her lip as he began to lick her again, drinking her arousal mixed with his ejaculate, until she was almost begging for him to take the knife from her possession and take her again, whenever and however he wanted. Since she did not have his shoulder to help muffle her cries, she had to resort to her hand again, and as he brought her to orgasm for the second time that night, she could not help the high moan that escaped.

He licked his way back up her body. When he reached her mouth, she muttered against his lips, "I'll still have him shoot you."

"That's my girl," he replied, rewarding her with a thorough kiss. "Now, I remember I said something about playing all night..."

Chapter Seven

She was not sure when she'd finally fallen asleep. Neither of them had lost energy after sex like Jake did. Grant had been amazingly voracious, intent upon enjoying every inch of her until he'd simply been unable to continue. And she'd seemed unable to stop herself now that she'd had a taste. It hadn't been that Grant was better than Britt, but sex — sex like this — had been so new, and feeling normal had been new, and she had not wanted it to stop. It had been exhaustion that did her in, not boredom.

She had been so lost in the present that night that everything crashed down on her in the morning.

At first she burrowed closer to the furnace that was Grant's body. They had barely made it under the covers, but they weren't really needed when he was the best kind of heater. Once Renee realised that the heat came from Grant, she opened her eyes. And once she realised what she had done the night before, she jerked out of his enveloping arms and sat straight up. Grant did not move, but when she looked back, he was watching her.

Sunlight was coming through the window above her bed, enough for her to see that she would not be able to sneak out of the room without the others seeing her. Or smelling him on her.

She began frantically trying to create an alibi, but her mind came up blank. There was not one single excuse she could come up with that would explain her being out all night, smelling less like herself and smelling like sex, to boot.

But excuses could be made later. Since no one had burst through the door looking for her, Renee assumed that her friends were not too worried about where she was. They probably assumed that she had decided on a whim to sleep with the dogs, or had fallen asleep at her computer. Leslie would know better, but he probably would not be asking the questions.

Right now, she needed to clean up. There was the tiny en suite bathroom that she had used as a kid. She found cheap but unopened shower gel under the sink. As she turned the water on hot, she knew that she could wash and wash and still be unable to get rid of his scent from her clothes. Then again, she had not had them on for very long. She would deal with that if it became a problem.

"So keen to leave me, love?" Grant asked. He leaned against the door frame as she whirled around. The closest towel was pink and flowery, and for some reason, that was the only reason she did not reach for it to cover her. He might have seen her naked—he was largely responsible for that state—but it was another thing entirely for him to see her naked like this. The magic spell had ended, and she wanted layers between his eyes and her skin.

"I need to get you off of me," she said. She tested the water with her hand before pulling back the curtain and stepping into the spray.

He leaned into the shower, and Renee was conscious of the fact there was nowhere to go in that little stall.

"Even if you were able to wash me from you, you do realise that you are all over me," Grant murmured. He pushed her wet hair from her face and held it in his hand like a rope. "And I am not so quick to shed that scent from my skin."

"And what would you say?" Renee asked. She wanted to back into the corner, but he would follow her into it, and she would be more trapped than she already was. Even now, though the impulsiveness of the night was gone, she saw his mouth and wanted it on her. They both had morning breath and they both smelt of their cum, but she felt her cunt twitch at the thought of rolling over the bed sheets wet as she was, clinging to his body with the water slicking his way over her, into her.

She did not know whether she would be able to stop.

"I'll tell them the truth." He stepped under the spray with her, bringing in a rough washcloth for her to use. "I'll tell them that we rolled around like dogs and that we did it with your knife to my neck. And balls."

"They won't believe you," Renee replied.

"No, they won't. But you'll tell them that it's true."

"I will?"

"If they're going to rip me to pieces, it better be because of something I really did," Grant said, as he poured the gel onto the washcloth and rubbed it into lather. "Your conscience will keep you from lying to them. You'd sacrifice yourself for me before you would lie."

He moved the washcloth from her shoulder blades to her waist to the curve of her buttocks. Then between, stroking her and washing away the scent from where she was sure it was most concentrated. He pressed her against him to get a better angle.

"This isn't helping," she muttered. But even though she knew she should push away, she kissed along the line of his shoulder. She found the place where she had bitten him—the skin was raised and slightly bruised. There was a scab where she had bitten through the skin. She traced the raises and ridges with her tongue. The knowledge that she had hurt him in some way, and that he had let her, made her squeeze her thighs around his hand.

"If your little bitch were here, too, we could really get things...clean," Grant whispered. He circled one erect nipple with his short fingernail, and bent it back and forth before flicking it. She was sensitive enough there that the action was a little uncomfortable, but she somehow still enjoyed the sensation. Like the way her thighs ached from the night's activities, but every time she used the muscles, she was reminded of *why* they ached. Like there were bite marks on her breasts and bruises on her hips and arms. But she had marked him as much as she had been marked by him. And she had held the poisonous knife too close to his skin.

An image of Britt had surfaced in her mind when he'd mentioned her, and though Renee knew that she would never come near Grant, she imagined for a second that Britt was behind her, that she was the one with the washcloth.

She thought sex would be just as good with Britt, and she let Grant kiss her as she imagined it. It helped that she had some practical experience to draw from—

she had not known how much of a difference that made.

His cock was half-hard against her hip, and she took it in hand as she kissed him. The wildness was coming back. She thought she could drain him dry and still want more. She canted her hips with the movement of his hand, rubbing her clit against his slick thigh. She was too sensitive, and the orgasm came with more pain than pleasure, but it was release nonetheless. She clenched her fingers around his cock as the orgasm wrenched from her. He gave a muffled shout when she squeezed too tightly, but he reached down and covered her hand with his, pumping himself over her fingers with the same too-tight grip. His breathing was harsh in her ear, and he came onto her stomach. A few small spurts hit her breasts. He looked at her as if she were breakfast, bent down to taste himself on her, his teeth drawing blood to the surface and his moans humming through her body.

When she turned around to let the water wash the cum off her breasts, another dose of morning-after reality hit her like a fist in the stomach—perhaps a little lower.

"Shit," she whispered. She went rigid when Grant ran a hand gently down her spine.

"It's going to get awfully old if you regret what you do with me every time," Grant said. She could practically hear his grin. "For you. Do you really think you'll be able to stay away?"

"That's not it," she said. Although she thought she could manage regret after every encounter, no matter how tiring it would be, because she was *supposed* to feel guilty about this. She was *supposed* to feel guilty about not being able to say no to him, about going behind Britt's back to have sex with someone she hated. "It's just that I didn't think…"

"That was the point," Grant murmured, his growl trembling over her skin.

"About protection."

She felt his mocking smile against her shoulder. "There are many things you need to fear from me, Red, but that ain't one of them. The only way we reproduce, the only—let's call it 'disease', like the bitch said, though I hardly think so—the only disease I spread is lycanthropy."

He curled his arm around her, pulling her to him and spreading his fingers over her stomach possessively. He flicked his tongue against her ear. "No regrets," he whispered before taking the lobe of her ear between his teeth. "It feels good, doesn't it?"

Renee finally pushed him away. So she had one regret she could cross off her list, but there were still a slew of others left twisting inside her, and his touch wasn't doing anything to make them disappear. Nor were either of them doing anything to make her clean.

"You need to go," Renee said. "Run in the woods through the snow."

"Put my energies into something other than making you scream, then?" Grant asked.

"Get my scent off in the air," Renee replied.

Grant hesitated, looking almost angry. But he smoothed his expression out, removed traces of annoyance or attraction. "Sounds practical," he said. "But I won't be your dirty little secret for long, love. Can't keep secrets in a place like this."

Renee held her shoulders, crossing her arms over her breasts. Shielding herself from him, creating a barrier.

"Fine." He reached for a towel and stepped out of the shower, drying off as he went.

* * * *

She did not know whether he did what she had told him to do. She only knew that he was not there when she finally got out, after scrubbing herself hard. Her skin was an angry pink in the places to which Grant had paid the most attention. She wrapped a towel around herself and considered her clothes on the floor. She could just walk out in the towel—the odds were that none of her shapeshifters would be in the house at this hour. But they *could* be, and a towel would be suspicious, to say the least. The clothes, though, might give them a clue as to where she had been, which they were probably wondering about anyway.

In the end, she chose to get dressed and hurry out and up into the loft.

Britt came in after her a few minutes after she got in, catching her changing between her old clothes and new, clean clothes.

"Where were you last night?"

The question was innocuous, Britt's face innocent. She was not even thinking of anything near what Renee had actually been doing. Maybe she did not smell Grant on her because she wasn't trying to smell him.

"In my room," Renee said, caught in the headlights of a direct question.

Britt nodded. "Needed a little alone time? I can understand that. Things have been a little stressful for you lately."

And, like that, Renee's indiscretion was buried under Britt's trust.

* * * *

The snow storms came in, blustered and calmed down. Getting to and from any of the buildings became a chore in itself, but the shapeshifters who gave their time and effort to keep the sanctuary running provided their invaluable services by shovelling paths. Fortunately, the house was the farthest building—once you reached the barns, it was easier to manoeuvre between them all.

Another full moon passed—the dogs were somewhat agitated, and Renee and Jake made sure to keep everyone locked in tight. She stayed all night with them without complaint, calming the dogs and sleeping intermittently on one of the couches. Jake was with her in his golden retriever skin, his alpha presence as calm as possible to help soothe the rest of them.

In general, Grant kept away from her these days, and Renee thought that was that. He'd had his taste and now he was finished with her, despite him talking about more. She was not too disappointed, although it would be a lie to say that she wasn't at all—if anything, though, she was relieved. It meant no more sneaking around, no more pushing herself outside what she knew, no more impulsiveness she knew could not last.

But the morning after the full moon, when the circles were deep under her eyes, he came to her outside the dog barn in a tattered pair of corduroy pants that he must not have been able to remove in time before he'd turned. Before she could even close the door behind her, he crushed her against it, slamming it shut with their bodies. The snow pressed in from all sides, except the partially obscured walkway that had been dug the day before. She thought she would be cold until she again felt the heat of his skin under her fingertips.

He did not seem to care that she'd just woken up from a bad few hours of sleep, or that her hair was messy, or that she smelt like dogs and was covered in dog hair. From the way he pressed against her, all he cared about was feeling her. His hands were rough, rougher than she remembered them, and she wondered whether what he did in wolf form affected his human form—it was different for the shapeshifters, although their dog forms aged proportionally with their human skins.

He found his way under her three layers of shirts to squeeze one breast hard enough to make her yelp. Then he thrust his hand into her sweatpants and under her panties to start fingering her with more finesse than the previous roughness would have suggested. As he did, he thrust his hips against her thigh, using her for friction and nothing more. Renee twisted her hand in his hair for leverage, and she thought she felt some of it come out, but he only bit her lip, almost too hard, before taking control of her mouth.

It was all fast. Rough. Hot. Wild. If Renee had been more awake, she might have initially protested before finally giving in, but he had caught her by surprise, just at the right time, when she was too emotionally raw to even think of protesting. All she could do was feel, from the deliberate painful reminders to the steady climbing of pleasure and the pressure of his fingers playing her clit.

"Do you know why I'm here?" he asked against her mouth. Her gasps blew frosted breath between them, and he tasted it with a curl of his tongue. "Do you know why I came here? Why I come to you?"

She pressed her nails into him as the swirl of orgasm rose.

"I want you," Grant murmured. "So much. I want to bite you."

She knew she drew blood when she came, thrusting her leg up against his hardness to try and make him rise with her. He rutted against her madly, but his voice was still soft, still intent, intense.

"A wolf has to have his pack," he said. He marked her mouth, her chin, her neck, anywhere he could find skin. And it hurt, but then he was jerking in short, tight movements. Then he was still, and she looked down at him from where he pressed her against the door.

"I could run for a hundred years from this place, and I would still want your flesh in my mouth," Grant said. He let her down slowly until her feet touched the ground, but he did not release her.

She wanted to whisper at him to let her go. There wasn't love or anything approaching it in his eyes. There was desire, yes, but also a need that went beyond hunger. Whatever it was, it was not insatiable—it had an end. It was as though he wanted her to burn without being consumed. With his body still tightly against hers and Jake just on the other side of the door—*Did he hear anything?*—she already felt consumed. She felt high, her head six inches above where it usually was, as though she was dosed on medication or had a particularly bad fever.

"Say something," Grant said.

That was the trouble. When she did not know what to say, she did not know how to fill the silence. She drifted her fingers, then her lips, over his neck, waiting for something to latch on to.

"Do you want me?" he asked, muscles bunching under her hands as he drew her closer.

"Yes," she said. She tasted the affirmative with a little bitterness.

"I can turn you," Grant hissed into her ear.

She did not jerk away, but she paused, pulled back slightly so that the icy air swept in where her mouth had been, cold on her lips.

"You can have this. All the time. The heat, the intensity. They can never give you this. You can't be domesticated, Renee. You're either broken or you're free."

"Like you?" she said. "Were you broken?"

"Your skin cages you," he replied. "I didn't know I was broken until I was freed. You *know* that you're broken, and no matter how much they try to put you back together, the only answer is magic. And their magic is weak."

She pressed her hand against his chest. Not pushing him fully away, but enough that there was space between them. She could only imagine the sight she was after sleeping with the dogs, then fucking a werewolf.

"I don't believe in magic," she said. Each word was enunciated without being angry or insulting. Just matter-of-fact.

Grant paused. "You're kidding, right?"

"No." She pulled her jacket up from where he had pushed it down her arms and began making her way down the snowed-over path.

"You run a sanctuary for shapeshifters who turn into dogs," Grant said. "You're harbouring a werewolf."

"None of this convinces me of the supernatural—at least, supernatural the way most people mean when they talk about it," Renee said. "Only that there is natural that is yet undiscovered or unexplained. They change into dogs. But that's all they do. Their families have conferences and wear suits and ties and go to work. They grow old with their dog skins, and they die. The dog skin and the human skin are unimpressive, except that one can turn into the other. And even that seems to be genetic. There's no fancy light show. They can't pass it on to me or anyone else." She finally reached the cabin and pulled herself onto the porch.

"I can," Grant said. "I told you." He swung himself up next to her.

"Then maybe they're the mutation and you're the disease," Renee said. "Like you said. Like Britt said."

He smiled, the grin spreading over his face in an almost ominous way.

"You really have no idea, love," he said. "But I promise, I'll show you."

* * * *

"Christmas is in a few weeks," Britt said, nudging Renee's shoulder as the core pack played Monopoly in the great room. Each of them balanced bowls of chili precariously on their laps, silverware clinking against the ceramic every time one of them leaned over to roll or move a piece. Leslie, in his quiet way, was winning without trying. Malcolm had already been bankrupted out of the game, but Renee and Ki were gamely soldiering on. Max, Jake, and Britt were beginning to buckle under the strain.

"Mm-hmm," Renee hummed. She was watching Ki getting closer to her housed Pennsylvania Avenue property. Another five steps forward, and Renee would be able to breathe for a little longer.

"So what are you getting us?" Britt asked.

"Yeah, Renee," Ki agreed. "What are we getting for Christmas?" Most of the shapeshifters had no bank accounts or credit cards, and their payment for whatever they did in the sanctuary was simply living there. Jake, Leslie, and Ki were the only ones other than Renee who had access to money. Britt didn't even have a driver's licence. As far as the government was concerned, she was a runaway, presumed dead. Renee always took great pleasure in getting them things for Christmas and birthdays. She could not buy them the best and most expensive presents, but she could get them things they'd find uses for. Jake usually contributed to the cost, although he had been adamant when he'd told Renee that he did not want any of the others to know that his family was rich. Renee respected his wishes. She was not sure even Britt knew just how much money Jake's family donated to the sanctuary every year. Not that money had ever meant very much to Britt.

"What makes you think any of you deserve anything from me?" Renee said.

A chorus of 'oooooh's followed the remark, and Britt cocked her head with a slightly surprised smile on her face.

"Did my girl just crack a joke with a completely straight face?" she asked.

"I'm not telling you what I got you," Renee said. "You guys do this every year."

"Leslie said he heard you fooling around in your room a few weeks ago," Ki said. "Must be some pretty heavy stuff you're hiding."

For a moment, her heart beat against her lungs, but no one was looking at her as though anything was out of the ordinary.

"Just doing a bit of cleaning," Renee said after a beat. She hoped the lie didn't show too much on her face. She could always blame the fire for the blush if it did. "You're all getting sculpted dust bunnies under the Christmas tree."

"A very popular art form these days," Jake added, moving his top hat ten spaces and going straight to jail. "It'll be worth millions ten years from now. We should all be flattered."

"What I've never figured out is why none of us ever just open the door and look," Malcolm said.

"That would spoil the surprise," Ki said.

"So would me telling you." Renee bought another two houses in anticipation of Ki's approaching game piece. She rolled for Community Chest, missed it, and hit the railroad instead.

"No," Ki replied. "*That* would just be like getting Christmas early."

"Who wants Christmas early?" Renee muttered.

A crunch, a bump, then the opening of the front door with the storm raging outside made them all stop what they were doing and look around. Grant, who had the appearance of someone who had been swimming through snow, shook the excess from his head and shoulders, leaving it to form a small puddle near the front door after he closed it behind him. His motions slowed when he realised everyone was watching him, and his lips twitched.

"Go on. Don't stop on account of me," Grant said.

Max reluctantly rolled the dice, but none of them really stopped keeping their eyes on him. In the middle of a snowstorm like this, the fact that he had worked his way to the cabin meant he was there for a purpose, not just for the pleasure of interrupting them.

"You landed on St James Place," Leslie muttered. Max handed him the money, and Jake took a turn trying to get out of jail.

"You and me, Renee, we're going on a road trip," Grant said behind her, unnecessarily loud. She felt her stomach plummet to her feet. "As soon as this storm settles, I'm taking you to Minneapolis. Actually, to a place right outside Minneapolis, but I'm sure we'll spend some quality time in the city, too."

"Wait, what?" Britt said.

Grant continued as though Britt hadn't said anything. "I know a pack that runs out there. It's no sanctuary, but you learn where the hot spots are once you're turned. It's the biggest pack you've ever seen. You'll believe in magic by the time I'm through with you."

"Was that a threat?" Jake asked.

"No." Grant did not even look at him. Every part of him was focused on Renee and her reaction. "The snow should only last a day or two. Be ready." He started down the hall towards the kitchen.

"Wait," Britt said. "You can't just come in here and order her around."

"Why not? I think she likes it," Grant replied.

"You *can't* order her around."

Grant grinned slowly. "I noticed that she didn't tell me no," he said.

"Renee?" Britt asked, turning Renee to look at her. Renee felt trapped, her brain frozen in a too-bright panic. She did not know what to say, what to do, how to respond. She did not know what Grant was trying to do. She wasn't going to say no. Couldn't seem to say no. Her mouth opened, but nothing came out.

"You think shaking the answer out of her is going to change it?" Grant said.

"She can't leave without me," Britt said. "She's agoraphobic. She can't leave this sanctuary without me."

"She seems to do just fine when she's here," Grant replied. "And even better around me. Although you're welcome to come along with us, pet, if running with wolves is your thing."

"She's *not* going with *you*," Britt snarled. Renee thought she saw a ghost of fur bristle over Britt's face and arms.

Grant looked interested briefly. "Well, well, maybe wolfkind is just the sort of thing you need."

Britt closed her eyes, taking a moment. When she opened them, she repeated, "Renee's not going with you."

"Now who's ordering her around, bitch?" Grant said, suddenly right behind them, his face between the two girls. His teeth glistened and looked sharp as he smiled.

Britt whirled around, back arched and teeth bared as she raised her hand to strike him, but Grant caught her wrist and squeezed, still grinning.

"I'm faster and stronger than you. You couldn't beat me in a fair fight, and I don't fight fair."

"We outnumber you," Britt said.

"I'd kill someone if it came down to that," Grant countered. "And I don't want to do that. Yet."

Renee put her hand on Britt's shoulder to calm her down and tugged on Grant's arm. He yielded Britt's wrist without a fuss.

"I'm not asking you to choose between your precious dogs and me," Grant said to Renee. "We'll be back before Christmas. I promise. But you will come with me. You *need* to come with me."

"You have no idea what she needs," Britt said, taking Renee in her arms, shielding her.

"And you do?"

"I've known her for eighteen years," Britt said.

"You *love* her," Grant said.

"Yes. And I know what she needs. I help her. When we go into town, I help her." She tightened her arms around Renee, and all Renee could do was let her, because she had a feeling the storm in the room was going to get worse than the one outside. "When she has a panic attack the first time she comes in contact with people outside the sanctuary fences, what are *you* going to do about it?"

There was a glint in Grant's eyes that made Renee perfectly clear about what he was going to say, and she stiffened. "I may just kiss her. Hell, I would fuck her against a wall in front of everyone if I thought it would help."

Jake leapt over the couch and took Grant's neck in his hands. All Grant did was laugh through the choking.

"Now that's really burned you, Junior," Grant rasped. "Don't start something you can't finish."

They hit the dining table and Jake bent him over it, still pressing his thumbs against Grant's throat. "You're never going to touch her, you slimy son of a —
"

"Stop!" Renee screamed. She ducked out of Britt's arms and ran around the couch to push Jake and Grant apart. Grant was still laughing as Renee put herself between them, facing Jake. "Stop. I'm going."

"What?" Jake and Britt said simultaneously, followed by similar interjections from the rest of the dog pack, who had jumped to their feet when Jake attacked Grant.

"Renee," Britt said, coming around the sofa, too. "You can't go with him."

"I am." Every part of her hurt, but she knew she was going. It wasn't even a question, even though the looks on the pack's faces were enough to tear into her. No matter how much she did not trust Grant, she knew she had to go with him. She *wanted* to go with him.

"That's right, love," he murmured behind her. His voice was husky from the pressure on his larynx.

Britt looked confused and more than a little hurt. "Going to a werewolf pack is bad enough," she said slowly. "But going with him... You heard what he said. The minute you start feeling what you always feel, you're not going to have me there. He's going to... You heard him."

"She didn't seem to mind it the other day," Grant said smugly. His breath rippled over Renee's neck, and he pressed his lips there, sucking briefly on the skin before pulling away. Renee could not help it as her eyelids fluttered with the frisson that came from the heat of his mouth. She was already tense, already aroused in one way enough that she shifted into the other way without trouble. She swallowed against it, but it was too late.

There it was, the eye of the storm when everything was silent for just a moment, waiting for the wind to return. And it did, but quietly.

Revelation dawned in Britt's eyes, followed closely by pain and betrayal. "So that's... I knew I smelt him on you before, but I thought it was just nothing. And you never said anything. Never told me. You never told *me*."

Jake was furious. He did not look at Britt or Grant, just backhanded a wooden chair against the wall and stalked out of the room.

"Well, it's clear why she didn't tell us," Leslie said. He, too, looked shocked, but perhaps not as shocked as the rest of them. "None of us approve. She was ashamed of it."

Renee could not speak up to defend herself because she *was* ashamed of it. She wanted Grant, and she was ashamed of herself for wanting him. But it was the clear betrayal that Britt felt, looking like a little girl when she was supposed to have the presence of a goddess — that was what made Renee feel that there was nothing under her skin but air. She stared imploringly at her friend.

"When you were with me, I could smell him all over you," Britt said, her lips drawing up in disgust. "Was that what you were doing that night? Letting him touch you, letting him see you? You haven't even let me…" Britt covered her mouth to press in either sobs or vomit. "Why?"

Renee tried to talk, but nothing came out for a few seconds. Then finally she said, "Because I needed to."

"Did he threaten you?" Ki asked, taking over for Britt. "Did he tell you that you had to do it or else he would do something to you, to us? Renee, if he —"

"Hey," Grant interrupted sharply. "What kind of monster do you think I am? I distinctly remember her attacking me the first time, not the other way around. And the second time, she had a knife. Don't you *dare* suggest I took her by force. If I'd done that, I'd be clear about it. And you know I'm right."

"Is that true?" Malcolm said. "You went after him? Is he telling the truth, Renee?"

Renee raised her right shoulder in a half shrug as she tried to come up with a better justification than that she had felt like she needed him. She opened her mouth, but she could not find words to describe the reason when there *was* no reason.

Britt nodded slowly. "Yes, he's telling the truth. He wanted her, but he wouldn't get the satisfaction of rubbing it in our faces if she hadn't been perfectly willing to do what he's been wanting all along. Isn't that right? She's going with him."

Renee began to step away from all of them, backing away until she could see the entire tableau in front of her — the lost faces of her friends as they stared at her as though they didn't recognise her, and the man on the other side of the room who was completely at ease with where he was and how things were.

"I'm coming back," she managed to say. But she still could not seem to get far enough away from the situation, and the backs of her heels found the stairs to the loft.

"Why him, Renee?" Britt asked, in little more than a whisper. "Why *him*?"

"I'm still here," Renee said. "I haven't changed. I promise. Nothing's changed. I need to get ready."

She went up the stairs. Not running, just walking at a normal pace. Though she was fleeing, she was relieved she was managing to be so restrained. She closed the curtain behind her and tried to breathe. She opened her closet door, opened her dresser drawers, and stared at her clothes. She needed something she could do and packing seemed like an idea, yet everywhere she looked, she could not find anything right. So all she could do was stare impotently at her clothes and hear bits and pieces of what was going on in the living room. She thought that Grant had left when she had, and if Jake had not killed him on the spot, he had probably gone back to the shifters' barn, waiting for the time when he would have her all to himself.

And she was here, alone, with a wilderness of distance between herself and her friends. And Britt. Britt seemed further away than ever.

The voices downstairs grew quieter. A line of light split the room. Renee did not look back to see who was there, who had pulled back the curtain.

"What are you looking for?" Britt asked.

Britt's bare feet made little whispering sounds on the wooden floor.

"Looking for things you can take with you on your little trip? Low-cut tops, short skirts, sexy lingerie? It's what he's expecting from you. His little piece of human arm candy that he's bringing along to show off to everyone. Looking good on the fur carpet."

"I don't have those things," Renee said. Everything she had in her closet was functional. Most of the time, she was getting dirty or getting fur all over everything. If it looked marginally good on her, that was just a bonus. But there was nothing for a night on the town because she had never had one, or had expected to have one.

There was a rustle of cotton and the sound of a zipper. Britt was undressing behind her.

"You don't need those things," Britt said. "You never did. You could be covered head to toe in clumps of mud and still have those bedroom eyes."

Britt slid her arms around Renee's waist and cupped her breasts, rubbed lightly at the peaks until Renee felt them grow harder under her bra. Britt pressed her mouth where Grant had kissed her on the neck, covering the sensation with a new one, a new mouth. Renee held the dresser drawer tightly with her left hand.

"Is it that he doesn't care about you? Because you know that he doesn't. And you know that I do. Is it that he's rough?" Britt asked. "Is that why you'll let him be with you? I can be rough. If it's what you need, I can give you what you need, Renee. I always have."

"I don't need that from you," Renee answered.

Britt stroked a hand down Renee's stomach, brushing the waist of her jeans and slipping under. "From the beginning, I've honoured your boundaries because I knew that they were important. I knew that this is the way you are and always have been. But he just blasted through like an explosion, with no consideration, no understanding. What did he do to you that makes you feel like you need that?"

Britt was not considerate or gentle as she began to press with her fingers, trying to find the place that made Renee's breathing hitch. When she did, Renee leant back into Britt's arms and closed her eyes.

"He's everything I'm not. It's not permanent, and I don't think he's fixing me. But for the moments that he pushes me past all the circling thoughts and paralysing fears, I can do things I've never done." She tightened her grip on the drawer again, but this time because she could feel the pleasure inside her tensing her up. "And in those moments, I feel like I think a normal person does."

"I can *be* what you want," Britt said urgently.

"You are," Renee said, pulling Britt's hand from her jeans and turning around. She drew Britt down and kissed her, drawing her in, tasting her, taking her mouth. Britt moaned, losing herself in the passion

Renee only occasionally showed. Renee was completely clothed, and Britt was completely bare. Renee stroked down from neck to thigh, feeling every curve as though memorising them.

"Don't you understand?" Renee asked. She kissed a line down Britt's sternum and bit lightly at her left breast. "You *are* what I want, and I don't know why you ever stayed here when you could have been so much more with someone better than me. I don't want you to be anything other than what you are. I've told you that I appreciate everything that you do for me, even if I don't always have the words for it."

"You seem to be doing very well right now," Britt said. She tucked Renee's hair behind her ears, scratching her nails across the scalp the way she knew Renee liked.

"I know you can be rough," Renee said. "But you aren't with me. And if I needed that to change, I would say something."

"Then why *him*?"

"I don't *know*," Renee said, just short of shouting, which was unusual for her. She continued at a lower volume. "I don't know why I do these things with him. I'm not used to not knowing why I do things. Even when I'm illogical, I can usually point to my craziness as the reason. But I don't know why I want him. I don't know why I let him do what he does to me. I just know that you aren't him, and I never would want you to be him."

Britt led them to Renee's bed so that they could speak on a more even footing. "Look, you know it isn't that you found someone else you wanted to be with. You know I wouldn't care if you wanted Jake or, hell, Leslie seems like an interesting match for you. Or someone in town that you trusted. Or you could meet someone online. I don't mind you with someone else. You aren't just mine. But Renee... Him. I can't stand you with him. Nothing good can come of that because *he* is not a good man."

"I know," Renee said.

"Then why?"

"I want him," Renee said. "I can't explain why. It's just there. And I don't think it will always be there. But it is now, and it's strong. I don't think I want it over yet. Because I *like* it, Britt. I shouldn't, but I do."

Britt sat back and stared at Renee, but her eyes were just a little beyond what was right in front of her. Then she lifted her head a little, and she breathed in decisively. "Okay. It's not my choice. And I've said what I needed to say."

"I know it all already," Renee said. "But you see..." She crawled to the centre of the bed and knelt. "It doesn't all have to be bad."

"Oh?" Britt said, mouth quirking a little.

Renee beckoned to her, and Britt was quick to oblige and climb onto the covers, meeting Renee in the middle. Renee kissed Britt once before swiftly pulling her shirt and jeans off, leaving her in just her cami, bra, and panties. Then she looked at Britt as she brought the cami over her head.

"Are you sure?" Britt asked.

Renee nodded and began to unhook her bra, but Britt stopped her and did it herself before helping her remove the last bit of clothing.

"Are we ready?"

Renee pushed Britt gently back and held herself above her. "I know I can now. You'll tell me if something's wrong?"

"That's supposed to be my line," Britt said, laughing.

"Remember, I won't break."

Renee lowered herself down onto Britt's body, feeling her skin where there had only ever been clothing. She rubbed her cheek on Britt's chest, her breasts against ribs, the bareness of her sex against Britt's tangle of thicker curls. They tickled her clit in the perfect kind of maddening way. She felt like a cat, just feeling without really touching, getting used to being naked with Britt. It felt different, she supposed, with different people. It was never really the same because they always wanted different things and they had such different textures. But as she had said, although it would be different with Britt, she knew that she *could*.

She pulled back and brought her hands between Britt's thighs, pushing them open so that she could slip between them. She bent down to lick the crease behind Britt's knee. Britt half-laughed, but clenched her hand in the sheet. Renee knew how sensitive Britt could be in the creases behind her knees, in front of her elbows, the tops of her legs, the backs of her feet, the place right under her jaw. What Renee thought to be the most unlikely places to make a person shiver like Britt did.

She drew a path with her mouth up the length of strong thigh until she could smell Britt's arousal right in front of her. It was not so much that what she saw was unfamiliar. It was more that it was almost surreal to see her up close — as though the strange loveliness of a woman's genitalia could not be associated with the familiarity of the rest of the body. Of course, Renee had her own and had seen it in mirrors, but it was not as if she had ever had the chance to really look closely at herself. As with her reaction with Grant, she was not sure whether she felt one way or another about the appearance or scent, strong and strange to her. All she knew was that she could give Britt pleasure there, and that she wanted to.

She threaded her thin fingers through the thick hair, touching the lines of Britt's labia until they reached the hood. Britt hissed, lifting her hips slightly. Renee stroked the revealed nub with the curve of her nail. Her clit was a little bigger than Renee's and pinkly swollen. Britt hissed again.

"Does it hurt?" Renee asked.

"A little," Britt said. "You know it's sensitive."

"I know." Then Renee dipped down and surrounded her partner's clit with her mouth, sucking lightly with each breath, then swirling her tongue at the tip and down beneath the hood. She gripped the tops of Britt's legs, stroking at those creases that only made Britt mewl just a little bit louder when she found a particularly sensitive spot. Renee was neither lost in her actions nor unaffected. She undulated her hips slowly against the sheets, but her main focus was on the act itself, learning from every cant of Britt's hips, from every cry, as she tried something new just to elicit a reaction and determine whether what she was doing was right.

She explored Britt's folds, tasting the slightly salty moisture from her entrance. Renee was not sure whether it really tasted like anything—it was a much weaker taste than Grant, and Renee was fine with that. She took one hand away from Britt's leg to slide one finger, then two into the slick, soft flesh. It was so much like touching herself, except here she could see everything and simply remember what it did to her and *know* what it was doing to Britt. It wasn't the same, of course. Britt's fingernails on her scalp weren't usually there, for instance, or the steady stream of sounds from Britt when Renee was used to being quiet herself.

Quite by accident, she curled her fingers once, twice, and she thought Britt was going to hurt her as she came, almost doubling over.

Britt gave a dry laugh as Renee pulled her wet fingers out.

"I didn't think you'd find that on the first try. It actually took me ages," Britt confessed. "I was a little embarrassed that I hadn't found it sooner. Here, I know you'd like to clean that off." She started to get up for a washcloth or towel, but Renee stopped her with her clean hand. Drawing Britt back down, she sucked her fingers into her mouth and cleaned them right there, beneath the curtain of Britt's luxuriantly wild hair.

"I can clean up later," Renee said.

"You know, my dear, if I thought you'd be this receptive, I would have pushed your boundaries a long time ago," Britt said, grinning and taking Renee's fingers into her own mouth. Renee was surprised how the same action could feel so different when Britt was the one doing it. As soon as they were free, Renee replaced her fingers with her lips, kissing Britt hard and wrapping herself around the long, lithe, firm body, finally starting to lose herself in the feeling.

"So do I get an A?" Renee asked.

"Undoubtedly." Britt laved her ear just the way Renee liked her to, then nipped her way down the cord of her neck. For a moment, Renee almost told her to bite, but she thought Britt might take it the wrong way. Instead, she pressed her thighs harder around Britt's hips, her heels crossing as she brought her nails up the back of Britt's thighs. Britt practically purred as she took one of Renee's nipples into her mouth, then moved to the other, letting the cold air tighten the first. Renee squirmed, wanting the heat and softness of Britt's tongue again. She rolled her nipple between her own fingers, circling the areola, but it was not quite the same. The darker look in Britt's eyes, however, with her pupils dilated... That was good.

"Over me," Britt directed, falling back and pulling Renee kneeling over her. Then she pushed herself down so that her mouth was poised underneath Renee's cunt.

"I can still smell him here," Britt murmured.

"I can only clean so much," Renee said. "You all have a better sense of smell."

Looking up at her, Britt looked oddly vulnerable, younger again. But there was nothing young in the husky voice as she commanded, "Ride my mouth."

Renee wondered how—and with whom—Britt had practiced something like this as she dove right in, fingers and tongue working in tandem around and above Renee's clit, focusing more on the clitoral hood and the bone beneath rather than the oversensitive clit itself. When Britt did give that little piece of flesh her attention, it was all soft and wet, the flat of her tongue or the velvet of her mouth. She could be rougher elsewhere, and she was. As she pressed her fingers in circles above the clit, she began to give Renee a taste of her own actions, fucking Renee's cunt with her tongue, and while the feeling was not quite as intense as she'd thought it was going to be, she still fell forward to brace her hands on the bed. Britt's technique was so different than Grant's, and the direction of her pleasure seemed to have found alternate routes so that when Renee's orgasm came, it was unexpected, like going over a waterfall. Renee's breath came out in short gasps as Britt drank the small rush of moisture.

When the pleasure had passed, Renee lowered herself down beside Britt, tucked against her. They were facing the wrong way on the bed, with their feet near the pillow.

"Your bed is not big enough for this," Britt said. She was staring at the ceiling with a smile on her face. Her lips were wet, and Renee licked the moisture off with the tip of her tongue before settling back. Britt stroked Renee's hair, combing through it.

"You don't say much, but you're a quick learner, babe," she muttered.

Renee just hugged herself closer. She was starting to get a little cold, and they were not facing the right way to get under the quilts.

"I'll help you pack," Britt said. "I'm not okay with it, but I can't force you to stay. I mean, I could. We could tie you up inside the dog barn, drive Grant down south and stake him to a fire ant pile, but I don't think you could ever forgive us for something like that."

"Seriously?" Renee asked. Sometimes she couldn't tell dry humour from when her friends were being literal, and considering their intense and bordering-on-violent dislike for Grant, Renee was not quick to dismiss the threat.

"No. But I've thought about it. On a fantasy level. I'd never really do it. I think. Anyway, I know there's not much in the closet, but you never knew what to do with it anyway. I don't know how, with over a decade of mainstream socialisation, you don't know how clothes go together and I do." She stood up from the bed and began rifling through Renee's half of the closet.

"You watch more movies," Renee said. "Why do you want to help me? You don't want me to go."

"It's important to you," Britt replied, not meeting her gaze. "And if you don't come back in a week without calling us, I'll get the National Guard to search every town outside Minneapolis. And this time, I'm being serious."

"I'll bring the cell."

Britt began taking things out of the closet and putting them on the dresser. Renee wrapped the top quilt around herself and watched.

"Do you know that Grant likes you?" Renee asked.

Britt paused in her chore. "I know," she replied. "I'm careful with him." When Britt continued going through Renee's clothes, Renee noticed that her hands were shaking. Renee furrowed her forehead. She was not sure what that meant—whether Britt was really afraid of Grant, or angry, or something else. Britt usually divulged everything to her, as much as Renee divulged very little. She was not used to fishing for clues how Britt felt or why she was feeling it.

"Does he hurt you?" Britt asked, with her back turned to Renee.

"No more than I hurt him."

"That's not very reassuring, Red."

"What do you want to hear? That he's a kind, caring, loving man? You know he's none of those things," Renee said. "I can't gild him for you."

Britt turned around to look at her, dark eyes fierce. "He's taking you to the largest pack this far north. If you think being with Grant is treading on the dark side… I think he wants to turn you."

"I know he does."

Britt raised her eyebrow in more than just a question, but a touch of horror.

"He's not going to turn me unless I want to be turned," Renee said.

"And do you want to be turned?"

"I don't know," Renee replied.

Britt dropped what she was holding onto the dresser top. "Is this the same kind of 'I don't know' as wanting Grant?"

Renee did not think she had ever seen Britt quite so mad at her before—angry, yes, but not at her.

"No," Renee said. "I just don't know my decision."

"How can this even be a question?" Britt shouted, shaking her. "How can you even be thinking about becoming a werewolf? By choice? You know what they are, you know what they do."

"They invade personal space and rile dogs up," Renee said. "I don't have the benefit of a sense of smell that discerns character or…mystical monstrosity or whatever. I don't know werewolves, and I want to see for myself. I don't want to just condemn an entire group of people because of the nature of one I've met. I don't even want to outright condemn him. He's not a good person, but I'm not convinced that he's a bad one."

Renee shrugged out of Britt's grip, which was beginning to hurt, and touched Britt's cheek lightly. "Do you really think that Grant is going to deliberately get me killed? Do you think he'll turn me if I don't ask him? He's already had that opportunity. Many times. And he hasn't."

For a moment, Britt resembled Renee as she tried to answer, but clearly could not answer the way she wanted. Finally, she shook her head.

"Look," Britt said, trying a different tack, "Jake didn't want to concern you when we didn't have any evidence of anything, but you know the dead hare and a few other animals? The ones killed but not eaten? There've been more that we haven't told you about. There were some rabbits, rats, a hare, some squirrels, bird feathers all over. They've all been on the edge of the sanctuary. This was not just an isolated incident or something a sick animal did. Some*one* sick did this, Renee."

Renee did not have to be told that they thought the animal killings were Grant. She believed they were, too. But as Britt and Jake said, they had no proof one way or another. For all they knew, it could have been a rogue shapeshifter.

And if it was Grant? He was keeping those impulses away from the compound, away from her dogs. Renee was disgusted by the idea that Grant could do that, although she was not surprised, but maybe he had come for sanctuary because of that impulse. It was possible he was trying to control it, but he couldn't. In any case, they could not do anything about it for now.

Renee nodded, took in and filed the information. "I need to know, Britt. I need to see what Grant is for myself."

Britt sighed. "I know you do. I'm just... I'm worried that it'll make me lose you. If you become a werewolf, I'm not sure if this, *this*, can continue."

"Because of the smell?"

"Because of everything," Britt said. "The whole package. I don't think you really understand what werewolves are to us. Humans who don't shapeshift...you have the bogeyman. We have werewolves. Except we know they exist. Other creatures aren't even on the radar. To them, we're animal prey *and* human prey, no matter what shape we're in. You *can't* know. You can't know how it is between us."

Renee stood on her toes to kiss Britt on the side of her mouth. "I need to know."

"I don't want you to know," Britt said. "I'm supposed to protect you, babe. That's what I was called to do. It's what I am. And I won't be there with you. I'm scared. I'm scared you won't come back."

"I'll come back," Renee promised. "I'll be back before Christmas."

Chapter Eight

She hadn't worn this skirt since high school, and although she hadn't grown since sixth grade, she could not remember it being quite so short.

Britt had found a few skirts under the oversized T-shirts that Renee sometimes wore for pyjamas. Renee had completely forgotten about them. They weren't exactly practical for her work, and they weren't exactly practical now with the weather as it was. Her floor-length coat was not going to do much to keep the cold from going up her legs. But Britt had taken her best friend job to heart, no matter what the lover part of her was thinking. She told Renee to wear the skirt the first day at least.

Renee could wear a tank top and torn jeans during the summer when she was working in the sanctuary, no problem. But it was another matter to be going into town with her legs showing. In the dead of winter. With a man that no one in town had ever seen. She was not concerned about her reputation, which she knew had already been ruined by her quirks. But people would be looking at her a little more closely.

She buried her hands in her coat pockets and wrapped the coat around her.

Grant didn't talk to her. She didn't mind. He had thrown his duffel and her vinyl suitcase into the back seat of the truck, then taken her keys from her without fanfare. When she had asked for his driver's licence, he'd grinned a little and dug it out of the duffel. It was nice to have someone else drive for a change. He'd turned the radio dial to a classic rock station and occasionally tapped out a beat on the steering wheel. She was surprised at how comfortable it was. She was just nervous about what would happen when they got out of the car.

That morning, she had woken up to an empty house. When she'd walked down the stairs, all she'd heard was the click of dog claws on the wooden floors, and when she had opened the doors to the porch to a surprisingly tolerable morning, she had seen Jake's golden retriever tail over the top of a snow bank, heading towards the barns.

Renee had anticipated that she and Grant would be leaving that afternoon. Her truck was tough and had weathered her through harder winters than this. Her dog pack must have known that, too, because all she'd seen of them were glimpses of dog fur. It was their way of ignoring her.

As Grant had turned the key in the ignition, then eased the truck down the dirt driveway, Renee had seen Britt sitting on the porch in her dog skin, watching them go. It had been the first time in years that she had left the sanctuary without Britt at her side. The early flutters of panic had begun to climb up her throat, and she'd clenched her hand in her over-the-shoulder bag, where she'd stored her anti-anxiety medication. She had already taken some, but it had felt good to be reassured.

Grant had distracted her with a hand high up on her thigh, where her skirt covered skin, and she had turned back around to look through the windshield.

Her stomach found her throat again when they reached downtown Antoine.

"I need to go to the bank," Grant said. "You don't have to come with me. But when I get back, we're going to a bar and having a drink. Maybe five. You'll eventually want to take off your coat. I can't be the only one in town who wants to see those legs." He pulled into a parallel parking space with surprising ease, then looked at her. "It won't take long. Don't run away." If it had been anyone else, she would have thought he was considerate. But the look in his eye was not quite mocking. Close.

If she'd had control of her muscles, if she'd had control of her brain, she would have been able to get out of the truck and pace the sidewalk. Maybe look in a window or two while she was waiting for him to come out. Instead, all she could do was sit meekly and wonder if she could get away with taking off her seatbelt and sinking down into the foot space below. She felt like every passerby was looking through the windows, which were not even tinted. She knew logically that even if people were looking, they'd forget her almost as soon as they saw her, but her legs still felt locked in place. She waited and wished that she had Britt's fur in her hands.

She noticed Marcus on the sidewalk, heading her way. She ducked her head so that her face was hidden, but she realised too late that her hair itself was enough to identify her. He slammed the flat of his hand into the window in greeting, and she jumped. He had done that on purpose.

"Hey, gorgeous," Marcus said. His voice was muffled through the glass, but his leering grin was easy enough to see. "In town early this season, aren't you? Decided you needed to see us after all?"

She unconsciously checked the locks, glad to find all the buttons were down. Marcus caught the direction of her gaze, and he grabbed the car door handle, jiggling it threateningly, all with a smile on his face. As if he thought scaring a woman was the way to her heart.

"Come on down to the bar with me," Marcus said. "It'll be fun. You can unwind. Maybe give us a dance or two. Loosen up."

He bent down to peer directly at her. His eyes were a little red—not enough to indicate that he was drunk, but he had certainly been drinking.

"You don't seem to have as much to say now that you're out of your little piece of land," Marcus muttered. "Can't function unless you have an iron fence and barbed wire between you and everyone else?"

He looked down both sides of the street to make sure that he was not being watched, then leaned against the window and pressed his tongue right where her face was, leaving a trail of saliva on the glass.

"All you need to do is wrap your pretty little self around me, and I promise I'll screw every thought out of that pretty little head." He laughed as he grabbed his crotch. He gave an exaggerated moan, just loudly enough for her to hear it through the glass. "Come on, Renee, it's all in good fun."

She was seriously contemplating climbing to the driver's side — if she could convince her arms and legs to move — when she saw Grant coming out of the bank, tucking something into his back pocket. The relief must have shown on her face because Marcus straightened and turned around. She wished she could have seen his expression, but she did see Grant's — a perfect combination of glee and savagery that made Marcus jerk away from the car and stumble back around the front of the truck. In comparison to Marcus, who had been a linebacker in high school, Grant was about half his width and barely reached past Marcus' chin. But it was undeniable who would win if it came to a fight, just by virtue of self-confidence. It was really no wonder that Marcus backed away in the presence of a far fiercer predator.

Grant took Marcus' place outside her window. "It's all right to come out. That cretin won't lay a finger on you with me around."

"Like hired muscle," Renee muttered as she undid the lock and stepped out. Grant locked the door behind her.

"Not quite." He wrapped his arm around her shoulder with what would appear to outsiders as affection. He was only wearing an olive-green T-shirt, but he was warm enough that the coldness on her legs seemed insignificant. She still wrapped her coat around her so that no one could see them. But with Grant there, she did not think she would have that luxury for very long.

"They'll be in the bar," Renee said as Grant led her right into The Benefit. At this time of the evening, it was just beginning to get crowded. Locals frequented it often in the evenings, more often than tourists, although the bar wasn't entirely without them tonight.

Hopping in small-town bars wasn't the same as hopping in a big town, but it was still the first real crowd that Renee had been in since her high school graduation.

Marie looked up from the bar and raised her hand when she saw the familiar coat and face to go with it. She paused upon seeing the man who took the front of the coat and spread it, pulling it down Renee's arms. Renee wanted to give Marie a reassuring smile, but she was afraid all she could manage was a grimace, so she just lifted a hand back.

She felt a few eyes on her that she was not accustomed to having, but it was not as though her arrival had stopped the world so that all eyes were on her, even if it seemed that way to her rapidly panicking mind. Marcus had come back to the bar after his scare and joined his friends at a booth. Will and Josh were there. Josh nursed a mug of draught beer and stared at her thoughtfully, taking in the length of leg and the flash of skin at her neck. What she was wearing was nothing really showy. Just a slightly smaller shirt than she was used to, which actually fitted her rather than gave her room for working movement, and a skirt that she wasn't used to at all. But it was different. And Josh was no fool. He knew that the man she was with was the reason. So even though he had a girl talking to him and hanging on to his arm—Renee thought her name was Melanie—he regarded Renee with a blank expression.

Marie came over, still surprised and even wary.

"Do you want your usual, Renee?" she asked. "Samuel Adams and chicken strips?"

"The chicken strips and fries sound good," Grant said. "But let's try a bottle of Jack Daniels and glasses for the two of us."

Marie looked to Renee and raised her eyebrows at the way he ordered for her.

Renee nodded an okay. She knew what it looked like from the outside, but nothing that the outsiders saw was true.

"Can I have a water while we wait?" Renee asked before Marie left.

"Sure, hon, be right back," Marie said.

"Do you have to be so creepy?" Renee asked, after Marie had gone back behind the bar.

"It's just an experiment, the drink," Grant said.

"Not the drink. Ordering for me when she was asking me."

"I knew what you meant."

"You won't get me drunk," she said.

Grant cocked his head curiously with a strange slant to his smile. "And what makes you think I'm not going to get you drunk, a little girl like you?"

"You can give me a hangover in the morning, but I don't get drunk." She shifted in her seat, pulling the hem of her black skirt down. It did not move very far. "I don't know what you're after."

"Well, the aim *was* to get you drunk, but I'll settle for pleasantly buzzed."

"Why?"

"For the sake of it."

"It seems like a stupid pastime. I've never understood why people do it."

"It is," Grant said. "Sometimes it's good to have a few stupid decisions under your belt instead of playing everything so safe and ordered."

Renee stared at him and wished that he couldn't stare right through her clothes and know exactly what she looked like. It made her think everyone could. "Not *everything* is safe and ordered."

"No," he said smugly. "Not everything."

"What next? A shot of heroin and a hold-up at a jewellery store?"

"If it strikes your fancy," Grant said. He found her fingers at the hem of her skirt and pushed them aside before sliding familiarly underneath, clutching at the whole curve of her thigh. "Although I thought we'd try getting drunk and having sex somewhere unexpected for tonight."

"You won't get me drunk, and I don't want a headache in the morning," Renee said. Marie walked up with the water, and Renee knew she'd seen Grant's hand under Renee's skirt. She did not say anything, just set the water on the table and went back to the bar.

But she thought Marie was watching her out of the corner of her eye. And she knew that Josh was watching her, and sometimes his friends would crane their necks—it was as though their gazes bored holes into her. Her clothes were too tight, clinging to her like leeches, and everything on the inside tightened away from where they touched her skin. She sensed the panic attack coming before the physical manifestations really started, such as the cold sweat and the shallow breaths, her heart pounding against her ribcage.

Grant saw it coming, too. "And you were doing so well," he muttered.

If she had been able to open her mouth, she would have said that if he had really intended her to do well, he would not have brought her here, where he had an excuse to claim her in public.

He pulled the rubber band from her hair so that it could fall over her shoulders—just one more way he wanted her to draw attention. His lips seared the thin, pulsing skin of her neck, and he pressed his other hand unapologetically between her legs, cupping her in his palm. If Marie had been looking, she could have seen exactly what he was doing to her with his hands. All the men in Josh's booth could see were his lips and the glimpse of his tongue and teeth on her, making her head fall back as air rushed into her lungs. Her heart was still racing, but now it was for a different reason.

She was finally beginning to attract attention from some of the other patrons. Although some were dancing in the open floor area on the other side of the booths, separated by a wooden railing and glass plating, they would be able to see the shoulders and heads of people in booths. Which meant that they had an unobstructed view of Grant making love to the stretch of a woman's neck. They'd see her threading her thin fingers through the man's hair and bringing that searching mouth to her own. She kissed him slowly but thoroughly. In this setting, neither of them was as impulsive and lost in the feeling as they had been at the sanctuary. But it was still perhaps beyond propriety, especially in a small-town bar that still got its music from a jukebox.

The clearing of a throat broke Renee from her trance, and she realised belatedly that Marie had caught her with Grant's hand in an obviously compromising position. This was one of those times when her blush was well qualified. Marie did not look disgusted or like she was going to call the cops, but she certainly looked as if someone had hit her in the face with a two-by-four. There was probably nothing in the world less Renee-like than sucking face and getting fingered by a man like that. As embarrassed as she was, Renee could not help the swell of giddiness in her chest. What she wouldn't give to be un-Renee-like all the time, not just when Grant was kissing her or screwing her. Not that those things didn't get her giddy in another way.

Marie put the two plates of fried chicken strips and fries under their noses. Then she put down two tumblers and poured them each a drink.

"Leave the bottle," Grant said.

Marie looked to Renee again, and Grant leant forward as though he was going to have a say. But Renee suspected that any say he had would only dig the hole deeper.

"It's fine," Renee said. "Really. He's not taking advantage."

"I'd say different, hon," Marie muttered.

"He's not *forcing* anything," Renee reassured her. "If I didn't want the drink, I'd say something. I promise."

"You wouldn't be the first woman with her man pushing his luck in this place. Nor the first woman who might get a shiner the first time she says no," Marie whispered.

Grant snorted impatiently. "Why does everyone think I'm some kind of demon who's looking for innocent flesh to corrupt? Look, lady," he said, "she said she's fine. Give the girl a little credit."

Marie checked Renee's expression. When Marie did not find any indication that Renee was there against her will, she took a step back. "All right," she said. "When you're ready to pay, just come to the bar. But I'm going to be watching you." She glanced pointedly at Grant. "Just in case."

Grant leant back, hooding his eyes in shadow but unable to hide a certain amount of smugness. "You do that."

Marie reluctantly left them in order to tend to some other patrons.

Renee bit into a fry in annoyance. "Now everyone in town is going to think I'm in an abusive relationship. Thanks very much."

Grant began to eat his own meal. "What difference does it make? You'll know better."

Renee was not so sure about that. She'd told Britt that the relationship was not going to be permanent, and that was true. The question was when it was going to stop being such a thrill ride, when the other shoe would drop. And if that shoe was going to end up a kick in the face. The silver knife was secured to her hip, and she was sure that Grant had felt it while he was feeling her. But she did not know whether she would actually use it. She had never been tested like this, and she did not know when she would eventually be tested properly. When, not if.

And what does that say about your state of mind, if you're still here in this bar with him rather than calling the police on his ass? He probably has a record. You don't know. You don't do background checks. You don't know exactly what kind of man you've let into your bed.

The only thing that Renee could think in response to that was that she had let in a man whom she needed. At least for now.

They mostly ate in silence, although Grant sometimes hummed with the music if he heard a harder-edged, old rock song that he liked. Sometimes his fingers tapped on the inside her thigh. He never let go of her. Not many people could see the legs she had been so nervous about showing, but it was as though he was telling anyone who happened to bend over just to look at them that those legs were his, not theirs. And Renee did not particularly mind. It reminded her that he was there. Much as her hand on Britt's malamute fur grounded her, his warm hand on her thigh kept her fairly calm in spite of the crowd, and Renee thought that Grant knew it.

"That boy is still looking at you," Grant said. "The lug isn't any threat, but the boy, the scruffy one, wants you more than he thinks he does. Oh, the envy in him is absolutely delicious. I can smell it even in the midst of all this."

He put down his food, wiped his fingers on the paper napkin, then held up his tumbler of whisky.

"Time to start, love," he said.

Renee paused, considering whether it was a good idea, especially since he was the one who would be driving. She could always insist on driving herself if it came down to it. She suspected, though, that it was not easy for him to get drunk either.

She raised her glass.

"Here's to rubbing it in their faces," Grant said. "To the smell of sweet success and the promise of a long night ahead of us. And no reason to stay quiet."

Renee leant backwards a little as the intensity that naturally came to Grant intensified even more. If his eyes could be said to smoulder, she could almost swear they were glowing lantern-hot. She tilted her head back and downed the entire glass. The bottom of the glass hit the table with a sharp knock. Grant quirked his lips, then slung back his own drink.

Renee closed her eyes against the burn of the spirits at the back of her throat. She was used to beer, and it had been a while since she had taken something stronger. But it had more flavour and more heat to it in her stomach. She thought the next one would go down more easily now that she knew what to expect. She felt the alcohol in her head for a moment before it cleared. It would definitely be easier the next time.

She had once finished an entire bottle of good vodka, courtesy of her couriers, without slurring her words—what few words she had spoken. Britt and Jake had shared two bottles with Ki and Malcolm—Max never drank—and all of them had ended up fairly zonked by the end of the night. It did not make much sense, since Ki was the only one who weighed less than Renee, but she supposed some people just had a tolerance. There were people who could smoke for years, then stop cold turkey because they wanted to. Britt said it was a gift. Renee had replied that a gift wouldn't let her get hangovers in the morning, no matter how much she drank water after drinking alcohol. Britt, who was often fuzzy-mouthed and headachy herself, did not have much to say to that.

"Think you can drink me under the table?" Grant asked in unhidden amusement.

"No," Renee said. "I think we'll both be sitting up and lucid when this bottle is finished."

"Tell you the truth," Grant whispered, "I think I'd like that. It'll make everything else so much better. Have you ever done anything impulsive while stone-cold sober?"

Renee stared at him.

"Besides me."

"No."

"Well, *this*..." He poured more whisky into their tumblers. "This is the perfect way to allow yourself to give in to your impulses. You can tell everyone you were drunk."

Renee did not think that was advisable, since getting her drunk—even fake drunk—was not a way to endear him to the few in the crowd who actually cared about her wellbeing or who were vindictive enough to get Grant arrested.

It must have shown on her face. "You can tell everyone you were drunk, and you liked it and would absolutely do it again," Grant amended.

Renee swirled the amber liquid in her glass and watched the dim light move through it before swallowing it all down.

"How much could I get away with?" Renee asked, staring now into her empty glass.

"A lap dance and sex in the bathroom," Grant answered without hesitation.

Renee blinked. "Are you serious?"

"I don't think you're a whore."

"That's not what I asked."

"I want you," he murmured, sliding closer to her in the round booth, "to let go. I want you to know the freedom of simply...not...caring. If those boys think I'm the luckiest bastard in town and wonder why they never tried to hit that before, it's a bonus."

He moved closer, wrapping an arm around her waist and pulling her so that her leg was flush with his. The knife was between them—not sharp in its small sheath, but just a reminder. He bit the flesh beneath her earlobe hard, once, twice. As though he wanted to give her his own kind of reminder.

She turned her face to catch his mouth with her own. She gripped his hair—it was not quite as easy to hold as Britt's, she thought, as she struggled to control the angle of his mouth. Without the knife actually pressing into his skin, he was much harder to control at all. Every movement he made was as though he were three times larger, faster, stronger than her, enough to overwhelm her. She could taste the whisky on his tongue, and she fought for some kind of purchase. At every effort, he pushed her down, held her under the water until she was gasping into his mouth. She felt naked, as if he was above her and readying her just with his tongue in her mouth and arm around her waist.

Renee yanked on the hair at the back of his head. His teeth clicked as his head snapped back. He did not look annoyed at her at all for it.

She tucked her knees under her, mindless of the possibility that the wrong angle might leave her ass under her skirt exposed. Then she swung one leg over his hips until she straddled him. Right there in the bar with the Rolling Stones playing in the background. Where she was fully aware people were watching. A little necking was nothing, but the stretch of leg and the show she was giving them now... That didn't happen very often, and it certainly did not happen with Renee.

It was not really a lap dance. Her hips did move, and so did his. It might have even been to the beat. They were not quite frotting. The sway of her ass, his hand moving over the back of her thigh, they were too orchestrated. She reached back to pour herself more whisky and threw her head back to offer him the line of her throat to taste as she drank the burn down.

He sat there watching her. His body language was not that different from a john getting his twenty-five dollars worth, but his expression was. He was not flaunting his find before the crowd, winking collaboratively at the competition—if that was indeed what they were. Grant was not just captivated. He was hypnotised, oblivious to anything around him. That booth was their world, and that was perhaps the only reason why Marie didn't tell them to take the show outside. Theirs was a show for themselves.

Renee was drinking the air, a drop of sweat sliding down the side of her face. Grant caught it with a flick of his tongue, and the sudden jolt of what had previously been a slow, warm rise of arousal caught her by surprise. His lips were an inch away from hers, as though he wanted to kiss her again but would not let himself.

He untangled her from him reluctantly and deposited her next to him again. He poured them both another drink as her flush became more embarrassment than sex. She could not look anywhere but at his hands on the bottle. They shook—only slightly. She might have imagined it.

He held the glass out to her, then poured one for himself. She was half-finished with it by the time he poured the last bit of whisky into his tumbler.

"As soon as you finish that," he murmured, "go to the bathroom. Stay there five minutes."

She shivered and drank the rest, but as she slid out of the booth, she stopped. The bathrooms were at the back of the bar. That meant that she would have to walk past booths and a few tables to reach them. That meant that she would have to walk past people, past Josh and Marcus and their companions. After what she had just done. And she would then have to walk past them again after doing what they were going to do. It was enough to freeze her feet to the floor.

"You don't have to fear them," he whispered in her ear.

"It's not exactly rational, Grant," she shot back. Her teeth were clenched. It was as though every muscle in her body was stretched tight, too tightly to move her bones. She felt as if she were a violin string stretched almost to the snapping point.

"I'll be watching you. If anyone dares come near you, I'll be there to stop them. You don't have to fear them."

He pressed a kiss to the back of her neck, burying his face in her hair and inhaling.

"Just imagine the reward," he said.

With one firm hand on her shoulder and the other on her hip, he pushed her standing, then gave her a slap on the ass to get her moving. Her foot had to push forward so that she could keep her balance. Then she took another step, and another. She could feel Grant's eyes on her, tracing her calves, her thighs, the black fabric over her ass, up the curve of her spine. She felt the click of her heels more than she heard them. Her ears roared with the sound of rushing water that muffled everything around her. She barely noticed as she passed by one booth, two, three, past Josh. If he did anything when she passed, she did not see it.

Before she even knew it, she was at the women's bathroom door. She sighed with relief as she pushed it open. There was no one in the bathroom, and when she closed the door again, she saw that the door did lock. But she did not lock it yet. The rushing in her ears began to subside.

She walked to the sink and peered into the mirror. It was neither a rule nor a principle, but she did not look into mirrors very often. It wasn't important to her, the same way as dressing sexily was not important— when she rarely went out and when all she did during the day was either sit at the computer or get dirty, there was never any reason to care what she looked like. And honestly, what she saw usually did not impress her. She was almost indifferent to her appearance. She would notice when her posture was hunched over. She was self-conscious about her inability to make eye contact. But she did not know whether she was pretty or not. She was so used to her reflection that she never thought she was qualified to give that opinion. As far as a reflection went, it was not a horrible pairing. She could live with it.

It was strange, then, to look in the mirror and see herself as others saw her. Maybe it was because she had actually been concerned about her appearance when she'd got dressed that morning. Maybe her reflection was so unlike its usual self that she gave it a second look.

Renee still didn't know whether she was pretty, not in the way that she could tell Britt without question that she was gorgeous — some things just were the way they were, no opinion needed. But Renee thought she looked sexual, if not sexy, at that moment. Her hair was mussed but not tangled. Her lips were pink and swollen, and already she could see red marks on her neck that might bruise. Her shirt was not low cut, but she could still see the shadow between her breasts over the neckline. It was not as sexy as the shirts of some of the women on the dance floor. But her skirt was even shorter than she had thought it was, and maybe that made up for her higher neckline. She touched her cheek lightly. She had more freckles than she used to have because of all the time she spent outside, but her skin was still very pale.

The door opened behind her, and she whirled around. There was something almost narcissistic about looking so closely at herself in the mirror when she wasn't doing something like brushing her hair or applying makeup.

Grant came in and slammed the door, turning the lock. Renee had wondered whether he would give them privacy or whether he would leave them at the mercy of any woman who needed to pee. It could have gone either way, but she felt a certain measure of relief that he had locked the door. Although when she thought about the alternative she felt a quiver of electricity through her fingers, a combination of fear and excitement.

"You wanted me to leave that door unlocked," Grant said. It was as though he could read her mind, or at least notice how turned on she was. The lighting was not very good, but Renee could see how dilated his pupils were, and she was sure that hers were just as huge.

"And if I had?" he continued. "You would still be eager to have my hands on you like this." He was before her in a heartbeat, lifting her onto the counter. "You would still cling to me like you are. You would still let me fuck you, hard, fast, filthy, like a slut who would sell herself for a drink and a room."

Her stomach roiled at the word 'slut', but she knew that, even as he roughly palmed her breast under her bra and yanked her underwear down her legs, he did not see her that way. Not when he *had* to taste her, had to drink in her shallow breaths, her little gasps. It was as if nothing had happened between the booth and here, as though she were above him again. She braced herself on the counter with one hand while she wrapped the other arm around his neck tightly.

He had barely opened his jeans before he was inside her, the teeth of his zipper pressing into her sensitive flesh, but not enough to distract her from what he was doing. Each thrust was hard and uncontrolled, and his mouth was all teeth, finally drawing little cries from her when the force of his thrusts made him bite down hard. And Renee... She was pushing herself down onto him with one hand and pulling herself down with the other. Her panties were caught on one ankle, her shirt and bra pushed up over her breasts.

She thought she heard the doorknob rattle, then a knock on the door, and she shook her head from side to side as she held in her orgasm, holding her bottom lip between her teeth. She slammed down just as he held her tight against him, his hips snapping in short jerks as he came. She undulated through her aftershocks to draw them out. When she was finished, she bent to the side to retrieve her panties before they hit the floor. He winced at the odd angle she was bending him, and she could not help but laugh a little when he slid out of her and stepped back so that she could pull her underwear back on. His cum began to wet the fabric almost immediately, but she resisted the compulsion to clean herself.

Grant unlocked the bathroom door and pulled it open as he zipped up his pants. A startled woman took in Renee's dishevelled appearance and Grant doing up his button, and she stammered a completely unnecessary apology. Renee straightened her shirt and ran her fingers through her hair. For some reason, she was not even embarrassed. And it was not because of the whisky. Her head was still clear, although she was a little tired.

Renee followed Grant out, and he took her hand to lead her to the dance floor. She resisted once she realised where he was taking her, but his grip was firm. He always knew where he was going and what he wanted. And he wanted her. Sometimes it hit her as simply and completely as that. It was not so easy to describe as desire, sexual or otherwise. He *wanted* her. Her neurosis, her voice, her eyes, her cunt, her legs, her fingernails, the crook of her elbow. He *wanted* her. Her skin hummed, and she didn't know if she liked it.

Grant pulled a quarter from his pocket and chose a song from the jukebox. Renee had never heard it before, and as the music began to pulse from the speakers, smooth and wicked, she wondered how a song like that had got onto a jukebox in the first place.

He brought them to the dance floor — not the middle but half in shadow near a corner. He twirled her around until she was facing away from him and pulled her against him. His arm was a vice around her shoulders, and it felt almost uncomfortable until he began to move them with the odd rhythm of the song. He was not hard, but she could still feel him against her, pressing into her with every beat. Every second of the song was carnal, down-low dirty, and she found herself swaying with him, subtly moving against him until she reached one hand up behind her to pull his head down. He kissed her neck obediently. He was unusually collected, unusually slow, careful. She did not doubt that he had an angle, but she had never known him to be subtle. She hadn't thought he had the patience to do something that wasn't bump and grind. All she knew was that, whatever was going through his mind, she thought she could like this kind of attention. It was almost more arousing than the scene in the bathroom. What they did could never be termed making love, and this was no exception. But it wasn't quite fucking.

Even so, they were not just dancing. They had on all their clothes. They were in front of everyone. He was not really touching her, and she was not really touching him. But they were still having sex.

For a brief moment, the rush of blood between her legs was enough to make her go literally weak at the knees, moaning softly, and Grant had to catch her before she caught her balance. She could feel him smirking into her neck.

"Mind if I cut in?"

They both turned their heads to see Josh with his hands in his pockets, eyes on the floor. Renee could almost see the glow in Grant's eyes as he imagined what he could do to Josh. The hand flexing on her shoulder was strong, and Renee feared that Grant would make a scene for the one time in forever that Josh seemed to be behaving himself.

But Grant sounded civilised as he replied, "Why cut in? Who said we couldn't share?"

Renee froze in the middle of the instrumental bridge.

"This is a dance floor, boy. You don't cut in. You just dance." Renee looked up to see his expression, and he was looking up at Josh with an almost predatory eye — different from the one he gave her, more like the way he looked at Jake. It wasn't competition — he did not even dream that Jake was a worthy adversary, much less Josh.

Josh's lips curled in reactionary disgust. "What's that supposed to mean?"

"She doesn't trust you. And she's right. Ergo, I don't want her with you. Alone."

"But it's okay for you to be alone with her. For ten minutes. In the girls' bathroom," Josh sneered.

"I'll say," Grant murmured against her cheek. He licked her with his strong tongue. Claiming her. Josh's eyes almost bugged out, but Renee did not know whether he was turned on by what Grant was doing to her or whether he was surprised. Probably a combination.

"You afraid of me, boy?" Grant said. "Afraid to be caught dead by your boys dancing with the girl you want while she's still with her man? This may be the closest you'll ever be to her without her bitch with her. But you don't get her all to yourself."

"Why?"

"If she really wanted you, she would have spoken up by now and told me to take a walk. Instead, she's still with me. Against me." Grant was gloating, dangling her before Josh. And it was beginning to make Renee feel slimy. Dancing with Grant in front of everyone, letting them all see what they were doing and letting them guess... That was all right. But saying it out loud like that made it something else.

She ducked under his arm. "Stoplight. Enough."

When she was finally able to see both of them, she saw the tail end of Josh's smirk. "Just because I'm done with him doesn't mean I'm interested in you. Not for a second." She raised an eyebrow at Grant. "Are we finished?"

"Here?" Grant asked.

"Yes."

"Then yes," he replied.

"Wait," Josh protested as Renee took the lead on the way out. Grant threw a few bills on the bar for Marie, not bothering to count out the money, but by the look on Marie's face, she must have received a considerable tip.

"What'd you do?" Josh asked Grant. "How'd you prise open those legs? Didn't the icicles get in the way?"

Grant's smirk made Josh's look like false confidence. "You really don't know, do you? Maybe I just had a pair."

Josh pushed his face into Grant's, jutting his jaw in challenge. "You know, I was her first kiss."

"Bravo. Quite a champion," Grant said. "But I live in the here and now. And you'll never know how wrong you are about her. That's the victory. I'm the one screwing her."

The punch hurt her hand. She must not have done it right, or maybe hitting that part of his jaw where the bone was strong was a bad idea. She was, however, irrationally pleased at the way Grant stumbled back. She didn't know whether she had actually hurt him — whether anything hurt him — or whether she had just startled him enough for him to fall away.

"God, is this what happens when two men thinking themselves alpha males get together? It's ridiculous," Renee spat. "I'm here, Grant. With you. But I don't have to be. One phone call."

"Ouch, love." Grant rubbed his jaw. He looked conspiratorially at Josh. "She's got a lot of power for someone so little."

"Quit while you're ahead." Renee started for the door without him. She stopped at the threshold. She had made it twenty feet and a right hook without feeling claustrophobic from the crowd or completely mesmerised by Grant's overbearing personality.

But now that she'd realised it, she could not walk out of the bar. She always had to realise exactly what she was doing and count the ways that it was somehow wrong. All in a matter of seconds. The room was suddenly too small, but the world outside was too big. She stared at the wood grain until he was there behind her. Hot and aroused in a way that the dancing could not account for.

"Just push it open, and you'll be out there. And I'll be with you," he whispered.

She pushed her way out into the cold. But she barely noticed it.

Chapter Nine

She was halfway to the car before she realised she had to wait for Grant because he had the truck key in his pocket. When he caught up to her in his own time, she thrust her hand into his pocket and grabbed them.

"I'll drive," she said.

"You drank half a bottle of whisky."

"So did you. I'm not slurring. Am I?"

"No," Grant said. "And you're walking in a straight line. But you don't know where we're going."

Renee opened the driver's side and pulled herself in. "Then direct me." She slammed her door and watched him through the glass. He shrugged before running around the front of the truck to the passenger's side.

"Just keep going straight. There's a motel where the street meets the interstate, about an hour west. We'll stop there."

* * * *

The motel was not prepossessing. Renee had read about 'seedy motels', but she had never seen one right in front of her before. The building looked solid — it had that going for it, at least. But the paint was peeling, and the structures themselves looked as though they were trapped in the previous century. They did not have the staying power for a retro label. If not for the cars outside the front office and a few lights on, she might have thought that the place had been abandoned and left to the trees.

Grant went to check them in, and Renee kept the car idling while she clutched her coat around her. She thought that this should be that time when she was wondering what she had got into and whether this was a good idea. After all, she was out of her sanctuary and away from friends, some of whom had always been fiercely protective enough that she had not had to worry about her safety. She was away from anything resembling a town, at a seedy highway motel in the middle of nowhere, with a man of questionable scruples, if any at all. But in spite of the fact that she knew the entire situation was grounds for a teen horror movie if she'd ever seen one, she could not bring herself to properly *feel* the concerns she should have been having.

He came out with a standard motel key and fob dangling from one finger. After he opened the passenger door, he knelt on the seat to retrieve their bags.

"Room one-oh-six," Grant said, dropping the key in her lap.

The motel door needed a little shove before it unlocked, but when she opened it, she was pleasantly surprised that everything looked clean. The paint was old and faded, the print over the queen-sized bed was of a Santa Fe landscape and easily dismissed, and the carpet looked lightly stained, but not by anything recent—nothing a steamer and shampoo could not have fixed. The room would serve its purpose—a temporary place to stay, nothing more and nothing less. For sleeping, soaking, screwing, shooting up...whatever your peace or poison.

She was coming out of the bathroom when Grant threw their bags in a corner behind the small writing table. He grabbed her wrist to bring her against him in an impromptu kiss that felt that much different in these walls than it did in the bar, at the sanctuary. He was always different, but always all-consuming. She fisted his shirt, holding on for the ride and making sure he was as close as he could be. She touched his jaw, and he pulled away for a moment. She realised that it was the place she had hit him. It had not left a mark.

"Did I hurt you?" she asked.

"No." Grant grinned. "I had just forgotten that you'd hit me there."

Renee had not even known she was pouting until he sucked her lower lip into his mouth. His teeth were sharp for a moment. She whimpered as pleasure trickled slowly down her spine. She touched his jaw again where she had hit him, pressing.

"It doesn't hurt," he murmured against her cheek. "Just a little pressure. But it was good. What you did, it was good. The whole night, my dear."

"It was inexcusable," Renee said. "I shouldn't have hit you."

"But I deserved it?"

"But you deserved it."

"The night wasn't as bad as you thought it was going to be, was it?" Grant said.

"I wasn't expecting anything," Renee replied. "I didn't know what was going to happen or where you'd take me."

"When you were there, though…"

Renee sighed and leaned against the wide dresser.

"It wasn't as bad as it could have been," Renee said. She had not been without Britt as a service animal for five years, and prior to that, she just had not left the sanctuary after her father had died. She'd had worse outings.

The expression on Grant's face was neither a grin nor a smirk. It was quieter than that, which was unusual, and he took off one of her shoes, then the other. He slid his large hands up her bare legs until he found the edge of her skirt.

"In fact," he murmured, "I think you were a proper little minx who knows how to put on a show. My God, woman, do you know the things that you did? In front of people who terrify you? Do you know that I can smell you right now?" He leaned in until she wrapped her legs around his and he loomed over her. She pressed her head back against the cheap dresser mirror. "My filthy girl. Braver women than you would never dream of being able to do the things that you did tonight."

"I'm not a terrified little girl, you know. Not really," Renee interrupted, pushing him enough that she could slide off the dresser and get between him and the door. "I'm nervous around people. I have a phobia of being in crowds. It's irrational—that's the definition of a phobia. But just because I'm afraid of people doesn't mean I'm afraid of everything."

"You did just fine in a crowd," he said. Now he was smirking.

"When you were—"

"Distracting you."

"Yes."

"Protecting you."

Renee did not have anything to say to that.

"That's why you like the bitch to be with you," Grant said, advancing on her. "She may just be a dog, but she's large, and she almost looks...well, like a wolf. And you know that I'm a wolf. You feel safer. You feel safer with a little bit of teeth."

Her back was against the door before she realised it.

"If you want to leave, Renee, you've had plenty of opportunities."

"I don't want to leave."

She could smell the whisky just underneath his breath, and if she could smell it, he could probably smell it on her, too. "Then what do you want from this?"

There was no answer she could give.

"We're away from anyone you could possibly know. In the middle of nowhere. The managers and our fellow transients are used to any sort of noise that could come out of this room. You can do anything you want here. Anything. No junior alpha to get in the way, no loyal bitch, no propriety, no rules."

"Stop calling her that," Renee said. Only part of the meaning was what Britt really was, and Renee could taste the sourness of the insult. Grant might have liked the quality in Britt, but that did not take away the taste.

"Calling her what she is?" he whispered before running his tongue over her neck.

"It's not all she is," she replied.

"It's all she's been to me."

"Stop."

"Make me."

She almost hit him again. Her hand flew up and was inches from the side of his head before she stopped. She slowly lowered her raised hand onto his shoulder. His kisses on her neck paused.

"Why did you stop?" he asked.

"I'm not going to do it again."

Grant laughed, drawing a growl from that deeper place inside him. He took her face in his hands, drawing his blunt nails over the skin lightly, suggestive of so much more he could do to her. "Silly girl. I want you to."

His eyes were glowing in the lamplight, and she could not look away.

"Hit me," he hissed. "Hit me, Renee. Just do it."

He took her wrist in his hand and drew it up, as if she were a marionette with strings. Her fingers were limp, but she could feel the tension in her palm. The readiness, a subtle flex.

"Hit me. Claw at me. Bite me. Make me take you. Scream for me, my dear. Do anything you want. Just hit me."

His grip grew harder, and her hand shook.

"Hit me, bitch!"

Her other hand, her weaker hand, shot up to punch him in his jaw on the other side. She heard the click of his teeth closing, and he actually shouted. He brought his hand to his mouth. Renee saw some blood as he brought it back—he had bitten his tongue. Grant smiled with his teeth stained red.

"There's my girl. Hit me again. I know you want to." His words were slightly slurred. She worried about how hard he had bitten himself.

As though he knew she was beginning to drown in her thoughts, he pulled his shirt over his head and came at her. His whole body language was menacing, predatory. She just reacted, shoving at his chest. It was like trying to move an oncoming car. They tumbled onto the bed. He shoved his hand under her skirt, fingers clumsy and forceful against her cunt.

"Love the easy access, by the way," Grant said. "And I'm sure the rest of them loved to see what they were missing. What I have."

She was still pushing at his chest, but the angle was all wrong, and she could not find purchase.

"Come on," he hissed. "Is that the best you can do?"

Renee clenched her teeth. She curled her nails—not particularly long, but they had not been cut in a while—into his skin, pressed, pressed harder and deeper, and she thought she felt something give.

He gave a low shout, but there was no mistaking that he was hard again, jerking his hips against her thighs. She hit his shoulder with her good hand, but when that got no reaction, she struck the side of his head with the palm of her hand, and he fell to the side. But he had a grasp on her shirt, and when she struggled to get up, she had to bend over and let him keep it. She stood there in her bra and skirt, not knowing where to go, not knowing if she felt threatened, if she should run and call the police about a man attacking her, or whether this was a game.

Then he was coming at her again, unbuttoning his jeans with one hand and holding the side of his head with the other. She yanked open the drawer of the nightstand and pulled out the Gideon Bible. She held it between them like a weapon, even though the knife was still under her skirt. He actually laughed, but the book still had sharp corners that took his breath away when she shoved it into his stomach. He kept coming at her, gasping for breath, and that was when the fear began to flow through her fingers until they were like ice. His hands were hard on her as he shoved her into the curtains. Her shoulder struck where the wall angled into the window, and she was sure there would be a bruise there. She hit him again with the Bible, but he batted it away. The carpet muffled the impact when it landed on the floor, but the sound was still loud in her ears as he pulled her bra straps down, baring her breasts without taking the bra off. He rubbed the sandpapery skin of his unshaven face against her nipple before he took it into his mouth, teeth tugging slightly, enough that she cried out— whether it was because it hurt or because she liked it, she couldn't say anymore. She looked down and saw a slight bloodstain where his mouth had been. He worked his way down her stomach with his teeth, taking flesh and testing it, sucking it, breathing her in, drinking her in as if she were the perfect snifter of liquor. Nothing she had done seemed to have even slowed him down.

She brought her knee up and caught him between the throat and the chin. He flew back, and she facilitated his fall with her heel to his chest. It was only when he wasn't holding her up anymore that she realised she was shaking. And scared. And inexplicably, irrevocably aroused. If he really took it upon himself to attack her, she knew now that she could do nothing but take out her knife. But right now... Right now she did not know whether she *should*.

He coughed and gagged for a few moments, and she took those moments to skirt around him, pulling her bra from its tangle around her and throwing it onto the dresser. Her hand flew to her side where the knife was under her skirt when he finally pushed himself up and rid himself of his pants until he was just a man. His cock was rigid, bumping against his stomach as he walked slowly towards her. A thin thread of pre-cum ran from the head to just above his navel. He raised his hands between them as a sort of truce, his gaze on her hand grasping the knife.

"You're afraid of me," he said. His voice was raspy from her hitting him, and from the growl that was making its way from deep in his throat. The sounds that meant he was as turned on as he could be. "That's good. It's smart. I'm bigger and stronger than you. But you've been doing so well, love. You don't need that. You don't need to fear me tonight. Unless you like being afraid. Then I'll scare you as much as you want."

Renee brought the knife out, but it hung limply in her shaking hand.

"You don't need that, Renee," Grant whispered, stepping a little closer. "You're doing everything right."

"What is this?" she asked, tremulous, and she hated the sound of it. "What do you want from me?"

"I need you to hurt me." He placed gentle fingers on her wrist. She did not let go of the knife, but she understood the restraint he needed to be gentle at all. "I need you to fight. It's good when you fight back. Make me earn your body, love."

"Why?"

He smiled toothily. "Because it's fun."

Renee rubbed a hand over her face and through her hair, pushing it back. She brought the hand holding the knife away from Grant.

"So this is fun?" she asked.

"Were you confused?" He came closer still, but he was careful not to move too quickly. She didn't bring the knife up, which he took as encouragement to wrap his arms around her, tugging her skirt and panties down until they pooled on the floor at her feet.

Renee let the knife fall with them.

"You like it when I hurt you," she said. "You liked it in the bar."

"You have no idea," he whispered in her ear.

She moved her fingers up his stomach, tickling the muscles so that they jerked in her hand. She circled his areola, feeling his hair there crinkle slightly. His small, flat nipple hardened almost the way hers had, and she bent forward to take it in her mouth, much like he had hers. Then, she opened her eyes to look up at him as she began to clench her teeth around the small bit of flesh in her mouth.

His cock jerked between them, and he threw his head back in a loud groan before fisting her hair and yanking. It must have hurt like hell when she pulled his nipple with her teeth on the way, but as she went stumbling back into the wall between the bedroom and bathroom, he only seemed more aroused, if that was possible.

This time, instead of running from him, she let him come to her. She almost struck his face, but he caught her hand in time, then the other. He was amazingly fast, and she had to suspect that some of her blows had either been unexpected or he'd simply let her hit him. His palms and fingers engulfed her wrists until she could feel her muscles and bones scrape together, and his breath was hot on her mouth, drawing muffled moans from her as he kissed her with her arms against the wall, as if she were crucified. Even though she wanted him to keep kissing her, keep making her moan—keep her forgetting that there could be anyone hearing them, forgetting that she should care—she brought her teeth down hard on his lower lip, then his chin. When he broke away, she tried to dig her nails into his hands but she was at the wrong angle, and she could do nothing as he brought her wrists together, then threw her bodily onto the bed.

For a moment, as he filled her vision with his too-large, bloody smile and glowing eyes, that fear of him came back. But unlike before, she let that fear thrill her, electrifying every nerve cell in her skin. She was shaking again as he attacked her shoulder, then the top of her breast, but she finally managed to twist her wrists so that she could grab his skin between her nails. She must have reached a pressure point because he let go of her hands, his own falling to each side of her. She brought her knee up, and he dodged a painful bullet by shifting to the side.

The movement conveniently let her curl herself around him. He rubbed his cock between her legs, his pre-cum and her juices mingling. His head fell next to hers as he began to rut against her without entering. She pressed her mouth to his shoulder, then slid beneath him a little so that he was frotting against her stomach and she could take his abused nipple into her mouth again, biting and licking in turn until he finally came on her, semen smearing over her stomach and her breasts. He did not even try to hold back as he shouted his orgasm, slamming one hand against the headboard and almost breaking the frame.

She held him through the rocking until he finally crawled down and kissed her again, as though he had worked out none of the sexual energy all night. He plunged his fingers into her hair and kissed her until she was gasping. His skin was so warm that she sweated beneath him, and she could taste her salt on his lips.

"You think we're through?" he moaned into her mouth before enclosing her throat in one hand and pressing—not enough to choke her but enough for it to feel like it. "You think I want you to stop fighting me? You're only just getting started."

His eyes were fierce, and her fear was back, drawing her legs together and her nails to his eyes, his Adam's apple. Blood was rushing through her head and away—she could feel it, thick and heady. She finally managed to get her knees into his ribs, and he let go with a feral grin. Air rushed into her lungs. She coughed and crawled, but he trapped her beneath him, covering her back with his body and nipping down each of her vertebrae. He covered her hands with his and pressed them into the comforter on the mattress.

She could see the two of them in the mirror above the dresser. There were places on his face that were a little swollen, and there was dried blood in the corner of his mouth. Her red hair was tousled, tangled, and wet at the temples—it looked almost too bright against her pale skin, which set off the marks he had made on her body, places where his teeth had been. She felt his cock stir between her legs as Grant made his way down her back, and he pulled her hands back until her face was against the comforter and her ass was in the air.

She could still see herself in the mirror. Renee could not believe that the woman was her. For all that she was small and hurt and beneath him, she thought she saw someone with strength there. It was all backwards, but she could not stop the whimper, the startled 'O' her mouth made in the mirror as his tongue circled the puckered hole of her ass. It was such an unlikely place for her to find herself wanting to cry from the sensation. He made his way down over her perineum until she was mewling for some kind of force. She squirmed, pulling against his grip as he drank through each clenching of her cunt. He swirled that moisture around her hole again, and she cried out, pressing her face into the mattress.

He let go of one of her hands to force her head back up as he moved up her body again, pulling her upright by the hair so that she could see her body before her in the mirror. She looked almost in pain as he grasped one breast tightly, pinching the nipple near the webbing between two fingers. He used that leverage to help lift her up so that he could enter her cunt. But she could feel his pubic hair where his mouth had been, and just the memory of it made her moan more every time he slammed into her.

"God, Renee, yes," Grant growled. He did not bother lowering his volume. If there were people in the next room or outside—or maybe a few doors down—they all knew that her name was Renee and that she was a wild bitch and that he wanted her more than he had ever wanted any slut. That she was going to keep screaming for him and that people were going to think he was murdering her for the way she was going to love every second of this fucking. He punctuated his declarations with pinching and biting and pulling her until she was just a bundle of aroused nerves, with not a single thought left in her head.

When he pushed her forward a little so that she had to brace herself on the footboard of the bed, he found that place that did make her scream, over and over and over again, as he hit it without any mercy. She shook with the force of the orgasm when it finally came, the pleasure hitting her over and over with every scream and every brush of that cock until it was too much, and she flung herself around, elbowing his ribs where she had kneed him, then his stomach. His head hit her shoulder, but his cock slipped out of her.

Renee was a little embarrassed at the fluid beneath her. At first she thought she had peed, but it wasn't right—it didn't smell right. Grant grinned as he noticed her notice the stain.

"Oh, I made you come all right. Now if only I can get my name out of that pretty little mouth next time," he murmured, pulling her back into bed by the back of her neck. His back curved, almost too much for a human, as he whipped around to cover her again. He buried his face against her breasts, licking at the places where he had come on her until all she was covered with was sweat and saliva and her own moisture dripping down onto the comforter. It was messy, and she should have hated it, but when he came back up to take her mouth, she delved her tongue into the corners of his lips where the blood had dried, cleaning him, too.

The vibration against her grew as his growl became more pronounced, and Renee swore that his teeth were sharp against her tongue. She jerked back and stared into his mouth. She wasn't wrong. The shape of his jaw was altered, slightly elongated to accommodate the new structure.

"Turnabout is fair play," he said in a guttural voice, the consonants slurred and sharpened at the same time. "For the silver."

She hissed as he began to bite, taking flesh between his teeth and worrying it with his teeth and tongue, to bring blood under the surface but not enough to break the flesh. He was a fraction of an inch from turning her against her will with every bite, just as she had been too close to poisoning him at the edge of a blade.

And perhaps she knew what had made him quiver with restraint as her fingers threaded through his hair to hold him close, but not pushing him down like she might have done. He was the only one with open wounds, but he avoided places that he had bit down on her before, just in case. It was strange that with all the things that Renee couldn't trust Grant with, she could trust him not to bite her unless she told him to. She knew forcing her into wolf skin would not be nearly as satisfying to him as Renee choosing to defy her dog pack. Just as letting her choose to come with him on this trip in spite of the commanding tone he had used had been satisfying. Just as every time she let him in or played his games was more satisfying than forcing her to do anything.

He dipped his tongue into her navel, and her hips canted up of their own accord. The slick surface of his lupine teeth slid against skin. "Careful, love. You don't want me to slip, now, do you?"

"Son of a bitch," she muttered, throwing an arm over her eyes. She bit her lip as he began to move lower, where it would be that much harder to keep still. His laugh came in waves of vibrations through her body.

"You'll find it's easier to stay still if you let yourself scream," he said, tracing lines up and down the inside of her thighs with clawlike nails. "Let them know which wolf is in your bed, Red."

That's what Britt calls me, she thought, though he'd called her that before. But her thoughts were tenuous as he began to bite and suck the folds of pink flesh between her legs. She could feel him breathe her scent and his in, as if he were determined to make it stronger. His tongue was a little longer and flatter, but still thick and powerful, and he reacquainted himself with the sensitive nerves of her perineum and lower. She couldn't clutch at him, couldn't bring him closer to her, and she found that all she had left was to fist the comforter and let the sounds out—wailing, begging, crying. They shattered the already broken barrier in her throat. There were no words but his name. There was not even enough of her in her mind to think that she would be embarrassed by how loud and needy she was being once he was finished.

His body below her rocked with every lick, every tease and taste of wet, fragrant flesh. He was rubbing against the comforter, growling into her and making the most obscene noises with his tongue. He seemed to draw passion from how vocal she was. What he did hurt as much as it made her blood pulse strongly through her clit and her cunt, and when he drew the orgasm from her, he also drew his claws down the outsides of her legs, so hard that they broke skin. But she was biting her arm through her second climax, which was quicker but almost as strong as the first.

When he crawled up her body and thrust his erection into her, forcing her legs up until her knees were against her breasts, she could finally wrap herself around him again. It was oddly soothing to hold him when he was as wild as he was. His feral teeth were clenched, holding his growls in his throat until he finally came.

The room was now strangely quiet but for their heavy breathing. Renee surprised herself by squirming, her clitoris still swollen with arousal. Grant gave a short bark of laughter as he rolled his hips down, giving her a little pressure. He pressed his human mouth to her shoulder and slid from her to rest next to her on the bed. They would have to get rid of the comforter eventually—it was filthy.

"And they say alcohol decreases the libido," he muttered into her skin.

"I told you I don't get—"

"Yes, you did," Grant said. "And I can handle correction."

"Then here's another. *Tell me* when you're playing a game. I'm not good at telling the difference. Not with you." She circled the pads of her fingers gently around his nipple—the one she had bitten and left marks on.

"Oh, my dear, you fear me when you shouldn't, and when you should, you only hold me closer," Grant said, chuckling. "I have to confess, it's attractive."

She looked at him, drawing her eyebrows in over the bridge of her nose.

"I could have bitten you and torn your life to pieces. Hell, I could have transformed and had you for dinner until you were a bloody mess on the bed sheets," he murmured. "And you knew it. And you know that I very much want to. You know that I am far less scrupulous than you...with your knife and Junior's big gun. But you didn't even fight me when you felt my teeth. Admit it, love," he said. "You liked it."

"You're not going to bite me," said Renee. "And if you killed me, my pack would know. And they'd hunt you down and kill you. You'd destroy your life by ending mine."

"Maybe I just want to bring you down with me," he whispered.

Grant rolled over to turn off the light, but Renee kept her eyes open as the afterimage faded.

* * * *

When she woke up, it was still mostly dark outside, although it did not seem to be as dark as when they had come in. She could not believe her sleep had been broken. Even as she stirred, she was exhausted. While the first time she'd had sex with Grant had left her aching, it did not compare to waking up now. She winced with every movement that she made, felt places tear anew that had only just begun to heal.

Grant's arm was around her stomach, but he wasn't too near her, and she was easily able to slip away, biting back the urge to groan as her body protested. But Grant's breathing was still even, so she assumed she had not woken him.

And even if she had, Renee thought, *Screw it*.

She bent over, hissing through her teeth, and pulled out the toiletry bag she had packed. Once she was in the bathroom, she shut the door and turned on the light. As she started the water for a bath, first cold for a while, then hot, she took a cursory look at herself.

If she had not known that the marks on her body had been made during particularly rigorous and sometimes violent sex, she probably would have been even more concerned, but as it was, she was only moderately so. She stood up to look at herself in the mirror. It was even worse that way—there were bite marks all over her body, some of them just bruises, others bordering on broken skin. Bruises where he had held her too hard or where she had hit herself on furniture. Claw marks all down her legs. The place on her arm where she had bitten herself. She thought she should be ashamed of them, and although she was slightly horrified, it was more because of their appearance, not because of what had caused them. At least it was winter, and there would not be much cause for someone to ask about places on her body that they would never get the chance to see.

She looked into the mirror until it began to fog up. She opened the bathroom door so that some of the steam would escape into the bedroom rather than get all thick in the small bathroom. She briefly turned the running water cold to cool it down a little bit, then shut the water off and lowered herself in.

She was unprepared for the stinging of the wounds all over her body, from her legs up to her neck. Breath slid through her teeth in a prolonged hiss as her skin pulsed in protest before settling down. She could breathe again. She clutched at the side of the tub when she stretched out her legs, pulling at sensitive, stinging places. Finally, she was able to lie back and reach for the soap. She lathered it up on a washcloth and began to wash the dried sweat, blood, tears, and other things from her body, cleaning the clotted places and staining the rough white cloth a little pink.

The steam, the roughness of the washcloth, the smell of her soap, the movement of her aching muscles — it all made her feel a little better.

"You don't have to wash my scent off yourself anymore," Grant said from the doorway. "You're not where they can smell you. And you're not around them. You're with me."

"It's not about that," Renee said. He had startled her, but she was glad that she had not shown it. "Not to get you off of me. I just hurt."

Grant stepped into the tub. Renee drew her legs up against her chest to let him in. They were cramped, but aside from the bones of her ass pressing against the porcelain, it was not uncomfortable.

"The good kind?" Grant asked, leaning to the side to avoid the faucet.

Renee stared at him for a minute, running the washcloth over her arm. Then she nodded. "The good kind."

"Good," Grant said. He slid his legs between hers until the two of them overlapped in the water. He did not try to initiate anything else—he looked tired himself, as though the sound of the water filling the bath had woken him up. It was just his hot limbs against hers, his toes under her thighs, the hot water rocking around them. "It's a good kind of hurt for me, too."

Chapter Ten

She let him drive in the morning. Her suspicion that she was going to wake up with a hangover had been spot on, but she had had worse hangovers in her life. And in spite of the soak in the middle of the night with Grant, her limbs and cuts still ached and protested when she tried to move. They had managed to remove the dirty comforter to sleep under the cleaner sheets after the bath, though, so she had not felt the need to shower when she woke up. Grant seemed unaffected both by the liquor and the rigorous sex, even though there were livid marks where she had bitten or scratched him, and there was a small corner-shaped bruise where she had hit him in the side of the head with the Gideon Bible.

He broke away from the highway once, making for an out-of-the-way diner that he had apparently frequented in the past. He knew exactly what to order — waffles, eggs sunny side up, hash browns and sausages. She let the waitress choose for her. What she brought out was just right — two pancakes and a smaller side of scrambled eggs. Renee stole one of

Grant's sausages, surprised that she was so hungry. She usually ate plenty, but a breakfast as big as these pancakes wasn't her usual fare. Even so, her stomach was still growling halfway through one of them. Grant looked amused as he watched her eat.

Renee could tell when they got closer to the city. The clumps of small towns started getting denser, and buildings began getting bigger and shinier. And there were more billboards and intersections, more cars, more people than Renee was used to seeing at once. It was all right while she was in the car, but she began to play with the buttons of her coat as she wondered how she would be when she had to get out of the car.

At least she was not wearing that skirt anymore. Grant told her that something more practical would be best for that night—they would be in a wooded national park area in the cold. So she was able to wear her long jeans and boots, but she also chose a nicer dark blue blouse over one of her usual camisoles. She didn't care if it got dirty—she had not even known it existed until Britt had found it behind everything else Renee owned. Then there was her coat and scarf. She was not going to be walking into a warm bar, and it was important for her to cover up. But Grant moved his hand over her thigh to the slight flash of skin above the waist of her jeans. He was not insistent—it was as though he needed to touch her. As long as he was able to drive in a straight line and the weather stayed clear, Renee did not mind.

There were some thick, high clouds in the distance, but the weatherman on the rock station said that all the storms would be south of Minneapolis, and Grant said that the place they were heading was to the northwest, although he did want to take her into the city after a night with the pack. He insinuated that they might not be alone. There was an odd glitter to his eyes—not tears, not sadness, not anger. Just memories. Renee wondered what he had left behind. And why he had left it behind to come to a dog sanctuary, where he knew there would be canine shapeshifters but no werewolves.

She knew they had to be getting close when Grant turned the music down.

"Imagine, if you will," Grant said, "a community of people who may not be completely like me, but they have many of the same traits. I don't think I have to tell you to stay near me. Werewolves tend to be leery of humans in their space, even more than weaker shapeshifters or other magical creatures. Our instincts are trained to see humans as prey more than any other animal. You will have wolves circling you."

He looked at her, keeping his eyes on the road with his peripheral vision. There weren't many people on the road anyway. "You'll handle it, love. You'll do just fine."

"As long as I stay close to you," Renee said.

"I'll keep them from tasting you, yes. I mean you'll do fine when they're trying to intimidate you."

"Like what you try to do to me?" she asked.

He looked at the road again, but not before his lips twitched. "Exactly. And my original plan for calming you down is still in effect. If you start to panic, I *will* kiss you. Believe me, though, the wolves love an exhibition, so you have some motivation to stay calm. Unless you want to give another performance, in which case, I only have more ideas what we can do."

Renee rolled her eyes and looked out the window, but she knew he was serious in spite of the laughter in his tone. She always had to be the most attentive when he was the most amused.

* * * *

Her truck was not the only vehicle in the gravel parking lot, but the area did not look nearly full enough for the largest werewolf pack in the north.

Grant must have noticed her looking around, because he said, "Many members of the pack stay in the woods permanently. The rest run all the way here from wherever they live nearby. Or they carpool. And then there are the few like me—just a visitor from time to time."

"Were you always a visitor?" Renee asked.

There was a beat before he answered. "No. I was once in one of the subpacks here."

Grant got out of the car and threw the keys to Renee. She slipped them into her coat pocket and buttoned them in. When he opened her door, she slid her legs to the side to step down, but he stopped her.

"And other rules still apply," he murmured. "The game's still on, my dear. If you need to scream, then scream. And if you need to hit me, then hit me. There are no holds barred here. There are no rules. Particularly the ones you seem to have assigned to yourself. With the exception of 'stay close to me'. Because if I'm dangerous, what do you think seventy-five wolves are to you?"

"Fine," Renee said. She tried to get out again, but he took her face in his hands and pressed his mouth to her cheek, licking the skin in front of her ear. She shivered, in spite of her layers and his warm body.

"Do you still hurt?" he asked in her ear.

"If I say yes, is that good?"

"Yes."

She stroked his dark hair before touching his face. He pulled back from her and let her touch him. As he watched her, she dug her nails into his rough, prickling, unshaven jaw. "Of course I still hurt."

He grabbed her hips and pulled her down from the seat, before pushing her against the outside of the truck and kissing her as though he hadn't kissed her in weeks, rather than just hours. She kept her nails pressed into him, digging furrows under his facial hair—she knew that the last thing he wanted was for her to stop. He pressed against her existing bruises, but she still found her hips canting against his, trying to bring him closer even though there were layers of fabric between them that were not easily shed. Grant was shaking as he took a step back—not from fear or romantic notions. The muscles of his forearms were quivering with restraint.

"You'll have your hands full with that one, girl," said someone at the front of the truck. Somehow, twenty people had come to investigate without her hearing a step in the crisp, brown grass. Renee found herself tensing—not necessarily from self-consciousness, but because of the scrutiny. The people around the two of them practically vibrated with energy. Renee was not good around those kinds of people, especially in these numbers.

She broke away from Grant and got back into the car. Grant made as if to snatch her back, probably thinking that she was running. But all she did was kneel on the seat and reach over it for her bag. She took her Xanax out of the side pocket and downed one dry. The overwhelmingly bitter taste made her face twist. There wasn't any water in the car, though, so she just kept swallowing as she turned around again and slid down the seat onto the ground.

Only to find that the werewolves were even closer, enclosing Grant and Renee in a semicircle around the truck. More than twenty, now that she could see them all up close together. Most of them could have been mistaken for members of an ordinary group visiting a national park for a weekend. Maybe a youth group or an environmentalist gathering or even an enthusiastic family reunion—*if* that group or family had been meeting in the early chill but sun-warmth of the fall rather than December like these people. Most of them were wearing short sleeves, some jeans, some shorts. Then there were a few here and there who would have stood out in any ordinary crowd. Some had already removed their clothing—others were in various stages of undress. There was more than one who was heavily scarred.

"I never thought I'd see the day when Grant, of all people, would bring walking meat to us," said the alpha. At least, that was what Renee thought he was— he was positioned slightly in front of the others, given more prominence. Just looking at him, he did not seem particularly special. But then again, neither did Grant. It was what they could be—whatever power they had boiling under the surface—that was so important to the dynamic of the pack. Jake, for instance, was alpha over his pack as well as over the entire sanctuary compound, although he deferred to Renee in everything. Jake was mostly soft-spoken, and although he was a big man, it was not his size that made him a leader. It was a quality that was given to a few—the knowledge of what had to be done and the power to do it. The man before them had that.

"She's not meat," Grant said. He kept himself in front of her, his expression casual but the set of his shoulders tense. He was being defensive, but not deferential. Renee knew from experience that dogs—or wolves—who did not submit to their alphas were either ignored or kicked out. And Renee had the sense that execution was not unheard of among werewolf packs.

Her hand involuntarily reached out to touch Grant's back.

The alpha's nose flared and he moved forward, pushing through Grant's space until he was too close for her to look directly at him. "Smells like meat to me," he said. She could feel his breath ruffling her hair as his nose followed the path of Grant's tongue. "And you. Do you think that marking the girl as yours is enough?"

"She's mine," Grant hissed.

"No," Renee said. "I'm not."

The alpha blinked. He was not surprised at what Renee had said. He was surprised at the tip of the knife she had aimed directly at his navel.

"You know you can't kill me with that, girl," the alpha said softly. He did not seem angry with her. Just a little intrigued.

"This conversation sounds familiar," Renee replied.

Grant leaned against the truck and stroked Renee's hair in something like pride. "It's silver, David."

David jerked back so fast that he almost stumbled. "You brought that into our pack?" he asked incredulously.

"Oh, stop your whining," Grant said. "I've had that thing a hair's breadth from poisoning my balls. And if you think you can get it away from her before she can gut you with it, do you want to take the chance that she'll nick you?"

David gazed with new interest upon her. There was some muttering among the pack members, and Renee saw that most of them weren't aggravated. Some of them were even trying to hide laughter behind their hands.

"If you want to walk freely with us," David said, "you're going to have to put that away." It was as though he were talking to a small child, and Renee bristled. It was the same kind of patronising tone that Josh used, as though her maturity and intelligence were as defective as her social skills.

"Am I off the menu, then?" she asked.

"Honey," David replied, "if you managed to get this one under control with that little thing, you can do whatever you want."

When David relaxed, the atmosphere among the group changed dramatically, although they were still the most highly strung, intense people that Renee had ever met. Most of them broke away from the semicircle to join the others in the distance. A few stragglers stuck around, curious but not too invasive.

"She didn't get me 'under control'," Grant said, as Renee tucked the knife back into her jeans.

"Hell, if she slowed you down, she deserves a medal. Isn't that dangerous?" David asked, referring to where she'd put the knife.

"It hasn't hurt me yet. And I don't mind a little blood," Renee said.

"It's a commodity here," David said. "I don't recommend shedding it on these grounds."

Renee did not respond, but she pulled her coat around her so that the knife was out of sight.

"Then let us get this out of the way now," David said. "The bastard hasn't changed, but you seem to be a decent sort of person. Which means that you'll probably be horrified by things that happen out here. We have other humans with us. Not many, but some.

They won't be walking amongst us, with the exception of you and one other boy. He, like you, is a potential recruit. The rest are food. Do you understand that you are not to free them? We aren't humans. We are not subject to your laws. It is your *privilege* to walk among us rather than being attacked. Any attempt to save them will be treated as an expression of hostility, and you *will* join their status. Your little knife may be good to protect you against one, but I can guarantee that it will not save you from all of us. Do I make myself clear?"

Renee's hands clenched into fists in her pockets. She was not angry—it was a reflex from the mounting panic in her muscles. David was not like Grant at all. He was courteous, controlled, good-natured. What she didn't like was what he was saying while being so courteous, controlled, and good-natured.

David pushed her hair behind her ear and looked at her face in the light. "Such beautiful big eyes. You're frightened. That's good."

She felt the vibrations deep in her body before she realised that Grant was growling, and not in that almost purr that he had when he was aroused.

"Watch out for this one," David whispered to her.

Renee thought that she would just watch out in general. This was all beginning to be worse than a very bad idea.

"You look vaguely familiar," David said, giving Renee her space again. "Have I seen you before?"

"You're not familiar to me," Renee said.

"It's one of those little niggling memory tricks. You probably look like someone I've seen on TV or something."

She wouldn't be able to help him with something like that, so she just let it go.

"You don't say much, do you?"

Renee shook her head.

David smiled. It was odd to see something so genuine on the face of someone with all that energy and intensity. Maybe it was just odd to see it on someone whose energy levels resembled Grant's. "If I didn't know better, I would have immediately pegged you as easy prey. So I have to wonder what it is he's found in you."

"None of your damn business." Renee actually jumped. That richly guttural voice was unlike anything she had ever heard from Grant. She turned to see him with glowing eyes, a toothsome maw, and fur growing over his skin.

"No," David said. "It's not. But if you turn her, it will become my business." He started to walk towards the rest of the pack.

"Doesn't have to."

David paused about twenty feet away. He turned around to face Grant fully. "You can't possibly be thinking about making your own pack."

"You aren't in control of anything that werewolves do when they run outside your pack. You aren't alpha to me," Grant snarled.

David's flesh rippled, and Renee had a glimpse of the werewolf that he was. Like Grant, his human form was not an analogue of his werewolf form. She began to realise part of the reason he was alpha—after all, size did matter in a power struggle, even though it was not everything.

"You don't have what it takes," David said.

"I could have been alpha here," Grant replied.

"Could you beat me in a fight?" David said. "Yes. You're stronger and faster than me. But you wouldn't be able to beat all of us, and that's what kept you from competing. The pack is afraid of you, and that doesn't make a good leader, Grant. Really, honey," he said, turning his attention back to Renee, "if you can handle this one, more power to you."

"You're lucky none of the packs are looking for a new alpha," Grant muttered.

"If you fought, you would lose," David replied. "Don't push your luck here. You're welcome as long as you remember your place."

"And if I do make my own pack?" Grant asked.

"The same natural laws that govern our packs would govern yours. If you can't respect that, you're welcome to throw down the gauntlet. But I repeat—you will lose. Have a nice evening."

"Colossal prick," Grant said after he left. The fur, fangs, and glowing eyes retreated slowly, as though he was reluctant to be rid of them.

"Aside from the killing humans, not so much," Renee said. When the fur flared up again, she continued. "He seems to be an okay guy."

"He's not worthy of his position," Grant snapped. "It wasn't his place to come over here and claim you."

"He doesn't want me, Grant. He was just…smelling me. You know that's normal."

"It wasn't his *place*."

"Hey," Renee said, "it's not your place to claim me either. I don't belong to anybody. Not to you. Not to Britt. Not to him. Just myself."

Grant brought her against him—not hard, just to have her there. He was becoming less angry, and Renee felt her own brand of tension draining out of her now that he wasn't as tight as wire.

"You're doing better. With me. With them. Can you tell?" he asked.

Renee nodded.

"I don't think I've ever been a *good* influence before," he said.

She wouldn't have said that he was a good influence, but he was just bad enough, maybe, to help her. She pulled him down, and he kissed her again, this time with the sure knowledge that no one was watching. And if they were, they were too far away to care. He slid his arms underneath her coat, his left hand pressing against the knife on her waist. She could feel its sharper edge slide threateningly against her hip bone.

"I have to claim you here," he murmured. "If I hadn't, there might have been a feeding frenzy. It's our way, love. You will always be prey. And prey with exceptionally pretty legs, at that. You and your own little pack don't get how it is out here. They're dogs. We're werewolves. And our natural prey is more human than anything else."

"And I'm naturally opposed to it," Renee replied. "I'm not exactly happy when anything else eats humans, you know. It just seems worse when you spend about half your time in human form, to see yourself when you're eating someone."

"As long as you're consistent." He was being facetious, but she didn't much mind because he found her neck, the bruises that he had made the night before, with his tongue and sharp teeth. She hissed as she arched up into him. She was almost surprised at the strength of her reaction, and he exploited it to the best of his ability, bringing the blood to the surface of her skin until it pulsed with her heartbeat. But he did not break the surface, not when the rest of the werewolves could smell fresh blood well enough without him making it more accessible. He finally just stood there, letting her kiss him, breathing in her scent and holding tightly to her arms.

"We have plenty of time for this tonight," Grant finally said. He sounded out of breath. "All I'll do by claiming you this way is to make you far more interesting to the others than you'll want to be. You already smell too good for words like this. If I were to just push down your jeans and wrap your coat around us, I could have you against your own car. And you'd be more than ready. You like it when I bite you. And I promise you'll like it when you finally let me bite you with my real teeth."

"So," asked Renee, in a rare coy moment, "what do you plan to do about this then?" She slipped her hand under his waistband and gripped his cock. "Think about David until it goes away?"

His cock twitched when she said David's name. She raised an eyebrow and looked at Grant inquisitively. Her strokes were long and slow as she considered him.

"I don't care who I dominate, my dear," Grant said. He wasn't stopping her, although he wrapped his hand lightly around her wrist as though he knew he was supposed to.

"I'm not all that surprised," Renee said. And she wasn't.

"Do you know that I'd like to take that junior alpha of yours and turn his world upside down?" he asked softly, the words almost a moan. He finally pulled her hand away from him. "Your pack doesn't know what an alpha is."

"Don't go near Jake," Renee replied, her voice just as soft as his, but for different reasons. She looked straight at him, forcing herself to confront him

"Don't worry, love," Grant said. "If I go after him, it'll be because he went after me first. And if I give him a new perspective in the process..."

"*Don't*—" she began.

"Have I ever done anything in your sanctuary if someone didn't already want it?" He undid the button and zipper of his jeans and began jerking himself off, fist flying over the dark red flesh. His words were shorter, more clipped, as he continued. "I may be a monster, but I'm not that kind of monster."

"Yet," Renee muttered.

"*Yet.*" His forehead fell to hers as he came. She angled her head to suck on his lower lip, drinking in his shallow breath. He rubbed his hand on his shirt, then pulled it over his head. When he threw the garment into the truck, she could see the scratches on his back from her nails.

"I think you'll enjoy tonight," Grant said, closing his jeans. "I know I will. But for now, love, you're just going to have to stay frustrated. It'll make it better."

Renee shrugged. A little arousal could make her squirm, but with so much stimulation around her, it was not on the top of her priority list. It was almost pleasant. Grounding.

"Hmmm," he said, "if you're able to shrug it away, maybe I haven't done enough." He kissed her again, quick and hard. Just the feel of his soft skin under her hands was enough to inspire a little more frustration. "At least you know that when I promise you'll be more than satisfied, you know that I'm not lying."

She knew he wasn't.

* * * *

The event really was like a family reunion. Renee could not figure out what was so special about the night. It was not a full moon or a new moon, or any particular moon day that she could think of. It was almost one of the pagan holidays—Solstice, if Renee remembered correctly—but the people around her did not strike her as Neopagan. There was a barbecue. Someone had taken out a guitar and was strumming to something from the Seventies. They were in various stages of comfortable undress, the werewolves unconcerned about their bodies much as the shapeshifters at the sanctuary were. Renee only noticed it anymore because of all the years she'd spent in school—had it been eight years already since then?

The only things that stuck out in the midst of almost stunning normality were the werewolves in wolf form, who walked through the crowd like huge, hungry dogs. They were somehow more menacing in the dying light than in the darkness. They were like some facsimile of wolves, an alien attempt and failure to mimic something existent. As natural as an animal was supposed to be, the wolves looked too disconnected from their environment, as though the world around them knew that they did not belong.

Then there were the humans. There were only six others besides her. She could tell who the other recruit was by the way the werewolves seemed to stare as he passed by. They would give him wide berth. Renee wondered if it was because he smelt like prey, and they did not want to tempt themselves. Renee could not tell if they were treating her the same way. She stayed too close to Grant, and most of them avoided him as much as, if not more than, they were avoiding her.

The others, though, were handcuffed to a bike rack that had probably been pulled from the parking lot. Most of them were gagged with cloth, and one had a ball gag. There were four men and one woman. The youngest was the woman—she appeared to be in her late twenties. The men were anywhere between their early thirties and late fifties. It was not a demographic that Renee would have expected, neither easy prey nor particularly difficult prey, based on the appearances of the victims.

Renee did not like just standing by and saying nothing, but her survival instinct and her natural proclivity towards keeping her mouth shut kept her from doing anything about them. She counted around one hundred and ten werewolves around her. She could not hope to help the humans who were going to be eaten.

She was startled by her impotence. Usually, when she felt out of control, it was in regard to herself. She was not used to having control removed from her from an external source. It was part of the reason why Grant was such a strange anomaly, giving her control by taking it away. David and the werewolves around her, however, were not giving her freedom with their restrictions, and she did not like how small she felt behind Grant. Like a lost little girl in the big city right before nightfall. Not even the knife against her hip could provide her any comfort. *Maybe I need a silver grenade*, she thought wryly.

There were not many things in her experience that Renee would call odd—too much of her life was odd for her to have an average scale of oddity. Watching people laughing and barbecuing pork while gagged humans struggled against a bike rack in the middle of an open field... That was near the top of her list.

"There is someone you should meet," Grant said. He led her behind a rusty pick-up to where some of the younger men and an older woman were lined up in front of a young woman. She was dealing cards on a small wooden table. She had beautiful, long, dark blonde hair, and her face was pale, almost colourless but for a touch of peach on her lips. Even her eyebrows and eyelashes were much lighter than her hair colour – almost invisible. Her eyes, though, were the most vivid green that Renee had ever seen.

As Renee watched what the woman was doing, she recognised tarot imagery on the cards. Rather than wanting to get closer, a wave of scepticism made her almost reel back. Grant turned around when he noticed that Renee was not still following him.

"Oh, she has her fun," Grant explained quietly. "But when she puts away the trappings, she's the real thing."

"The real what?"

"She was handpicked by David. He turned her two years ago. She's a witch," Grant said.

Renee shook her head in confusion.

"Not the spiritual kind," Grant said. "You said you didn't believe in magic, in spite of all the shapeshifting around you. And me. I think you may just need a different kind of magic to convince you. Kelly will fucking blow your mind, the things she can do."

"Are you saying she does *actual* magic?" Renee asked.

"I float things, turn them into other things, and also make julienne fries. And if you call now, you get this vibrating crystal for only five-ninety-nine." Kelly had spoken up from her place behind the table.

When the people in the line saw Grant heading for them, they scattered, in a casual but intentional way.

Not for the first time, something in Renee's stomach turned. Maybe the fact that she seemed to be the only one who wasn't afraid of him was actually a commentary on her sanity. Or her perception. Then again, Kelly was still sitting on her stool and absentmindedly shuffling the cards. She looked tired.

Grant took Renee's shoulder and led her forward to meet Kelly. Now that she was closer, Renee could see that underneath the voluminous sleeves of her sheer robe—which was all that the woman had on—the entire lengths of her arms were tattooed. When the woman stood, she revealed that her legs were similarly inked. Even her sternum was tattooed with part of a black and white design. Renee could not determine what any of the designs were—it was as though she could only see a part of the art at a time, never its entirety.

The woman let Grant kiss her in greeting, but there was something in the tightness of her features that Renee could not place. Her shoulders were loose, not tense, around Grant, yet her expression was profoundly negative.

Kelly reached out to greet Renee. At first, Renee's arm was heavy and tight against her side, the way it usually was when someone offered to shake. But then she slowly extended her arm and let Kelly clasp her hand. It was somehow easier to squeeze back once her hand was actually surrounded by someone else's skin.

Kelly's strange expression dissolved into something with which Renee was much more familiar—puzzlement.

"You're…human," Kelly said.

"So people tell me," Renee replied.

Kelly smiled a little. "Sorry, I'm sure it's quite obvious to you. But what the hell is a girl like you doing with a man like him?" She looked sidelong at Grant, who seemed unaffected by the continuous questioning of her—and his—judgement.

"So people ask me," Renee said.

"No, wait, I get it," Kelly murmured. Her eyes were piercing. Renee didn't like it, and she found herself aggressively avoiding the woman's gaze. "I get why someone like you might want to be around someone like him. So maybe I'm asking the wrong person."

Kelly looked at Grant—she was around the same height as he was, but it still seemed as though she was looking up at him.

"So what was it, wolf?" Kelly asked levelly. "The quiet air of desperation, that no one could come to her rescue out there in those woods, or that she owns a shapeshifter sanctuary and you simply have an overdeveloped sense of irony?"

"You're the mind reader. You tell me," Grant said. His feet were shoulder-width apart, his arms crossed, but not defensively. He wasn't threatened by Kelly's interrogation. He was not threatened by her at all.

"If you wanted someone weak to control, there were much easier ways to get what you wanted." Kelly narrowed her eyes. Peering into Grant, Renee realised. Into his mind. Grant hadn't been exaggerating. "Nor, it seems, did you actually get it, if that's what you were looking for. That's interesting."

Grant was unable to maintain eye contact, and he looked down at his feet. "No," he said.

Kelly's lips thinned a little. She beckoned to Renee and led her to sit down on the stool. "Your pills aren't going to help you much in this kind of environment. Perhaps it's best if you take this time to brace yourself. The darker it gets, the more they're going to take from you."

"Don't suppose you have a vibrating crystal for that," Renee said.

"I was kidding," Kelly said. "Although I do have some crystals in the truck. They soothe me. I like the colours. No, mostly I just take a drink now and then. But since that doesn't work for you..." When Renee twisted around at the suggestion of common experience, Kelly shook her head. "Nowhere near as bad as you. My difficulty being around other people comes from another problem."

Kelly looked at Grant and said, "Go take a swipe at someone. You want a fight if you can't have a fuck. You've heard all the stories I have to tell, and no one will come at her while I'm here."

"What if you're the one she has to worry about?" Grant asked.

Kelly gathered her hair into a ponytail and pulled it behind her shoulder. "You know better than that," she said quietly.

Grant uncrossed his arms, uncharacteristically serious. "Yeah, I do."

As Grant headed towards the denser part of the crowd, Kelly sat on the small table in front of Renee. Renee was surprised at how she did not feel anxious around this perfect stranger. But Kelly did not seem dangerous or threatening, although she was not without the quality that all the werewolves seemed to share. If anything, though, Kelly struck Renee as a little more human.

Kelly continued as though she hadn't spoken with Grant. It took a moment for Renee to catch up with the conversation. "I hear what people are thinking, and sometimes they're loud, obnoxious, alarming—even violent. There were times when I would go out and think that a man was going to kill his wife or that a woman was going to kill her boss. Just the passing thoughts would be loud enough that I couldn't tell the difference between a brief fantasy and a legitimate plan. Then there were the things that would go flying across the room when I was too nervous — which got worse as the thoughts got louder. Lights would go out over my head. I would awaken from a trance where I had been drawing on walls — drawing things that were going to happen or words of prophecy that I had no memory of writing or even thinking. Then there were the times I'd have strong urges to make things. I'd spend a fortune on things at the grocery because I absolutely had to make some kind of potion right then. None of these were conducive to a normal lifestyle.

"In that way," Kelly added, "you're almost lucky. You don't need a normal lifestyle. Not with your sanctuary. But I was an office assistant at a newspaper. It required a certain amount of normalcy. Which I couldn't have as long as all this was just happening to me with no rhyme, reason, or control. I couldn't even have peace in my own home. I kept blowing out lights, and I didn't trust myself with candles in case they decided to fly about on their own and something caught fire."

"I'm not lucky," Renee said.

"I said 'almost'."

"Why are you telling me?"

"When David found me, I was a mess, but I had begun to control it. Once I stopped trying to get it all to stop, I was able to learn how it felt to move with it, then manoeuvre within it. But only after David turned me was I able to find the strength to control it fully. And I didn't even know that magic existed and that magic was what was happening to me. Once I knew that werewolves were real, I was able to find other people like me. Not here in the packs, but in other places.

"The reason why I'm telling you this is because David found me when I was out of control. And he and Grant are not as different as they would like, at least when it comes to the company they want to keep. When David saw me, he saw an opportunity to change my world. Maybe thinking that it would buy him my undying devotion. It's tempting to give in to that kind of personality, the kind that's overwhelming and charismatic and unyielding. They're like one of those waves on a beach, the one that doesn't look as big as it is, then it hits you until you're drowning and can't reach the surface again because the tide's going out. I got my control, Renee Chambers. But now I play cards with creatures who think I'm a parlour trick and who would eat me in seconds if I didn't smell like them, since I don't eat with them."

"You don't eat humans?" That made Renee a little less nervous about being alone with Kelly.

"You should worry more about being alone with Grant," Kelly said. "I don't hate what I am, but if I could function without being a werewolf...I would. Look, Grant's good for a while. When you spend your life like you do, without any chances, taking a chance can be addictive. And maybe you think that if you keep him around, you'll always get better. But let me let you in on a secret." Kelly bent down and cradled Renee's cheek in her hand. "Grant's not giving you anything you didn't already have. He's not your key. He's simply the catalyst."

Renee jerked her head back. Kelly pulled away as though burned, even though it was her body that was hot. "I'm sorry," Kelly said. "Did I say something?"

"You don't know," Renee said, standing. "It's not the same. You don't know."

"I can see it, Renee," Kelly said, with an earnest expression. "I can see you in my head. The way you go about your life. The way you need someone there. It doesn't have to be him."

"But you *aren't* me," Renee said. "I don't need him, maybe. But I... I don't believe in magic, anyway."

Kelly's chin rose as she took a deep breath. She guided Renee's hand to her hair. "But you want him. For a while. You think you'll be able to let go when that time comes. But that's the difference between desire and addiction. I know that you like sex rough with him. I know about the scratches on your thighs. I know that Grant wants to turn you and that you're considering his offer. I know that you have a malamute, not a Siberian husky, and that the dog turns into a woman who loves you. And I know that you like my hair."

Renee leaned in angrily. "I'm not convinced," she said.

"Then look at where we're not standing," Kelly replied.

Renee looked down and saw that she and Kelly were floating three feet off the ground. She snapped her mouth shut before she could scream, but she did fall backwards when she pulled her hand away from Kelly's hair. Her arm broke the fall.

"Sorry," Kelly said as she floated down to the ground. "I didn't know you'd pull away so quickly or I would have made that fall softer." She pulled her robes back so that she could kneel on the ground with Renee.

"Sometimes I use words, sometimes I don't. Sometimes I use potions and wands and herbs and whatever. Sometimes I don't. I'm not all-powerful, but..." If anything, Kelly looked paler. "There's no way for this to end well. Not with him."

Kelly sounded like Britt. Too much like Britt. Renee knew this part already. Being careful on her arm, she stood up.

"I'm fine," she said. "It'll end when it ends. But right now — *now* — he's helping."

"Being a werewolf doesn't make you normal," Kelly muttered. Her bright green eyes were fixed on Renee's hip, and it was only when Renee knew where Kelly was looking that she realised the fall had forced part of the knife into her hip. It began stinging the moment she knew. Kelly licked her lips and curled a hand around the back of Renee's thigh.

"I'll settle for half-normal," Renee replied, with a slight tremor in her voice. As Kelly drew her open mouth closer to the wound, Renee added, "The knife is silver and might have poisoned the wound for you."

Kelly did not pull away, but she did close her mouth. She closed her eyes tightly, and Renee could actually feel the skin re-stitch itself and the blood completely disappear from around the wound. Kelly's teeth clenched, but then she forced herself to stand, using Renee's leg as leverage. But she did not immediately let go, and ran her fingers up the back of Renee's thigh to her spine.

"Think about what I said." Kelly brushed her lips against Renee's cheek before stepping back. "Maybe you would prefer a half-normal life where the smell of human blood doesn't make you go a little crazy. Honestly," she said, a little louder, "I think you both bit off more than you can chew."

Renee felt Grant wrap his arms around her, his teeth on her ear. There were fresh claw marks on his arms.

"Don't you two stop on my account. It looked like you were getting more than acquainted," Grant said.

"You would think that," Kelly replied. "I suppose you'll take her to a vampire next. Then it'll all sound like a bad joke."

"I don't know any," Grant said. "It's not on my agenda. I think you've effectively proven to her that magic exists."

"Don't bet on it," Kelly said wryly. "I'm a bit unremarkable these days—I don't even give a satisfactory light show out here. Besides, she's already couched everything in pseudoscientific terms in her mind. When the supernatural is natural, it is hard to convince the jaded of the existence of magic, Grant. And what you now want of me can probably be explained as pharmaceutical." The door of her truck squeaked as she climbed in for something in the passenger seat. She came out with four small three-ounce bottles filled with a brownish liquid. "This is what you wanted, yes?"

"You're a goddess," Grant answered, taking two of the bottles.

"Make sure she knows what it is before she drinks it," Kelly warned.

"She won't drink it *unless* I tell her what it is." Grant held the bottles up into the sunset light. The brown became a dark cognac colour with the light shining through it.

Kelly cocked her head.

"Come on," Grant said, still staring at the bottles. "The best things happen when the sun goes down."

"Most people know that," Kelly said. She held up the other two bottles and said to Renee, "I'll put one of these in your truck, but you should take one now."

"What is it?" Renee asked, accepting one of the bottles. She held it up to the light.

"One of my potions. It'll keep you from conceiving for about six months," Kelly said.

Confused, Renee said, "But Grant said he can't..."

"It's not for Grant," Kelly replied, ignoring the way Grant glared at her. "Just a precaution. Just in case."

Renee was not sure whether it was safe or whether she should trust anything Kelly gave to her. However, whatever she thought about magic, she *did* trust that Kelly cared about her welfare, even though Renee did not agree with her conclusions. She did not think Kelly would give her or Grant anything that would hurt her.

She opened the bottle. The contents smelt faintly of cucumber. Kelly nodded encouragingly, and she swallowed it down. It tasted the way it smelt.

Kelly smiled. "You'll thank me later."

"Renee," Grant snapped. His sharpness was not directed at her. "We have to go." He tucked his bottles in his jeans pocket.

Kelly touched Renee's shoulder before Renee left.

"I'll see you again," she said. There was complete conviction in her voice, and her eyes seemed brighter in the shadows than they should be.

* * * *

"How do you know Kelly?" Renee asked.

"Are you asking whether I slept with her?" Grant replied.

"No."

"I did."

"I don't care," Renee said.

"She was David's bitch. She's got power beyond what David could ever hope to have. And she had a spark of interest for me, too. He was furious. Not so much that she was with another wolf, but that she was with me. God, I loved it."

"Is that why you got thrown out of the pack?" Renee asked.

Grant snorted. "Hardly. I got thrown out because I had one too many fights with the alpha, and they knew I was stronger than he was. They always get so nervous when I come back. It's part of the reason I come back at all. And they only let me come back because I don't do it often enough to piss them off too much."

Grant was leading her into the thick of the pack. She pressed herself against his side, trying to get as far away from the rest of the crowd as possible. If she could have crawled into Grant, she would have done it. Her fingers were tightly clenched, one into his side and the other on his arm. He pretended that she was not hurting him, but he flinched now and then if she squeezed a little harder.

The other humans were in the centre of the pack, wide-eyed and naked, while the pack was hungry-eyed and naked. Grant tried to disengage himself from Renee's hands to shuck off his own pants, but she wouldn't let go. It was as though her hands were stuck that way.

"Renee, I'll give you something to calm you down in a minute, but you're going to let go of me now."

"I can't move my hands," Renee said.

"Let me try, then."

He prised her fingers off him, one at a time, and her stomach clenched for every finger that released. They ached when she flexed them.

Grant pulled his pants off and took the vials from the pocket before kicking the denim to the side.

"They won't eat you," Grant said, letting her come close again, pulling her in to press her cheek to his chest. His heartbeat was strong and a little fast. "You know I won't let them."

"They're people. You know," Renee said.

Grant laughed. "You're the only woman I know who would be more concerned about the crowd than the werewolves about to turn."

"Yeah," she muttered. "I'm unique."

Grant found one of her hands and slipped a vial into it. "Drink this. Things are going to get interesting as the moon rises, and I think you'll enjoy being a part of it. With me. Not with them."

"Does everyone start humping or something like that?" Renee asked.

"Or something like that," Grant said.

"You won't be able to scratch me or bite me," Renee murmured.

"At least, nothing that breaks the skin," Grant said. He leant down and whispered in her ear, "But you can scratch and bite me all you want. And I think you'll want to."

Renee looked up at him, pushing her hair behind her ears. "In front of them?"

"You won't care," Grant said. "And they'll be distracted by their own activities. We can leave when they start to run, run our own path. The potion will have worn off by then."

"I can't run with you."

"Then ride me," Grant said. His cock was beginning to rise, in spite of the cold in which Renee could see her breath.

"The potion's an aphrodisiac," Renee said. It was not a question.

"Naturally." Grant's smile was sharp, and he opened his own vial. "We don't need it, but it's fun. It's out of control. It's better than drugs."

"Does it make *me* hump anything that moves?" Renee asked.

"Only if you want to," Grant answered. And he downed his vial.

It smelt like maple syrup, and when he licked his lips, she was compelled to try it there. At first, he just let her lick—it tasted like maple syrup, too, although the taste was so faint that it could have been nothing. But then a shudder went through his body, and he shoved her coat off her shoulders, pulling it down until it fell around her feet. His tongue plundered her mouth and stole her breath. The low growl was back, rumbling through his chest and into her until she was gasping.

"God, woman, drink that potion now if you're going to do it." His eyes were glowing a dark red, and the pupils were dilated almost to the edge of the expanded irises. Fur crawled over his skin, but he was not changing—his teeth and nails were still human. It was as though he was trying to let something of his other nature manifest if he couldn't release the sharper parts, for her own safety.

Her tongue tingled from where she had tasted the potion on Grant, and she could feel herself growing warm even as the night got quickly colder. She opened the top of the vial and swallowed the entire contents down, barely aware of the urgency of Grant's fingers on the fastenings of her jeans or of the way that the wolves were transforming around them. As she dropped the vial, Grant whipped her around so that she could see the melee in front of her. The first scream of the night pierced through the wind rustling leaves and grass. But instead of horrifying her, the sound made her bones themselves sing. Every nerve thrummed with each minute stimulation.

"Oh...my...God..." She moaned low in her throat. Even that felt too good for words. Her panties were wet when Grant pushed her pants down and palmed her, rocking the heel of his hand against her clit. His breath was fast and hot in her hair. He found her nipple with his free hand. He had rid her of her shirt at one point, although she was damned if she could remember when. Her brain wasn't working—all there was was the world, and the way it gave her pleasure.

She watched the wolves begin to transform, fur sprouting and bones cracking, fur against fur against fur as they ran against each other, drawing solidarity from the friction, circling the humans with great grinning mouths.

She quickly looked away just as Grant shoved another finger into her, spreading her juices and stretching her open. He tore her panties off and pushed her down onto her coat. He used his tongue on every part of her that it could—the hollow of her armpit, the shadows under her breasts, her navel, until he was devouring her between her legs and she was screaming and coming, so fast and hard and strong.

As other screams cut off, Grant rose on all fours and howled. His fur was rough on her over-sensitised skin as she pulled him back down. His limbs lengthened for a second, but then he was in that still mostly human state again.

"You could have this every night," Grant groaned. "Every night, like this."

"Stop talking and fuck me," Renee snapped. She pulled too hard on his hair and pushed him onto his back. Her knees pressed into the grass as she thrust her tongue into his mouth, drinking in his new moans. She needed every inch of her skin on him, and she rubbed her cunt against his stomach, against his rock-hard cock, coating it with the moisture from her first orgasm and the new one building in every flutter of her inner muscles. "For God's sake, fuck me."

She reached down between them and took his cock in her hand to position him right where she needed him to be. Then she pushed down as hard as she could. He howled again, his teeth growing sharp and claws sliding from his nail beds. His lips were too wide, a perpetual grin, and he pulled her down with arms that were too long. He did not kiss her, though — somewhere in his muddled mind, he must still have known that if he were to kiss her, he would bite her, and he could not do that. Not only to keep from changing her, but also to keep the others around them, the whirlwind of fur brushing maddeningly against Renee's feet, from seeing her as available prey more than they already did.

Instead, she bit into the flesh of his thinly furred shoulder, almost whining from each thrust he gave even as she pulled herself down, rolling her hips so that she could get some sensation on her clit. The fur on her feet, the fur rubbing against her stiff nipples, the flesh under her mouth and the slightly salty taste of droplets of his blood...all of it was too much. Her nails scrabbled for purchase down his stomach as she came again. She felt her muscles clench so hard that it was as though she were squeezing Grant in a vice. His glowing eyes rolled back in his head, and he came into her, body thrashing underneath hers until she fell off him. His limbs twisted and cracked, muscles groaning as he became the wolf, larger than life and teeth flashing to catch the muzzle of a passing male getting too close to Renee's vulnerable and still too aroused body.

She cried out as Grant crashed into the other male, rolling around with him on the rough brown grass in twist of fur, flesh, and teeth. Her hands travelled over her body as she watched. She couldn't help herself. She needed to feel, she needed hands on her. She forgot how much she did not like touching herself when she was so filthy. Her fingers worked furiously on the sensitive place above her clit as she rubbed her neck, her breasts, her arm, her stomach, her thighs—anywhere she could reach to watch and stimulate herself at the same time. Just watching Grant fight with the other male—undoubtedly David, if the ferocity and longevity of the fight was any indication—made her bare body warm enough in the winter night. By all rights, she should have been hypothermic, but every inch of her was hot. Was this how Grant was all the time?

A wet nose on her shoulder startled her, and she cried out, twisting around to see a wolf with green eyes and fur so light that it was almost white. The shape shifted almost gracefully into Kelly, and she crouched over Renee.

"Just until they get it out of their system," Kelly said. But in spite of the fact that Kelly must have seen what Renee and Grant had been doing, she still seemed surprised when Renee rolled around and kissed her, plunging her free hand into Kelly's hair. Kelly tried to say something, a muffled protest against Renee's mouth, but eventually she just sat there and let Renee get it out of her system.

Finally, Renee yanked herself back, gasping through another orgasm that was powerful but short. And it still did not seem to be enough. "Please," she begged hoarsely.

"I would," Kelly said, backing away from Renee's reach but staying by her side enough to make sure that no one was going to attack her. "But you would regret it in the morning. And I don't swing that way. Sorry."

The shriek came from Renee's throat before she could stop it. Not at Kelly, but just in mounting frustration after the brief satisfaction.

"Not long now," Kelly reassured her. "And your wolf is coming back."

His side was bloody, but he was transforming even as he walked towards Renee.

"He's alive," Grant rasped through a ravaged throat. It was already clotting, and he took the crouching position over Renee to relieve Kelly of her vigil.

Kelly's eyes flashed bright green, but not from the wolf, Renee realised. The glow came from human eyes. "I should hope so." She stood and began to run. Her body transformed mid-stride.

Grant's kiss was more languid against hers, although she was still urgent. She clawed at his wound and he growled, nipping sharply at her lip. Renee did not care whether he broke the flesh or not as she tried to pull him over her and into her at the same time. This time, it was her who was thrashing, just wanting it to be over, just wanting the pleasure to finally peak into satiation.

Grant threaded his fingers into her hair, holding her head in place as he pressed his mouth to hers and consumed each moan, swallowed each scream. One of his legs spread hers, and he slid into her, drawing out her desire. She willed him to go faster, but he kept a slow and maddening pace, forcing her to stay still beneath him. Tears streamed down her face as he changed his angle and found that spot again, the one that rocked her body and made her legs cling tightly around his hips until she was sure that his hip bones were leaving bruises on her inner thighs. It seemed like forever before he began to increase his pace, rubbing against that spot until she finally came again. Light exploded on her eyelids. Her scream must have made it sound as if Grant was attacking her. And this time the coil began to unwind and her body relaxed. The crest had been reached. She was finally satisfied. She could let Grant take her through the oversensitivity because the satisfaction was just that good, all on its own.

When he slumped over her, crushing her into the grass, he licked her ear and whispered, "Ready to run?"

If she was honest with herself, she wanted to sleep. She was not usually tired after sex, but after sex like *that*... But she could run with him. The cold would keep her awake.

Renee let Grant pull her up, and it was only when he let her go that she felt just how cold it was. She did not much care that she was naked—if any of this had happened a few weeks ago, maybe she might have felt differently. But she pulled on her clothing quickly— the clothing that was still intact, anyway—just to get herself warm. Grant did not bother. He did not need to. His legs and arms were beginning to lengthen again, as though he really wanted to change, the way a person might stretch before exercising.

"Look," he said. "Behind you." There was that vulpine glow in his eyes again. His arms were furred when he embraced her clothed body. His jaw jutted out for a moment before returning to normal. "Look at them."

Grant was looking at the other human recruit, his skin almost white among the dark forms around him. Three werewolves circled him like prey, but the man was not running away, nor did he look afraid. He did flinch once, when one of the werewolves darted out of the circle and bit him on his arm, just below his shoulder. It looked as if one or two of the teeth had pierced his chest, as well. The man stumbled, doubling over and clutching himself. Dark blood seeped through his fingers and dripped to the ground, but when the man looked up, the strained expression on his face was not pain. The man was smiling, his mouth wide and teeth shining. Sharpening. He burst with fur, and even from where Renee was standing she could hear the cracking and straining of flesh and bone. Grant's arms were protective, and his own teeth were sharp, as though he was prepared to challenge the new werewolf if he lost control and went after Renee, simply because she smelt like prey.

The group of werewolves paid her no notice, though—they took the new one into the woods, and were gone in a matter of seconds.

"That could be you," Grant rasped, the shift in his mouth and vocal cords not meant for speech. "It would be so easy." He lapped at one of the healing wounds on her neck from the previous evening, the teeth dangerously close. She could feel them, dry on her skin.

"No. No, not..." Renee stopped before the 'yet' could leave her lips, but she knew Grant heard it anyway. That low growl travelled from the base of her spine to the place where he held her unbroken skin between his teeth. She arched her back slightly, surprised into a flash of arousal even after the aphrodisiac had basically milked her for as much as she thought was possible. *Maybe there's even more*, said a little voice in her head, and she was as intrigued as she was a little horrified.

He released her, inch by inch, as his body began to groan. "It'll take work to stay on," Grant said. "Have you ever ridden a horse bareback?"

Renee shook her head. They had only ever had cows.

"You'll have to use all your muscles. It'll be tiring, but once I get into a stride, you'll get used to it. You'll love it." He finally fell forward and could no longer speak to her. He was huge—he always looked so big when he was right there in front of her, looking down just a little from his great height. He lowered himself to the ground to allow her to figure out how to climb on.

Renee had ridden a horse once before, but it had worn a saddle. Grant was as tall as a horse, but his frame was a little slimmer. She found a place just below his ribs to clench her knees. Grant was telling the truth when he said it would take work to stay on him, and her jeans were rough against her crotch without panties underneath. She shifted her coat so that it could pad her against his spine. She gently leant forward, laying herself against his back and wrapping her arms around his neck, away from his face. The muscles of his front legs shifted beneath her as he stood, an unusual and unfamiliar feeling. Almost as soon as he began walking forward, she felt as if she were beginning to lose her balance. Her legs clenched harder, and she dug her fingers into his thick fur.

She was still struggling to stay on when Grant started really moving towards the dense trees. His thick, defined muscles moved seamlessly under his fur in a decidedly odd feeling on her legs and arms. She was surprised that as he started running faster, it actually got a little easier to hold onto him, as long as he kept himself level. When he ran down into a valley and jumped over a tree root to lower ground, she had to hold on more tightly. While she could not relax and had to be extra vigilant as to where he was going, she did not always have to hold him hard enough to crush a lesser creature.

I'm going to hurt more tomorrow than I did today, she thought. After the rigorous activity of the present and previous evening, her muscles were still sore, and they were only going to stiffen even more after all this work to stay upright. It was insane, and it felt strangely satisfying—every ache, every inch she pushed herself. Grant's pace created a breeze from the still night, and his huge paws hit the ground like thunder. Riding him like this, when he was a lone wolf running, it felt as though he was some kind of creature beyond the world. Some kind of god or a demon—more than anything that reality was supposed to render.

Her nose and ears were freezing, and the run seemed to deafen and dull her hearing, but she was warm from holding onto Grant. The trees rushed past her, and sometimes the littlest branches or pine cones brushed against her cheek. One or two of them might have scratched her. But it happened too fast for her to notice, and the cold was already stinging on her face.

She kept herself close against Grant. His fur and the toughness of his skin shielded her from most of the wood's reaching arms.

In so many places, the forest was almost pitch dark. Renee knew that Grant could see or at least knew how to find his way, but she herself could not see much farther than the coarse fur under her nose. She could barely see that her own hair, loose around her neck under the coat, was red.

Then the dense trees would open into clearings for a momentary break, and the moon would be almost too bright. It was hard to believe that its light was so weak when it hurt her eyes during the times it broke through the darkness.

She was almost lost in the rhythm—the sounds of Grant's breathing, the pounding of his feet, the rustle of the foliage and the rasp of needles as Grant disturbed the forest. Then a snarl ripped itself from his throat. Her heart was racing, but it felt like her blood had stopped moving through her veins. She locked all of her limbs around him, which was good because he lunged forward even faster than he had been running, diving on top of a deer and bringing it down to the forest floor. His teeth closed around the throat, crushing the windpipe and piercing the main artery until it spurted up. Renee reacted instinctively, her locked muscles releasing so that she could leap off him and onto the ground, rolling until she hit the base of a tree with her lower back. The impact was like being kicked.

But she was out of the way, and as she watched Grant ravage the animal until the bleeding slowed, she shivered there under the tree, wrapping her arms around herself and pressing back into the trunk.

When Grant had finished with the animal's neck, leaving the head almost completely severed from the rest of it, he started in on the belly, ripping into the intestines and yanking them out. Renee could not even tell whether he was eating anything or just destroying it.

She was not afraid that Grant was going to turn on her and attack her. She was not morally opposed to him attacking the deer. But it was one thing to know something, to understand it, and another to see it just a few feet away from her, new sounds in her ears — moist tearing and dripping blood, the sounds of Grant's growls as he tore at the flesh.

Finally, Grant seemed to settle down, chewing on a part of the deer he'd pulled from inside its body. He lowered himself until his belly was on the ground, haunches bent and eyes half-lidded. He had never looked more like an actual wolf to Renee as he did then. She could smell the blood now. She was no stranger to it — Jake sometimes slaughtered something outside the kitchen or drained blood into the stainless steel kitchen sink. Death was simply a part of life, especially for carnivores, and Renee could accept that. But it made her stomach turn every time, no matter what she thought. There were just some things that she couldn't help. The shivers that racked her body now that she wasn't holding Grant was one of them. The fear that made her skin tingle was another. The nausea was simply another symptom of being human. And from where she was sitting right now, she did not know whether that was something she was willing to lose.

Grant coughed, stepping away from the carcass and changing into human form as he came towards her. She shuddered as his breath flowed over her face, his tongue licking her cheek where blood had struck her. He tried to kiss her, but she shoved him away.

"Don't take it personally," she said, "but I can't kiss you like that."

Grant spread his arms. His entire top half was smeared with the deer's blood. "It's part of the package, love."

"A part that I don't have to like," Renee replied.

He crawled to her again. "A part that you'll enjoy as a werewolf."

"But I'm not."

"No, not..." The repetition of her unspoken *yet* lingered in the air between them.

"Every existence has its drawbacks," Grant whispered. "The skin I'm in, the skin you're in. The price for strength, power, freedom... It's a small one. I don't even call it a price."

"Kelly does," Renee said.

"Kelly is an exception to the rule, then."

The strong smell of the animal's insides filled her nostrils once again, and she winced.

"When the thing you once found disgusting tastes very nearly like the thing you've been craving all your life, it does not seem like too high a price."

"I don't care that you killed it," Renee said. She gestured to the pile of meat. "I know better than that. Maybe I care that you kill them. Us."

"Humans are our natural prey," Grant explained. "Everything in a werewolf's instinct tells us that humans smell good and are meant for our teeth."

"Then why haven't you eaten me?" Renee said.

She could tell that he was biting back a lascivious reply in order to answer her question honestly. "Because we have another instinct—to propagate. This instinct is sometimes closely linked with the impulse to mate, even if procreation isn't possible that way between us. Procreation requires sparing some humans. You should feel fortunate that I'm affording you any time and choice in the matter."

Renee pulled her coat more tightly around her. "Really? And if my answer is no?"

"Why would it be?"

"If it is?"

"We'll just have to see, won't we?" Grant said.

"No," Renee said. "If I say no, does that make me prey to you?"

Grant tangled his fingers in her hair, caressing the patch of skin under her ear with his mouth. "I don't know," he murmured.

If Grant told her that he didn't know, Renee had to accept that he didn't know. There was no reason for him to lie when he felt no compunction to lie to her about other unsavoury aspects of his character and lifestyle. The only trouble about Grant telling the truth was that it did not always reveal everything. Renee knew that a distinct possibility was that she could become prey—he could kill her if she said no. But he could also disregard her decision. Or he could force the decision in some other way. She would have a little bit of protection if she said no in the company of her shapeshifters, but she did not want any of them to be taken down protecting her just because she was mostly unable to protect herself. Even her knife would not be a sure defence if or when it came down to the wire, she thought.

She was almost sure that if she gave Grant the wrong answer, he would find a way to make her give the right answer. Or get rid of her. She thought that he would feel disappointment, maybe sorry that he had to do it. But he would get over it.

Grant could get over killing her.

Chapter Eleven

Renee had slept outside before, usually in a tent and a sleeping bag. But with the cushion of her coat and half-curled on Grant's body, the ground was surprisingly comfortable. Or if it wasn't, she was unable to differentiate between the aches from lying on the ground and the ones from the sex and the ride the night before.

At first, she did not know what had awakened her. She didn't ache unless she moved. She wasn't cold as long as she held onto Grant, who was more than warm enough for the both of them. Then she felt something hot on her belly, wet and sharp through her clothing but not quite piercing her skin. A threat, a hint of something that could be.

Renee's eyes flew open. The morning was a deep golden yellow, and there was something surreal about seeing a werewolf in the morning light. She guessed that the wolf, who was a little bigger than Grant's wolf form, was David. She thought that no other werewolf would dare, and there was a quiet, cruel intelligence in those bright eyes, which were almost sardonic as they stared at her.

Renee shrugged Grant's arm from her shoulder and tried not to move her stomach as she reached for her knife. But David had her at an angle where she could not reach it without possibly puncturing herself on his teeth. Which would make her decision for her.

"Let her go." It wasn't Grant. The voice was too high, and Grant would never have spoken so gently to David.

A pale hand touched Renee's head, then David's neck. Renee looked above her to see Kelly staring intently at David.

"Let her go. Don't blame her for what you hate about Grant."

By now, Grant was beginning to stir.

"David," Kelly said sharply. "Release her now."

His jaws snapped open as though something had yanked them apart, and the werewolf whimpered in pain as he jerked back. His expression was no longer sardonic. Instead, he looked hurt by what Kelly had done.

"You know it's not her you want to hurt, no matter how good she smells to you," Kelly continued. She stood up and held out her arms to David. "Come to *me*. Forget him."

Kelly gave one last glance behind her, a silent apology and farewell on her lips. Renee nodded. When she settled back into Grant's arms, she saw that he was awake.

"Do I need to kill him?" Grant murmured.

"No." Kelly had David well under control. Renee pressed her cheek to Grant's chest and wished she had that same reassurance with him.

* * * *

She drove them back to the sanctuary a few days later. Once she reached the highway, it was easier for her to find her way back to Antoine than she thought, and Grant was actually sleeping. She kept the radio on the old rock station anyway. She kind of liked it.

For a man who had pretty much been running high for the last few days, she wasn't surprised at just how hard Grant could sleep when he put his mind to it. Even when the sun was in his eyes, he did not budge from his position with the side of his head against the door window. She wished she could say that he looked cute when he was sleeping, or that he looked older or younger. But he simply looked shut down. And she thought that it was healthy for him to shut down now and then. He might actually be healthier if he did it more often. She did not know how werewolves could maintain that kind of intensity without burning out at one point or another.

She felt relief when they passed through Antoine and headed to the woods on the way to her sanctuary. This was familiar territory—and even though the driving had not been as hard as she'd thought, she felt her muscles relax. The closer she got to her sanctuary, the less small she felt. Everywhere she had gone over the last few days, she had needed Grant right there with her, or Grant to push her beyond almost every boundary, dominating her world. But in her sanctuary, she knew what she was and where she was going. She did not need someone by her side, twenty-four seven. Perhaps it was sad that the only place she felt good—after seeing places and people she would have never dreamed of seeing and doing things she had never dreamed she would do—was home. Or maybe she felt good there because it *was* home, and home was simply the place you always came back to in order to feel that.

Grant woke up as they were headed up the long and bumpy driveway.

"Let me out here," he said, his voice rough from sleep.

Renee looked at him quizzically.

"You're going to have something of a welcome home party, I'm sure, and they won't want me to have any part of it. I'll find my own way back once the streamers clear."

"You sure?"

"They'll have my hide if I have you for one more second than I've already had you this week," Grant said. "Just slow down and I'll jump out."

She stopped for him anyway. When she put the car in park, Grant reached over and took her face in his hands, kissing her slowly but thoroughly. He was not doing it for anyone's amusement or notice. Just hers. Just so that she knew what he could make her feel, just so that she knew that some part of her was his. And that no matter how much her own pack wanted her, they could not have all of her. She did not like how he had to have the last word, even if his tongue made her tingle in remembrance of everything that they had done.

Then he pushed open the door to the truck. He kicked the door shut with his back leg and ran into the woods, still in human form.

Renee wiped her mouth thoughtfully and continued up the driveway. Some of her shapeshifters would know that she was back, but she was not expecting the fanfare that Grant expected. The memory of Britt on the porch and all the other shapeshifters nowhere to be seen as she'd left with Grant was etched in her memory. A very low part of her would not have been surprised to discover that they had all gone, vanished, moved on, gone back home...anything to abandon her if she was going to betray them like that.

The rational part of her knew that while it was not impossible, it was unlikely. Many of the shapeshifters did not have very many other places to go. Britt did not even have another home, as far as Renee knew. For many of the shapeshifters, the sanctuary was their last hope.

Another low part of her hoped that she wouldn't be run off her own land. That was slightly more likely than the former scenario.

As she drove up to the log home, she avoided the free dogs, who were all ecstatic to have her back—it was the longest she had ever been away from her home, as far as Renee could remember. The less controlled ones leapt onto her, and she had to work extra hard to remind them how to behave around her.

When she looked up, she saw Malcolm crossing from the dog barn to the log home. He raised a hand to her, and Renee felt a wave of relief that made her lightheaded. Even if the others were mad at her, at least one of her own was okay with her.

Malcolm whistled between his fingers, and most of the dogs reluctantly ran to him. She must have caught him right before a run.

She pulled her bag from the back of the truck, then headed up to her house.

The living room was empty when she opened the front door, but she thought she could hear someone in the kitchen. Adjusting the bag on her shoulder, she headed up the staircase to the loft.

She tossed her suitcase on the bed, and a creak of the floorboards was the only indication that there was someone else there before their hands were on her. One on her mouth, and the others dragging her to the bathroom.

They did not even bother turning on the light, which meant that everything was almost pitch black because there were no windows in the loft or the bathroom.

"You smell like him," Britt's voice murmured. All on its own in the darkness, even the murmur seemed loud. "You stink of him. You have no idea."

The larger hand over her mouth had to move in order to help Britt remove Renee's clothing.

"What—?" she began.

"Look, I'm not going to argue with you," Britt said. Her voice was clipped, but not hard. "Jake and I are going to get you clean so that we can stand to be around you. And then we are going to make you forget that ass for the rest of the night. I swear that we'd smell it if he even crossed your mind."

Renee was completely naked now, the first time she had ever been naked with Jake, who was obviously also naked behind her. It made her skin break out into goose bumps—whether that was good or bad was anyone's guess. It was certainly different, unexpected, and she was not used to things being unexpected. Except Grant, from whom the unexpected was expected. But her shapeshifters were not that way. At least, they never had been before.

Britt turned on the water and waited for it to get warm as she continued, "After we get out of this shower, you have a choice. You can give in to whatever we come up with to make up for the torture that you've put me through these last few days. Or you can walk away, and I'll move into another room. We'll leave whatever we were creating before behind.

"This isn't an ultimatum," Britt added. "Until now, all I've ever wanted was to be what you needed. That's what I've devoted myself to for the last eighteen years. And now I'm feeling a little selfish. I need to know whether you're committed to this or whether I'm just your afterthought. This time, *I'm* the one who needs reassurance. You need to make that decision, babe. I can only do so much. Especially when you smell like this."

She tested the water, made a little adjustment to the temperature, then led Renee in. Britt positioned herself in front of Renee, and Jake stepped in behind her. It was a tight fit, but Britt and Jake seemed to know what they were doing. They found the shampoo and the soap and loofah. Jake threaded his large fingers through her hair, rubbing them against her scalp as the lather ran down her back between them, making his body slippery against hers. The sponge was rough against her skin as Britt soaped her up. Renee held onto Britt's shoulders when the taller woman bent down to clean her legs, her stomach, working her way up and being painstakingly thorough, as if she refused to miss a single spot. Everywhere she smelt Grant, Britt scrubbed him away. The sponge scraped between her legs, but Renee was too turned on for it to matter. She was only glad that neither of them could see where Grant had left marks, although she supposed they would notice eventually.

Britt passed the sponge over her breasts, where it caught and tugged on her nipples, and she couldn't help but cry out with both pain and the way it made her clit begin to pulse. She hadn't known she could be aroused by the anger of her friends—of all the things to get her squirming. Her cry was what made Jake's cock begin to twitch against her. Renee wondered what had taken it so long.

Britt's mouth was near hers. Renee could feel her breath, cold on her wet cheeks. But Britt did not kiss her, just ran the sponge over Renee's arms, palms, between her fingers, then turned her around so that she could do Renee's back. Jake seemed so much taller as Renee rested her cheek against his chest. In the darkness, it was so much easier to get close to him, when he wasn't protesting or treating her like porcelain. She knew he loved her very much—first it had been like a brother to a sister or like a dog to its master, and now it was like a friend who could not help but be more than a friend. His body was unfamiliar to her, but she held it close anyway. He was not as hot as Grant, but his skin was warm, his heart beating beneath her ear. His hands were firm as he pressed them against her shoulders, digging his fingers gently into the muscle. His hardening erection made Renee a little anxious, but only because it was new. It was all new.

Except for Britt, who dropped the sponge and slid slick hands up the front of Renee's thighs, slipping between Renee and Jake until Britt was stroking both of them, her breasts pressed up against Renee's back. But she still would not kiss Renee as the showerhead rained down on them, slowly washing the soap and scent from their bodies and down the drain. They stayed in there like that until the hot water began to cool down.

Britt shut off the water, and Jake reached for one of the towels. They did not dry off completely, just enough that they would not drip too much as Britt and Jake led Renee into the bedroom. Water from her hair trickled down her back, like cold fingers. She shivered.

Renee was on her back on Britt's bed before she knew it. Her heart leapt to her throat, though, when Jake pulled her arm to the side, where he tied her to one bed post with a piece of nylon cord. It was rough, but not chafing. Britt did the same to her right arm. Britt trailed her nails down Renee's leg, and Renee thought the two of them were going to bind her ankles as well—she might have really protested if they had tried that, because she needed to move, needed to have *some* kind of out. To have her legs spread, her entire body at the mercy of anyone, even her friends...

She was already at a disadvantage. Several disadvantages, in fact. She did not need to have everything taken away from her.

She could see a little bit more now. The light from the living room made it through the loft curtains, and Jake and Britt were moving figures of dove-grey skin. Jake watched from the foot of the bed as Britt stroked Renee's legs with her fingertips. Renee felt her weight shift as he sat down, his hand encircling her ankle. But his presence was soon less of a concern for her as Britt bent down to take Renee's big toe into her mouth, sucking lightly and swirling her tongue around the tip. Renee's light arousal spiked into something a little more fervid. Her breath caught, and Britt moved on to the next toe, running her teeth over the oddly sensitive nerves, then moving to lave the in-step, rubbing the arch with her knuckles. Renee's clit throbbed and tingled with every stroke.

Following Britt's initiative, Jake bent down to do the same. Renee bit her lip as she received similar but somehow completely different stimulation from both

Britt and Jake. And they were only at her ankles now, their tongues tracing her veins until their hands found her calves. Britt nipped lightly, pulling at the skin and sucking with the most obscene noises before withdrawing into an almost chaste kiss. She more than made up for Renee's silence with deliberate slurping and sucking sounds, deliberate moans, deliberate movements to make the mattress creak. She was a writhing and undulating ivory ghost, and just watching her was enough to make Renee want to squirm. Jake used his lips to feel the outline of her kneecap, tickling the crease behind her knee with his tongue, making her leg jerk involuntarily, but he still held her ankle firmly.

Now they were at her thighs, taking their sweet time, as though every inch of her skin were covered with a thin layer of fine, dark chocolate. When their mouths found the scratches on the insides and backs of her thighs, Renee hissed. They didn't sting anymore, although the healing skin itched a little. It was more that she did not want them to see what Grant had done, what she had been perfectly happy to let him do. She did not want them to get the wrong idea...or to look at her as though she had somehow disappointed them. But she couldn't cover herself up, although she reflexively pulled her wrists against the rope.

Britt and Jake traced their tongues over the rough lines where Grant's claws and nails had torn the flesh. There was a pause. Jake pulled away, and his breath was cold where he had licked her. The tip of Britt's tongue stayed against her, sliding over each slightly raised hill of healing flesh. She seemed to be counting. Renee tried not to count with her—she wondered if the wounds tasted salty or bitter.

"He didn't...?" Jake began.

"He did," Britt answered him before Renee could. "But she didn't mind, did she." It was not a question, but perhaps the tone in Britt's voice was not as bitter as it could have been. "No, my dear, we already know she likes things rough. But let's leave him out of it. I don't want to even smell his name."

She bit the top of Renee's inner thigh hard, and Renee cried out at the sting. But it was close to where she was aroused, and she was not surprised that the warmth after the pain only made things better. Air swirled against her wetness as Britt breathed in.

"See," Britt murmured. "She likes it. She'd beg for it if that was what I wanted to give her. Or what she wanted me to give her. But for now..."

Jake's mouth was on Renee's leg again, though he seemed a little hesitant. Renee thought that Britt had guided him down again.

But although she could feel their breath against her, they paused when they reached her folds, the open lips of her cunt. Britt only licked at the crease at the top of her leg before she took Jake's mouth and kissed him. Their chins rubbed against the top of Renee's mound. Britt was still making those noises, and Renee could almost see the details of their faces after growing used to the darkness.

Slowly, Britt laid their heads against Renee's stomach. Their wet hair tickled and tangled against her as they kept kissing each other. Only their hands remained on her, stroking the length of her legs as though stroking each other's bodies. And sometimes, they did touch each other, breaking away from her altogether, but always coming back to her. Renee could feel Jake's erection hard and high on the side of her leg, rubbing lightly. She pulled against the restraints, but not too hard. All she could do was wait until Britt was ready. All she could do was lie there with her cunt clenching in the cold air, waiting for something that Britt was not going to give her yet.

Renee felt Jake's leaking pre-cum on her leg before he and Britt broke apart. Their tongues dipped into her navel in a swirl of hot, wet velvet flesh. It was so sudden that Renee gasped, her hips canting up into nothing. Jake groaned, biting lightly at the thin skin and tugging. It was as though his groan went straight to the bottom of her spine, spreading in warm pleasure between her legs.

They continued to move their tongues up her body, along the lines of her ribs until they reached the undersides of her breasts. Britt began to circle the skin around the areola. She slid her hand up Renee's leg and her stomach until it cupped the underside of her breast, lifting it so that the hardening nipple pointed to the ceiling. Renee whimpered as Britt bypassed her softly aching nipple entirely, but Jake had no intention of ignoring her. He took the tip into his mouth, sucking it hard before loosening his lips to taste the entire nipple. Renee's head fell back against the pillow. She did not care if he could feel the scabs there on the edge of the areola, or whether Britt did not approve. The cold air between her legs only accentuated how much she wanted something — anything — there to satisfy the urge that she would have thought had been quenched over the last week.

Britt moved on, licking up Renee's sternum to dip into the hollow of her throat before following the line of her collarbone, teeth testing the length of the bone. Jake released her breast reluctantly and took Britt's lead up Renee's bound arms, licking underneath in the oddly sensitive and arousing place, to her elbow, to her wrist where her pulse thrummed. She could feel it there, feel her heart in her hands as they tasted her palms, then took her fingers in their mouths the way they had her toes.

Renee watched Jake watching her as he slid his mouth up and down her forefinger. She thought of how Grant had said something about wanting to put Jake in his place, show his dominance. Renee had a vivid image of Jake fellating Grant—he would never do it, but the image was explosive. A minor tremor rocked her body with arousal. Her fingers clenched in reflex.

"You smell like us now," Britt whispered in her ear, pulling Jake down from Renee's hand to lie next to Renee on the bed. "I couldn't stand the smell of him all over you. It's like walking into the barn on a hot day. And you'd been with him for a week, rubbing that body all over him, letting him mark you and do all sorts of nasty things to you. I almost worried that the smell had reached all the way to the bone. And I was even more worried that you were lost to me. I was worried that you wouldn't come back, that you would have let him change you and you'd leave us behind. That you'd leave *me* behind.

"But you came back." The words hummed through the skin of Renee's throat. Britt's mouth found bruises where Grant had bitten, and she knew where Renee was still tender when Renee winced. "You came back."

Britt guided Jake to Renee's lips, and although Renee had kissed him before, it somehow seemed new again. Unlike Britt, who knew what Renee could and could not take, and unlike Grant, who didn't care, Jake was still hesitant, soft. The slight stubble on his chin brushed against her lower lip as he took a shallow breath before bending down again. His chest was broad and his body stretched even beyond her feet. He seemed indeterminably large to her—he could cover her like a great, warm, smooth blanket. As he tentatively touched his tongue to hers, she wondered what his cock would feel like inside her.

Lying between the two of them, here and now with their combined scent all over her, the darkness making everything seem unreal, all the time since she'd last seen them...she felt free. Her body was completely separate from her mind, although her body still gave her pleasure. And, free from her body, her mind was free from all anxiety. This was so much different than the way that Grant had taken away her fear. Here, she was simply separate.

Jake pulled away, breathing heavily, and Britt took over without the hesitation Jake had shown. She consumed Renee's mouth until Britt was the only thing that Renee could taste, smell, see, think of. The weight of her breasts against Renee's was beautiful, as was the slow rub of her nipples on Renee's skin as she moved. Renee had not forgotten how much she'd missed sex with Britt, but it had grown fuzzy in her memory. In real skin, real time, it was still amazing. More than ever, Renee wanted the use of her hands, and she whined when she could not wrap her arms around Britt and pull her closer.

At the sound, Britt pushed herself up and settled herself between Renee's spread legs. She gripped Renee's thighs firmly, holding them still, and looked at Jake. "Fuck me," Britt ordered.

As Jake positioned himself behind Britt, his hands near hers, dipping the mattress, she looked at Renee. "Watch."

Britt moaned as Jake slid into her, tossing her head and pushing back into him. "Yes, just like that. So wet for him, Renee. Just…" Her breasts lifted and fell with Jake's every thrust, and Renee could see the light in Jake's eyes, enough to tell that he was already halfway to heaven and it wouldn't take much for him to finish.

Looking straight into Renee's eyes, Britt lowered her head and closed her mouth around Renee's clit. Every time Jake pushed into her, Britt sucked just a little harder, moaning until Renee could feel the vibrations everywhere and it still was not enough. Renee's breathing was shallow as she tried to bring her hips closer to Britt, tried somehow to speed things up, but her legs could not go anywhere, she couldn't move her hands, and Britt was just teasing her now, even though Jake was fucking Britt even harder, losing control. Britt circled Renee's clit with her tongue, dipping under the hood and pushing against the sensitive flesh against her pubic bone.

But there wasn't *enough* pressure, *enough* speed, enough anything. Renee bit back a shriek as her pleasure began to build into an orgasm in such a way she knew it was going to be a disappointment, like going under a wave rather than riding it. And she had to bite it back again when Britt pulled away, voicing her orgasm and pulling Jake into her as far as he could go. He grunted, his hands tightening on the sheets to Renee's sides, and pushed into Britt hard enough for Britt's mouth to hit Renee's stomach. Renee could feel Britt's catching breath as Jake stroked her through the rest of her orgasm. They slumped over her, Jake's weight made all the more apparent in comparison to Britt's.

But Renee was still wet, still clenching, still waiting for her climax and immeasurably frustrated. She was not used to waiting, not used to teasing, and she didn't think she liked it like that. She wanted to pull Britt up to her and kiss her, to wrap her legs around the woman's thighs and press her hips against her, to find just the right place to *press*.

"Please," Renee begged quietly, her voice small in the room, almost unheard under the pants of the two shapeshifters above her.

"Please what, Red?" Britt asked, fingers brushing against Renee's stomach in gentle affection.

"Please let my hands go."

Britt looked up, as though that was not the request she'd been expecting. "Does that not work for you?"

"Not for too long," Renee said evenly. She tried not to squirm as Britt disentangled herself from Jake and moved to untie the ropes on Renee's wrists. As she was released, Renee realised that they had chafed her wrists in spite of the smoother material. She had not noticed it until the air hit the place where she had rubbed the skin off. It was not too bad, and it only stung a little. Her upper arms ached more than her wrists. Renee flexed her fingers to make sure she had feeling. Jake was stirring on the bed, making his way upright.

"So...you're still human," Britt said. It was not a question. She would have smelt werewolf if Renee had turned.

Renee threaded her fingers through Britt's hair and brought her lips down. Where they were on an emotional level was up in the air, but their sexual spark was still there, and Britt's shoulders dropped with a release of tension as Renee kissed her, needing to feel her and taste her completely. Not just in the slightly sticky way that Britt had claimed her.

She lay back on the bed, pulling Britt over her and curling a foot around Britt's thigh. There was the weight she needed, the sensation of being covered. Every possible inch, she could feel her lover. Ejaculate and female juices dripped onto Renee's leg, but she was already filthy, and the smell of sex had already permeated the room. The bed lowered and creaked beside them, and Renee felt a warm, slightly furry arm slide under her neck.

"Is it all right?" Jake asked tentatively. Renee laughed a little into Britt's mouth, then turned to kiss him almost chastely on the cheek.

"Fine," she answered. Britt settled on the other side of Renee, letting Jake take her place. The penultimate time Renee had kissed him, she had still been new to the whole sex experience. She had been fucked six ways to Saturday since then, and it was hard to fear sex with people who she trusted absolutely.

She was right about the oddness of Jake covering her. The oddness of everything—the smooth softness of the body hair on his chest and arms and legs. The press of his mostly flaccid cock on her leg, bigger than Grant's, as Jake was bodily bigger than Grant. She knew it didn't always work that way, but in this case, it did. She was caved in by his body, her skin tingling as it touched his, sensitive to each and every little hair. And he was gentle, so very gentle. With Britt and Grant, Renee knew there was passion there, an undeniable attraction to her. What Jake did—while he was very good at it and while it was clear that both he and she were enjoying themselves—was more like a deep sexual massage. By a good friend. A friend. Not a lover. But God, if he wanted to, she would let him inside her. She thought it would feel nice.

His palms were flat and dry against her. He could cover her face with just one hand, and yet his hands were soft as they held her face, her neck, sliding down to her chest to cup one breast. He was so very vanilla, not rough at all, that the bruises on the sides of her breasts, and the places where Jake's hair brushed against new skin, made her feel almost ashamed. She knew that he could be much less delicate with Britt, fucking her into the mattress, yet he was delicate with her because she was Renee. Not because she was breakable, but because he cared so much about her wellbeing and because he was still worried about hurting her in any way, perhaps in a way that associated him with Grant. But she did not have any need for him to hurry in spite of the arousal between her legs that still yearned for some kind of release. She gripped the wide expanse of his back, but she did not curl her nails into the flesh. She wrapped her legs around his hips and brushed her heels against the firm muscles of his ass. His breath caught in her mouth, and she began to feel the first real sign that his erection was recovering.

Renee gently pushed Jake away, down onto the covers so that she could straddle him. Her legs protested the angle, but it was worth it for the way that Jake stared up at her. His golden eyes were glistening, glazed over as his eyes and fingers strayed over the curves of her breasts, her stomach, her lips.

Britt came up behind Renee and wrapped her arms under Renee's breasts. She teased the edge of Renee's ear with her mouth as she helped balance Renee to slide down around Jake's still growing shaft. Renee gave a soft cry — she hadn't thought that a bigger cock would feel much different since most of her sensitivity was nearer to her clit, but Jake was stretching her, straining that sensitive flesh. Her nails caught on his skin reflexively, and the muscles under her fingers fluttered at the sensation. She clenched her pussy around him, getting a sense of just how big he was. He threw his arm above his head and arched his back as she did. He was engorged inside her, and she dripped down between them. Britt spread her fingers and pushed her hand down Renee's stomach until her forefinger and third finger were poised just above her clitoris, right where Renee needed them to be. Renee began to rock. It was not quite the sensation of riding cock—she was teasing herself mercilessly now, as much as she was teasing him. But he had already got off once, and as long as she did not have the ropes around her wrists, she was going to enjoy herself and set her own pace.

It was a little harder to focus on teasing as Britt began to massage that area above and around her clit, pressing deep under the hood, her mouth finding all the ravaged, sore places on her neck that made her nerves tingle. Pleasure dripped down her spine as surely as she dripped around Jake's cock. He was beginning to moan, long breaths low in his throat as his hips sometimes snapped up in reflexive need.

"I've felt what you feel," Britt murmured. "I've had his cock in me. Just a few minutes ago. He was in me, and now he's in you—my juices are mingling with yours. It's like you're surrounding me. Come on, Red. Come for us. All tight around him, squeezing him until he pops and calls out your name. We want you to come for us."

Britt's fingers were more insistent, circling the place that made her hips buck. Then she wrapped her other arm more firmly around Renee's stomach, and Jake braced one of his hands on her hip. Using her own hips and the strength of her limbs, Britt lifted Renee up and brought her down hard around Jake's erection. Then again, until Britt and Renee seemed to be one woman riding him. His groans grew louder—Renee almost imagined she could feel his blood pulsing through the piece of him inside her.

The orgasm came suddenly after so much build-up. It ripped through her, and she simultaneously went limp in Britt's arms and tense around Jake's hips, her hands clenching in time with her cunt. A soft whine escaped her lips, but that was all as she shook through the orgasm. Britt stroked her and rocked her on Jake's still turgid erection until he too came through Renee's aftershocks. Renee gasped when her pleasure rose again in a smaller orgasm, like driving over a swell. She almost hit Britt squarely in the jaw as her head snapped back through the last shudders of her second climax.

Jake didn't have to collapse back, since he was already on his back, but he did make a noise of protest as Renee twisted around to kiss Britt. She belatedly noticed that she was bending his cock in ways it did not want to bend, and she lifted herself off him.

All the combined fluids dripped down her thigh, and her first impulse was to go straight back into the shower now that she was covered in her sweat and theirs, their saliva, their combined fluids. But Britt pushed her onto the covers, and Renee told herself that if she could resist the impulse to clean for Grant, she could resist it again for their sakes. And besides, this was Britt's bed instead of hers, and Britt was not so concerned about such things.

Their breasts were sticky as they rubbed against each other, and Renee's nipples were oversensitive, tight and tingling, but she wasn't ready to let Britt go.

This touching was not about getting anywhere, it was just being able to touch and feel that clenching warmth without fruition. It was as though neither she nor Britt wanted to let go, for very different reasons. Britt because she did not want Renee to go away, and Renee just because it was nice to be home. And it *was* home.

Chapter Twelve

It was both strange and familiar to go back to her normal routine after the last week and the welcome home. Grant stayed scarce the following weeks, more out of a sense of self-preservation than of courtesy, Renee thought. And maybe it was a welcome return on his part as well, since they had been in mostly civilised areas following the meeting with the werewolf pack, and here he had hundreds of acres to run without having to rein himself in. However, when he did come up to the compound, he did not let Renee relegate the two of them to private areas where no one could see what they were doing. The shapeshifters would have known what she was doing with him anyway. So while they were not screwing around in plain sight, Grant made no effort to hold back his groans as she went down on him in the greenhouse, or when he invited her to his cot in the shapeshifter barn. Mostly, though, they had sex in Renee's old room, where it was comfortable and private without really having to hide.

Renee did have one demand she did not compromise on. The loft area was off-limits for him. Only Britt and Jake were allowed there, and Renee would not protect him from them if he invaded that space. Grant had not agreed to the rule, but he never went up there anyway.

At first, the atmosphere between Renee and her shapeshifter pack was tense. She went into the computer room with Leslie the day after coming home and started working at her station, and although neither she nor Leslie were normally talkative with each other, Renee felt the silence more keenly. She would sense him looking at her, but when she turned around, he would be looking at his monitor again. Only the creak of the chair would indicate his pretence.

Still, she had more emails to wade through than she had expected, and she had to update the sanctuary website and blog and get back to the people who wanted to adopt dogs for Christmas. She apologised for it being last-minute to many of the potential adoptive parents, and they were mostly understanding, if a bit frazzled. She set up a few appointments and welcomed a few people the very next day.

Britt, Jake, Malcolm and Max had kept the sanctuary running fairly well in her absence, although when Jake was not in the loft bedroom, she noticed that both he and Malcolm were a bit on edge. Jake dismissed it when she asked, but Malcolm got that look in his eyes that told her he was lying. However, none of them were telling her what was going on, so she knew it was not a problem with the sanctuary itself. She decided to leave it alone.

As the pack got used to her being with Grant as well as with them, they calmed down a little about it and stopped skirting around her as though she were going to transform on them by the power of sex alone. The fact that they regularly saw her with Britt as well reassured them that Renee was mostly the same Renee they knew.

* * * *

Jake had actually bought security cameras for the front gates while she'd been gone, an early Christmas present that had been installed the day before she'd come back. It was how he and Britt had known when Renee had returned.

She was not as shocked as she thought she should be when she saw a police car on the screen next to her computer. A plainclothes policeman was ringing the bell at the gate, and she could see that there was another person in the passenger seat. The man's stance was too casual for Renee to be too concerned over the safety of the shapeshifters in the sanctuary, but there should not have been policemen at her gate at all.

Struggling to breathe slowly, she pressed the button to let them in, then pressed the button on the compound intercom.

"Roll call. Repeat, roll call." It was one of the codes that she had developed, and it was one that she had never had to use before. She hoped they remembered what it meant. They had heard the gate bell, so they knew someone was coming, but 'roll call' meant that there was an outsider emergency, and they needed to act quickly to hide the presence of as many shapeshifters as she had in the sanctuary. Enough to qualify as workers and volunteers, nothing more. She had encouraged the shapeshifters who did not have identification to go canine so that they would not draw suspicion.

It was something that she wished she had never had to plan for, but even now she realised that they had not planned enough. There was the whole second barn set up for human comforts, and if they locked it up, it would look suspicious in the case of a search. As it was, she knew that the shapeshifters still in human form were hurriedly folding beds down and stacking them against the wall to look as though they were only brought out when necessary. But that wouldn't hide the fact that there were that many beds in the first place, or that there was a kitchen in that barn, or that there were people out of their dog skin who no one knew were there in the first place. For someone already suspicious, the circumstances were a bit shady. Renee was not doing anything wrong, but she did not know whether a suspicious person would see it that way.

Renee pulled on her coat and went outside to meet the policemen. The dogs ran to greet her. Her heightened emotional state made them anxiously excited. Britt ran with the rest of the dogs as the malamute. Jake, Leslie and Malcolm came out of the cabin as their human selves, though, as they sometimes interacted or used to interact with the world. Jake's and Malcolm's faces looked grim, and Renee suspected that the thing they were not telling her might be what the policemen were coming up to investigate.

All Renee could hope was that Grant was hiding somewhere. The last thing she needed was Grant ringing alarm bells. Of course, this entire thing could just be routine, or maybe one of the policemen wanted a dog.

Renee snorted. *Dare to dream*, she thought. She gripped the edges of her coat. Britt bumped her cold nose against one of her hands, showing her canine support.

The police car drove up the steep incline. The snow was wet and the weather had gone uncommonly above freezing. Only by a few degrees, according to the porch thermometer, and it kept drifting under now and then, but at least it made getting to the compound a little easier for strangers. Renee wished it had been icier, but then they might have only tried harder.

The plainclothes cop got out of the car. He looked a bit like George C. Scott, in affect if not fully in appearance. The other policemen got out in full uniform, and Renee amended her initial assumption that she was a man. The woman looked young for her occupation — about Renee's age. Renee did not recognise her, so she assumed that the woman had either not been raised in Antoine or that she was older than she looked. Their demeanours were not accusatory, and Renee's panic about possible criminal activities from the sanctuary lessened, leaving only a marginal social anxiety.

"You'd be Ms Chambers, then," the plainclothes cop said, holding out his hand. After some measure — and the encouragement of a cold dog nose — Renee took it and shook. "I'm Detective Ebon, and this is Detective Benoit."

"Renee Chambers," Renee said. "Jake, Leslie, Malcolm."

Detective Ebon pointed at Leslie and said, "Leslie Cannon? I've read your book. Not bad at all. Good to meet you."

He turned back to Renee, and while he put on a fairly affable expression, Renee was not sure what to make of the dark beadiness of his eyes. This was a man who could be on two levels at once, and that might mean that things could be worse than she thought, and she would not even know from looking at him.

"And of course, we know who you are and what you do," he said. "We don't want to make you more uncomfortable than you already are, so we'll make this quick. The National Park Service has noticed some animal deaths that are, as they say, atypical in nature. They say that the animals are ripped apart, among other things. While they didn't find any sign of rabies, they are worried about a wild animal that could be diseased. They hoped it would be taken care of in its own time, but no such luck. Since this is, after all, a dog sanctuary, we wanted to know whether you've had any similar experiences with strange animal deaths, or if one of your dogs has escaped."

"You think it's one of my dogs?" Renee asked.

The detective shrugged. "It's unlikely, but we have to cover all the bases." His words said one thing, but underneath, Renee swore she heard, "It's a possibility, and that's why we're here and not calling you on the telephone."

"I have over seventy dogs in the sanctuary, and we let them mostly run free," Renee said, bristling. "But they can't leave. The fences that run the circumference of our compound are specially built so that they can't break through or jump over it. Even our Great Dane couldn't make it out."

But a shapeshifter could. Or a werewolf. The thought surfaced like a dead body, and Renee shuddered. She looked at Jake. What exactly were they not telling her because they thought she would be too sensitive about Grant?

"We each patrol part of the perimeter every week," Jake said. Detective Ebon took a good look at him, as if taking in his size and the strength evident underneath his clothing. "We've had some strange deaths, but none of us have seen any broken fence. You can check it yourself if you would like, but we're secure."

"If you're secure," Ebon said, the mild expression belying the shrewdness in his eyes, "then why have you had a few animals torn apart on your property?"

"He means that our dogs are secure inside the sanctuary. They can't get out," Renee said. "We sometimes get deer stuck in the fences, and I've seen wolves right outside the perimeter, but we built the fences with even the biggest dogs we have in mind. Sometimes small animals get in, and anything that flies or climbs is a given. But whatever is killing those animals is either big enough or smart enough to scale the fence."

"Yes, that's what we thought, too," Ebon replied. "All the same, if we checked your fences and brought in a tooth mould to compare to your bigger dogs, you wouldn't mind, right?"

"Not at all," Renee said. She knew they wouldn't find anything wrong with the fences, and if they could indeed make a workable tooth mould from ravaged animals, they would not match any of her bigger dogs. But while she did not get the impression that Ebon suspected her of any wrongdoing—he was sharp, but not aggressive—she thought that he suspected *something*.

"Very good." Detective Ebon drew his coat closer around him. "And quite unrelated to this messy business, Ms Chambers, I do have a complaint from a few citizens in the city regarding poor animal treatment and threats directed at them."

"Excuse me?" Renee was a little surprised by the iciness of her own voice, and if she was not mistaken, so was Detective Ebon. But *no one* accused her of being cruel to her dogs. She could be accused of a lot of things—some of them could even be illegal—but not of hurting her dogs. There were only a few people who would say something like that to spite her. "Josh and Marcus?"

"I do believe those are the concerned citizens, Ms Chambers."

"They harassed me at my gate on my land, and yes, I threatened them. I threatened to protect my property and to protect my animals from them. I would never let them in this sanctuary for any reason." Renee found the scruff of Britt's neck and massaged it, feeling the fur between her fingers to calm herself down. "If they saw anything, which they didn't, they would have been trespassing."

"So people can get in and out," Ebon said.

"They might have a few scratches and scrapes, but yes, people can climb over the fence if they know what they're doing and put in enough effort. The fence is there to protect the dogs—it was not built to keep people out, although common courtesy should do that. We have had a few trespassers over the last few years, maybe one or two. They've all had a bite out of their ass for their troubles. I've had to put down two dogs because of two trespassers, and I don't want to have to lose any dogs because of those inbred bastards."

"Well," Detective Ebon said, giving a hearty sniff from the cold weather. "We didn't hold much stock to the claim, since you've got a better reputation here than those two boys. But we had to check anyway. Two birds, one stone. Or maybe it's two in the bush."

"Well, if you want to patrol the perimeter, go ahead. I'll have my people look over it as well. I'm sure they'll tell me if something's wrong," Renee said, closing her expression off.

Detective Ebon noticed it and immediately stepped back. If he knew of her reputation, then he probably knew that she was not very good with people. Especially, Renee thought, when they were antagonising her sanctuary. And that was exactly what Ebon was doing, even if he was doing it under the guise of simple enquiry. She had no doubt that he would have people patrol the entire circumference of the perimeter, and if he had to use that complaint against her in order to get in without her permission, he would. All the more reason why she would be having a talk with Jake and Malcolm after the police left.

"If you discover anything or have any information for me, here's my card." He slipped it out of his coat pocket and handed it to Renee, who put it in her own coat pocket. "Hope you have a good holiday season," Detective Ebon said, nodding at no one in particular. He beckoned to his partner, who had not said a word, but who had been looking around more actively than Ebon. The dogs who had come up to greet them had probably distracted her a little. None of them had gone near Ebon—they had not barked or growled at him, but they just kept their distance. Renee could not blame them. He might pretend to be pleasant, but he was decidedly unapproachable. Dogs did not always have to be told.

Renee waited until she could not hear the police car anymore before she turned to Jake and Malcolm. She did not have to say anything. Whatever they had been keeping from her was out in the open now, like frozen breath.

Jake touched her shoulder. "This will probably be easier for you if you take one of the four-wheelers." They had a few stored in a small, makeshift garage outside the shapeshifter barn. At least a quarter of the shapeshifters were too small in their dog forms to move quickly at greater distances, the way Jake, Britt, Malcolm or Leslie could as large dogs, and Renee herself could not get her truck everywhere in the sanctuary.

Renee followed Jake, Malcolm, and Britt to the four-wheelers, turned one on, and backed out of the space. Jake and Malcolm had already shrugged out of their clothes and transformed.

Renee could barely hear anything over the roar of the four-wheeler. She followed the shapeshifters as they led her into the western part of the forest. She did not drive very quickly. The forest did not have many paths cleared for it, so she had to improvise her way through. There were some places where it seemed the dogs liked to run, which opened up a few spaces for her, but other times she had to do some careful manoeuvring so as not to flip the vehicle over. The shapeshifters were patient.

She was so focused on the uneven forest floor in front of her that she almost did not notice when she arrived. The burst of red halted her right on the edge of the clearing. The colour was first. The smell was next. She had never smelt so much rot all at once.

The clearing was about twenty feet in a rough circle, with a few smaller trees in the centre. Some of the trees from there had been removed completely by the roots and thrown to the edge of the clearing. Bodies were strewn in the sunlight in a rough spiral from the centre. That could have been dismissed as pure coincidence, a rare, unusual act of nature. But other bodies were hung on branches, the skin attached and spread in such a way that suggested macabre artistry. No animal could have done that—hung the animal corpses a little higher than her head. Only something with hands and fingers, something large enough, could have positioned the gutted animals, which looked like sacrifices or strange ornamentation. Renee might have thought it was ritual, except there was nothing in the clearing but the light, blood, maggots, cockroaches, ravens, and the bodies.

Renee turned off the four-wheeler, and the silence made the massacre even worse. Her stomach twisted, clenched, then heaved. By simple reflex, she managed to turn her head and let it out in a bush. She didn't get anything on herself except a drip down her chin. She rubbed it off and swallowed, wincing at the sharp acid in her throat and the bitterness on her tongue.

"How long?" Renee asked. Her throat clicked as she swallowed again. She wished she had some water or something to wash it down and take the taste out of her mouth. When she looked at Jake and Malcolm, who had transformed back into human form, she saw how taut their skin looked, pebbled against the cold. But they suffered through it, wrapping their arms around their chests and rubbing.

"We noticed it on a run three weeks ago," Malcolm said. "It wasn't this bad then. We weren't sure enough."

"You let me go off with him after seeing this?" Renee asked.

"You didn't exactly leave us a lot of choice," Jake said dryly. "You're a big girl, figuratively speaking."

"I would have appreciated the information."

"Would it have changed your mind?" Jake asked.

Renee looked at the rabbit on the tree closest to her. It was open and spread like an anatomy lesson, the insides ravaged beyond recognition although its skin was largely untouched. The eyes had already been eaten by the ravens. Its head had fallen back so that it seemed it implored for mercy to the sky, its empty sockets looking straight at her. But she looked beyond, saw the birds, the rabbits, the vultures, the hares, the deer. No dogs. He had not touched her dogs. And there were no humans in the small, bloody pocket of ruin. In spite of the fact that this kind of destruction spoke of a deranged mind, she'd already known what Grant was. She'd known he was a wolf, vicious and impulsive. And that was what had made her go with him.

"No," Renee answered. It still would have informed her decision, Renee thought. She would have been even more on her guard.

She walked around the edge of the clearing. She knew there was a fence nearby—this was the edge of her land. But she could not see the fence unless she walked a good way, and when she did reach the fence, she could not see the clearing. There was a bit of blood on the barbed wire, and the area looked worn and used, but maybe not enough to alert a green policeman, or one that did not know what he or she was looking for.

She walked to the clearing again and swung her leg over the four-wheeler.

"Are you just going to let him keep doing this? The police are noticing," Jake said. He spoke a little louder as she turned the four-wheeler on.

"It's what he is, and I can't change that," Renee said.

"Do you really want to let him do something to one of your dogs or one of us before you do something?" Jake snapped, moving in front of her and grabbing hold of the handlebars. "Or maybe to you."

"I'm not going to kick him out for something that he *might* do," Renee said. "Any of us *might* do something. He may be more likely to, but I still can't do it on a *might*."

Jake's eyes were hard, his jaw tense. Renee's fists tightened over the handlebars. "You're making a mistake," Jake said.

She wanted to thumb the throttle, make the vehicle growl, but she restrained herself. She waited until he let go of the handlebars in his own time, the way she would treat a tense dog. He stepped aside and let her drive back. Britt followed her. She had stayed in her dog form the entire time, just watching Renee. When they arrived at the house, she transformed back into human form.

"Jake's right," Britt said quietly. "You're making a huge mistake. And you know it."

She did. Renee knew there was a mistake, a flaw in her logic, but she could not quite put a finger on it. Any way she turned it, she felt she could not make a pre-emptive decision, even if she *knew* better.

Her mouth opened, but nothing came out but a cloud of her breath. After her lips tried to form words for a few moments, she eventually gave up and went into the house without saying anything.

* * * *

She did not see Grant all day, and all things considered, it was probably a good idea on his part. When she went to bed, mostly avoiding a subdued Britt and Jake, she slept in the loft rather than in her old bedroom. It was freezing — Max was working on the breaker, and it meant that she needed about four quilts and one crocheted blanket on her bed, not to mention her warmest pyjamas. It was fairly warm under the blankets, but her nose was still cold enough above them that she was easily awakened by the loud thump against the front door. At first, she thought she had dreamt it, although the tendril fragments of her dream were already slipping away. As time passed, the thump didn't return, but she became more convinced that it hadn't been a dream at all.

Her skin immediately tightened and broke out into gooseflesh when she pushed her blankets down. She wrapped a quilt around her, and though it did not work as well as she would have liked, she did not think she could manage more than one blanket at a time. Max must have fixed the heat, because she was not quite as frigid as she had been going to sleep, but it still took time to heat up a house that had been freezing before. The spicy woodsmoke that they had used until the heater came back on stung her nose, but it was still one of her favourite smells — it saturated the walls from all the winters. Her slippered feet brushed quietly against the hardwood floors.

When she opened the front door, she winced against the wind. The warm spell had run from this front. Renee could almost feel the moisture in her eyes and mouth turn to ice.

The door opened wider. There was a burst of red out of the corner of her eye, and she saw where the carcass of a racoon had stained not the door, but the wall right next to it, a macabre declaration. Grant stood as still as a totem at the bottom of the porch steps.

"I could smell you at the blood grounds," Grant said. The air was rarefied, and it was as if he were right next to her ear.

She didn't say anything, just stood there with the cold getting into the house, wrapped in a wholly inadequate blanket.

"If you're looking for an apology, I'm not giving one," Grant added.

"No apology," Renee replied. "But the police are looking for you."

"I was wondering how long it would take the pups to tell you what I was doing," Grant said, as though he hadn't heard her. "They've known for a month. What does that say about how much they respect you and your opinions, I wonder?"

"They thought I was attached to you," Renee said.

He climbed the stairs, his right foot almost against the animal's body. "But you're not."

The blood was bitter. Fresh, it smelt stronger than the woodsmoke. Grant was all shadow in front of the door, but she saw enough of him to know he was naked and ready. Her quilt slipped down her shoulders and onto the floor when he reached for her with the hands that had thrown that animal carcass against her house. She tried to recoil, but his grip became stronger.

He grabbed hold of both of her wrists, yanked her out onto the patio, then shut the door behind her. He had to let her go to rip the front of her sweatshirt apart, but by then, she could not go far—it was too damn cold. Her nipples felt hard as rocks, and they hurt terribly when he pinched, but even so, she felt her cunt soften inside. The moisture made her colder there between her legs, even as her blood tried to make it warmer. Grant's skin steamed, and he was slow but insistent in pressing her against the door. When he pushed too hard, tiny splinters slid, stinging, into her shoulders. She should have run then. But then he closed his mouth around her right nipple. In contrast with the cold, his mouth felt as if it was at boiling temperature, and she bit her lip, choking in a rising cry.

His nails lengthened into claws as he yanked her pants down, tore off her underwear and clutched her hips. The tips thrust through her skin. The pain was sharp and warm. When he pushed his thigh between her legs, lifting her from the ground, she found herself riding him. She hadn't known just how hot he had made her — her skin had been too cold for her to feel the pulse of veins beneath — but now there was no mistaking it.

He was growling between her breasts, really growling. His mouth was too wide, and his teeth too sharp. He was trembling, as though he was trying not to lunge down and rip open her stomach like he had all those animals, like the limp animal on the ground in front of her. She squirmed, trying to move away from the door, but she only succeeded in digging splinters deeper into her back. She hit his shoulder even as she thrust her hips towards him, but he was as immovable as rock. Then the heel of her hand found his mouth and smashed his lips into his sharp teeth.

She could feel the hot blood drip from his mouth and fall on her shoulders as he pulled back. He ran the back of his hand — too-long fingers — over his mouth, and when he put his hand down, he was grinning toothily. Her feet found the ground, and she turned the doorknob, then pulled the door open. She was now keenly aware of the fact that her sweatshirt was torn apart, and her sweatpants were halfway down her legs. She tugged them back up with one hand, held her shirt together with the other.

He followed her in while she was deciding whether to slam the door in his face or yank him in with her. His lips were on hers again as they stumbled blindly to her bedroom. Every time her shoulders flexed and her shirt moved, she could feel the drying blood and the stinging of the splinters.

Grant kicked the door closed behind him. When he came after her again, she sidestepped out of the way.

"No. Not yet."

Grant gave a short, quick sigh. "I suppose you want to talk about those animals," he began.

Renee shook her head. Pulling her shirt off down her arms, she bit back cries as some of the splinters came out, and others stayed in. The shirt was ruined. She was glad it was not one that held any sort of sentimental value to her. Some of the sweatshirts she wore had belonged to her mother or father. She sat down on her bed and presented her back to him.

"Fix it," she said.

She felt like a pincushion, a strange hybrid between a porcupine and a human. She thought that it probably didn't look as bad as it felt, but she couldn't see her own back, and she didn't think she could reach most of the splinters anyway. Sure, she liked a little pain when she fucked him, but she didn't like the way the splinters felt inside her at all, like stiff-legged spiders burrowing into her.

Grant joined her on the bed. She shivered as she felt his tongue trace around and catch on them, as he tasted her skin beneath the blood.

The first splinter out startled her, a sharp tug and a sting about five times more painful than she'd expected, but it faded almost as soon as she registered it. Renee looked over her shoulder and saw Grant spit the particularly large splinter into his hand.

"You should sand your door," Grant said.

"I'll put that on my list," Renee replied.

He continued about his business, sometimes just using his teeth, and other times having to use his fingers to pinch her skin swollen so that he could find the splinter. When he was finished, he ran his hand over her skin, asking her whether she could feel it sting anywhere. She shook her head. His tongue found her skin again, this time just the tip so she could feel him trace patterns over her, clean his blood from her shoulder, clean her blood from the wounds. It would probably be more sterile for him to put rubbing alcohol on, but her head was fuzzy, her cunt wet, and she was swaying in place, half asleep from his ministrations.

He made her stand, pulled down her pants, and guided her down over his dripping erection. A moan escaped her as he warmed her from the inside out, moving slowly, drawing out each second so that she could feel him completely. Swiping her tongue over her dry lips, she twisted around. It took a little flexibility, but she eventually manoeuvred herself so that she faced him without letting him pull out of her. Her muscles grasped his cock in a steady rhythm, and his dark eyes burned. She pressed her small hands on his chest until he lay on his back with her riding him. She stirred herself in slow, sinuous circles with his cock, making sure he touched every inch of her cunt that he could. She eventually found that spot that made her buck. He ground himself into her, trying to continue hitting that same spot. It was an awkward angle, but he was strong and determined, rock hard and hot inside her, his legs quivering.

"Come with me," he murmured, edged with a growl.

The orgasm climbed strong and slow, clenching and clenching more than she'd thought she could, until it felt as if she was constricting dangerously tight around him. His eyes rolled back into his head, his mouth in a blissful, sharp smile. He filled her, twitching and coming as the warmth swirled within her, pulsing all the way to her fingertips and toes. With her head thrown back, she could feel the ends of her hair brush the small of her back as her body shook through the prolonged climax, her back arched and tight. He slid his hands up her sides before pulling her down until her breasts pressed against his chest. She breathed and listened to him breathe until she felt like she could move her limbs again.

Then she rolled off him and grabbed the modified rifle from under the bed. She had attached the silver knife with duct tape to the end like a makeshift bayonet. Completely naked, she cocked the gun and pointed it at Grant.

"You need to leave," she said.

Chapter Thirteen

A smile broke over his face, crooked and somehow disbelieving. After all, she had pointed the knife at him before. But a knife in foreplay was very different from a knife attached to the barrel of a gun.

Grant stood slowly, his smile frozen. His eyes were dark and aggressive. The smile did not quite reach there.

He took a step towards her. "You won't shoot." But even Renee could hear that he was not completely confident in the statement.

Renee just kept the barrel trained on him, keeping her arms as steady as possible although the gun was a little big for her, and she was not one hundred per cent sure that she would shoot him either, or even prick him with the knife. If he got close enough, he could knock the gun from her hands without too much effort. She had to commit to act on the threat if it came down to it.

"A bullet won't kill me," he said.

"Maybe. If I don't hit you in the head. But it'll stun you long enough for me to stab you. And that *will* kill you."

The smile was beginning to become more genuine as he came closer. One more step, and she would have to do something. As long as he didn't...

His dark eyes ran over her body, dwelling like claws, appreciating the picture of such a vulnerable little girl holding a big gun. His cock began to twitch.

"Just when I think I know you, you surprise me. I like it." He began to reach for the gun. He should have just swiped it away from her, but she took a step backward, angled the gun slightly away from him, and pulled the trigger. The kickback made her hit the wall, and she did not think she was ever going to hear again. The benefits of actually shooting the gun were that Grant knew she was serious, and that she woke up everyone else, every single one of them eager to see Renee kick him out.

Grant stumbled back, hitting the bed with his calves. Renee might not go out and hunt, but she did know how to shoot. After Jake had finished teaching himself, Renee had asked him to teach her. She had not practiced in two years, but she went through the motions as though it had been yesterday. She popped the shell casing, then cocked it again, pointing it straight at Grant's chest.

"Still like it?" she asked.

He stood straight again, but for the first time, his nakedness made him seem as vulnerable as she must seem to him. "I don't understand." But she knew he understood perfectly.

"My answer is no," she said. "I don't want to be a werewolf. I don't want to be the bitch in your pack. And I don't want you endangering anyone else up here with your behaviour. You need to leave. Now. If you have anything you're attached to, send me a postcard, and I'll mail it to you." She pushed herself off the wall with her stinging shoulder blades and began to advance on him.

He bared his teeth — silver and sharp. He was beginning to change.

"And if I feel even a little bit threatened by you, I will shoot. You, this time. I swear."

"You actually think you had a choice?" he snarled, the claws lengthening over his nails. But that was as far as he went. His muscles did not shift, and he did not begin to sprout fur. What he did was back away to the door. It opened from behind him, hitting his ass and making him scramble to the side so that he did not have his back to an enemy. Jake and Britt were the first to appear in the darkness of the hall, then Malcolm, Max, and Ki. Renee was fairly sure that Leslie would be at the back, watching but not prepared to engage. She was also fairly sure some of the other shapeshifters would be trying to make their way to the log home after hearing the gunshot, but the weather would probably be enough to deter some of them.

"You had me in your bed, and you knew what I was," he growled. His voice had dropped about an octave, growing guttural and rough. "What could have possibly changed your mind? Do you really want to be the only one here without the magic I've shown you?"

"I can live with that," Renee said. She continued to advance, and Grant stumbled out into the hall, avoiding the shapeshifters who would attack if he touched Renee or them. Renee followed him out, but when Grant opened the front door, she realised that although he could survive the weather, she could not possibly walk out there without getting frostbite. Jake put his hand carefully on her shoulder.

"I can take that," he said.

She shook her head. "Someone get some clothes and my coat," she said. "I'm going out there."

Britt ran up the stairs to the loft to get her what she needed. She gave Jake the gun only to put the sweatshirt and pants, shoes, and coat on. Grant refused to budge from where he stood, as if waiting intently for some kind of advantage.

Then she took the rifle back and forced Grant out onto the porch, then into the field.

His eyes burned red. "I will have you, Renee. That was never a question. You'll run with me."

She did not even bother telling him that he had given her the choice. She just kept the gun trained on him.

They heard voices from the other shapeshifters heading towards the cabin, and that was when Grant turned and ran.

Renee did not even stop to think. She dropped her shoulder, keeping a hold on the gun, and began to run after him. Jake and Britt had to change into their dog forms in order to run alongside her.

After years of running with the dogs herself, she had good speed and endurance, the air frigid and fresh and sharp in her lungs. She slipped once or twice in the snow and lost track of Grant now and then, but he was using the driveway, and she did not have to work to find him again. When they finally reached the gate, he undid the latch and pulled it open. He closed it on himself and watched as Renee closed the lock, then set the security code so that it would not open again for four hours, with no exceptions. He stared at her heatedly, his muscles finally changing and the fur running over his skin like water.

"I'm what you need," he hissed with the last of his human vocal chords. He ran into the woods, ostensibly away from the sanctuary.

When Jake and Britt changed into human form, practically freezing in the process, they moved close to Renee, hugging her as much for warmth as for reassurance.

"You know he's coming back," Britt said. "He's not going to just leave." Neither she nor Jake said anything like, "I told you so," or that they had been right all along. Because Renee had been right, too—she had never doubted that Grant was going to have to leave the sanctuary. The only question had been whether she was going to leave with him.

"I know," she said. "We have to get all the dogs. It may be tomorrow, it may be the next day, but the next thing he'll try for is one of the dogs. And then he'll try for one of you. So you all need to be ready, and we need to get all the dogs locked in their barn. Tonight, if we can."

Britt nodded at Jake, and he went ahead to get the other shapeshifters to work together to get the dogs in. Most of the dogs stayed inside during this kind of weather, but a few of them were more open-air than others, and those were the ones who would be vulnerable to Grant's attack.

Renee let Britt hold her a little while longer. Britt's feet must have been turning blue, and Renee could feel her shaking from the cold, but Britt did not seem to want to let go, knowing that Renee had chosen them over what Grant offered. And some part of Britt must have known that Grant had offered Renee something that Renee believed had great value.

Finally, Britt changed into her far more practical form, circling around Renee as she made her way back to the home, making sure nothing came at her. The malamute was snuffling with the effort to not miss a single whiff of werewolf that got into Britt's olfactory range. Renee did not run back up the hill, but she was not walking slowly. She did not think that Grant would come right back for her, but she was still jumpy, ready for doors to be locked and lights on. She had not thought much further than threatening him off the property.

She tightened her fingers around the rifle, clinging to it. Her one defence against anything that came after her. The shapeshifters and dogs had their teeth, and Grant had everything he could possibly have to be dangerous. His body was a weapon. But all she could do was hope that a bullet slowed Grant down long enough for her to infect him with silver, presuming that he could not just knock the knife away from him when he was in terrible pain from a bullet wound, and presuming that she could shoot him where it would hurt. She was a good shot, but it was easy to shoot a bull's-eye when there was nothing making her nervous. Those were the best possible conditions. Someone like Grant, who inspired deeply ambiguous, torn feelings within her, and who was wickedly violent when he wanted to be… It was understandable that Renee might not shoot him well enough when the shot counted.

Britt's hackles were still raised as they reached the house. Leslie held some winter clothes in his hands. Jake had told him to give them to Britt. Britt brought the clothes into the house with her and changed in the warmer living room. Renee went to put on more clothes than the basics she had, then grabbed a few more outfits, unsure how long they would have to stay in the barns before Grant made his move and came back.

* * * *

At the very least, some of them would have to go back and forth between the shapeshifter barn and the dog barn. The dog barn was not set up to be hospitable to the shapeshifters who preferred their human shape to sleep in, and besides, the dog barn was already crowded when it was just the dogs living in it. Also, the dog barn did not have a kitchen.

Renee stayed with the dogs, while her shapeshifter pack split into two groups, one to help protect Renee and the dogs, and the other to make sure that the other shapeshifters were okay and knew what was going on.

The weather wasn't helping. The snow was back, so although the biting wind of the day before was gone, the cold only seemed to be getting worse. The snow had built up between the barns so that moving from one place to the other was difficult, and they could not always see their surroundings.

The dogs were restless, and they knew that the people around them were stressed. They barked at nothing, paced near the door, peed in corners, and begged to go out and relieve themselves. The shapeshifters took them out a few at a time throughout the day, but without their usual exercise and freedom, the dogs became overexcited or belligerent.

Renee had not showered in two days. She smelt like dog, slept on one of the couches with at least three dogs near her, plus Britt, who stayed in dog form most of the time. Two days, and they had not heard anything. Jake, Malcolm, Max and Ki shuffled to and from the shapeshifter barn, bringing food for the rest of them, keeping a lookout, and asking the other guards if they had seen anything.

What if Grant was basically going to wait them out? Maybe he would wait until they came out of their own accord, sure that he was really gone. It would take too long to starve them out, but Renee could see them getting cabin fever if things stayed this tense for much longer. Dogs weren't meant to be cooped up, and Renee could not stay away from the world outside forever. There were things that needed to be done, an organisation that needed to be run. She couldn't stay. But how long *could* they stay like this? Was Grant patient enough to wait? Or would he crack before they did?

* * * *

It was midnight on the fourth day in. Renee, who had had a hard time leaving the log home for months after her father had died, was ready to get out of the barn. She could not get comfortable on the couch, tossing back and forth and disturbing the dogs around her. She wondered whether anyone had contacted the sanctuary. She wondered if anyone would even notice if there was radio silence from them. She wondered if Detective Ebon would notice, and if he had found anything from his search around her perimeter. Most of the barn was dark to simulate night, but they kept lights on in the loft so that they could see if they had to move about.

There was a loud, sharp thud on the barn door, familiar. Renee jerked straight up, and all the dogs began barking. Now that they were awake, they could smell something that made their hackles rise. Renee stood up and headed towards the door.

"No, don't go near it," Jake said, striding past her and putting himself between the door and her. "You think we've been keeping you in here for your health?"

Malcolm, Max and Leslie came up behind them and joined Jake at the door. Max held the crude bayonet that Renee had made, his face unusually grim. Ki would not be going out with them—she was Renee's size soaking wet. The only reason Max was going out was because he was big enough in human form. And the only reason Leslie was going out was because he was big enough in dog form. However, he looked terrified.

"We'll come back in and tell you what it is," Jake reassured her. Britt touched Renee's hand with her muzzle, and Renee jumped. "Just stay in here. Promise me."

She did not promise anything. Her entire body was shaking inside out from the cold, but she could not help but remember that Grant had wanted to show Jake what a real alpha could be. She had come to the thought then, but she was not aroused now, and instead remembered with foreboding.

The four went out, Leslie in his dog skin, closing and locking the door behind them. Renee listened hard beyond the barking, but she could not hear anything. She looked down at Britt, whose ears were trained on the door, but Renee could not tell if Britt could hear anything either. Ki was going around trying to calm the dogs down, but although their barking began to subside, they were still more restless than usual, running along the walls and pawing at the dry dirt floor as though trying to get out. Their ears and tails were erect and tense.

Renee did not even realise just how tense *she* was until the shivering in her neck hurt and her hands protested being clenched so tightly. She kept expecting Grant to burst in through the doors. She kept feeling his teeth on her, tasting her, preparing her for the real thing. Although he was hardly a restrained person, he had forced himself to wait until she told him to bite her, and now it felt as if she was only a hair's breadth away from being changed against her will. She was terrified for herself and her friends, but what felt even worse was that she would not have given up the last two months for anything. She hated and loved and wanted Grant all at once, and she didn't know whether, when the time came and he leaned over her with his teeth bared, she would fight too hard.

Her legs locked as she heard two screams—one of which might have been a howl—and a gunshot, then nothing. She thought she would fall, but her body was paralysed. Britt transformed back into human form and ran naked to the door, unlocking it and pulling it open. She was halfway through the change back into a dog, but then Jake and Max carried a bleeding Malcolm—in human form—into the barn. Leslie ran in after them, transforming back to human skin, pushing Britt back and locking the door. His normally placid face was drawn and white, his mouth a dark gash on his face.

Ki came running over, clearly thinking her Max was hurt at first, but after seeing that he was okay—if scared and furious—she ran to get a first-aid kit. Renee helped clear off one of the couches and kept the dogs from sniffing at the wound in Malcolm's leg.

Malcolm was staring at the ceiling, his face slack as he clutched at the wound in his leg. His dark eyes were glazed.

"I got off a shot, and I got the bastard. But not good enough. He bit Malcolm," Max said, throwing the rifle on the ground, too angry to care about gun safety. "The wolf bit him when Malcolm was human. Goddamn it."

Renee gently pulled up Malcolm's pants leg. Malcolm winced as the fabric pulled away from the wound, but he didn't say anything. The bite was still bleeding, and while it looked shallow, it had done its trick. Grant did not have to kill one of Renee's pack in order to destroy his life.

"So...what does that do?" Renee asked. She did not make a habit of asking questions to which she already knew the answer, but she just had to hear it out loud.

"If he had bitten Malcolm's dog form, it would have hurt like hell," Jake said. "But that's all it would have done. But Malcolm was human. Which means that, come next full moon, he'll transform into a wolf. I don't know whether he even has his canine form anymore. I don't know how this works." He collapsed on the couch next to Malcolm, clenching his hands into fists and hitting his thighs with them. Ki ran over with an open first-aid kit, and Max helped her dress the wound. Malcolm just let them do whatever they wanted, neither helping nor hindering.

"But you shot him. You shot Grant," Renee said to Max.

"I hit his stomach," Max said. He put pressure on the wound as Ki began wrapping gauze around the calf. "But it would take a direct hit to the heart or head, I think, to slow a werewolf down. Or the fucking knife, but he wouldn't let me get close enough."

Leslie staggered over, his coordination limited through his shock. He held out a wallet. The wallet was blood-stained and left Leslie's hand red. "There was a body," Leslie said. "He threw a human body at the door. That's what made the noise. We didn't recognise who it was, but it was hard to really see…what he once looked like. His face…"

Renee took the wallet slowly. If it was not one of her shapeshifters, there were only so many people Renee knew — and with whom Grant had seen her interact. Even before she opened the wallet to see the dead man's driver's licence, she somehow knew.

Ki climbed onto the couch next to Malcolm and held him, just giving him something to feel even if he did not react to her presence. Renee also wanted to reassure him, but she had nothing to reassure him with, since the situation was her fault to begin with. Instead, she walked around the couch and stepped a few feet away, distancing herself even though she knew that was probably the worst way to respond to Malcolm's problem.

She opened the wallet. She had been right. There was a photo of Josh Beall on his driver's licence, a few years younger than he had been when she'd last seen him, but recognisable. She also found a Visa credit card, car insurance documents, and sixty-seven dollars in cash, plus change.

By the time she dropped the wallet, her hands had become even more stained. She did not have to be a shapeshifter to smell the blood, as strong and fresh as it was now. Renee toed a dog away from sniffing the wallet, then forced herself to pick it up and throw it in one of the sinks on the wall.

Then she strode over to the couch and picked up the rifle from where Max had thrown it. She found the box of bullets near the sink and reloaded it full. She was halfway to the barn doors when both Britt and Jake whirled her around.

"What the hell do you think you're doing?" Britt asked, at the same time that Jake yelled, "No way you're going out there!"

"This didn't have to happen," Renee said. "He wants me. That's all he wants."

"So you're just going to go out there with a gun and try and shoot him before he bites you?" Britt asked. "Seriously? Have you gone crazy?"

"He's fast," Jake said. "And it's both a blackout and a whiteout out there. You can't see anything, but he doesn't need to see well to find you. God, I don't even know why he let us come back in here. He could have slaughtered us all."

"And that's what he's going to do if I don't go out there," Renee said. "Josh—the body. And Malcolm. Those were just warnings. He'll escalate. Soon he won't even bother waiting for the door to open. It was stupid to try to hide from him, and I'm not going to let him hurt anyone or anything else. If biting me is going to make everything else go away, I'll do it. I don't even care anymore. It's better than watching him turn my friends and kill my enemies."

"We're trying to protect you," Jake said, his grip hard on her arm. "I'm not going to let you go out there. What if he goes after the rest of us while you're out there, huh? Destroy all your connections until you have to go with him? Have you thought any of this out?"

"There's no time to think!" Renee shouted. "If you want to protect me, have my back. But I'm not going to just sit in here while he plays his games with us. He already changed Malcolm. Getting the two of you would be a plus to him. But I'm the one he wants. And I don't matter."

"If you didn't matter, we wouldn't bother. And he wouldn't bother," Britt said. She let go of Renee, but although her voice was quiet, that did not take away from the weight of it. "If you had let him bite you because that was what you wanted, I would have at least understood that. I wouldn't have known what to do about it, but I would have understood. It would have been your choice. But you're letting him decide for you, which is what he's been trying to do ever since he came into this place. He thinks he can force you into doing anything he wants. He thinks that you're his, that because he's marked you, you belong to him. But you don't."

"I'll try to shoot him," Renee said, shrugging off Jake's hand. "But we can't stay here forever. There's no need to risk everyone else, just because he wants his teeth in me."

"I'm going out there with you," Britt said. She was shaking in spite of herself, but she managed to stay standing as she went to get something to wear outside.

"If you insist on going out there, I'll go, too, but I swear, I'll tie you to a chair before I let you go out there," Jake said.

Renee brought the rifle up and cocked it. The tip of the knife was inches from Jake's chest. "Please," she said. She did not want to hurt Jake in trying to do the right thing. "Help me end this. One way or the other. But I'm going out there with or without you."

Jake peered down at her, a little girl from his height, and his face was tight with pain—from seeing the body, from being cooped up in a barn for almost a week, from feeling helpless against Grant, from watching his friend get bitten, from thinking that another friend would be bitten against her will. Renee had a feeling it was all of the above.

She did not even feel the anguish anymore. She was past that now. All she wanted was for it to be over. If that meant offering herself to Grant even though it was not what she wanted, she would do it for her friends, and for the sanctuary.

When Britt came up behind Renee, dressed in a tan cable sweater and two layers of pants, Jake took a step back. "Fine, I'm going out with you."

"Behind me," Renee said.

"No fucking way."

"If he can get to me more easily, I don't have to worry about losing you to him."

"If you don't trust us to protect you," Jake said, "how can you trust your own reflexes?"

"I don't," Renee said. She pulled the gun closer to her and started to head towards the barn door. "But I've got to try."

"Renee," Britt said softly as Renee reached for the barn door lock. "If he turns you... Turn me."

Renee turned around and stared at Britt. "You hate werewolves. You're afraid of them."

"And if you're trapped as one, I don't want you to be alone. Not with him. Okay?"

Renee lowered the gun, pulling Britt down for a rushed, desperate kiss. It felt as if she was walking out there to be executed. Depending on Grant's mood, she might be. And Britt was offering to be executed with her. Grant had told her that the shapeshifters could never give her what she needed. But this was what she needed—someone who needed her, whether that person could change into a dog or a wolf or nothing at all. It was all she could do to step back and turn around, turning away from Britt. It took even more effort just to undo the lock. Her hands were shaking, making the lock rattle, and when she took the gun in both hands, she could hear the gun rattling, too. Jake took the initiative and pulled the door open for her.

The cold was biting, and she realised that she had forgotten to put on her coat. However, she did not bother going back in for it. One way or another, things would be over quickly. At least she was wearing boots.

She curled her finger around the trigger and held up the gun in the darkness, prepared to shoot or thrust it out into whatever body came at her. It was practically pitch dark outside except where the light from the barn shone in a cylinder of limited vision. She was hyper-vigilant. Not a single snowflake escaped her notice. Nor did the dark, slumped shadow of a body reclining against the side of the barn, but she could not allow herself to be distracted by that.

She heard the growl the second it began. Her head jerked to the left, but she could not see anything. And the growl seemed to be moving, left to right, then all around until it filled her ears. But she still couldn't see Grant. He had to be close, but the shadows were not moving. She had no idea where to even look.

"Goddamn it, just come out and do it," Renee shouted. Her voice was lost in the snow. It sounded small and tinny to her ears.

"Just a few days ago, you were throwing me out at gunpoint to keep me from turning you," Grant said. Like his growl, his rough voice seemed to be everywhere. "You've got your dog pack behind you.

And I see the gun, love. You think they can protect you? You think you can shoot me fast enough?"

"No," Renee said. "But I'm willing to try. You try to get me, I try to get you."

He laughed. The sound was not cruel. He seemed genuinely delighted. "I would not expect anything less, my dear. You'll turn fighting. And that's good."

Her cold fingers gripped the gun everywhere but the trigger, not ready but prepared. She was still shaking, but she was not paying attention to that. Every sense was straining to hear where he was coming from.

Someone's hands yanked her backwards as Britt screamed, "Above you!" A giant shadow dropped where she had been. At the surprise, her trigger finger clenched and shot randomly in the dark.

The shadow unfurled into something that was half-man, half-wolf. His mouth was still human enough so that he could speak to her, but the teeth were sharp, and Renee suspected that he could turn her in this form. He was just three feet away, and he could have darted forward and taken her then, but he didn't. He stood two feet higher than he did as a human and stared down at her.

"Go ahead and shoot me, Renee," he said. Even closer, his voice seemed to fill her head as she tried to get her balance back.

"Shoot him," Jake urged. "Come on, he's not running. Shoot him before he gets you."

"Can you do it? Can you really be that kind of person?" His long, flat tongue caressed his teeth as he looked over her with red eyes. "You came out here knowing that you would fail."

"I came out here so that you wouldn't have to go through my people to get to me," Renee said.

"Of course. You own a sanctuary. It wouldn't provide much sanctuary if the owner is the reason for its downfall."

"Why won't you come at me?" Renee asked tightly.

"Why won't you shoot me?" He reached one furred arm out slowly. It was about as long as her leg. The claw stroked a harsh line down her cheek but did not break the skin. "Dare I suggest that you harbour something like love for me?"

Renee would have said that was a bit of an overstatement, but she did not give him the satisfaction of an answer. Snapping the gun up, she cocked it and shot straight at his right shoulder. It wouldn't kill him. Somehow she couldn't. She couldn't kill him if he wasn't attacking her. But she was damned if she was going to let him draw this out when all she wanted was for it to stop.

He stumbled backward, clutching his right shoulder. His mouth elongated as a howl transformed into a roar, and she reeled back, slipping on the snow. Britt caught her, pulling her farther away from that giant mouth, dark pink and glistening as he screamed at her. But it was the teeth—those two-inch long fangs that snapped down—that had her undivided attention. But he still didn't attack. He panted, then pulled in his muzzle until the mouth was human again.

"Fucking bitch," he gasped. "That hurt like hell."

"For Malcolm," she said.

Those sharp teeth locked in a glinting smile. "The fool who wanted to be a hero? He tried to kill me with his bare human hands. I let him off easy. I liked the man."

Renee struggled to stand up again, although Britt kept her hand curled on Renee's arm to keep holding her back, keep protecting her. She fought against Britt, her stomach sinking with each inch she put between her and her lover. She set the rifle again, held it between herself and Grant almost like a spear. The cold was beginning to get to her. Her knuckles were white, and while she knew her fingers were moving and clenching, she could barely feel them.

"Think you can shoot to kill, love?" he growled, breathing heavily. Black blood dripped from the wound in his shoulder and gleamed wetly.

"Kill him," Jake hissed. "You've got the time."

The gun was ready, her finger trembling on the trigger. She would have hit his head if she had taken the shot, and that might have been enough. But her trigger finger would not press down. His eyes glowed red, and her stomach dropped to her feet. His teeth clicked into a wide smile as he began to bear down on her.

In his half-wolf form, he towered over her. She knew now why he had never taken his lower than average human height to heart. Down the dark grey fur of his stomach, she could see his cock, dark red and rising as he reached for her. It pressed into her stomach when he wrapped his arms around her and pulled her into him. The gun was forced upward and to the side, the knife pointing past his neck and into the air.

His heat kept her from the frigid weather, but she still trembled as though it was thirty below. And heat dipped between her legs. She was terrified out of her mind, and still her body reacted to Grant, wanting him to take her and free her. She wanted out of her body and mind. She had denied him because she knew that she would be going from one complicated life to another, from one unacceptable extreme to another. But with him covering her, swallowing his scent, it was hard to remember the reasons she wanted to stay herself when he could make her feel like this. She loosened her hands on the gun to feel the broadness of his furred chest, and she could not stop her hips from canting towards him, wanting him.

"You need me." His voice rumbled through her like the vibration of an old train. "They can't give you what you need. I will free you."

Her head tilted back as she struggled with each wave of feeling that he always brought to her. She was going to give in to him, not because she wanted to, but because he was all there was, and she couldn't think at all. That was bliss—not to think, just to feel him, to touch him, to want him to fill her.

"Renee, please," Britt cried from behind her. It was as if Renee heard her from a mile away.

"I heard what she asked you to do to her when this is over," he whispered in her ear. His breath was hot and wet, and her fingers clenched again. "I have no objection. I could use another bitch in the pack."

His teeth were on her shoulder now, massaging the skin under her shirt, getting ready to clamp down. She thought of the woman behind her, afraid for her and afraid for herself. That woman was willing to become a wolf if she did.

She still wasn't thinking clearly, but her hands found the gun. Her finger found the trigger again and pulled. The bullet went into the air, but she was not expecting to shoot him. She had taken a gamble that at the deafening noise, he would either clamp down his teeth and bite her by reflex, or jerk back.

Grant jerked back.

And when he did, Renee thrust the rifle forward as hard as she could before she could stop herself. If she had hesitated, she might not have made it through the mat of fur and the skin beneath. But she did not hesitate, and she felt a spurt of almost boiling blood on her face from the force of the blow, and she stumbled back. She had caught him under his rib, possibly puncturing a lung. But it would not have mattered if she had just grazed bone or scratched him. The silver had made it in.

Grant opened his mouth to scream at her, but somehow it was like the jaw didn't stop, gaping wide as though the bone was unhinged. The entire face became like a wolf, then tried to transform back, then tried to transform again. He was a mass of change and creaking bone and sinew, but no matter which way he turned, he could not escape the trace of silver sweeping through his bloodstream, subject to each contraction of his heart. His mouth foamed and snapped, but he was in too much pain to walk the three steps to bite her—not that biting her was a priority to him now.

He stared at her with glowing eyes, seeming blankly stunned that she had actually poisoned him. In spite of the crimson glow behind the blue, those eyes looked terribly human, terribly taken aback.

Renee could lower her arms now. She was shaking and cold, but that wasn't what was important. She couldn't believe that she had done it, either. She couldn't believe that he was falling to the ground in a growing pool as the stab wound and gunshot wounds continued to pour blood. While he was writhing, the human side of him finally started to emerge, the wolf slowly being eradicated from his system. Finally, he was simply a man—naked, screaming as if acid was moving through him. But his eyes never left hers.

Not even when he finally stopped moving and his gaze became marble.

The rifle fell from her hands, and the bloody knife stained the snow. After that, it was a blur. Jake went back into the barn to tell everyone what had happened. Britt took her to the log home—there was no reason to fear now—digging her way while Renee tried to figure out whether anything was real.

The log home was still warm, since the heater had been working steadily while they'd been gone. Britt tried to get her to the upstairs bathroom to wash, but Renee, her thinking mind finally surfacing, told Britt that she shouldn't wash yet. She went back out and stopped the shapeshifters from moving the bodies of Grant and Josh, which the snow had already started to cover. She might have been sleepwalking. Her voice was even and monotone, and she thought her demeanour scared them enough that they listened when she told them to cover the bodies with a blanket so that the scene could be preserved. Then she went back to the log home and found Detective Ebon's card in the computer room.

"Hello, I'm calling for Detective Ebon," she said.

"That'd be me. Who's calling?"

"Renee Chambers, from the dog sanctuary. I know who was mutilating the animals. He killed a man. Josh Beall."

"You mean Josh Beall killed the animals and murdered a man?" Detective Ebon asked. He sounded distracted, and Renee could imagine him scrambling for a pen and paper to write things down.

"No. Grant killed Josh Beall. Grant's dead. I shot him when he was coming at me, and my knife got him when the gun didn't work. He's dead."

There was silence on the other end. Then, "So there are two dead bodies at the sanctuary, Josh Beall and Grant...?"

"Grant Heath. He's been staying at the sanctuary to help out. But..."

"You were hiding him," Detective Ebon said. He didn't sound accusatory. Instead, his voice was just as flat as hers.

"No," Renee said, and she did not think she was lying. "I didn't know it was him, not until a few days ago. He started stalking me. I kicked him out of the sanctuary, but I knew he hadn't gone far. I couldn't call you before. We ran to protect the dogs, and we don't have cell phones."

"You don't have cell phones."

"We don't *need* cell phones. At least we didn't, until... I kept my people from cleaning up, but the cold will freeze everything by the time you get here."

"That's very considerate of you."

"I got his blood on me. Should I wait to wash it off?"

Another pause. "On your clothes, or on your skin?"

"Both."

"I'll requisition a helicopter. This needs to be done now. Don't wash off."

"Okay."

"You're not alone?" Detective Ebon asked.

"No. I have my people with me. There were witnesses."

"Good. Try and hold it together until we get there. I know how awful this kind of thing can be. And Ms Chambers?"

"Yes."

"I'm sorry this had to happen to you."

She hung up.

Britt tried to get her into the shower, but she shook her head. "Not yet," she told Britt. "They're coming for the bodies. They need pictures."

Britt looked at Renee with more than a little concern in her eyes, but she stayed at Renee's side while they waited for the sound of a helicopter. All Renee did was sit on one of the dining room benches and stare at the darkness on the other side of the window.

Her shapeshifter pack slowly filed in. Max and Leslie were helping Malcolm because he couldn't quite put his weight on his bitten leg. Malcolm looked just as empty as Renee, and the room was almost completely silent while they waited. Britt explained what was going to happen, and Renee asked whether someone was watching over the bodies, but other than that, there was not much more than the snapping of the fire that Jake had built in the living room hearth.

It was three o'clock in the morning when they finally heard the muffled thump-thump-thump of the helicopter. There was enough open space on the top of the hill for it to land with safety, if a little precariously. Jake got the door when Detective Ebon knocked.

Detective Ebon shuffled in, brushing snow from his shoulders. He looked even more awkward and bumbling than when he first came, but he was all business.

"If you could direct my partner to the bodies, that would be a great first start. Ms Chambers, if you could follow this young woman, we can get some pictures of your...clothing, and talk." Behind Detective Ebon came an officer with a camera, followed by an ME.

Detective Benoit poked her head in, and Jake and Max led her back out towards the bodies. The ME was taking a look at Malcolm's leg as Renee and Britt followed Detective Ebon and the officer into the kitchen—a neutral, out-of-the-way room for their purposes.

"This would be better if we could talk to Ms Chambers alone," Detective Ebon said pointedly.

Britt knew that the pleasantries were laced with an order, but she stood her ground, and at an inch taller than Detective Ebon, she managed to stare him down.

"All right, then," Ebon muttered.

The officer, a young woman named Laura, asked Renee to stand still as she took pictures of blood spatter and new wounds, scratches on her arms and bruises on her shoulder where his teeth had pressed until the flash of the camera illuminated them to her.

The officer stepped to the side when she was done, another silent advocate for Renee in her trauma. Renee supposed it was procedure when dealing with women. It did not annoy her.

"If you're ready, Ms Chambers, we can get this over quickly so that Laura can take your clothes and you can clean up," Ebon said.

Renee nodded.

"Please take me through the events of the night."

Renee explained, in vaguer terms than she would have liked, how they had been in the barn keeping the dogs and her friends safe from Grant. She had kicked him off the sanctuary when she had learned what he had done to the animals, but had fully expected him to come back for some kind of revenge, since he had developed an obsession with her.

"Did you return any of his advances?" Detective Ebon asked. He looked straight at her, peering at her face, and she knew that if she lied on this matter, he would know.

"At the beginning," she answered.

She went on to say that they had been alerted to his presence when he'd thrown the body of Josh Beall against the door of the dog barn. Three of her people had gone out to confront him, as was their right to protect the property, which had led to Malcolm's leg wound. She, of course, did not explain that the wound was a bite.

Renee continued by saying that she and some of her people had gone out to confront him head-on, since Renee had known he would not stop until he encountered her. She was honest when she said she had gone out with the knife on the gun, just in case she had not been able to manage what she needed with a gunshot, and in case she used up her ammunition. She gave the bare minimum of details of the attack, saying that Grant had come at her, and while she had hesitated to begin with, she'd shot him in the chest when he'd grabbed her. Unfortunately, he had kept coming and hurt her even more, so she had stabbed him in the belly with the knife, and that had finally seemed to stop him.

"So you're saying it was self-defence," Detective Ebon clarified.

"What would you say it is?" Renee said. She was tired, and she did not want his games. "He stalked me, murdered Josh, hurt a friend, threatened more of them, and then came after me. In what universe is that not self-defence?"

"Witnesses?" Ebon asked, evading the question.

"Me," Britt said. "And Jake. Jake, Malcolm, and Leslie were witness to the first attack. And Grant admitted to killing the animals and the man."

Detective Ebon gave Britt another look. "I don't believe we've met."

"No, we haven't." Britt didn't continue.

Ebon kept an eye on her for a minute, then flipped his notebook closed. "Well, I need to go out and look at the crime scene. If you could remove your clothing and give it to Laura before you take a shower, we would appreciate it. Laura, if you could follow Ms Chambers to her shower and make sure she doesn't walk into it with her clothes on. She's looking a little out of it. Thank you. I'll speak to you again after you're finished."

Chapter Fourteen

When Renee came down, she was wearing sweats and had her wet hair back in a ponytail. She wrapped a quilt around her shoulders and waited for Detective Ebon to come to her as she sat down in an armchair. Britt did not crowd her—she sat on a nearby sofa, willing to be there for Renee if needed.

Ebon came over and sat down in the armchair across from her. It was some distance, but Renee was fine with that. The other shapeshifters must have been taken elsewhere, because she, Britt and Ebon were alone in the living room.

Renee noted that Ebon looked a little pale.

"Miss Chambers, I'll say first that I think you are telling the truth…to a point. And I have a sneaking suspicion that you know what that point is."

Renee just waited.

"The evidence doesn't add up. There is no way that the wounds on your shoulder were made by human teeth, and the animals were mauled with animal teeth as well. Same with the wounds on Josh Beall and your friend Malcolm Delancy. Yet there is evidence of blood and skin underneath Mr Heath's nails, and there is blood and flesh in his mouth. There is no way it could have been placed there. Then there is this."

Detective Ebon pulled an evidence bag with the silver, bloodstained knife inside.

"This is not an ordinary knife, is it?" he said.

Renee shook her head but did not elaborate.

"See, the ME says that the gunshot wound to Mr Heath's chest might have been a killing blow, or at least a stunning one. But it did not kill him, you say?"

She shook her head again.

"Stabbing him with this killed him."

Renee nodded.

"And how did Mr Heath make the marks of a larger animal with sharper teeth?"

She looked directly at Ebon. "How would I know?"

Ebon turned a little paler, and he put the knife back in his coat. "Yes, well, the rest of your people are corroborating your statement, and most of the details of the attacks seem covered. I suppose we'll have to put the rest down to mystery. It sometimes happens."

He put his hands on the arms of the chair and pushed himself standing with a grunt. "Good evening, Ms Chambers. I'll have to talk with the assistant district attorney, but I hope we never see each other again." He headed towards the door, his walk brisk with his strong desire to leave as soon as possible. But he stopped at the door and turned around, his curiosity getting the better of him.

"Ms Chambers," he said, "is this knife made of silver, by any chance?"

Renee turned away from him and stared into the fire. "Yes," she answered. "Sterling."

She heard the distinct click of his dry throat as he swallowed. "Well..." His voice drifted off, and he closed the door behind him.

There was quiet, and Britt and Renee sat there, waiting for the tension in the room to dissolve. When Renee's eyes began drooping from exhaustion, Britt slid closer.

"Are you ready to sleep?"

Renee had not known whether she would even be able to close her eyes tonight, but now she knew she could. She nodded, and Britt led her up to the loft and into Britt's bed. Renee kept her quilt around her, but she loosened it a little as Britt changed into warm pyjamas and joined her in bed, then wrapped her arms around Renee and held her close.

Renee began drifting almost immediately, surrounded by warmth that smelt of cotton, skin, and Britt's shampoo. Jake joined them later, and Renee jerked awake briefly as his weight shifted the bed and made the mattress springs creak, but his strong, warm hand on her hip only reassured her, and she slipped easily back into sleep.

* * * *

When she woke up, she, Britt and Jake were still wrapped together. Renee could not believe that they could go downstairs and there would be no Grant. It was too early for her to know how that felt, whether she missed him or felt guilt or regret or relief. Maybe she would never resolve that contradictory tangle of emotions. She pressed herself closer to Britt and waited for them to wake up, too.

The first sign that Britt was awake was when she kissed the top of Renee's head. Renee looked up and into the dark pools of Britt's eyes, there in the shadows of the loft. Then she stretched herself up to kiss Britt tentatively, as though unsure whether Britt could be there with her without Grant pulling her in the other direction. It was morning, and their breath was ripe, their faces a little oily, and their hair was a mess, but Renee did not care. She deepened the kiss, pushing thoughts of Grant away. She would not let him force his way into her life now that he was gone. Not between her and Britt.

Britt met Renee's kiss, pulling up Renee's shirt. Renee gasped, her arousal building languidly. She needed this. Just this — knowing that they were alive, together and unbitten.

Britt crept her fingers under Renee's pants and began to press and rub above Renee's clit, drawing that arousal into a more urgent pitch. Renee returned the favour, pushing Britt's pants down her thighs and bringing her hand down until their fingers worked in tandem, their wrists bumping against each other awkwardly, but they did not want to stop. They did not care if it was awkward. They just wanted to feel each other, reassuring one another.

Their coming was quiet — a few bucks, a whimper, and the sweet sound of tongue on tongue, then tongue on flesh as Renee licked Britt's neck.

"I can be what you need," Britt whispered. "Anything you need. Anything you want. And what I can't give you, Jake can learn."

They both looked behind Britt, where Jake was still fast asleep.

"Okay?" Britt added. "All you need to do is ask."

Renee stroked Britt's hair. "Here's what I need," she said quietly, slowly. "Don't always wait for me to ask."

* * * *

It took two weeks before the bits and pieces of Grant's influence on the sanctuary were cleaned away, with the exception of Malcolm. Ki and Max were beside themselves at the way that Malcolm shut himself away in a room, ran the woods in his bare feet and human skin, the way his personal energy seemed to hum with anger and resentment and something he could not even describe. They all knew what it was — it was the werewolf in him. He dared not change in case he became the wolf, but the shapeshifters who knew him less began to avoid him because of his smell, and so did the dogs in the sanctuary once they stopped barking at him and learned that he was not a threat in spite of the scent of danger. All of those dogs had been his life — he had known every single one of them, and now he couldn't go near them.

Renee wanted to stop him, wanted to tell him that it was okay that he was what he was, but she was not sure how to broach the subject without him snapping her head off. After all, she was responsible for what he was. All she could manage was a short exchange in the greenhouse when he came back from a run. His feet were bloody and covered in dirt. A few weeks ago, his toes would have been blue, but she could feel his heat as he passed by her. He was as hot-blooded as Grant had been.

"Malcolm," she called before he went into the kitchen.

He would not turn around, but he stopped, the muscles under his white, worn undershirt tensing.

"You are still welcome here," Renee said. "I hope you realise that that's not even a question."

Malcolm gripped the door frame. Renee could hear the wood grain crunch slightly.

"Yes," Malcolm replied. "I know this sanctuary is welcome to werewolves." The blame was pointed, and Renee ducked her head as Malcolm went into the house.

Ki came to her a few days later with her own concerns. "He's not just mad at you," Ki explained. "I hope you know that. And he shouldn't be mad at you to begin with. He's frustrated with himself. His nature has changed, and he needs to be the wolf but doesn't know whether he can control it. He doesn't want to deal with the change. I've told him over and over again that we still want him, but...he's ashamed. He doesn't know where to go if he can't stay here."

"He can. I told him that I wouldn't think of turning him out," Renee interjected.

"I know you wouldn't. I mean, you wouldn't turn Grant out until you knew he was a threat to us," Ki said. Renee wondered whether Ki really believed that or whether she just knew that Renee had done it all with the best of intentions, as most roads to hell went. "But he doesn't know where he belongs anymore. He doesn't want to be with other werewolves, not with the way we are about them. He wants to become his canine form again, but he can't. He wants to stay, but he's not sure he should. And I don't know how to fix things. Not between him and Max, and not between him and me."

Renee could not give her anything. She was just as lost as the rest of them. All they could do was let Malcolm make his choice in his own time. Only he could figure out what was best for him.

* * * *

After enough time passed, things surprisingly went back to as close to normal as they were before Grant had come. Four weeks after the attack, Renee got a voicemail from Detective Ebon that no charges were being brought against her, which Renee had expected, but hearing it was still a relief. Following another trip into town, Britt told Renee that she thought Renee had got a little better in crowds, if even quieter than usual.

Renee wanted to tell Britt that it helped that the town knew she had killed a man, but she did not think it was prudent to add that some of them probably believed she had killed both Grant and Josh in cold blood, during a psychotic break. She was more than just an eccentricity now.

Those who knew her better than a stranger, like Marie at the bar, knew it was complete bullshit that she would kill anyone for reasons beyond self-defence, and they welcomed her into their places of business without question and defended her to the rest.

Still, because of the rumours and the little exhibitionist show she had put on when Grant had brought her to town, Renee felt that the walls did not close in so much, and that the people — just ordinary people who might or might not stare at her — were not a threat. Not in comparison to what she'd had to face. In the end, Grant was dead and she was the one still alive. That resonated with her, and she reminded herself of it every time she felt she couldn't take the eyes on her or the crowds around her.

Things were not perfect. She still wanted Britt with her when she went into town, but she found that she did not endure full-on panic attacks anymore. Strong anxiety on occasion, but even that was beginning to be manageable.

Britt. When they were at the sanctuary, Britt began pushing Renee, just like Grant had done. But Renee knew she could trust Britt completely, with anything and everything. And it did help her. Not to mention that the sex was great, occasionally rough, sometimes more so than Britt was expecting. But even when Renee was bruised and scratched, and Britt not looking much better, the sex was more than satisfying. With enough coaxing, Jake, too, learned that he could squeeze Renee's wrists without breaking them. However, mostly Renee just stayed with Britt.

As spring began to thaw the earth, all of them — even Malcolm, in one of his rare moments of wanting to be a part of the old crowd — were sitting down to a meal when they heard a vehicle crunching its way up the driveway. Renee and Leslie looked at each other. They had not heard the gate bell ring. Either the gate was broken and open, or someone had broken in without setting off the alarm.

Renee wiped her mouth with her napkin, her brow furrowed, and threw her legs over the bench to see who could possibly be coming. Since dinner was mostly over and the rest of them were curious, they followed her out.

It was an old, rusty, pinkish pick-up. Renee thought it looked oddly familiar.

She recognised it when the woman driving came into view. The truck stopped near Renee's, and the woman got out.

"Sorry I had to open the gates on my own," Kelly said. Her blonde hair was braided, and most of her tattoos were covered with surprisingly conservative clothes. She had good, almost vintage taste. If it had not been for the tattoos that were still visible, Renee might have thought she worked in an office.

"Did you close them behind you?" Renee asked. She stroked the head of the medium-sized mutt next to her in reassurance. The dogs who would usually rush upon any car that came into the compound were watching the woman from a distance, but strangely, they didn't bark.

"Yes, don't worry." Kelly shut the truck door, then took a look at the shapeshifter pack behind Renee, who were watching her warily, having recognised what she was the minute her scent had reached them. Her gaze stopped on Malcolm, whose brown eyes had locked on her. He knew. And she knew. Her expression turned to one of distress.

"I'm sorry," she whispered. "I'm so sorry. I heard he was dead, and I... David was thrilled, you see," Kelly said, turning to Renee. "I thought he might have turned you already. David said to bring you back with me, that they could use another bitch, especially if that bitch had killed Grant. I told him that you might not want to come. He told me to force you.

"And I killed him." Kelly's light eyes were pale and hard. Her face, usually soft, became angular as she almost transformed in anger. "He never knew. He always enjoyed the change. And I knew that you wouldn't, that you would be miserable in our pack. I saw it in a dream. I knew I would have to kill him eventually. The alphas always need to change.

"They drove me from their pack after that, as a traitor. They won't follow me, but... I didn't know where else to go." Kelly held out her hands to Renee. "Can you help me?"

Renee turned her head to look at Britt. Britt and the other shapeshifters were looking at Kelly differently than they had looked at Grant. Kelly had the same undeniable energy and, Renee assumed, the same werewolf smell. But the shapeshifters were not showing the same automatic dislike for Kelly as they had for Grant. It was as though they knew Kelly was a completely different kind of person, and Renee could see that it perplexed them.

But it was Malcolm's face—the recognition in his expression—that made Renee take one of Kelly's hands and draw her towards the log home. Renee smiled at Britt, who was shaking her head in quiet amusement, and they all began to head into the house. Britt kissed her cheek, clearly thinking Renee wouldn't be Renee if she didn't open her home to someone who needed it.

Renee noticed how Malcolm fell into step with Kelly, and that Kelly slid her arm around Malcolm's waist, giving him reassurance.

Renee thought that this could work.

About the Author

Aurelia T. Evans is an erotic writer with a fondness for horror and the supernatural. In addition to writing, Aurelia enjoys baking, taking late night walks, and listening to almost every genre of music.

Aurelia T. Evans loves to hear from readers. You can find her contact information, website details and author profile page at http://www.total-e-bound.com.

Total-E-Bound Publishing

www.total-e-bound.com

Take a look at our exciting range of literagasmic™
erotic romance titles and discover pure quality
at Total-E-Bound.

www.ingramcontent.com/pod-product-compliance
Lightning Source LLC
Chambersburg PA
CBHW022026260626
47156CB00017B/347